A STRANGER TO COMMAND

Sherwood Smith

Copyright © 2008 by Sherwood Smith

Cover Design Copyright © 2008 by Vera Nazarian
Photographs Copyright © 2008 by Sherwood Smith
Cover Model: Thomas Lembke

ISBN-13: 978-1-934648-55-1
ISBN-10: 1-934648-55-8

FIRST EDITION
Trade Hardcover

August 1, 2008

A Publication of
Norilana Books
P. O. Box 2188
Winnetka, CA 91396
www.norilana.com

Printed in the United States of America

# A STRANGER
# TO COMMAND

**YA Angst**

an imprint of
## Norilana Books

**www.norilana.com**

**Other Books by Sherwood Smith**

Crown Duel

Inda

The Fox

King's Shield

Senrid

Over the Sea: CJ's First Notebook

A Posse of Princesses

Special thanks to Tamara Meatzie
and to the Long Beach Writers' Group

This was written for my friends at Athanarel,
who asked "what happened before?"

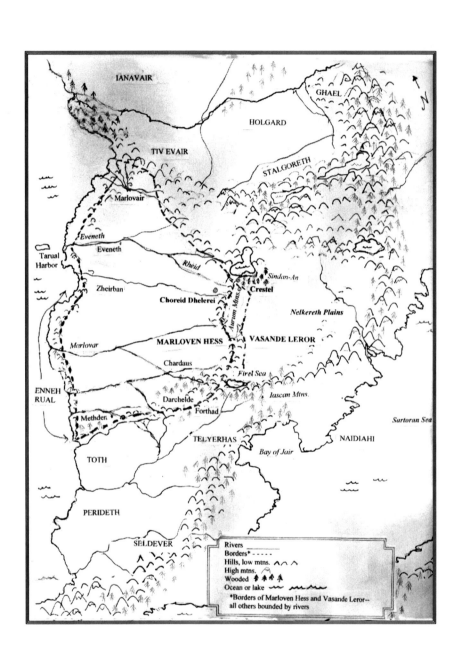

# A Stranger To Command

A Prequel to Crown Duel

# SHERWOOD SMITH

# One

"You're a new one."

The 'new one'—a boy of fifteen—paused just inside the courtyard, mentally translating the words.

"Yes, I am," Vidanric Renselaeus said carefully in the language he'd been studying so hard since winter.

For a moment the Remalnan boy and the Marloven man regarded one another. The Marloven had short fair hair, square cut in back, his clothing a fitted gray tunic over loose riding trousers that were tucked into high blackweave riding boots, belted at the waist with plain blackweave. Everyone Vidanric had seen so far in this enormous castle built of honey-colored stone appeared to be dressed in gray. They all wore blackweave riding boots, their hair—mostly variations of light colors—square-cut in back. They looked bewilderingly alike.

To the Marloven, on duty to sort out the academy boys, the newcomer was obviously a foreigner. He was weedy, as fifteen-year-olds typically are. Under his wide-brimmed riding hat his long pale blond hair was tied back with a ribbon. He was dressed in foreign clothes that looked well made but fussy to the Marloven eye: over a fine cambric shirt he wore a long split-tailed riding jacket of brown linen, trousers to match, lace edges at cuffs and neck. You heard about people wearing lace, but this was the first time he'd actually seen it.

At the boy's shoulder stood a bearded minion of some sort, holding the reins of two horses loaded with baggage.

This boy had to be the foreigner everyone had heard rumors about. Some foreign toff invited, no one knew why, to attend the cavalry academy. But the king was just a boy himself. Maybe that had something to do with it.

He said, "You'll be with the colts."

Vidanric repeated the word, then said doubtfully, "Young horses?"

"Your class." The Marloven turned his hand toward the inner courtyard. Didn't the foreigner know anything? Obviously not. "You're called colts." With rare consideration he added, "You won't call yourselves that, of course. That's what you're called."

Vidanric's misgivings about this journey had worsened at the first glimpse of the enormous castellated city. And here was this man making no sense whatsoever.

The Marloven now just wanted the foreigner out of the way, and under someone else's eye. "This would be your first year?" he said slowly and distinctly.

"Yes. First year," Vidanric repeated, wondering why the man sounded so ironic. He tried to enunciate clearly; the sides of his mouth and his jaw felt tight.

"That. Building." The Marloven extended his hand again, palm open toward a stone archway that led to another peach-stone courtyard, from Vidanric's limited view, exactly like the one he stood in. "Through. There."

The words were flat, the consonants precise, but at least Vidanric understood. He turned to Leffain, his courier.

The Marloven added, "No. Servants. Beyond. This. Wall."

Vidanric realized he was being mocked, but the man had already moved on to a group that just entered the court, their rapidly-spoken Marloven beyond Vidanric's ability to untangle.

Leffain was busy with the saddlebags. Vidanric blinked against streaming sunlight. The Marloven capital Choreid

Dhelerei rose around him, a bewildering complexity of mighty towers surmounted by snapping flags and high walls prowled ceaselessly by sentries—walls within walls. Three times on the way in he and Leffain had encountered massive gates. Sentries had assessed them at a glance, saying, "Academy that way."

The last wall had been so thick the archway through was more of a tunnel, one blackish green with age underneath, but they had reached the academy at last. Or at least the academy's forecourt, crowded with people, horses, carts.

Now it seemed Vidanric was to go on alone.

Leffain held out Vidanric's travel bag. "Marlovens. I told you, my lord, they don't have courtly manners. Just speak out when you have to."

Vidanric hoisted the bag over his shoulder and walked slowly through the archway into the next court. Leffain followed a few steps, leading the horses by the reins. He owed no duty to these Marlovens, but he did to Vidanric's father. For the Prince of Renselaeus's sake, and for his own, he would see the boy acknowledged by constituted authority, or the closest semblance possible in this infamous academy.

Several boys peered over the stone wall opposite, their shorn heads looking exactly alike on their bare necks. One of them yelled what sounded like insults to someone unseen, but his words were too quick, too flat, too slangy for Vidanric to follow.

Another young man—short, fair-haired, dressed in gray—emerged from the low wood-and-stone building adjacent the wall. He gestured toward the doorway and said to Vidanric, "First year. Upper school."

Though the man had spoken as if making a statement rather than asking a question, he seemed to be waiting for an answer.

So Vidanric said, "Yes."

The man's mouth soured at the edges. "Take your gear inside. Choose a rack. The nags go with the servant." The man gave the horses, standing there in their Sartoran-style saddles and bridles, a contemptuous glance.

Vidanric had already encountered this attitude toward outland horses. The Marloven breed really was as beautiful as the histories claimed, the saddles were scarcely more than what Vidanric thought of as saddle-pads to support stirrups and sword-sheaths. No bridles at all, only the briefest of halters to attach reins to. Marloven riders and their animals seemed to understand one another without words.

So he ignored the look, and hastened to explain about the courier, lest Leffain feel he had been insulted. "He's not—"

The man turned away just as he spoke, addressing another gray-tunicked man. They vanished through the same archway Vidanric had entered.

"—a servant, he's—" Vidanric stumbled to a halt. "What now? Did I do something wrong?"

Leffain handed him a second bag, one that clanked. "Let it go, my lord."

They had spent nearly four months together, first on board the trade vessel—which at first had made him vilely sick—and then on the long ride up from the Bay of Jaire, speaking Marloven every day.

"As you say," Vidanric assented, with a polite gesture.

"My lord Marquis. I have seen you to your door," Leffain responded—in Sartoran, the language of formality. "And acknowledged by constituted authority, as your father decreed. Now I will leave you here."

"I thank you, Courier Leffain. Please tell my father I'll write as soon as I find out how letters are sent from here."

Leffain bowed, mounted his horse, and gathered the reins of Vidanric's. The animal huffed, ears flicking, and shouldered against Leffain's mount. The two animals had snapped and snorted at one another for most of the days of travel. Now they seemed ready to bicker again.

A raucous laugh from behind brought Vidanric's attention round; one of the boys peering over the wall pointed at the horses. He and the others exchanged fast, scornful words, then all the heads turned sharply as one to glance back. They vanished. The sound of running feet echoed from the court beyond.

Vidanric turned. Leffain and the two horses vanished into the tunnel archway beyond.

Vidanric was alone.

He hitched his clothing bag over his shoulder, gripped his gear bag, and trod inside the low building.

It was dark inside after the bright sun in the courtyard. The faint but distinct odors of horse and boy-sweat caught at the back of his throat. He was used to big, airy rooms on a mountain-top, or the clean, subtly perfumed rooms of court.

Low beds made of slatted wood frames lined the room on both sides, head against the wall and foot forming a central aisle. The beds all had thin mattresses on them, stuffed (he would soon discover) with old armor quilting. Some were made up with plain cotton sheets, quilting-stuffed pillows, and coarse-woven cotton-wool summer blankets, others were still bare mattress. Stored beneath were sturdy wooden trunks with iron-reinforced corners.

The walls, beds, trunks, doorways, were gouged, slashed, nicked and rough, looking to Vidanric as if mad wolves had chewed the wood. The plank floor was swept clean, but utterly unadorned, and it, too, bore scrape and gouge marks. To someone raised to cherish wood this room seemed crude, almost savage.

A thump against his shoulder knocked him stumbling.

"Here." A boy exclaimed from behind. "Nip a rack or not. Don't sit in the road like a horse apple."

Vidanric translated the gist and stepped aside. The boy pushed on past without a look back, throwing his bag onto a bed midway along the wall. Vidanric realized the beds were fast filling. If he wanted fresh air, he'd better claim one under a window, and fast.

One was left, at the end farthest from the door, next to the open cupboard that appeared to contain the bedding. He dropped his bags onto this bed.

The muted *ching!* of the weapons bag caused a sudden silence.

Every boy in the room stared at him.

Someone said, "You're asking for a breeze."

Vidanric whispered the words. They still made no sense. The Marlovens talked fast, those precise consonants, sharpened vowels, flat tone. Leffain had warned him that his own accent was marred by Sartoran intonations.

Vidanric said carefully, trying to mimic the others' accent, "Breeze?"

Laughter. Sudden and loud.

Then a tall boy walked in, and the laughter stopped. Vidanric could not see why this boy would so instantly command such a reaction just by his presence, unless it was his being older, for he was dressed exactly like the others. No, he wasn't. He was dressed like the two men Vidanric had just seen. His gray tunic fitted him, and a brass-topped long stick stuck slantwise through his belt, a blackweave weapon belt. The other boys wore loose, lighter tunic-shirts, belted by sashes.

The boy with the stick looked around, then said, "Inspection directly after callover."

The boys Vidanric's age launched into action, some unpacking, others changing, a few dashing through the door as the older boy continued down the aisle between the bunks, looking neither right nor left. Everyone got out of his way.

Vidanric still hadn't moved. The older boy gave Vidanric a fast, assessing scan, which he returned, gaining a swift impression of a square, bony face—a facial structure he was to find repeated in infinite variety in Marloven Hess—dark blue eyes, sun-bleached yellow hair cut short in a line below the base of his skull just above the high collar of his tunic, parted in the middle on top, sweeping back over his ears.

"You're the new one. The foreigner," the boy said, observing and not questioning, at least to Vidanric's ear; his last word did not end in rising inflection the way he was accustomed to hearing questions posed.

"Yes."

"Name." It sounded like a demand, but the boy's attitude was not that of a demander, and Vidanric wondered if he was hearing the question mode after all.

"Vidanric Renselaeus, Marquis of Shevraeth." Very aware of the silent but listening boys in the room, Vidanric spoke his name quickly, automatically—thinking when it was too late that adding his title, as was proper at home, might sound pompous here. Then he remembered Leffain had told him titles were completely different in Marloven Hess, organized along old military hierarchy. There was no such thing as a duke or a marquis or baron. Or, for that matter, a lord.

Sure enough, the older boy frowned, an ordinary human frown of puzzlement. He seemed less daunting. "You have many names, it seems. Vih-DAWN-rik. I want to say VIH-dunrid," he added with a brief, wry almost-smile. "Vih-dan-rik. RenSLAY-ahsss." The sound was too heavy, too harsh. He stumbled over 'marquis,' an old Sartoran word that obviously had no equivalent here—he mistook it for a third name, ending with, "Shev-RAY-eth." The 'th' sounded hard, almost a 'd' but at least it was recognizable.

The boy lifted his chin again. "King wants only names used. Family names. SHEV-ray-eth." This time he switched the emphasis to the first syllable, the way of most names in Marloven.

Vidanric was about to correct him, then decided not to. The thought of hearing 'Renselaeus' mangled over and over in that braying, hissing *Ren-SLAY-ass* prompted Vidanric to agree. No one need know 'Shevraeth' was a territorial name, part of his title as his father's heir. He ducked his head, mentally adjusting: he was now Shevraeth, with the emphasis on the *shev*.

The boy said, "Shev-ray-eth, I am Janold, the aran radlav for this colts barracks." He indicated the room. "Colts are first and second years in the upper school."

Shevraeth frowned. *Aran* meant house, though they had several words for 'house' that obviously had different meanings, but Leffain hadn't been able to define them more precisely. *Rad, radr,* meant lieutenant. *Lav?*

Janold saw his question. "'Lav' is specific to the academy. We use the same rankings as the cavalry and army, only with *lav* appended." He grinned. "We don't have real rank out there. Only in here." A thumb jerked over his shoulder, then down at the floor.

Shevraeth closed his eyes, rapidly translating. Leffain had wisely given him military vocabulary first, so all those words were familiar by now. He said, trying to match the Marloven question mode, "How shall I properly address you?"

A soft whisper from behind, instantly silenced when Janold glanced to one side. "Janold Radlav will do under orders. My name the rest of the time. We use rank as part of our names only for parade. Big games. Inspection. Punishment. *Radlav* is actually several academy ranks—*aran* means I'm in charge of this barracks House—and we almost never use the *lav* except when we're outside the academy." His voice lifted just a little, which stopped the hiss of whispers somewhere in the back. "The king has given me specific orders. He wishes you to be made comfortable, and for your questions to be answered. There will be an interview when you have settled in."

Silence behind, a reflective silence on the part of the new barracks mates. Obviously the foreigner didn't know what that meant, but they sure did.

Janold turned his attention to the bags on the bunk. "Did you bring weaponry from your homeland?" he asked, indicating the gear bag.

Shevraeth nodded. "I thought I was supposed to."

"We are not permitted steel except in weapons classes, and then it is furnished us," Janold explained. "We can store your gear for you."

Shevraeth said, "Very well."

Janold gave him a sharp, considering glance, wondering if the foreigner was mocking him. 'Well' what, or was that foreign-talk for agreement? "Well?" he repeated, and this time his voice rose incrementally at the end.

Shevraeth had been trained by his parents not just to listen, but to watch. Not that you could always tell what people were thinking, but sometimes their bodies provided clues that their words, their tones, even their faces did not. Janold had stiffened, and Shevraeth realized he'd somehow said the wrong thing.

His hands gestured in peace mode, fingertips touching then opening out. "It is a common expression where I come from, an agreement. It sounded odd when I said it," he added. "The Marloven 'well' seems to relate to being and doing, was my first impression." And on Janold's open-handed gesture, "What say you for agreement?"

"Yes will do," Janold said, somewhat wryly, but with less edge than before.

Both were aware of the silent listeners. Janold added, "You had better get your things stored into the trunk there under the rack." He pointed to the bed. "And you'll need to get kitted out before the bell rings for noon mess, so I suggest you make it fast. Baudan! You appear to have nothing to do. Get him—" A side-glance at the other new boy standing uncertainly at the bed across from Shevraeth and one over. "Get him and Faldred there ready to ride by the bell."

Janold hesitated, his gaze on the foreigner's hair. By regulation everyone dressed the same, a rule going back to a bloody dispute in the past when the sons of commanders had expected perks just because of birth. But there was no rule about hair. Everyone in the military wore their hair the same, it was a mark of distinction.

He found himself reluctant to explain that to this boy with the toff clothes and manner. The fellow couldn't be an idiot or the king would not have invited him here. Let him figure it out.

So he picked up the gear bag and walked out, scattering the listeners to their supposed tasks.

# Two

As soon as he was gone, everyone started talking at once. They all looked so alike in their loose tunic-smocks, their hair short and pale. No, a couple of them had dark hair, three or four of them brown. And there were a couple of redheads, one tall, one short.

Shevraeth shut his eyes and tried to follow all the conversations, but only caught occasional words: "Sword . . . didn't get a squint at what he carries . . . 'well'? maybe it means sick, in foreigner-lingo . . . king."

The Marloven word for king—*harvald*—was the word Shevraeth heard them using most.

He opened his eyes.

Baudan was a short, solid boy with hair so pale it was almost white. He elbowed the others back without ceremony, picked up Shevraeth's travel bag and upended it.

Out fell all the expensive clothing that Shevraeth's mother had with loving care overseen the making of. Nothing ostentatious—from the point of view of a courtier in Remalna. Everything designed for movement, except for one formal suit, and that was in a subdued pearl gray, the lacing modest, the sash of raw silk the shade of straw said to be the latest fashion in Colend. Nothing, in short, at all inappropriate for sitting in court under the king's critical eye. But the colors, the fabric, the lines,

Shevraeth realized, were as out of place here as a peacock in a barnyard full of roosters.

More talk shot back and forth past him, broken once by a low whistle. Shevraeth did not know whether to protest, to get angry, or to laugh when a tall, brawny boy with unruly brown hair reached down to touch one of his fine cambric shirts.

Baudan smacked his hand away. "Get. Callover—did you hear? No time to measure. Stad. You're more or less his size and build."

A boy Shevraeth's height, with dark eyes and dark curly hair, mimed surprise. "Me? Me? Am I your runner?"

Four voices said, "Yes."

Stad sighed. "I'm going, I'm going." He sauntered to the door, but as soon as he got outside he took off at a run for the supply building.

Shevraeth repeated to himself: Baudan, that short one with hair lighter than mine. Stad, my height. Black hair. Who was the brown-haired one?

"Ventdor and Marec, you make up his bed." Baudan whooshed out a breath of relief. Evrec had already gotten the other newcomer, Faldred, mostly squared away.

Shevraeth whispered, "Ventdor—small, Marec—red hair," over and over as a scrawny fair-haired fellow and a boy with wild rust-colored curls swiftly and silently made up the bunk.

"Rest of you, pack him up."

Someone snatched Shevraeth's riding hat off, then he found himself shoved unceremoniously back as five pairs of hands grabbed up his belongings and sorted them into piles. Underclothes in one, the fine clothing in another, the pens, ink-bottle, and ribbon wrapped packet of fine paper in a third. They folded the clothes in a specific manner, and stored them neatly in the battered wooden trunk that a sixth pulled from beneath the bunk. His fine new clothes, with his flattened riding hat, were now on the bottom. Apparently no one expected him to use any of it. On top went his underclothes, and down the side were tucked the writing things as someone muttered, "Who has time for writing lessons?" To which Baudan uttered a loud snort.

Then Baudan said, "You'll have to learn to stow your own togs. Easy enough. Inspections will be every day for the first week. If we don't catch a fist—"

"Five defaulters," the redhead put in.

"—inspection goes to once a week, and no mess-gag."

None of that made much sense to Shevraeth, but the others did not wait to see if he comprehended. The same hands pulled bedding from the cupboard against the wall, and with the speed of several years' practice they made the bed up, corners neat, blanket flat and wrinkle free.

Stad returned at a hard run with an armload of gray fabric. Under Baudan's direction—the others who had finished their own work looking on critically—Shevraeth had to strip to his underclothes then dress fast in a sturdy cotton-linen tunic-smock that came down mid-thigh, loosely belted by a thin sash. The trousers, dyed gray, were not much different than his own. They were worn tucked inside of riding boots, as no one below seniors had formal uniforms.

A second, heavier, tunic and trousers were packed on top of his home clothing. Then the boys slammed the trunk shut and shoved it into place under the bunk, exactly squared.

The others held a quick, nearly incomprehensible exchange in slang-laden shorthand about his boots, from which he gathered they were adequate enough for now. He did not point out that they were very expensive, made by his father's own boot maker. But they didn't have the high heels of these others, or the severe line tapering to slightly squared toes.

A bell rang somewhere, echoing from all the stone walls, and the others stampeded out, Baudan pausing only to smooth the blanket and twitch at the flat pillow so it was exactly squared against the bare wood-slat headboard. He shoved Shevraeth behind Stad, who had the bed next to him.

*Baudan. Stocky. Pale hair.*

*Stad. Black hair, next bunk over.*

*Marec. Red hair . . .*

*My name is Shevraeth.*

They walked in line at a quick pace, hands at their sides. When they reached the stone corridor between walled off barracks, they fell in next to a line of boys from the opposite archway, these boys smaller, looking no more than ten to twelve.

No one spoke. Shevraeth was relieved. He tried to scan the territory, but the archways, flagged stones, courts, plain barracks buildings glimpsed through archways all appeared to be mirror images of one another, except for various colored flags hanging above the doorways of the battered barracks doors.

The line snaked across a big quad, a brisk spring breeze carrying the distinctive odor of horse. Then they passed through two double doors to a garrison-sized mess, tables on either side making a central aisle, mirroring the arrangement of the beds in the barracks.

His line filed in orderly manner to the right-hand side of a big table, on which tureens of food sat, shallow plate-bowls stacked at one end, with spoons in a tray. Spoons only, no forks. Shevraeth did as the others did, picking up spoon and plate, then waited as the front of the line helped themselves to the food.

Everyone was silent and more or less orderly. The only sounds were the wooden plates klunking on wooden tables, spoons clattering, and the shuffle of feet, as those who had their food sat down at the tables. Boys gave one another surreptitious nudges, elbow-knocks, and exchanged brief, covert hand-signals, but when one of those older boys with a brass-topped stick in his hand paused in his prowl and frowned, everyone straightened up, eyes forward, only little quirks at the corners of their mouths betraying inheld laughter.

Someone poked Shevraeth from behind. The line had moved on, leaving a large space. He grabbed a piece of bread, dropped it on his plate, then ladled out a soupy stew that smelled of cabbage, pepper, lemon, fish. Next was a big platter piled with a baked something cut into squares. It smelled like berry-tart. He took one of those, and followed the others to the table, where someone had already set out heavy wooden cups of water. A pitcher sat in the middle of the table, its sides frosty: more cold water.

Most of the Marloven boys ate noisily, using the bread to mop up the rest of the soup. Shevraeth did his best to eat politely, as he'd been raised, though he was puzzled by the heavy, shallow spoon and no fork. Every time he looked up he encountered stares from mostly light-colored eyes. Curious stares, sometimes indifferent, others narrowed, and a few with hostility.

Other than the clack of spoons against the dishes or the thump of cups on the plank tables, the only sound was the slow rap of heels as a big boy walked the center aisle, his gaze sweeping continually from side to side. He, too, wore one of those gold-topped wands thrust through his belt, and his tunic was fitted to his body, the collar high and stiff. He had to be another radlav, Shevraeth figured.

His barracks-mates ate swiftly, then sat back and waited. When Shevraeth was done eating, he put his hands in his lap, glad for an opportunity to just watch, and to mentally go over names and faces. *Short one: Baudan. Stad: black hair. Marec: red hair. . .*

Most everyone was done (after some surreptitious trading of bread, tarts, and once a hunk of cheese that Shevraeth hadn't even seen at the big table) when another single bell rang, and they all rose, and row by row carried their dishes to a big wooden bucket set at the end of the big table, from which someone had removed the tureens. Magic scintillated faintly as each boy ducked his plate, spoon, and cup into the bucket, shook it off, then stacked the plates onto the growing piles along the table, the spoons in a tray, and the cups into towers of exactly nine apiece.

Then they ran out the door, still in orderly lines. A susurrus of expectation rose in covert, short whispers as they formed up in their lines in the big quad outside the mess. The wind had turned cold, and snapped at their clothes and hair. Every barracks had eighteen boys. Eighteen: two ridings.

*Ridings.* It was the Marlovens who, centuries ago, had established nine as the perfect number for a horse-troop, called a riding. It could break into three threes, or two fours led by a captain, or ride as a unit. Four pairs under a leader—or nine pairs if they joined another riding.

Vidanric Renselaeus, fifteen-year-old Marquis of Shevraeth, was really *here*, in the kingdom with the most military influence of any in this hemisphere, a kingdom with a terrible reputation for centuries, until very recently.

And to Marlovens, there he stood, a foreigner, brought within the academy to be taught what had only been taught to Marlovens for centuries. Not that a few outsiders hadn't been here—one just a few years before—but there had always been some connection in high places, and a pretence of being Marloven. This time there was still the connection, but no one pretended.

A horn blew a three-note fall. The lines stilled, boys standing with feet slightly apart, hands at their sides, shoulders straight. Shevraeth sneaked a peek to make sure he was doing what everyone else did. To his surprise, he discovered at the far end there were four rows of girls! They were dressed just like the boys, their stances the same, their attention forward.

A big boy up front called out something unintelligible, and hard heels struck the stones, clump! Now they stood straight, feet closer together.

The radlavs moved up their lines, counting out their charges one by one, then reported to the boy at the head. He didn't speak back, or move until the last four rows were called out in high feminine voices. Then he turned his head, and once again the fanfare blared.

Then they marched back for inspection. Janold returned with them. Each stood at the foot of his bunk, at attention—feet apart at shoulder width, arms straight at sides, palms in—while

Janold went around smoothing a bed here, picking up a speck of dust, checking the squaring of a trunk under a bed there.

Footsteps rang on the courtyard stones, and that same boy who'd stood in front at the callover came in. The boys along the bunks snapped right hands flat over their hearts, all except Shevraeth. The big boy frowned, glaring at Shevraeth from pale blue eyes, then turned his head.

Janold said something in an undertone, and the big one flicked a hand in a gesture too quick to follow. "Teach him to salute," he said, and passed slowly down the row, looking closely at everything.

Shevraeth sensed relief in the others when he reached the wall by Shevraeth's bed without any further words. Then he spoke. "You'll test in riding and sword this afternoon. Bow, knife, hand tomorrow."

Thump! Again the boys performed the salute, and this time Shevraeth belatedly copied them. The big boy stalked back down the aisle and left.

Faces turned Janold's way.

"Let's get to the horses first," he suggested, again with that wry almost-smile.

The boys gave a wild yell, which turned into excited chatter. They ran out, but formed again into line in the court.

Shevraeth was grateful for the lines as they walked through the confusing maze of sand-colored walls. He felt apprehensive about the horseback riding. He would have preferred beginning with something he'd trained hard in, like dueling, or knife-throwing—though the latter was more of a sport. No one in Remalna threw knives, at least courtiers didn't.

He smelled the stable before they reached it. The boys lined along the back wall of a sizable paddock. The animals brought out were stunningly beautiful, small of head, heads and legs mostly variations of dun and gold and tan, paling to cream-colored coats. They had dainty feet and long beautiful legs, glossy manes and tails.

And not a one had so much as a blanket on its back, or even a halter.

The boys waited, poised to run. At a sign from someone unseen, Janold snapped his wand against his boot top and the boys launched themselves toward the waiting horses. Shevraeth followed more slowly, and discovered he was expected to leap to the horse's back. Grateful for the days he and his boyhood friend Russav Savona had dared each other to do just that (while being roundly scoffed at by some of the shorter boys at court), he took a series of running steps and jumped, scrambling upright on the animal's back. But when the horse sidled he clutched at its mane, and when it trotted forward, he tried to pull the mane, calling in his home language "Stop! Halt! Whoa!"

Scornful laughter hooted and crowed on all sides.

The horse continued to amble toward the stables, ignoring its rider with disdain. All the others were riding in what looked to him like perfect control, their hands on their thighs, the horses far more obedient than his. Shevraeth's face burned with humiliation.

A tall man in gray appeared, snapped his fingers twice, and Shevraeth's horse stopped, lowering its head and snorting.

"Go ahead. Dismount." The man waved in the direction of another part of the academy. "You'll be training with the scrubs."

The laughter around Shevraeth was the laughter of expectant superiority, of triumph. He retreated next to the wall and waited, hands behind him (gripped tightly, but no one saw that) as he endeavored to maintain the court mask.

Janold saw in his stiff posture the stolid blankness of someone who thoroughly hated himself and the situation. Time to end it. He put his hand to his wand, and half of the boys shut right up.

Janold eyed the rest of them. Sure enough, brawny Nermand was doing his best to fan the flames. Janold stepped behind him. The two boys on either side of Nermand immediately shut up, but Nermand was too busy trying to goad everyone into more laugher. ". . . he'll make us lose every game, just you see—"

Whack! The wand snapped across his shoulders, and he yelped and jumped.

From behind came a snort and snicker, quickly silenced.

"Two more for reminders," Janold said.

Whack! Whack! Nermand took those in silence, with only a wince.

Shevraeth watched, appalled. Caning! He'd heard of it, but had never seen anyone caned in his entire life.

"Line," Janold invited, and watched them instantly obey.

In silence they marched to the weapons court, where the small boys from the lower school were just finishing with the wooden practice swords. Ordinarily the Marloven boys would have made faces at the younger boys' clumsiness, maybe even called out an insult or two, but Janold was prowling the line with the wand gripped at his side, and so they stayed silent.

The scrubs' radlav signalled, the small boys scrambled into their line and marched out, most of them hopping or shoving at every other step.

*At least I won't disgrace myself here*, Shevraeth thought. *Not after eight years of tutoring.*

But as soon as the first pair had donned the protective gear and taken up the wooden swords, he realized with dismay that even these swords were heavier than the dueling rapiers he had trained with. They were made to resemble a type of sword he'd heard of but never seen, a cavalry saber with a slightly curved tip. The balance looked so different he knew his training would be next to worthless.

He waited for his turn, and when he was motioned forward, picked up the practice pads with the grim, slightly sick expectation of imminent mortification.

He slid on the gloves, straightened his shoulders, and picked up the blade, which felt just as strange as he'd feared. Determined to keep his emotions hidden behind the expressionless court mask, he took the dueler's stance, side on, left hand on hip, right wrist up.

Snickers broke out behind him.

"Hep," said the master, and Shevraeth attacked—knowing that he was too slow, the blade too heavy for the movements he used, that curved tip not made for thrust.

He did his best anyway.

The master tested him hard, dealing him stinging blows to both arms, to his ribs (he felt them even through the padding) to his front leg, but twice Shevraeth almost broke that guard, though he suspected the master permitted him. When at last he fell back, breathing hard, sweat running down inside his tunic, he realized the boys had gone silent, and were standing at attention. He stole a look to the side. They were staring at a newcomer, another blond boy, who looked very out of place in his civilian brown trousers and white shirt.

A stray city boy? A servant, maybe?

No, not with those silent, intent stares.

The master brought the sword up in a salute toward the newcomer, blade out, guard against his heart.

The boy said, "That is the best example of Sartoran dueling style I've ever seen." Then, without waiting for an answer, he walked on.

It took about two heartbeats before Shevraeth realized he'd just seen the Marloven king.

# Three

Most of the boys were asleep within moments of the glowglobes being clapped off.

Shevraeth lay in the uncomfortable bed and stared up at the shadowy wooden ceiling, which was such a contrast to the painting of the summer night sky on the smooth plastered ceiling of his bedroom. His parents had arranged for a theatre mage to add glimmer to the painted stars, probably at ridiculous expense. The sound outside his windows at home was the steady roar of the waterfall.

Here, the ceiling was rough wood centuries old. The noises were breathing—snoring at the far end—creaks of wood when someone shifted, the soft repeated thump of a fist into a lumpy pillow. Near the door someone farted and someone else smothered a laugh, followed by Janold's slow tread down the aisle. Though the windows were open, the still air seemed thick with the stale smells of exhaled dinner, faintly mildewed blankets, dust. Horse.

Shevraeth let his breath trickle out. His body was tired, but his mind refused sleep. His first night after an endless day. First night of how many?

*I hate this place.*

Shevraeth closed his eyes and tried to pretend he was home. But comfortable memories did not come at his wish.

Instead he relived that cold, wintry day when his father summoned him and said, "We are going to send you away."

How he'd struggled not to express dismay, to keep his voice even, because at court your emotions could be so easily used against you. He loved and trusted his parents, but practice at the court mask had to start at home. You did not want to err before King Galdran.

"Your reasons, Father?" he'd said, only the last word going husky, and his father had smiled with sympathy as well as approval.

"If you are away, you are less likely to suffer an accident here. And I will have the more freedom to conduct the tedious, exacting, and exceedingly delicate investigations I feel must be mounted."

Investigations. This was adult politics—until now words overhead, worried glances observed, but no facts.

"The Marloven Hess academy is where their commanders are trained. And though the Marlovens' place in history occupies an . . . ambivalent position at best," his father had said with a deprecating gesture, "no one has ever said that their commanders were weak or indecisive. Their kings are trained there, as well as their commanders, which argues for lessons in statecraft. It might chance that, in future, such training could benefit our kingdom."

"But is that not the responsibility of the king?" he had asked.

"The responsibilities of the king are . . . sometimes difficult to define," his father had said, taking him by surprise yet again. "I am about to tell you something that none of the young people your age know. We recently heard, again third hand, that Rannic Turlee didn't ride off on a wager, as we were led to believe. He was found murdered. And we are very much afraid that the mysterious disappearances and accidents of far too many outspoken heirs were murders as well. But though we are told the deeds were done by brigands, too many ordinary people have seen no highwaymen, brigands, or outlaws on our roads. Only the king's men riding back and forth."

"But that would mean the warriors are turned brigand?" he had said in disbelief. He personally knew some of the king's guard.

"Or they were given orders," his father had said.

Impossible! Except his father had never lied to him.

"For Rannic's death, for example, there appears to be far too much secondary evidence pointing to the king's own cousin. . . ."

Shevraeth shuttered away the memory. He'd agreed with his parents that it was a good idea for him to go away. Now he wondered again, why here? Why not a foreign court? Why not *anywhere* else?

And if it had to be here, why couldn't Russav Savona come, his cousin? They had been like brothers since Russav's parents suffered an accident—

*Their deaths were not an accident.*

His father had said, "I would send Savona with you if I could. But the king regards Russav as his ward. And dukes, even fifteen-year-old ones, don't usually leave their lands. We do not wish to draw the king's eye any more than we have."

Shevraeth rubbed his hand over his face. No use in whining, even to himself. He was here. He had agreed to it. He had even looked forward to it, he remembered, when climbing the ramp onto the ship back in Mardgar Harbor.

*That was then, this is now. So deal with the now.* He began reviewing all the words he'd learned that day, until they jumbled through his mind, chased by images from home, from here, and he slept at last.

It was fitful sleep, disturbed by unfamiliar sounds, smells, the lumpy mattress, until the clatter of a stick against the wall and a shout woke them all abruptly: "Rise up, get ready for inspection!"

# Four

Russav:

*I don't know if you'll ever see this letter, but I have what they call liberty for the first time and nothing else to do except think about home, and you did make me promise to write. At this point it's a tossup whether I carry it back and hand it to you, or pitch it in the fire. Liberty! Yet are you any more liberated, there under Galdran's eyes? Sometimes I think about just what 'liberty' means to different people at different times. Enough of that.*

*You asked me to tell you if the swagger in the history books about Marlovens was real or fart noise. It's not fart noise. Of course I haven't seen them at war. But I haven't seen anyone at war, so we both know how much my opinion is worth.*

*Their opinion of me? I'm a soft-handed, sloth-raised aristocrat and couldn't defend myself against a blind snake. An aged blind snake. And I should by rights be housed down with the ten year old scrubs, or pups, in the lower school. Apparently we are colts. That's the first two years in the upper academy. You don't call yourselves*

*these things, pups, scrubs, colts. They call*
*themselves men. Good practice in not laughing,*
*when you hear a boy of nine or ten squeaking*
*about the "men" in his barracks. Tradition says*
*the pups are as worthless as they are useless, but*
*when they cross from the lower school to the*
*upper, they add arrogance to their worthlessness.*
*At least, everyone seems to be determined to*
*spare us colts the peril of thinking ourselves*
*superior. No danger of that.*

*The only things that kept me from going*
*straight home and dedicating the rest of my*
*hollow life to the drinking, gambling, dancing,*
*and lounging that Galdran thinks I'm doing are*
*accidental. And both I lay at your feet, since you*
*harassed me into that game of vaulting on*
*horseback, and then that next summer, nagged me*
*into knife throwing just so we could impress*
*Rannic. Remember the monotony of that entire*
*year, practicing for two bells every day—and how*
*he thrashed us both for our gall in showing him*
*up? Yes I blamed you for all of it and yes you said*
*it would be useful some day. So go ahead and*
*gloat. The fact that most of the time I can hit a*
*target with a knife, either hand, overhand or*
*underhand throw, seems to actually matter here.*
*Unlike at court in Remalna-city, where the*
*daggers are all verbal, and no one is ever likely*
*to toss a knife, I least of all.*

*Otherwise, all those masters my father so*
*carefully chose and hired are apparently*
*untutored fools. No, it's not true, that's me feeling*
*sorry for myself because every bone and muscle*
*in my body aches, even when I sit here on my*
*bunk cursing you for lying at your ease at home,*
*your time your own.*

*Well, and Galdran's. Right.*

*So let me end with this observation. On the ship journey here I entertained myself with mental pictures of how brilliantly I would exhibit my skills, moving on to master statecraft while everyone around me tried to catch up with me. Statecraft! Reality is, I'll get about as close to statecraft as to the moon, and meanwhile I am told I don't even know how to properly ride a horse. But—and this is very important, worth crossing the continent for—I do know how to make a bed under the count of twenty.*

Clang-g-g!

This was his third morning. Shevraeth now knew what the bells meant.

He was already dressed, his bunk neat, his trunk packed just like all the others. He had been lying on his bed writing while those still in the barracks talked quietly. Some had vanished before dawn. He did not know where, and did not ask. As the unmelodic clang reverberated along the stone passageways everyone stashed whatever they had been doing, checked their beds and trunks one last time, then dashed outside.

He took his place in the silent line that marched to breakfast and went on mentally composing his letter:

*Observation. You don't ask questions unless you are invited to. At best you only get a retort as blunt as it is nasty for your pain. At worst you get scragged. Yes, they have that word. That is, they have three separate words for 'scrag.' Three that I know. Might be more. I wouldn't be the least surprised.*

*They have a lot of slang. A 'breeze' is a caning from one of the boy commanders, called radlavs, or just rads. The rads appear to be*

*limited to three hits, and only once in a day, but
anyone who tries anything after getting his one
breeze is reported to the senior radlav, and
apparently you don't want that unless you like
your shoulders 'measured.'*

*A 'dusting' is a fist fight between two or
more, and a 'brush' is an organized battle. All
are forbidden, of course, but are carried out just
the same, and it's interesting to see how
'forbidden' is interpreted in a place where
everyone, from the oldest master to the smallest
boy, seems to know that duels are fought in any
one of three places—*

Thunk! A sock on his arm broke into his thoughts, and he
realized space had opened between him and the boy in front. He
picked up a tray and piled food on haphazardly.

Yes, the food, he thought. That requires a letter all of its
own.

Not that the boys were stinted, or the food was ill-
prepared. But Marlovens did not seem to regard taste as a matter
of interest, judging from the lack of variety, the ever-present
bitter flavor of rye, the smell of cabbage, seasoned—if you could
call it that—by a light trace of garlic and onion braised in olive-
pressings. Only their cheeses were excellent, and judging from
how quickly those got grabbed up, others were aware of their
superiority. Their cheeses and heavy, layered berry-breads, very
tart, and crunchy with nuts, were both excellent. He'd learned
the night before that these nutbreads, baked very densely with
honey instead of northern sugars, were the Marlovens' travel
food in the old days. They were still used on certain types of
overnight expeditions.

He sat down with his tray.

*We eat in silence,* (he continued his
mental composition) *we march in silence, we do*

*everything that proves we're here not to think at all, but to be beaten into a shield wall of brainless warriors. How could this possibly be termed a school for learning command? More important, what was my father thinking?*

Everyone seemed edgy. Shevraeth, frustrated at not being able to discern why, felt his neck and shoulders tighten. The others in his barracks ate quickly, and so did he, plunking and thunking his dishes when the others did.

Despite a thin drizzle blown in chilly drifts by a sharp wind, the lines formed up earlier than usual. Pale-eyed Zheirban, the Danas Valdlav or boy commander of the academy, was there waiting for them, the rain plastering his blond hair to his forehead.

In rigid cadence the radlavs counted off their barracks, and then Zheirban said, "This year there are more changes. As promised. You no longer go with your barracks in the mornings. Your rad will give you new orders. There are new classes." His teeth showed briefly. "Such as history."

He paused, eyes narrowed, but no one spoke.

No one moved.

Shevraeth sensed tension zinging between the upper-level seniors, betrayed by subtle signs. He wouldn't have even seen them, his first day. He still couldn't figure out what they meant.

"Afternoon games are the same as last year." Zheirban nodded to one of the first-year seniors, who ran along the lines, handing out slips of paper to the radlavs.

When that was done, he signalled the dismissal, and they marched back to their barracks to wait for the morning inspection.

As soon as they were inside, Stad exclaimed, "Talk, Janold! Or I die. Right here. On the floor. And who knows how many defaulters a corpse nets us?"

Some of the boys snickered, but under their breath.

"The king wants us learning history." Janold studied the faces before going on. "Not just battles. Most of us already know all that. But what the kings did. What *mistakes* the kings made. Something about the neighboring kingdoms, and not just when they belonged to us."

Marec whistled.

Nermand muttered something under his breath, and Holdan, who did everything with Nermand and Gannan, snickered meanly.

Janold turned to Nermand, who was an ordinary boy of sturdy build, looking like the others except for his habitual scowl. "Well, you must have said something stupid when you had your interview last year, because you're assigned with the scrub class for the history. They'll be learning rough stuff like where the borders lie."

Several of the others hooted in derision. Janold, with an ear to the outside, began reading through the list. The boys stayed quiet, listening for their own names, and then afterward discussed in whispers what the class groupings meant.

Eyes turned Shevraeth's way when his assignment was read. He did not have a history class at all. He was with the younger boys for sword training and hand-to-hand combat, and he was to go with the next level above his own barracks for knife work. That netted some exchanged looks. Finally, for riding, he was to report to the girls' side.

Silence.

Shevraeth wondered what that meant. An insult? No, none of those faces—specifically Nermand's—were gloating. Janold's expression in particular was difficult to interpret.

No time for reactions or discussion. Through the open window behind Nermand's bed they heard Zheirban splashing across the flagstones, and scrambled to their places at the foot of each bunk.

Zheirban entered, they all saluted (Shevraeth still had to fight the urge to bow) and he tromped down the center aisle and back, but Shevraeth wasn't the only one who noted his absent gaze. His head might be turning, his eyes moving, but Zheirban saw nothing in front of him. Whatever he truly looked at was inside his head.

He was gone again in the space of three breaths.

Janold said, "Defaulters in the classes still mark against the House, so watch it. Anyone does anything stupid, you'll not only catch the breeze from the masters, you will from me, too. I want the gag off as badly as the rest of you." He opened his hand toward the door.

"Gag?" Shevraeth murmured as he fell in behind Stad.

The curly dark head half-turned. "By Restday, if we don't get over three defaulters, we drop back to one inspection a week. And we also get to talk in mess."

No time for further conversation. They had to run to their first class.

Shevraeth knew generally where the stables lay, and loped in that direction.

The stable area, with its training pens and runs, was the largest discrete segment of the academy. Despite his wet clothing and the rain in his face Shevraeth was warm by the time he reached the stable gate. A swift rise of notes on a bugle caused him to fall back just before he entered the gate. Galloping hooves approached, and a double column of third year seniors rode out, the horses' tails streaming, the high-held banner snapping. The boys rode with consummate skill, looking even close at hand like they and the horses were one.

Shevraeth whistled under his breath, and when the splashing hooves were safely past, he continued on inside. When he spotted a boy pulling a cart of hay bales, he said, "Where—"

"Main stable," said the boy, after a cursory glance.

Shevraeth grimaced as he loped round the corner and into the first big courtyard. Everyone seemed to know who he was, all right. Was it his long hair hanging wetly down his back? He didn't look all that different from most of the others, he was certain.

Mentally shrugging the subject off, he continued on his way. Because there were only a couple lines of girls, because the girls were apparently new to the academy routine, he assumed someone had given them a little side barn, so he was quite surprised to discover girls all over the main stable, the big one with the uncountable rows of stalls. It was the boys, he realized, who trained off-side.

As he crossed the dirt yard, packed hard as rock over centuries, several girls paused in their tasks. The younger ones under the big overhang stared openly, one giggling and a taller one fingering her hair. A thin, pale-haired girl of about sixteen said something in a clipped undervoice and they returned to pitching hay, their manner exactly like younger boys threatened with a breeze, though Shevraeth did not see a cane in the older girl's hands or in her belt.

This girl met his gaze, and without any change of expression tipped her head over her shoulder toward the great barn.

Shevraeth realized she was some sort of radlav and gave her a two-finger salute over his heart, just as he did the radlavs on the boys' side. Her face relaxed minutely just before she turned away.

Inside, everything smelled of horse and hay. Shevraeth walked slowly into the gloom, his eyes adjusting.

"Over here."

Behind him stood a tall girl with short black curls. She dropped the reins of a haltered horse into the hands of another girl and walked toward Shevraeth, her pace leisurely, her dark eyes narrowed in assessment.

She wore the loose clothes of the under-school, except her collar was the high one of the seniors' tunics. Her manner was that of a radlav and so he saluted, two fingers to heart, and she acknowledged with a wave, the corners of her mouth deepening. "Shevraeth?"

He began to bow, fought the instinct, and nodded awkwardly.

"I'm Senelac. Today let's see what you know, what you need to unlearn, before I figure out who's going to teach you."

He'd been silent so long that he just had to talk now. "You didn't hear the report from the first day disaster? Or do you need a laugh?"

At once he realized he had probably gotten himself into trouble. Boys were not supposed to talk unless they were asked a direct question. That much he knew. But here he had anyway, because it was a girl, not a boy, because she did not carry a cane. He realized he hadn't expected the threat of violence because women didn't use violence as a weapon at home. Of course Marloven girls wouldn't be like those at home, and he braced for reprisal.

Intelligent black eyes scanned him from head to heels, then back up to his face, before she said reflectively, "I do all my own evals." She beckoned to the waiting girl, who brought forward a saddled horse, a fawn-colored mare with cream-white face and lower legs. "Up you go."

No bridle. No bit. No real saddle, he saw when he stepped close. Just one of those quilted pads, securely attached to stirrups. And a halter, leaving the horse's mouth free.

Shevraeth vaulted up, settled himself, then took the reins in the way he'd been taught, and glanced back expectantly.

"Just as I thought." She crossed her arms. "Excellent seat. Just no grip, and once you get your forearms free and carry your reins, you'll do."

Grip? Carry? He looked at his hands, then back again.

"Grip here." She smacked her hands against her thighs. "Never mind. Get her to walk. No, not with the reins. Knees. One fast press. Your forearms and hands are part of the reins. You don't pull, you guide. The feel of the rein is enough, you never need to yank. Your arms and the reins are all one."

Shevraeth loosened his arms, barely holding the reins, and flexed his inner thigh, squeezing his knee against the animal's side.

The mare obediently walked sedately forward.

"Two quick ones."

He had to concentrate, but his muscles obeyed well enough, apparently, for the mare began to trot. She headed for the wall, and he felt the urge to yank the rein to guide her in a circle, but hesitated, sensing that he would at best confuse the animal.

Senelac had been watching closely. "Lower leg press. Either side."

He flexed his left calf—and the mare turned promptly.

Three or four more commands followed, all conveyed through his legs. He performed each and watched the horse's ears, her breathing, feeling her great muscles beneath him. Finally he was told to flex both legs all the way down, and the mare stopped.

Senelac gestured, a flick of the fingers, and he leaped down.

"Come here."

She led the way to a narrow door between two sets of stalls. They passed tack rooms, everything hanging neatly, and tables where girls and boys worked under the supervision of one man and one woman. Beyond that lay a room with stacks of bagged oats. At the other end they passed through another door that opened onto a courtyard.

This yard was enclosed by a high wall. It extended nearly the length of the front courtyard. On its far side he could just make out hoof beats and the high voices of smaller boys.

Before him was an amazing sight. Obstacles lay strewn all over this yard, about which three girls on horseback rode steadily. All three of the girls had their hands tied loosely behind their backs, and they were blindfolded.

And yet they rode as if they could see, as if they held reins—even when the animals leaped over low obstacles.

"They have to learn to trust their mounts, to understand them, listen to them, before they can truly guide," Senelac said.

Shevraeth nodded, so astonished at what he saw that he did not know how to respond. Presently he said, "Can you do that?"

A soft chuckle. "Since I was ten. We Senelacs have always been good, and I'm the best. My brother saw to that. Come." A whack from her palm against his arm.

He followed her back inside, but they did not go through to the barn. Instead she made an abrupt turn into the space with the feedbags, and when he stepped inside after her, she whirled around and shut the door, setting her back to it.

"You have a good seat, light hands, and you have the instinct to listen to your mount. I think I've reached a decision," she said. "But a question or two first. To be sure. See, the king wants you to ride. *They* don't." A tip of her head in the direction of the boys' side of the academy.

Shevraeth thought: why? It was easy to assume that the others had taken a dislike to him, except he knew that people rarely acted with one motive. Besides, only a few had ever seen him, and of those just a handful had actually spoken to him. No, the issue lay not with him, but elsewhere.

He realized he'd been frowning down at his hands, and looked up. Senelac was waiting for a response.

So he said, "What is it? Do they think I'll take the knowledge away and come back with an army?"

Her quick grin was both merry and a little wry. When she spoke, it was with decided approval. "Some fear that, yes. Others would love that. They know you come from the other side of the continent, but some of 'em are so ignorant for all they know that's a day's ride away. A few have the stupid reason of wanting to keep our military superiority just to keep it. Some are just afraid of change. We've had so much, of late."

He nodded. That made sense.

"So, do you want to learn to ride?" She jerked a thumb back toward the hidden court. "Really ride?"

"Yes," he said.

She grinned again. "Good. Then be here every morning before dawn. Every morning. I'll put you into the class with the little boys, as ordered, but in addition." She laughed softly. "You'll ride bareback, and learn how a horse moves, what their muscles do, how they talk to you. I will teach you myself."

# Five

*Russav: I think I have time for a couple of observations.*

Shevraeth did not add he hoped he had the strength for one. Every part of his body hurt, right down to the bone. Especially in the mornings when he first woke. But mentioning that even in a letter seemed too much like whining. He would let no complaints past either lips or fingers. It would prove what at least half his bunkmates seemed to believe, and what some of the older ones sneered, just within earshot: that he was soft. A coddled foreigner. Clumsy. Weak.

*The reason I have time is that this is Restday. Last week's Restday was taken up by punishment drill when three of my barracks-mates celebrated the lifting of the mess-gag and the inspections by breaking rules. Never mind which ones they broke. Too many to list. Angry as the others were, no one blabbed. So we all put in an entire afternoon cleaning, scouring, sweeping, then when we were really tired, various weapons drills. Not the fun ones, of course.*

*Today's Restday was mostly taken up by the first wargame of the season. They live for these wargames. Talk about them endlessly. This particular wargame was considered an easy one, that is, we march out to the field beyond the horse training paddocks, divide into ridings, carrying these grubby flags and nothing else. The goal is to protect your flag and steal everyone else's, and to that end we spent the entire day out under a heavy rainstorm chasing about after these flags.*

*We lost. The barracks one over won, the prize being our barracks flag, which is hung over their door, and they take precedence for a few days in mess line and at lineup for the colt classes. From the way they strutted and the rest cursed, this stuff really seems to matter.*

*All that by way of a reason for the week-and-a-half gap in writing, not my observations, which are these:*

*One, they use a lot of wood. I try not to show my dismay, because I know our Compact would be regarded as overly stringent by the rest of the world. They all have their own ways of dealing with wood that is acceptable to both the natural and magical world, and to prove it Fire Sticks are as common here as at home. The beds and benches and tables are all made of wood, though from the look and feel it is centuries old and has hardened into something not unlike iron. Doors, too, and my knuckles at first showed that tapestry habit can be harmful. (And some of the others assumed I'd been fighting. More of that anon.) But the wood that goes into arrows! Yes. They shoot arrows, not just on foot but from horseback. The sight of the seniors riding at the gallop and shooting at posts is impressive, make no mistake. At first I was not going to learn it (I was of course an abysmal failure at archery at the test) but the more I think about what my father said about the king's responsibilities and mysterious murders, the less I am convinced I'm right to refuse learning whatever they teach me. I don't have to use it. Or even to like it. But I think I had better know it.*

Janold entered, shaking rain off his hair. "Lights out soon."

The others looked up, one from reading, some from repairing their clothes, most from the card game taking place on Hauth's and Andaun's beds, which had been shoved together for the purpose. Shevraeth was the only one writing; two were already asleep.

*I will say they retrieve every arrow they can, and they reuse wood as scrupulously as we would.*

*I am running out of free time, and who knows if next Restday will afford me any. So my second is this. I can understand having places for quarrels, I can barely understand why some of the bigger boys or the ones good at scrapping would spend time prowling that area looking for fights. What I cannot get a grip on is what I first thought of as bare-faced hypocrisy: the universal emphasis on obeying the rules, enforced with those disgusting canes, yet everyone from the highest to the lowest participates in overlooking their breaking, when it comes to these same duels. There is something at work here that is not courtly lying, which until now has been my internal standard for hypocrisy.*

*The strangest thing of all is that the dueling has its own set of rules, strictly obeyed or you set off yet another round of duels. When I say 'duels' it does not mean two people with weapons of choice. Here there are no weapons (and now I know why!) it's all fistfights, and there can be any number involved—*

The lights-out bell tolled, the sour note reverberating down the high stone walls between the barracks buildings and then echoing faintly off the higher castle walls. Shevraeth knew by now that he would have just enough time to stopper his ink bottle, shove the on-going letter back inside his trunk, fling his clothes off, and get into bed before the glowglobe would be clapped out.

Some grumbled and griped, but silence fell almost immediately after. As had happened for the past two weeks, Shevraeth slid promptly into exhausted sleep, waking at first-bell, which was a full watch—what they called four hours—after midnight. Two thirds of a candle at home.

Once or twice Stad rose as well, dressing hastily then vanishing through the door without even looking Shevraeth's way. The others still had half a watch of sleep ahead, but Shevraeth pulled on his clothes, tiptoed to the cleaning frame and felt the sleep-grit snap from eyes, mouth, skin. He'd learned how to brush his own hair on the ship, as his father had wished, for there were no personal servants at the academy, he'd been warned. He ran his fingers impatiently through it, yanking through snarls, then tied it back with his ribbon. He picked up his boots and trod noiselessly to the door, as he had every morning since his first interview with Senelac. Sniff, listen. Good, no rain. He ran across the courtyard, and as soon as he was through the archway to the main passage he paused and shoved his feet into his boots.

Then he ran, for the morning was chill. The run was excruciating at first. He passed the archways leading to the other colt barracks, one, two, three, and then he began to feel warm, the ache in his muscles lessening to what he now considered bearable. Strange, that. At home, this much ache would have caused him to take an easy day at his desk, reading and writing. There were no easy days here. Ever.

He reached the great barns and looked around the globe-lit riding paddock, fighting yawns as he performed the by-now familiar tasks: locating the night watch stable hand, selecting a horse experienced at night training, mounting, riding round and round and round, attention to seat, grip of legs, and all the subtle signals the horse sent to him in response to his own body's signals.

When Senelac arrived just before dawn she stood in the still-dark barn, observing him. That made the fifth time this week he was there not just on time, but earlier than she was. As soon as she entered the yard she began issuing a stream of criticisms.

Business as usual.

The one good thing about getting up so early, he'd discovered, was that he was thoroughly warmed up by breakfast time. He followed the others inside, his thoughts as usual confined inside his own head. He was not the only silent one at those early meals, though the first-week mess gag had of course been lifted, and the mess hall filled with noisy voices at each meal—unless an entire barracks had enough defaulters to put them back under the gag rule.

After breakfast they ran to their first class. He had not expected to like archery, given the ban against it at home. The first week he hadn't done anything but practice drawing the bow and pretend shooting, over and over until his arms quivered like loose string. Already he could feel a kind of inward calm once he began the rhythm: raise, aim, draw, shoot—the arrow arm snapping back. He wasn't the only one practicing just the form over and over, at least. Sloppy shooting arms had landed several boys over scrub age in that class.

On his way to knife throwing he paused at the fence of the big paddock. A riding of older boys galloped in line. On command they drew their arrows and shot, arms snapping back to a straight line from fingertip to fingertip before arcing down to nip another arrow and in the same smooth half-circle bringing another arrow to the string. As the horses galloped along a track, the boys shot at spaced targets.

Their movements were so smooth, deliberate— accurate—Shevraeth decided to adapt that same circle to his knife throwing.

He rarely missed dead center that day.

He scarcely noticed the others watching speculatively. He was locked inside his head, partly from tiredness, partly from the rarity of conversation. Mostly from intense concentration. When the master dismissed the class, most of the boys took off running. Shevraeth followed more slowly, his thoughts still on that smooth circle, and how it also applied to the saber-fighting from horseback. He could see how effective it was, once you built up your strength and speed, but it required him to unlearn all he'd learned about point, about the narrow bounds of the polite duel of the east. If you could call dueling polite—

Whop! Pain—someone yanked his hair.

His arm came up in a block as he turned. He knocked the hand away, and looked up into unfamiliar pale blue eyes.

"Cut that hair off," said the boy. A senior, by his size, by the fitted coat.

Shevraeth fought against the haze of surprise, confusion, tiredness. He did not recognize this senior. He was not a radlav, because he did not have a wand.

The practice area was filled with seniors. He had forgotten one of his father's earliest rules: *Be observant at all times.*

Everyone stared at him, expecting him to respond.

His heart thumped. "What's it to you?"

"Your presence," came the retort, "is an insult." And on some laughter from behind, the senior curled his lip.

Shevraeth crossed his arms. "I'm desolated." Too late his muscles responded to old home habit, and he performed a slight, ironic bow, one hand up in mirror mode. It did not take much imagination for the Marloven boys to interpret that as a kind of airy dismissal.

Several of the seniors laughed.

The class Shevraeth had been practicing with, the boys next level down from senior, had backed up, all of them watching the foreigner, the seniors, the foreigner. The rules didn't cover this situation. Did they protect the foreigner, who wasn't really one of them yet, or let him stand alone, though he hadn't done anything to be gated out?

The seniors' laugh seemed to anger Shevraeth's opponent even more than his bow. He flushed with anger, then said, loudly, "The king says we all go by the regs. That means outlanders too." The word 'king' was delivered with a teeth-baring sneer.

*There's something other than my long hair at stake here.*

The bell rang for third class, and the younger boys broke and ran. Shevraeth turned away. His shoulder blades twitched, but he kept his pace steady and did not look back.

At sword practice, he was no longer locked in his thoughts, he was intensely aware of the reflective gaze of the seam-faced master, and the whispers and furtive stares of the little boys. Word of the strange encounter had somehow spread ahead of him.

While he stood there with the spring sunlight warming his body in its shapeless gray tunic, his mind returned to that wintry day. After his father had told him he was coming here, his mother had summoned him for her own interview.

"Will you promise me something, my boy?" she had said.

"Of course, Mother."

She was tiny and birdlike. He'd been taller than her at thirteen, and he was the smallest of most of the boys their age at court.

She hugged him against her. He felt the trembling in her arms, and a swoop of sorrow had gone through his middle. "I know you mean it, but I also know what I ask will not be easy," she had said. "It seems that you must learn something of war, if only to understand how best to prevent it, or failing that, how to control it with as little cost as can be. Too many of our records show that wars conducted by those who know nothing of the matter can be more bloody, and long-lasting, than fights against conquerors such as the Marlovens of the past. Learn, therefore, what they have to teach, but do not become one of them."

"I don't want to become any Marloven," Vidanric had protested.

"You know of course that they number among your ancestors," Princess Elestra replied, smiling at him. "And I don't mean any Marloven. I mean the royal family, the same ones who produced Ivandred the Conqueror."

*Whose descendent I am going to now*, Vidanric had thought.

"It was Ivandred's sister Theraez who came among us and married into the Calahanras family. Her daughter thus married the Renselaeus heir. You therefore have a kind of cousinship with the young Marloven king. That might, indeed, lie behind his decision to accept you into their training, which at least historically was kept very secret."

Vidanric had bowed agreement.

"I tell you only to give you perspective, and thus to come to my request. Promise me on your honor that you will endeavor, at least once a week—every day if you can—to perform an act of kindness. It will not count if it is meant to gain you something, whether praise, friendship, or material. It must be unseen, unspoken. Promise me."

He'd been trying to keep that promise, but without anyone knowing. It would be sickening to be caught at it, to force some boy who maybe didn't even want him here to say thank you—if he had manners. So he gave some surreptitious twitches to Ventdor's bed (he couldn't seem to ever get it straight) before inspection, put Stad's boots through the cleaning frame one night when Stad had fallen asleep without meaning to. Stad was up as early as Shevraeth, vanishing somewhere. It couldn't be punishment. Stad never did anything wrong. But he never said where he was in Shevraeth's hearing. He also stayed up late when they were offered extra practice after supper. He worked hard, he slept like he'd been knocked cold.

Shevraeth also left the last hunk of cheese for someone else, when he would have liked it. Little things all. But he meant them as kindnesses, and he hoped no one saw him at it.

This promise to his mother, so unexpectedly difficult to keep, was still on his mind at the midday meal. He felt the stares again, though when he looked around no one met his eyes. Round-faced Baudan set his tray down abruptly next to him, and said, "You gonna cut your hair?"

Shevraeth put his bread down. "I take it someone's been blabbing. Nothing better to talk about?"

Baudan snorted. "Everyone always blabs about Tdanerend Sindan."

Stad was sitting across from Shevraeth. He leaned forward. "Sindan was supposed to be Thanar Valdlav."

Shevraeth had learned that the Thanar Valdlav was the head boy commanding the academy foot exercises, as opposed to Danas Valdlav, the boy cavalry commander. Those were the exact translations of the academy ranks, but he still hadn't quite figured out the implied meanings. Zheirban—the Danas Valdlav—was supposedly the highest ranking boy at the school, but there were many who seemed to think Thanar Valdlav as high, or rather at least as important. Shevraeth couldn't figure out if this was because of some elusive attribute of the rank, or because of the boys themselves.

So was this foolishness just a matter of a sulky big boy who didn't get the promotion he wanted? Instinct, that nasty tone when Sindan said *harvald*, king, hinted at more.

He hesitated, trying to frame his question. He understood pretty much everything now, but he still had trouble expressing himself.

Dishes clunked on the table. Everyone looked up.

With a smirking glance Shevraeth's way, Nermand dropped down onto the bench, Holdan and Gannan on either side. Stad began eating. Baudan turned to skinny Andaun on his other side, and started talking about the foal born just that morning. Next to Stad, Vandaus pulled a grubby paper from his pocket, laid it between his and Faldred's plates, and the two began studying.

Shevraeth bent over his food, but his attention was not on it. He was aware, for the first time in days, of the clatter of the broad, shallow wooden dishes, the high, shrill small-boy voices at one end contrasting with the deeper, raspy burr of the teens at the others. The girls' light voices, behind and to the left, were just barely discernable. There were fewer than a hundred girls, and something like four hundred boys.

When the meal was done, Shevraeth waited until Vandaus finished, then stepped next to him in line to clean and stack their dishes. Vandaus and the other new boy, Faldred, read all the time, either books or papers. Vandaus had said on the second day, in a matter-of-fact voice, that he meant to be a desk jockey to a Jarl. Faldred looked like a Marloven version of Shevraeth—tall, weedy, gray-eyed, with pale hair, and very quiet. He had motioned agreement, and no one seemed to think anything of it. Those two, if anyone, would know the regulations binding the academy.

"Is there a reg for hair?" Shevraeth asked Vandaus, as Faldred ran off on some errand.

Sure enough, Vandaus didn't look surprised. He swiped a thick swatch of rust-tinged hair out of his eyes in an absent gesture. "No." He paused, brow wrinkling slightly as he considered. "No. I don't think it's ever come up. Everyone arrives with short hair, which has been the military cut since my greatfathers' days. Though farther back cavalry had horsetails. To mark 'em apart. But no longer. The horsetails are real ones. On their helms."

"Thanks," Shevraeth said, and Vandaus loped off in the direction Faldred had gone.

Shevraeth walked more slowly. If anyone had asked, he would have cut his hair. He didn't care if it was long or short. Hair grew.

But he would not cut it at the orders of a bully.

# Six

The afternoon was spent first in grappling, and then Janold took their barracks to one of the empty courts south of their barracks, hard against the wall dividing them off from the lower school. Over the wall came the high-pitched yells of small boys busy at some game, punctuated by laughter and insults.

Janold set them to sparring so he could assess everyone's progress.

Shevraeth watched closely, aware of looks his way from some, but no one said anything outside of Nermand's muttered, "You running to Sindan's rein?"

"No."

Shevraeth turned away, reaching for the cracked, dusty padded gear they all put on before handling wooden swords.

Nermand glanced aside. Janold was busy watching a match between Mondar and Alrec, calling encouragements, hits, and criticisms.

Nermand licked his lips. "Then you're gonna take a stroll, outlander." His usual scowl changed to a nasty grin of anticipation.

Shevraeth knew by now that *take a stroll* was slang for sneaking behind the second and third year senior barracks, where most of the scrapping took place.

He looked at Nermand in disgust, then remembered his mother's admonition. So he said only, "Your turn." And he indicated Alrec and Mondar, who were just finishing.

The rumble of thunder in the distance caused skyward glances. Clouds moved northward, making the glare especially white and intense. But there was no immediate threat of rain, so Janold shrugged and pointed at two more boys.

Everyone was sweat-drenched, hot, thirsty, and tired when the mess bell rang for dinner. Shevraeth followed behind the others, keeping a slow pace as other boys raced into the passage from various practice courts.

He was surrounded by a swarm of ten and eleven year olds. Gannan did not see Shevraeth among the crowd as he bustled up to Nermand. "Sindan jumped Lennac."

"Where? When?"

"After noon mess. Behind the stable."

Nermand gasped, and Shevraeth thought, *Against both sets of rules, the visible and the invisible ones.*

"Dol says Master Blackeye found Lennac—"

"Did Lennac rat?"

Gannan snorted. "Of course not. Fall from a horse."

"Why'd Sindan jump Lennac?" Nermand asked eagerly.

Gannan glanced back to make sure they weren't being overheard. Nermand also turned around. When they saw Shevraeth their excitement smoothed into the usual smirk, then they ran, Gannan whispering.

That night in their barracks Nermand stalked down the aisle between the beds and confronted Shevraeth. "You gonna cut your hair?" he asked loudly.

Shevraeth ached all over. He knew he'd be rising all too soon for yet another grueling day. The hot flash of anger he knew was mostly just tiredness, so he stayed silent, watching Nermand glance left and right. The room had gone silent, no one speaking.

"Are you?"

"No."

"Then you're gonna stroll."

"No." Shevraeth did not raise his voice, unlike Nermand.

Nermand licked his chapped, chewed lips as he furtively looked to either side. Now Shevraeth could put emotion to his expression and stance. Nermand was looking for support.

No one interfered, though they all listened.

"You're a coward." Nermand poked a finger at Shevraeth, without quite touching him.

The heat of anger flashed much hotter this time. Shevraeth maintained his breathing, concentrating on the court mask. When he could trust his tone to remain even and polite, he said, "You just go ahead and embrace that thought if it pleases you."

At home that would have caused the fight Nermand was obviously spoiling for, but here the others looked puzzled, except for Stad, who snickered. Baudan grinned as he undressed for bed.

Nermand hesitated, glaring at the newcomer, who just did not make any kind of sense. Was he a coward, or wasn't he? Why was he *here*? What else was going to change, and for the worse?

"You're a coward," he said louder. To make it absolutely clear even to a stupid foreigner, he added, "And it makes us all look bad."

Again the foreigner didn't react any of the ways Nermand understood. No threats, no shoves (and he was braced, Gannan behind him, breathing hard, as support), nor did he look afraid. Or give in.

Instead he swung around, his shirt in his hand. "Stad. Do you think you look bad?"

Stad waggled a hand.

Shevraeth lifted his head. "Evrec?"

Evrec, who had the bed directly across, just turned over and buried his face in his pillow.

"Baudan?"

Baudan wrinkled his snub nose and gave his characteristic pig-snort. "See me sweating? Shut up, Nermand."

Shevraeth glanced down the row of beds on his side of the aisle, met the eyes of bony, red-haired Marec. "You?"

Marec said, "I hate Sindan."

It was not an answer that Shevraeth understood, but several of the boys made little movements of involuntary agreement, and he realized once again he'd missed a clue—but right now, the important thing was that Nermand wasn't getting the backup he so obviously wanted.

When Janold's step sounded in the little hallway outside the room Nermand flung himself away.

Janold paused in the doorway, eyes narrowing. "Lights out."

ഇൽ C380 ൽ

Next morning, when their session was almost over, Senelac looked into Shevraeth's tight face, and against her better judgment said, "Are you—"

He whirled around. For the first time she saw him express a normal human emotion.

As usual, it was anger. In her experience, the first thing you saw out of stone-faces was always anger. Maybe laughter being second.

"No." His melodious accent was quite strong. "I am not going to cut my hair."

She laughed. "I was going to ask if you were aware of what's galling Sindan's saddle."

"So you know about it, too."

"Everyone knows everything about Sindan Hotears. He makes sure everyone knows his business."

Shevraeth let out his breath. "Then you'd know if whatever it was he did to this Lennac yesterday, whom I do not know, had anything to do with me?"

Senelac rubbed her hand across her grimy brow. "It's more that everything has to do with the academy. Or more like, the king. See, promotion is supposed to be on merit. Not on family. Sindan's family, which is an old one, was tight with the Regent. Sindan was named for him. In the Regent's day, they pretended it was merit, but it wasn't. Now it is. The king made Ret Forthan, whose family's mostly farm people, Thanar Valdlav. Everyone including Sindan knows Forthan is smart, fast, strong. A leader. But—" She shook her head, aware suddenly she was saying too much to this foreigner. It was one thing to be ashamed of the way things used to be under the Regent, and it was quite another to expose those things to outsiders.

Shevraeth said, "Tell me this. Did Lennac really fall off a horse?"

Her face changed. "No. Of course not. That's what—"

"Tell me. Please. Nothing makes sense." Again his emotions—his frustration—was clear.

It was that plain human emotion that prompted her to say, "It's what we say when the masters ask. Because we try to solve our problems ourselves. Aren't we here to learn to command?"

Shevraeth looked pained. "So let me get this straight. Lennac did not tell the authorities, an action that protected a bully. Who broke the rules. Not just the real rules, your regs, as you call them. But these w—" He bit off the word *weird.* "These unwritten other rules, concerning the fist fights behind the upper level senior barracks, which incidentally are also against regs. But no one does anything about them, and that's part of learning command?"

His long-repressed feelings made him sarcastic, and he saw as soon as it was out that sarcasm was a mistake. Senelac's expression tightened from interest to reserve.

"I don't know," she said, pleasantly enough. But her tone, her face, her entire countenance made it clear the subject was closed. "Wasn't there. See you tomorrow."

Shevraeth turned away, feeling a sudden brief, violent urge to smash something.

No one would talk, that was clear enough. Well, he thought as he ran toward the mess for breakfast, he supposedly was to have an interview with the king. Who was just another boy. *I'll ask him.* Anger flaring through him once more, he vowed, *And the next idiot who asks if I'm cutting my hair will get a fist for his pains. Not behind the barracks, or behind anywhere. Right then and there, and see if he tells anyone he fell off a horse.*

ЯО СЗ ЄО СВ

But no one asked him anything over the next three days, as the last of the storms departed, leaving summer weather upon them at last, with an unrelenting strength that left them all limp and weary at day's end, grateful if Janold let them go to the baths, which were like baths anywhere else: huge stone pools fed by diverted spring water. Only there was no magic heating them, but the cold water was refreshing. Houses only got to visit the baths if they did not earn House defaulters for the day.

Gradually Shevraeth found himself closing back inside his own head, so that third night he was not particularly wary or even interested when Gannan, Nermand's other crony, muttered just before lights out, "Messenger for you in the court."

Messenger? Maybe it was the king. *At last* was Shevraeth's first thought, and his hand fell away from his sash, which he'd been about to untie. He shoved his feet back into his boots and dashed for the door.

Stad called, "Shevraeth! Wait, Janold's not—"

But by then it was too late.

Before he'd gone five paces into the darkness beyond the door hard hands seized him. He started to fight, to be yanked off balance by someone much bigger and stronger. From inside the barracks came a confusion of muffled yells that abruptly stopped.

The hands shoved him out of the barracks courtyard and into the passage between theirs and the second year colts' barracks. He resisted with all his strength. The only sounds were the scrape of heels on stone, and heavy breathing. He smelled the sharp sweat of older boys.

The hands flung him against a wall. Stars flared across his vision, leaving him gasping. He was propelled farther into the passage. He fell painfully to his hands and knees, rolled to his feet as he'd been so recently trained, and glared at Sindan, who was faintly lit by the ruddy, beating light of the torches high on the castle walls.

Sindan pulled a knife from his sash, its steel shining blue in the moonlight, watermarks rippling down just inside the edges. "Kneel. I'm going to cut your hair. Free to all foreigners."

Muffled snickers from the circle: five, six voices. No chance, no chance at all.

"No," Shevraeth said.

The fist seemed to come out of nowhere. Again sparks flared across his vision, but he launched himself, with all his pent-up anger, emotion, even isolation, taking his assailant by surprise.

He bore Sindan backward, and they both crashed to the worn stone ground in a tangle of arms and legs, to the sound of muffled whoops from the watchers. But that was the last good blow he got in.

Sindan might not be the best in the academy but he was stronger, faster, and far better trained than Shevraeth, not to mention much bigger. Blow after blow sent red flowers of pain blooming through Shevraeth's body, punctuated by Sindan's breathless, husky voice: "Kneel."

"No."

After five or six repetitions, Shevraeth's lips were too numb and he couldn't speak.

"Kneel."

He shook his head. Mistake. Shards of bright color blinded him, followed by floating black spots. He staggered to his feet, though the world reeled so violently he wasn't quite sure he was standing any longer. His teeth all felt loose, he couldn't seem to move his left arm. But he made it to his feet.

Smash! He didn't even feel himself landing on the stones again.

"Kneel."

Anger alone enabled him to roll over, get one foot under him, his one good hand on the ground. His body shivered, the world tilted and whirled.

Distant noise. Buzzing, keening in his head. Nothing made sense, nothing except the whisper, "They're coming."

"Get him down."

He was just trying again to stand when the hands gripped his arms and legs and flung him face down to the stones. Then pressed him flat. Still he fought, though his movements were little more than wriggles, and the grip on him far less severe.

One vicious hand yanked his head back by his ponytail, and the other sawed hard at his hair next to his scalp. Then the tail of hair gave and his chin struck the stones.

The hands lifted away from his arms and legs, and he was aware of the urgent need to pee. He had just enough consciousness left to whisper the Waste Spell that everyone learns at age two, and the pressure in his bladder eased. Then darkness took away all the pain.

Not for long. Not nearly for long enough. He felt hands on him again, he was sick, dizzy, couldn't get his feet to move, wanted just to be left alone, but hands insistently bore him somewhere, until at last, oh, at last he lay flat on a bed. Voices buzzed, whispered, whirling slowly with the world.

Whispers, a cool cloth on his face, and someone else gave him a gift more precious than kingdoms, trickling cold water between his bruised lips. He sucked it down, choked, and the water withdrew.

The voices withdrew.

No. The voices silenced.

Light pressed against his eyelids, and he heard breathing. A man's low voice. Low. Kind. But urgent. "What happened?"

A man? So far, men had never entered the barracks, they stayed in the training courts and fields.

Shevraeth made the greatest effort of his life and opened his eyes. Despite the slowly revolving world he made out Stad standing at attention, a water mug in his hand. A bruise was forming on his temple and his clothes were all awry. Next to him stood Baudan with the cloth. Ventdor wiped a cut on his own cheek, Vandaus held the water pitcher. All at attention, all looking back at Shevraeth with the same expression of shock and anxiety.

Seated on Stad's bed was an older man. Graying. In a black uniform with a thin gold stripe down the trouser seam that vanished into high blackweave boots. "I am Commander Keriam," this man said slowly. "Can you speak? Tell me what happened to you?"

When Shevraeth tried to lift his head, more black spots swam across his vision, but he still saw details: Stad's white knuckles gripping the mug. Baudan's flickering glance of apprehension at the commander.

Shevraeth worked his lips, realized the water had helped, at least enough for him to draw a shallow breath. What could he say? *Try asking Sindan.*

*Or You people are savages.*

Or, most compelling of all, *I want to go home.*

*But my father sent me here. There is something I must learn.*

He heard Senelac's low, soft voice: *We try to solve our problems ourselves. Aren't we here to learn to command?*

He said, "Fell. Off. Horse."

# Seven

Three days later, Shevraeth painfully retrieved pen and paper.

*Russav: It's Restday at the end of my third week, and I'm alone here, with plenty of time—*

Shevraeth dipped his pen, hesitated, and while the ink slowly beaded on the end into a tiny black tear, he thought, *Plenty of time, but I don't want to write. Rather tell you. What I come back to is that my father sent me here for a reason. Two reasons—training and statecraft. The second is a wash, but the first—*

The ink was about to drip. He used it to scribble out the line he'd written, though the exertion made his ribs ache. He shoved the pen and paper down into his open trunk, lay back for three breaths, then forced himself upright again. He capped the ink bottle, dropped it into the trunk and flipped the lid shut. Time to rest again.

Next he'd force himself out of bed to shove the trunk back under, though he still had sweat on his forehead from the effort it had taken to pull it out.

"Nothing broken," the Healer had said, that first night.

"Sindan! That Norsundrian soulsucker's always known exactly how far he can run," Baudan had said after the man's departure. "Never breaks bones. Trouble in that. Always just short of it."

Shevraeth's jaw had been tingling too much for him to speak, or he would have said, "You could have fooled me." But the Healer had done some kind of sealing spell to hold his loose teeth in his jaw so they could heal naturally. The ache didn't lessen any, unless he drank hot, extra-strong brewed listerblossom, but at least he wouldn't be gap-mouthed when he returned home.

He'd slept through two days and two nights.

Shevraeth waggled his jaw experimentally now. Closed his teeth. Yes, much better. Too bad his ribs ached. Ribs and everything else.

But they weren't broken, he reminded himself. So next day he'd ride.

Having resolved that he wondered if he should try to sleep again when he heard noise outside the open windows, the racket of footsteps, yelling voices, and moments later the boys in his barracks ran in, smelling of grass, sweat, and clammy cotton. They took turns dashing through the cleaning frame. Shevraeth watched the faint scintillation of magic as each boy shot through, and some flung themselves on their bunks. Others went for the water pitcher and mugs, chattering about classes. All except Gannan and Nermand, who were generally ignored. Several others crowded around Shevraeth's bunk.

"Bored?" Stad asked, sitting on his own. As far as Shevraeth could remember, it was the first time Stad had ever addressed him first.

"Oh, no," Evrec retorted, flinging his thin, pale hair back from his eyes. "Everyone loves being stuck flat with nothing to do."

"I wouldn't mind three days of rack time." Alrec yawned.

"Apply to the Watch House. They'll dust your togs." Stad whacked his arm in a brushing gesture. "As long as you stay small and alone, of course." The emendation caused general laughter.

*Watch House.* Shevraeth had paid little attention to the ever-changing references to the various barracks, other than learning that his was officially known as Southeast, and their grubby flag featured a brown square at the southeast corner of a block of gray squares. Nicknames for the barracks had changed rapidly over the first few days.

But it seemed like Watch House was settling in permanently for Sindan's barracks, the oldest building, officially termed Senior South. If three days could be a sign of permanence. It was a typically Marloven sort of joke, too. Shevraeth had been informed by a gleeful Marec the day after Sindan's attack. "At morning callover Zheirban said that since the academy is getting so clumsy it cannot seem to get from one place to another at night without falling down, there will be roaming sentry duty for a month, from night bells to dawn, and Senior South will serve all the watches."

Baudan had added triumphantly, "They get to divide up the time, but everyone to serve. Every night."

"You know what that means," Stad had added, chortling. "That means no one, not one single one of 'em, is gonna get a full night's sleep for a whole month."

"The entire House," Vandaus said, with his quiet, pensive smile.

"Won't they love that," Stad had drawled, causing a general gloat: high, hooting laughter.

Then the four of them glared at the other end of the dormitory, where Nermand and Gannan sat on the latter's bunk, playing cards, and apparently unaware of everyone else ignoring them—even Holdan. Gannan and Nermand hadn't told Holdan beforehand that they'd agreed to be Sindan's messenger boys for the scrag. Holdan hadn't said anything to anyone, but they all had seen how he utterly ignored Nermand and Gannan.

Stad gave Shevraeth an uncharacteristic look, uncertain. Tentative. "You're sitting up," he observed, an obvious statement that Shevraeth realized had to be prelude to something else.

Baudan smacked Stad in the arm, jerking his chin toward Shevraeth. "Want one of us to even it up in back?"

"It?" Shevraeth realized they meant his hair. He almost laughed, but it hurt too much. "I don't care. I don't have to see it."

"We do," Evrec said, pulling a face.

They laughed more than the stupid joke warranted, their manners a little too off-hand, or too intent, and Shevraeth realized he'd somehow changed status. Even though he'd lost a fight. No, it hadn't even gotten far enough to be a fight. He'd been scragged, just like the untrained foreigner he was.

His head hurt too much to think it out, but again he followed instinct, and said, "Sure. May as well."

And saw the corresponding relief in their faces. Not that anyone spoke. In fact the group broke up, all of them going about their business, except for Stad, who'd found a very sharp knife somewhere, against the rules. Unless again there was complicit permission from on high.

Shevraeth realized he was seeing his second Marloven dagger. It was beautifully made, slightly curved at the tip, as if to be used from horseback. Stad reached behind him, tugged a little, made quick, even saws that testified to the extreme sharpness of that blade. Then he stood back, Marec made a flat-handed sign of approval, and Stad took away hair and knife. Now Shevraeth looked like everyone else.

The mess bell rang, and they all clattered out again, leaving him alone.

Janold himself brought a tray of food, his manner slightly less grim than it had been the first few days.

Seeing that Shevraeth was awake (which he hadn't been the first three days Janold brought in food) the radlav set down the tray at the foot of the bed then squatted down beside it. "I'm sorry I got blindsided."

Shevraeth thought back. "You were gone."

Janold grimaced. "False message. Should have smoked a ruse as soon as Nermand spoke, but I didn't stop to think. Just ran all the way to the first barn, to discover that Master Voln hadn't sent for me. There was no alarm. He wasn't even there."

Shevraeth was intensely relieved that the radlav had brought up the subject. So talking about it couldn't be breaking some unbroken rule, as he'd feared. "What happened in here? I heard noise."

He'd waited for the others to bring it up, and they'd waited for him. Though they'd done what they could, in fumbling, furtive ways, to make up for their having been blindsided, Shevraeth did not know them well enough to see the signs. Nor could they understand his foreign mannerisms.

Janold rubbed his chin, making it plain how much the subject grieved him. Most of the time he seemed so old and tough, but right now the three years' difference in their ages diminished to nothing.

The barracks was Janold's responsibility, and he knew he'd failed Shevraeth. If he'd said something to the foreigner at the outset, Sindan wouldn't have found him so easy a target in his quarrel with the king. "Sindan sent five of his pals in here to hold the House when you went out. Baudan got sat on. Stad tried to run to your aid. Got knocked on his butt. Though I'm told Hunker Rand took a kick in the crackers first." He laughed briefly. "Ventdor and Marec also tried to run to your aid, and got turfed. The rest stayed put." His tone lowered, and Shevraeth realized he was apologizing for them.

Shevraeth drew in a slow breath. He was still far from understanding everything, but he sensed that more had changed than he'd first assumed. So he opened a hand in assent, then picked up his spoon.

That seemed to be the right response. Janold looked relieved, and stood up. "Need anything else?"

"I wouldn't mind one of your history books." Shevraeth carefully took a bite. His jaw still ached.

Janold said in a lower, gruffer voice, "About Nermand. Gannan. It's up to you, when we ungate 'em from Norsunder."

Norsunder? At home, you didn't make such light reference to Norsunder, it was considered at the very least impolite. Some said it was dangerous, that the Host of Lords, the mysterious and powerful mages who lived beyond time in Norsunder, were always on the watch. You never wanted to draw their unsleeping eyes.

What was polite and not polite seemed to be different here, but one thing was clear: Norsunder was still the timeless enemy.

And so 'gating to Norsunder' had to be slang for being shoved outside by community will. Not physically, but by a deliberate silence. Not only did everyone not talk to Nermand or Gannan, they didn't seem to hear if the two spoke.

More invisible rules.

How to answer the question? Impulse formed words: *As long as my teeth ache.* Then he remembered his promise to his mother. He struggled internally, not believing that any act of kindness at all toward bullies, random or not, would do any good in the world.

But a promise was a promise.

"Don't gate 'em on my account," he muttered.

Surprise widened Janold's eyes. He opened one hand in a brief gesture. "See what I can do about a suitable book." Five quick steps and he was gone.

&#8272;&#10070;&#8276;

Shevraeth made it to the barn just before dawn.

Senelac was there overseeing the longe-line training of some young horses. She stopped, and with furrowed brown took one look at his slow, stiff walk. Then she ran to him, making shooing motions with her hands. "Don't even think you're getting onto the back of one of my—of our horses. You'll upset 'em all."

He let out his breath. "Mostly came. To see if I could do it. Get out of the rack for a time, without—" He groped.

"Fuss," she finished, giving him a wry smile. "Well, I can understand that. Here. Come inside. Sit. I happen to have some listerblossom all fresh-brewed for one of the girls who took a bad fall yesterday."

He followed her to a small room adjacent the tack room, where there were some comfortable old chairs, a table, a tiny fireplace. The listerblossom was still warm, faintly steaming, and the morning was not yet hot enough to make that an unpleasant sight.

She poured out a mug, then sat opposite Shevraeth. "They evened it up nice in back." She flicked a curling black lock of her hair that lay against her cheekbone. "You look like one of us now." She chortled. "Trade for trade. Sindan is gated. Whole academy."

"Would have cut my hair the first day, if someone had told me I should."

"Then it would have been something else. But hair was easy. You stood out." She turned her hand over, a gesture he'd seen a few times, but as yet could not quite interpret. "No one knew if you had some kind of toff custom, wearing your hair long."

"Toff meaning it was assumed I was . . ." He hesitated, then used some of their slang. "I was on the swank? Even though I've been doing everything everyone else does."

"Meaning maybe it was for the king or Commander Keriam to pass down word." Her smile went wry again. "As for you, well, you dress like us, and you even look a lot like us, but you don't . . ." She twitched, hands shaping air. "Don't move like us," she finished.

He drank more, not wanting to ask what he moved like. He wasn't sure he wanted to know, especially after he'd been trying so hard to fit in.

He lowered the cup, and jerked his head irritably, despite how much it hurt. Already he hated short hair, how the top part would fall in his eyes if he leaned forward. But he knew it would train back eventually. "I didn't realize I stood out. No mirrors here. At least in our barracks."

"Mirrors?" Senelac tipped her head to the side, and Shevraeth wondered if the girls didn't have mirrors any more than the boys did. Well, it made sense. In this kingdom everyone seemed to dress alike, either in uniforms or similar garments. She shrugged, then grinned. "I'll bet the others haven't told you what they're calling your barracks."

Shevraeth said, "No."

"Ponytail House."

He looked puzzled.

She laughed, seeing the unhidden confusion in his face. "It's partly a snap of the fingers under the seniors' noses, see. Because they didn't rein in Sindan. But it's also a ref to the past." She paused and when he shook his head, she said, "Way, way back. In our empire days, you see. The warriors wore their hair in what was called horsetails. The senior boys were ponytails. But when you first came to the academy, they cut your hair, and you were *in*. . . . Well, maybe it still doesn't make sense. Especially if long hair has some kind of meaning where you come from."

"Fashion. And habit." He flicked his hand out in matter-no-meaning mode.

She smiled; those movements of his were impossible to interpret, but they were kind of pretty. "The boys might not have understood you, but they did understand your back of the hand at orders from Sindan Hotears." She laughed as she held up the back of her hand in the direction of the boys' senior barracks.

The subject had not just gotten old, it made him vaguely uncomfortable. What could he shift to? History? But as yet he'd only parsed a single paragraph in the one Janold brought for him, as he'd first had to get Vandaus to write out the Marloven alphabet for him. Leffain had not taught him to read it.

She put her chin on her hands. "What are you thinking?"

He looked up in muted surprise. "About your alphabet."

"Ah. It's just that your stone face . . . reminds me of someone." She laughed softly. "Like him, you look human first when you get mad. And when you laugh. But you're a little more expressive now."

The conversation had turned strange, or maybe it was just his light-headedness from his first walk, and the strong listerblossom brew. "I don't even know the words in your language. It's how we're raised. We call it at home the *court mask*."

Senelac shook her head. "I don't know any other languages. Though the king speaks a bundle of 'em."

And Shevraeth said, "Is he your other stone face? Your king?"

Her eyes narrowed. "Oh yes. How did you know that? It probably saved his life—but it also got him into trouble." She paused, dropped her hands onto the table and gazed down at her palms, her straight brows furrowed. "I used to be a stable runner. In the Regent's day. He wouldn't let girls here. All we could be was servants and runners. But we all had to assemble for punishments. Once he had the entire castle assemble when he had the king caned. Not just welters, but weepers." She rubbed her fingers together, and Shevraeth realized, with intense revulsion, that she meant blood. "Kept trying to break him, but he kept that face right to—" Abruptly she stopped, and stood up. "Here I am blabbing away, and work is a-waiting. Don't come back until you can sit a horse."

She walked out.

Puzzle-clues. Everything was a clue, but as yet he didn't have the pieces to give him the sense of the entire puzzle.

One thing was clear. He had somehow slipped *in*, as Senelac had put it. That meant inside the community. Before he'd been outside. Not shunned—'gated to Norsunder'—not when he'd been invited by their king. But the king had not intervened since that very first day, which meant that aura of royal protection no longer held him apart. Instead his own actions had brought him in, whereas Sindan, who officially had done nothing and so officially could not be punished, was apparently being shunned by everyone else for stepping outside of those invisible rules. The particular verb for *scrag* the others used (only once in his hearing) he would translate as slang for *lynch*.

So the rules worked. Visible—and invisible.

He shook his head over the world's strangeness, then his thoughts moved to what Senelac had told him about King Senrid. In Marloven, Senrid-Harvaldar—the 'ar' being added when used more formally. This king was his own age, or near, wore the court mask, spoke a bundle of languages.

Shevraeth very much wanted to meet him.

# Eight

But as time picked up its normal rhythm again, Shevraeth wondered if he was ever going to have that interview with Senrid-Harvaldar.

The others talked more around him now. It wasn't obvious. He hadn't been gated, before. Gating was deliberate. It's just that the others had sort of lived around him, as if he was a tree on the path, or a rock in the stream. Now he found himself part of the constant flow.

Vandaus, the serious, scholarly boy, looked around one evening. Stad wasn't present. He said, "I think Stad's in command class."

Scoffing noises sounded all around. "He's over at the stable, nights, is all. Half the new stock were from his family's horse stud." Baudan jerked a vague thumb. "He knows most of the horses. I bet you anything he's over there with the girls, longe-lining the yearlings."

Vidanric said, "Command class?"

"It's hand picked," Marec explained. "You have to be invited. We think it's held at night, when everyone has rec, so nobody knows who really goes and who doesn't. Only the seniors get invited."

"Ri-i-i-ight." Holdan drew the word out. "No first year colt's ever gone into command class."

"So *you* say," Baudan retorted. He didn't believe for a moment that Stad was at the castle with the seniors, but he was annoyed with Holdan's derision. "Everyone says Forthan was in it his very first year here."

"Wait." Shevraeth put down his cup. "Isn't learning command the purpose of this academy?"

Everyone looked blank. Then Faldred, the other new boy, said seriously, "There is a command class above the academy, you could say. It's by invitation from Commander Keriam, and you're not allowed to talk about it if they have you in. But it's only for those they think will be wing commanders and above. The rest of us will be desk jockeys, like me and Baudan here, or garrison commanders. *They*'ll be at the top."

"Most of us will be just captains," Ventdor said, grinning. "Lots of garrisons."

"Or we'll be border captains." Marec yawned. "We'll be in the chain of command of the ones in command class."

"So no one knows if Sindan is in it?" Shevraeth asked.

"Some of the seniors say he drops hints like he is." Faldred opened his hands. "But the masters won't confirm or deny. They just laugh if you ask anything about it."

"And the seniors drop on him for swank," Marec said, grinning.

Shevraeth was pretty sure he could tell who was satisfied to be a desk jockey or garrison commander, and who longed for a higher rank. *After the little I've read of their history, I don't even want to know what they study in their so-called command class.*

Just as well he was a foreigner. No one would be wanting to teach him secrets of Marloven conquering.

◦⊰⊱◦

By the end of the fifth week he was riding again, just practicing communicating with the horse, nothing more strenuous. At archery he was kept moving without arrows, repeating the drill in draw, shoot, arm back—circle down, draw, over and over. The master would not let him loose an arrow until he had the circle as drilled habit. Some things hadn't changed. The younger boys in his class thought it extremely funny that he was so profoundly ignorant about any aspect of archery, and hooted at pretty much everything he did—when the master wasn't turned their way.

His first day back in grappling practice, the master motioned him to take his place as if he'd never been away. "You boys have gotten into the habit of scrambling. That's fine when you're having fun. But I want you to remember, in any fight when you're smaller and lighter than your opponent, you have one chance to strike. Make it tell. In fact, unless you like fighting, that should be your aim even when you get your height and growth." Then he demonstrated.

Even without the sidled looks Shevraeth knew the lesson was aimed at him. That was all right. He'd already resolved that no one was ever going to take him by surprise again—and the master later reported in satisfaction that the foreigner was shaping up just fine, just fine.

During free moments he kept grinding away at the history book, and slowly he accustomed himself to the new alphabet, so that reading gradually became less like decoding a secret message.

He attended parade, and inevitably he saw Sindan, and knew Sindan saw him, but they ignored one another.

Shevraeth gradually realized there would be no more problems with Sindan, unless he himself sought them. The senior had learned that making a target of a younger boy, even a despised colt, was bad tactics. The younger boys still continued to talk about him, and reports of a preposterous number of fights made their way to Ponytail House, as Sindan fought his way through the seniors. Some fights Sindan won, some he lost, but he had apparently decided to confine his quarrel—whatever it was—to his peers.

Meanwhile Shevraeth began to listen for gossip about the king. He couldn't decide if he was being ignored, or just not noticed, and for what reason? That the king rarely interfered directly in the academy was obvious by now.

He was seldom a topic of conversation. Not that his actions were not of interest, but the boys seemed to be reticent about indulging in speculation, at least in front of Shevraeth. There were levels of being inside, just like anywhere else.

Some stray facts Shevraeth gathered as time seemed to pick up speed, and the days turned into weeks. A month galloped by, and half another, bringing back spring rains and then another taste of the summer to come. Shevraeth learned that the king had never been permitted to attend the academy, had been forbidden to learn the sword, but he'd managed to master archery on his own, and knife throwing—all things he could do on his own secretly, when the Regent was still asleep. That meant he'd risen at an impossibly early hour, every single day. From a very early age.

He'd also been taught hand-to-hand fighting, overseen by Commander Keriam himself—at risk of his own life. And he'd had to use it, too, when he'd reorganized the academy a bare year before Shevraeth came: one of the seniors had challenged him, and lost.

Two Jarls had also challenged him, and lost. Not in fist fights held in a practice court, but in the political field. Both were tough men with private armies and a taste for warfare. One had backed down when Senrid-Harvaldar arrived at his holding with three wings of cavalry, but the Jarl of Methden had apparently decided that the advent of a boy king was a signal to conduct his own expansion to the sea, and there had been some kind of skirmish ("Dust," the others had called it) during which Senrid had shown himself quite able at command. At least at dusts.

This last conflict has been caused by the father of Jarend Ndarga, the former Danas Valdlav. Stories about Jarend's toughness and prowess were easier to come by than gossip about the king, but this much was clear: he apparently had a strong sense of justice, and he had supported the king against his own father (and not just to inherit, as there was risk of their family being removed altogether from their title and holdings) begging only after the revolt was over and the boy king won that his father be exiled, and not executed. 'Gated' out of the country, and apparently all the Jarls had agreed with the king's decision, judging it right.

This is a king who knows something about state affairs, Shevraeth thought. Whatever his age. But if he wasn't permitted to go to the academy, where did he learn it?

The night of the tenth week's Firstday, Janold entered grinning. "We've got our overnight."

A shout rang up the wooden walls. Two people were quiet: Nermand, who brooded on his bunk, and Shevraeth, who knew overnights were extended wargames, and why would anybody be excited about that? The Sunday chases out in the fields were bearable now that he'd lost his soreness, but they were still more trouble than fun, in his view. Everyone wild, hot and thirsty, just to get those stupid flags.

"Who's riding captain?"

"Who's rad?"

"What House are we going up against?"

Janold crossed his arms, his expression mock angry. The whispers of speculation died away at once, and he studied the expectant faces before him, including Nermand's sulky frown, and Shevraeth's polite impassivity. He still did not understand the foreigner, but to Zheirban and Commander Keriam he'd said, *He'll be all right.* Meaning *he's settled in.*

"Your enemy is Mouse House." (So nicknamed because a few of its boys had tried a little too hard to get people to name them for one of the great predator cats.) "Ponytail House's riding captains are Stad and Evrec."

The two were by far the best at everything, so no surprises there, but still the boys gave in to whoops, whispers, laughing insults.

Evrec said to the faces turned his way, "You watch out, you lazy slackers. You'll learn the meaning of real discipline."

Stalgred pointed a finger. "Oh, sure, Evrec. You'll just be inventing commands to see us have to salute your sorry carcass."

Evrec widened his blue eyes. "Well, of course!"

When the laughs and insults died down at last, Janold said, "If you actually get out of the rack and pass inspection before dawn, we have leave to march."

Stad snapped his fingers. "And scarfle us prime digs. We'll be up and ready before the Mice even crack an eyelid. Won't we?" He looked around, tapping a fist against his palm.

A cacophony of pungent insults, emphasized by a hailstorm of balled-up dirty socks, was his answer.

It took a long time to settle down. Shevraeth lay in his bunk quietly listening to the muffled conversations, and the snickers. Once again a divide had opened between him and the others—not one of will, or intent, but one of expectation. They all looked forward to the prospect of a cold night outside after a long day of running around to no discernable purpose, and he braced for endurance. He fell asleep wondering if he would ever understand the others.

The next morning they were woken by Stad. Janold stood by, effectively invisible, as Stad and Evrec nagged, threatened, joked, and pleaded the others into getting ready for the early morning march. Five boys were sent to the mess to get their cooking gear, for they would be taking care of their own meals.

The sound of the dawn bells shivered against the paling sky as they marched through the back gate of the academy and straight west along a well-trampled dirt path. The weak light revealed uninteresting countryside, mostly fields between wind-worn low hills with streams meandering among them, wild grass growing everywhere, speckled with flowers. Here and there clumps of trees formed darker green patches against the yellow-green spring grass and the mild blue expanse of the sky.

They marched fast to warm up, two or three boys thumping on hand drums and the rest singing marching songs; this lasted until the strengthening light revealed their enemies ahead of them. The boys in front passed back the word, causing groans of disappointment and a few curses and threats that no one paid any attention to.

"Let's catch up and pass 'em," Stad said.

Janold rode alongside his charges. He said nothing as the boys sped up their pace, only grinning when Mouse House promptly put some bustle into their own pace.

The two groups gradually increased their speed until they were all running, arriving hot and breathless just before noon at a site where two academy masters on horseback waited under a clump of spreading oak.

Blats on horns pulled up the two rival groups into more-or-less straight lines. One of the masters on the hill waved a flag. The boys broke line and ran, Shevraeth running with them, though as yet he didn't know what for.

Stad led, his dark head jerking from side to side with his effort to outrun a tall redhead from the rival House. They raced flat out for an outcropping of rock just below the hillock with the trees, the redhead reaching it first.

Around Shevraeth the Ponytails groaned but Stad just waved as he veered, running at top speed on the other side of the hillock to an ancient hedgerow running north/south.

"They got the prime digs," Evrec sighed.

Shevraeth realized that *prime digs* meant the campsite in the most defensible position, and with water nearby.

"So we turf 'em out," Marec piped up in his shrill voice, his flushed face almost as bright as his ruddy hair.

"We'll set up first, and see what's what." Evrec waved a hand, then yawned.

Stad called, "Water's still here." He pointed through a break in the hedge, through which they could hear the chuckle of a stream. "So at least we won't have to trade for water."

Shevraeth asked Vandaus, who stood nearby. "Trade?"

"Giving them some advantage," Vandaus said in his precise way, wiping back his sweat-slick blond hair. "Later in the summer, when this stream runs dry, or in springs when we get rains late, whoever gets the rock digs at the river has the best ground, and the others are forced to trade advantages to get water."

Shevraeth nodded, remembered that nods didn't mean anything here, and opened his hand in copy of their gesture for agreement or understanding.

The five who'd been assigned cook duty unloaded their packs and everyone helped them set up the cook tent that two other boys had carried rolled up. The knowledge that the sooner the setup was done everyone would eat (having skipped breakfast) made for willing hands.

Both teams served out food. This was Shevraeth's first outside experience of the ancient Marloven travel bread, a recipe that had not materially changed for hundreds of years. The dense, heavy rye bread was thick with nuts and berries, a blend of bitter and sweet that took some getting used to. Hunger helped, as did small bites of the sharp yellow cheese also served out. They washed this repast down with sweet, cold water from the stream, while Evrec and Stad stood off and planned.

When the cooks were done they cleaned up. Different boys would be in charge of the evening meal.

Evrec oversaw the camp setup and posted sentries, while Stad walked across the field to confer with the two masters and one of the radlavs of the Mice.

When Stad returned, he said, "Usual borders, and usual rules."

"Hurray!"

"What's that mean?" Shevraeth asked Vandaus.

"Means we can skirmish at night, which is fun—unless you're on guard duty. But night guards never have to do cook tent, so it's a trade."

"And our goal is to capture the others' flag, like those Sunday games, right?"

Vandaus had a lopsided grin, one side of his mouth curving up. "Flag," he said. "And prisoners. Game goes until either one side wins or the Master calls it, usually noon."

"Winning is getting the others' flag?"

"Either that or all their men as prisoners."

Shevraeth frowned. "Once you're a prisoner, then what?"

Vandaus laughed. "Try to escape, of course. And the others run a rescue. It's most fun at night."

"Oh." Shevraeth realized for the first time that the Sunday scrambles were some sort of practice, and this game here was what they practiced for, using the skills they drilled in the classes.

Evrec and Stad summoned the House, who lined up and were divided into half-ridings of four. The two masters rode round and round the perimeter, watching, as the game commenced. Tackling and wrestling were allowed, even open-handed strikes or blocks.

"Control, control," they'd yell if someone got too rough, or a group dog-piled someone. Strength was not as useful, Shevraeth realized, as speed. Otherwise the tactics, if there even were any, made no sense whatever as boys on both sides prowled the boundaries, testing, shoving, taunting, then assembling into forays.

As the light began to slant, plans were somewhere made and somehow conveyed, though Shevraeth did not see where or by whom. He responded to breathless barks of orders ("Feint over there!" "Guard the trees!" or usually just "Run!"), never understanding what the immediate goals were. And so time wore on as forays were carried out and repelled, back and forth, back and forth, until the agreed-on signal for supper, which was rice-and-cabbage balls, more of that sharp cheese crumbed over the top, and the whole fried in pressed olives. Shevraeth was hungry enough by then to find that more delicious than the most subtle Colendi sauces.

At sundown they put up torches at the campsites.

The night games turned out to be just as fun as the others had predicted, with dashing raids carried out by both sides, trying to break determinedly held inner and outer perimeters. Shevraeth was surprised when the midnight trumpet was blown. He was enjoying himself, though in a way he'd never experienced in his life.

He was asleep as soon as he hit the bedroll. Just before dawn the trumpets called them all out again. Breakfast was bread dipped in beaten egg and fried in the pressed olives. Then they ran out again for more games. At noon the horn blatted: they were finished. The Ponytails had pushed their front line almost to the Mice's campsite, but the Mice held more prisoners. The masters conferred, and declared the battle a draw, which drew howls of disappointment that didn't last. They were too tired to protest or celebrate beyond token yells, and there was still pack-up and the march back to the academy.

They made it in time for supper, and when that was over, they were permitted to retire early, after which came another surprise: a scarfle. From the anticipatory whispers going round as Janold went into his room and then emerged with a basket, Shevraeth got the impression that some high treat was in store, on the order of a king's banquet.

But what came out of the basket were plain nut-and-honey encrusted pastry twists, much like the ones common people bought from street vendors in Remalna-city, and munched as they went about their business.

Triumph, obvious pleasure in every bite and finger-lick—here was another of the unspoken rules that could be broken. Rads could, if pleased with their houses, bring in a treat. Raised in a sophisticated court, Shevraeth was astonished at how so lowly a sweet could cause such intense pleasure for these tough boys. But after listening to them, he began to see that it was not just the taste, it was the sense of reward, and the sharing of it with fellows, as well as the idea of eating in the barracks, otherwise strictly forbidden.

The sense of shared triumph, the good will, made the simple food taste as good as a king's banquet. No, better. Because at a king's banquet, despite the smiles, and the fine music, and the tables laden with rare dishes, everyone was in fear of his life.

# Nine

Next morning Shevraeth rose at his usual hour, thinking about the game as he loped through the silent passages for the great barns. He still saw it all as wild running around, except for some of the short raids. Those had clear purpose. He had run three raids, one of them to rescue prisoners; he'd been captured twice, escaped once, and was rescued once. Not bad for a first game.

Senelac was not at the barn, but he was used to the riding routine by now, and began his rounds without her. She showed up very late, and seemed distracted, though her eye was as sharp as ever as she criticized seat, wrists, jumps.

Just before he was about to leave a small girl ran into the barn, shrilling, "*She's* here!"

The effect on the girls was strange, as if for a moment or two they'd all been enchanted into stone. Then Senelac clapped her hands and everyone returned to work. Senelac herself vanished to her morning tasks before Shevraeth could ask who 'she' was.

The smaller boys were not the least reticent about talking. When Shevraeth arrived for his archery lesson, a scrawny, buck-toothed ten-year-old turned to him and piped up, "Sartora is here!"

Shevraeth stared. "Sartora. Not—"

"*The* Sartora," one of the other urchins declared triumphantly. Then he looked askance. "You foreigners didn't even know she was friends with the king? He was the one't *rescued* her!"

*You foreigners* as if everyone else on the vast Sartoran continent held exactly the same view. A laugh bubbled behind Shevraeth's ribs, but he hid it. The year of enchantment over the entire world by the Norsundrian Siamis had, of course, involved Remalna, but from an eerie distance, like the details of your own life were whispered by strangers in a fog, and nothing you lived yourself.

The only one who had actually seen Sartora—the young girl who'd released the world from the enchantment kingdom by kingdom—was King Galdran, and about her he'd just said, *She was a small, scrawny rat of a child. Didn't stay long enough to exchange two words.*

To which Shevraeth's father had said in private, *If it's true she is able to hear your thoughts as did our ancestors, what child, or adult for that matter, would linger in King Galdran's presence?*

"Are you going to yap all day?"

That was the senior rad in charge of archery, smacking his brass-topped stick against his palm.

The boys scattered.

When the noon bell rang and Shevraeth joined his own barracks, red-haired Marec said, "Did you hear Sartora is here?"

Shevraeth asked, "Will we see her?"

Baudan turned his thumb down. "She's only come to the Summer Games once. Rest of the time she rides with the girls, or stays up in the castle." Now the thumb hitched over his shoulder. "The people up there report she and the king blab about history, and all the other kings they know."

"Kings," Shevraeth repeated.

Stad poked him in the arm. "I'll bet you didn't even know our king got taken to the Norsunder base when Siamis first came. Escaped, too. It was after that he met Sartora."

"We didn't hear any of that," Shevraeth admitted.

"Are *you* ignorant!" Marec declared with the satisfaction of superior knowledge.

Vandaus snorted. "Truth is, Shevraeth, the king never talks about any of it. We only know as much as we do because some of us have relatives over in Vasande Leror. Next kingdom just northeast of us. And the princess there has the world's biggest mouth."

They all started chattering, and Shevraeth shook his head, laughing inwardly at himself. He'd arrived comfortable in his own superior knowledge. Remalna, so close to Sartor, influenced by Sles Adran and Colend, was sophisticated, rich with world literature, music, history, and these Marlovens were supposed to be ignorant barbarians, only good at war. The truth was, Remalna was a tiny kingdom lying at the edge of world events, and he stood now in a place where world events occurred.

So maybe he had his answer at last: what interest could a king involved in international affairs, whether his age or not, possibly have for a nobody from a small, unknown place like Remalna?

He was still laughing inwardly when they returned that night from supper mess.

Janold came to him, saying in a quiet voice, "There's a runner from the castle waiting for you outside the north gate."

"A runner?" Shevraeth repeated.

Janold opened his hand toward the door. "King wants to talk to you."

# Ten

Janold watched Shevraeth look down at himself, his customary expression of polite detachment lengthening into dismay. Then he looked up, his confusion clear. "Like this?"

Janold said, "What else? Only seniors get fitted uniforms. Everyone younger grows too fast."

"I have a formal suit of clothes meant for royal interviews," Shevraeth said.

The foreigner seemed to be uneasy, as if he'd made a mistake. So Janold didn't tell him what he could do with his formal suit of clothes. Instead, he laughed. "If you can still fit it, more'n I know." He jerked his thumb over his shoulder. "Runner's waiting."

Shevraeth dashed through the cleaning frame, then hurried out, not even stopping to answer Stad's "Where you going?"

He found the runner waiting in the corridor outside the barracks courtyard. The tall young woman had a stooping eagle stitched over her heart. She was not just a castle runner, but one of the king's personal runners.

"You Shevraeth?" she asked, and on his affirmative, "This way."

They walked along the walled corridor and into that low, dark almost-tunnel through the massive castle walls that he had seen on his arrival.

Dream-like, that was what he felt. He didn't fit here, just as one never quite fit in a dreamscape. It wasn't just the flickering torchlight at the street corners and high on the castle walls, he felt intensely self-conscious in this rough Marloven clothing, though he'd gotten used to it within the context of the academy. But surely one didn't dress this way for a royal audience. He frowned down at the stones so carefully fitted together on the street, worn from centuries of horse, shoe, and wheel. Maybe he was mistaking the rules again, and this sudden summons was some sort of oblique royal insult.

He remembered his father telling him once that personal interviews before the king of Colend required not just a nicety of formal apparel, but you had to be careful which colors you layered over which, and how your sleeves were draped, for all those things sent subtle signals. And then again, you had to enter certain gates, at certain times, for the gates and times all combined into layers of meaning before a word was even spoken. Even what kind of boat you used on the canals to approach the royal palace (for they apparently had few castles in Colend, and no walled cities) sent a message.

All dangers—without a steel weapon in sight. His mother had once told him, *The western barbarians duel with steel, in the east with silken ribbons.*

He and Savona had scoffed. Who could be afraid of a ribbon? To which his mother had answered, *When the weapon is a ribbon you discover your wounds in the scorn of the court. Humiliation can be far worse than mere steel.*

Well, here might be a world of steel *and* humiliation. Shevraeth laughed at himself inside his head, though he was careful to maintain the court mask. *Pay attention, or humiliation is guaranteed*, he thought.

The royal castle was enormous. Shevraeth was about halfway through the history book Janold had brought him. In it he'd learned that during the royal city's early days it hadn't been called Choreid Dhelerei, but Choraed Hesea, as the kingdom had been Marloven Hesea (the "ea" not the *AY-eh* of the east, but a breathy *yah* that had been lopped off a couple centuries ago). And way before that the kingdom, or empire, had had a different name altogether.

But from the very beginning, at least from the time the Marlovens had lived in castles, the armsmen of the various Jarls had been housed in this castle during what they had called Convocation, held every New Year's Week, and again for the summer wargames. Apparently, at least at certain points in their extremely violent history, the Marloven royal families had required a substantial private guard as well as the city guard. This was why the royal castle was enormous, made up of conjoined stone buildings, each three stories, the towers considerably taller.

Shevraeth had looked at the book's diagrams of the castle and its changes over the centuries, and recognized enough of their route to realize that at least the interview would not take place in the vast throne room, with its ancient and bloodstained war banners hanging on high, and the huge black and gold screaming eagle war banner suspended behind the throne. That chamber lay south of them, behind doors so tall and wide one could drive a team of horses through the opening. In fact, one of this king's ancestors had, during one of their many brutal internal conflicts.

Shevraeth knew that the eagle standard had once been the House standard of the Montredaun-An family, who had held onto the crown longer than any other Marloven family, losing it to treachery and regaining it again.

He knew that this king he was about to meet was the son of a man murdered by his own brother, when Senrid was barely out of babyhood—a fact Shevraeth had discovered by listening to vague references made by the boys in general chatter, and putting together the clues.

He had looked at the back of the book in hopes of finding out more, but the pages having to do with Senrid's father and whatever happened after had been ripped out.

They climbed at last up the stairs into the Residence wing and traversed long halls lit by glowglobes. On the smooth plaster some Marloven artist had created friezes of large, stylized raptor shapes, done in subtle shades of pale gray.

"Here we are," the runner said, and paused outside a door otherwise unmarked, no different than all the others along the hall.

She rapped twice, and a voice called, "Enter."

She opened the door, and waved Shevraeth inside a big room with a high ceiling, and a line of four tall windows on the opposite wall, overlooking the rooftops of the academy. Torchlight gold-washed the roofs along the castle walls just below eye-level.

The same blond boy who'd appeared so suddenly at that very first sword fighting evaluation sat at a fine desk facing the windows.

"Come in," Senrid-Harvaldar said.

Shevraeth's first instinct was to perform the royal bow, his second to strike his palm over his heart, then he remembered someone saying that the proper salute for kings was a fist over the heart.

Senrid stood, waving a hand. "Never mind protocol."

He was half a head shorter than Shevraeth, with gray-blue eyes set well apart in a face just beginning to lose the roundness of boyhood. He looked much younger than fifteen, except around the eyes.

"Would you rather speak Sartoran?" he asked, in that language. He spoke it with ease, nearly accent-free, except for the Marloven precision to consonants.

"Whatever you wish, your majesty," Shevraeth replied in Sartoran, using the courtesy title he was used to.

Senrid laughed. "Forget the title stuff in here. Out there we play the game by the rules." He jerked his thumb toward the windows. "Have a chair. Tell me what you think of your stay so far."

Shevraeth's long training in court politeness prompted him to bow a little before he took a seat. "Everything is most satisfactory—" He almost added *your majesty*, for Galdran Merindar required the courtesies to be observed at all times, and Shevraeth was in royal mode, despite all the differences of the past couple of months. This boy in the ordinary shirt rolled to the elbows, the dusty trousers and scuffed riding boots, was still a king.

Senrid's brows lifted. "That tells me exactly nothing. You have no observations to make, after nearly a season among us?"

Shevraeth's face did not change. He said in the same polite, level voice, "I came to learn what you have to teach."

Senrid crossed his arms and leaned against his desk. "Do you always yap out platitudes?"

Shevraeth asked, his voice still courtier-bland, "What do you wish to hear?"

"What you have observed during your months among the evil Marlovens, of course." Senrid's smile showed the edges of his teeth.

If a man had said that, Shevraeth would have kept silent, but this was another boy, even if he was a king. "If you wanted a spy, you should have made that clear to my father."

Senrid laughed. "A real retort, if not a real answer." His laugh was sudden, there then gone. For that moment he seemed much younger than his age.

It was that disarming laugh that prompted Shevraeth to say, "If you want some kind of evaluation of your training methods, I don't know how. It is so different from home. But different is what my father wanted." He looked down at his hands. "I'm still trying to understand things. Learn what's considered basic here. Nearly all of it is unknown at home."

"Fair enough. They speak well of you. Have you any observation to make on the method of teaching, from your perspective as newcomer?"

*Method of teaching.* Just how much did that compass? Shevraeth suspected Senrid-Harvaldar knew all about Sindan, but he wouldn't bring it up unless the king did.

"I found it strange that so much teaching is done by other boys. They're good at what they do, at least as far as I can tell. But we seldom see masters, except at the various types of fight training, and even then they mostly oversee. It's the senior boys who do most of the demonstrations."

"We have a long tradition of the older boys teaching the young, and girls teaching younger girls as well. There have been . . . changes," Senrid said, after a hesitation. "Some like them, some don't. As is common with any change most anywhere. Marlovens," he added with some irony, "tend to be less than courtly when they don't like change."

Shevraeth remembered the stories he'd heard, and the urge to smile doused in a heartbeat. So he shifted the subject, just enough to regain neutral ground. "The only thing I can offer is a question more than an observation, but why so much time spent on those games? The overnights are fun, and I can see they are practicing some of the things they experiment with on the shorter games, but playing around like that—no weapons, not even toy ones—doesn't seem much to the purpose of learning the skills of war."

"It is very much to the purpose of learning the skills of command."

Shevraeth said, "How?"

"Next game, try not to pay so much attention to your own riding, and what you yourself are doing. Get captured early, if you need to. Watch the bigger patterns. It won't make sense at once. At least it didn't to me. But—if you watch—you will start seeing the whole. That's the first part of command, just seeing what's there. Making sense out of what appears to be confusion. The rest of course is deciding what to do and then doing it."

'Part of command.' Shevraeth felt a shift in perspective that was almost like a moment of dizziness. It was followed by the heat of embarrassment. "Nothing was said. I take it everyone understands that purpose from the beginning."

Senrid flicked a hand open. "They grow up knowing it, knowing it so well, most of them, they don't really think about it. But then most of them will be middle-rank commanders. Masters. Captains at outposts."

Shevraeth began, "My father said—"

Senrid's mouth tightened. "So why are you using a territorial title rather than your name?"

Shevraeth stared, surprised both by the interruption and by the question.

Senrid's expression turned wry. "Do I look stupid?" Then that quick, disarming grin again. "Don't answer that. My uncle thought I did, and he saw me every day. Or I would not be alive now. Here."

He moved quickly, reaching inside a beautiful cabinet carved over with patterns of running horses. Inside were vertical rolls of paper, all with notations at one end. Senrid ran his finger quickly along them, then pulled one out and snapped it open, spreading it wide on the desktop with his hands. Shevraeth was distracted by faint white scars across both of Senrid's wrists. Wide scars. Strange. What would make such a scar?

"Here's the eastern end of the continent," Senrid said, setting an ink pot at one end to keep the paper from curling, and holding the other end down.

Shevraeth studied the skillfully drawn map, rivers and forests detailed with stylized clarity and then colored. Neatly lettered were all kingdoms, capitals, major cities. Sometimes trade cities.

He found Remalna, tucked away among the other small kingdoms surrounding it, there above Sartor. He saw his father's principality and all the counties named correctly, including his own marquisate. On the east, along the mountains forming the inland border, someone had printed *Goldenwoods—guarded by tree people*. He touched the lettering. "We call them the Hill Folk."

"Up north they're called the Hervithe." Senrid brushed his fingers over the mountains of Tlanth in the corner of Remalna. "What are they like?"

"My father says they aren't even remotely human, that the ones people occasionally catch sight of probably aren't even in their true form."

Senrid's face had gone wry again. He snapped the map closed. "People want to send boys here for one thing, to learn the Marloven war skills. Despite all the flattery and compliments they mouth out. Or write out, in your father's case." He glanced over his shoulder before he put the map away. "So of course I did some delving. Made sure the oh-so-polite and oh-so-flattering Prince of Renselaeus wasn't planning to do some throne grabbing after his son spent his time among the barbarians. Your—"

The door opened, and Senrid's head whipped round, then he relaxed. Shevraeth had only time to feel one pang of alarm at Senrid's instant tension, before he turned to observe the newcomer, carefully carrying a tray, who did not need to knock at a king's closed door.

She was short, slight, probably eleven or twelve years old, wearing a shapeless old tunic of blue-dyed cotton and loose trousers of a dull green that only came to the knees. Below the hem of these peculiar-looking trousers her skinny legs and feet were bare.

Shevraeth's gaze traveled up again to her face, which was unremarkable, round as children's faces are usually round, framed by thin, lank light brown hair. The short, ragged ends looked as if a hand like Sindan's had hacked it off with a knife. And there had been no one to 'even it up' for her.

She set the tray down on the desk. On it was a pot of hot chocolate and cream pastries of the sort Colend made famous, the first Shevraeth had seen in this country.

"Do you like pastry?" the girl asked in Sartoran. Her accent was somewhat flat, a foreign accent Shevraeth had never heard before.

Shevraeth felt the urge to bow, and restrained it. The girl's face was dominated by her eyes, which were so light a brown they looked golden in the lamp light, their expression steady and acute in a way he'd never seen before in adult or child. She seemed to be aware of his impulse and its correction, for he saw a subtle flicker in her brow, not quite a contraction, but a pucker, just for a heartbeat, and then she smiled shyly. "Please, have one. Senrid likes 'em and I brought enough up for three."

"To the rescue, eh?" Senrid asked, not saying whom she was rescuing.

The girl just looked at him, her manner still. Senrid turned away, busy rolling up his map. No words had passed, but Shevraeth sensed a challenge from the girl, one accepted by Senrid. He was astonished at this interaction, which was so unconventional—as was her appearance—he once again felt he'd slipped out of the world into dreams.

"This is Liere." Senrid raised a hand toward the girl, and Shevraeth saw the scarring was on the underside of his wrist as well.

"Lee-AIR-eh," Shevraeth repeated, trying to get the vowels right. Had he heard that name before?

"What shall I call you?" Liere asked.

"Shevraeth will be fine." And to Senrid, in answer to his question, "No one in the academy knows it for a title. They thought it was my family name, which they had trouble pronouncing. So I let it be."

"Fair enough." Senrid's mood seemed to shift again. He leaned forward and picked up a pastry. "Like hot chocolate?" He pointed at the pot.

Shevraeth bowed slightly, not wanting to say that he much preferred coffee—and hadn't had any for months.

Senrid said, "The academy will have coffee again in a year or two. Sartor seems to have reopened trade with their neighbors first."

The subject of coffee coming up when he'd only thought it, the casual reference to Sartor's reemergence into the world after a century of enchantment, all unsettled Shevraeth, and intensified that sense of nothing being quite real.

It was that off-balance sense that brought out the question he'd tried to find in the book—the question he thought he'd never ask. "Why do you break the Code of War?"

As soon as the words were in the air he wished he could catch them again, and stuff them back down his throat. But Senrid did not frown, or jump up and demand a duel—a beating—whatever. He opened his free hand. "We never agreed to it. So of course we never practiced it." He flashed that nasty smile, the one with the teeth. "It was forced on us, truth to tell, as part of a treaty, during the days when the empires were breaking up. That is, we could do whatever we wanted within our borders, but if we rode over the borders armed with bow and arrow, we had a fairly massive alliance of neighboring kingdoms ready for any excuse to come back in and take us apart down to the last stone. And I have to say the particular ancestor forced into this treaty deserved it." He laughed.

Shevraeth felt yet again that strange sense of the ground swaying, but he knew it was not a physical reaction, it was the mental whirlwind that results from long-held expectations blasted in a moment.

Liere handed him a pastry. He thanked her absently.

He was grateful to have something to do with his hands, and the pastry tasted better than any he remembered, probably because he'd gone so long without such things.

And his mind had a chance to catch up. Liere poured out chocolate for two—none for Senrid—drank hers right off, then poured a second cup in the time it took for Shevraeth to politely take a sip. He realized what seemed familiar. The words Galdran had used about Sartora—small, scrawny child—and the memory that she'd had another name, an unfamiliar name, brought him to realize that he was face to face with the world's most famous person, outside of the Norsundrian Siamis, whom she had defeated. This scruffy little girl was Liere Fer Eider, universally known as Sartora.

He stared, and saw a faint flush on her round cheeks. Her brow puckered faintly again, and he sustained yet another inward blow when he remembered what his father had said about her hearing thoughts.

Embarrassment, sharp and painful, was his reaction. The girl looked up, and words formed in his mind, as if spoken: *You have to learn to shield your thoughts. I can't always shut people out. It takes a lot of effort because I'm learning, too.*

The mental voice was that of a young girl, the tone one of slightly self-conscious kindness.

Out loud he said, knowing he sounded foolish, but he couldn't help it. "You're Sartora."

"Yes." She looked down. "But I really, really hate that name. That is, not the name—it's a good traditional name—but all the fuss that goes with it. I feel like a fraud."

Shevraeth stared at her, finding her reaction utterly beyond his experience. To have done what she had done, and to shun the admiration of others? But to him fame was a given. People recognized him when he rode into Remalna-city, or when he rode around Shevraeth doing his duty as marquis, which he'd taken over when he was ten. The fact that people would know who you were and look at you was a part of life, as unquestionable as having two eyes, or as the fact that winter follows fall. It just *is*.

Instead he struggled to find some connective reaction in people at home. He couldn't imagine Tamara, say, responding that way. She never got enough attention. Trishe would laugh and make jokes. Elenet, the quietest girl he knew, had wept last year when a foreign diplomat had mistaken one of her painted fans for the work of another girl. "Someone she thinks is less talented," Shevraeth's mother had explained. "Elenet's pride was hurt. She'll be all right, just leave her be—pretend it never happened."

He realized that Sartora, and Senrid, too, had experiences so wide and strange he had no way of comprehending them. He was now far too unsettled, he had to get away, to think. He finished the chocolate and set down the cup. "I had better return." And then, remembering who he was with, "If I may?"

"Of course." Senrid flicked his fingers open toward the door. "If you want to read more, you're welcome to visit the library. Anyone will show you where." His tone, so normal, was reassuring in a curious way, as though Senrid was unaware of all these hidden surprises. But as Shevraeth bowed to Liere, no, to Sartora, for she had done the world great service, he suspected Senrid, too, somehow knew what he was thinking.

The runner was waiting for him in the hallway. As soon as she saw him she tucked the scroll she'd been reading into a pocket and conducted him back down all those halls, and all those stairs, and through the tunnel into familiar surroundings, if not exactly home. He was grateful for her silence.

# Eleven

Upstairs, Liere and Senrid stood at the window. Presently they watched the two blond heads emerge from the tunnel, gold-touched in the torchlight. The runner's manner was alert, the Remalnan's head bowed as if he contemplated each step.

Liere said, "I came before your jealousy made you say something nasty."

Senrid's temper flared, to be immediately extinguished. The fact that her words could cause that reaction meant that they were true, and so he laughed at himself. "Jealous! Jealous. I've never been jealous before."

He turned away and wandered back to the desk, restless, unsettled. "Jealousy. All I recognized was annoyance. I thought if he mouthed out *My father said* one more time I'd knock him through the window." He turned his head. "What am I jealous of? I never met the father. Thought him a toady at first, until I recognized the style of his writing. It's very old-fashioned courtier talk. I saw it in some of the old Sartoran records, before the enchantment. But it conveys nothing of the man. Only something of his goals."

Liere struggled to put her thoughts into words. There were too many images to sort for an immediate answer: what she'd gleaned from Shevraeth's unguarded mind, the beloved older figure central there, kind, loving, wise. Then there were Senrid's own memories, cherished memories, glimmers he still probably did not know he had shared, so early in their adventures, before he mastered his own ability to shield thoughts. There, too, was a loving father, tall, powerful, smiling, a low, husky voice, a crushing hug, laughter, riding across the plains that smelled of summer sage, safe in warm, strong arms.

And there was her own bitter upbringing, her father's petty tyranny, his distrust of her interests, his dislike of her as a person—and his painful bragging to others now that Liere was both away, and famous. She would never go to that house in South End, Imar, ever again. It had never been a real home.

She looked up. Senrid was waiting for an answer, and she knew the answer would hurt him, but they both had promised there would always be truth between them. "*His* father is alive," she whispered.

&#8270;&#8270;&#8270;

At the end of the next week, Senelac said abruptly, "All right, enough practice. Before you know it we'll be up against the gymkhana, and the mouthier hounds are wagering you Ponytails will lose to Mouse House. You don't want to disgrace me, do you?" 'Hounds' being the last class in the lower school—next year's colts.

She grinned, and Shevraeth grinned back, but his heart began to hammer, because he knew what she expected him to try.

He wanted to say "I'm not ready yet" but you don't say that in this place, he'd learned. Nor could he say, "I'll never fight with swords on horseback, much less shoot arrows."

So he let her bind his hands behind him, not tight, but firm enough so he could not use his arms for balance, and he had to get up on horseback by running and using his legs to vault him high. Again and again his arms twitched and yanked, always instinctive reaction that he just couldn't control, not with all he had to concentrate on.

He tried to remember those drills he'd been practicing over and over and over as he rode the obstacles. He managed not to fall off, but the horse was made skittish by his desperate leg grip, the convulsive, abrupt signals, his jerky balance. He rode too slow, and at the end, he couldn't manage the jump—he knew it and the horse knew it, and she shied and sidled, and refused to go over.

Senelac was waiting. "Not bad," she said.

He stared in amazement. "It was awful."

"Not for the first time. No one is good the first time, at least no one here. You'll do better." She grinned. "Tomorrow." Then she stepped behind him, and gave the ropes one quick tug. They fell away. "Oh, better put some poultice on those, and wear your winter togs, with the long sleeves. You can go back and change again before breakfast."

He looked down, aware for the first time of throbbing and stinging from his wrists, but that was not what made him feel sick inside. These superficial scrapes would heal up in a day or two.

No, what made him sick was the memory of Senrid-Harvaldar's scarred wrists, and the conviction that they had not gotten that way by riding games.

# Twelve

"Brushfire!"

Shevraeth thought the whisper was in his dream. He said to Russav Savona, *What's brushfire mean in Marloven?* Savona's dark hair and eyes blurred, changing to Senelac's dark hair and eyes—

—and vanished.

Shevraeth sat up in bed, bewildered. He couldn't remember where he was. His mind tried to impose the enormous dimensions of his own bedchamber in Renselaeus, with its row of windows opening onto the roar of the vast waterfall, over this long, narrow room full of rustles and whispers and the drum of heavy rain—

—and the quiet thunk of heels hitting the floorboards. A hand knocked into his arm. A face, revealed by flickering blue light through the window, leaned over him. He was in the barracks in Marloven Hess. The face and dark hair belonged to Stad.

". . . going now," Stad whispered. "Want to come?"

Lightning flared in the distance again. All the boys were wrestling into clothes and boots as fast as they could.

"Janold asleep?" Shevraeth asked as he pulled on his tunic, his brain laboring to wake up.

"Gone." Evrec flung the word over his shoulder, pale hair flying as he dashed after a mass of boys.

Shevraeth grimaced, yanking hard; his boots seemed to get tougher to force over his feet every day.

Stad ran between the empty, rumpled beds and out the door into the dark courtyard. Shevraeth followed him, straight into a wall of warm rain so thick he gasped, ducking his head and raising a hand to cup over his mouth and nose.

Habit prompted him toward the archway to the main passage, but a sock on the arm made him stumble after the others in the opposite direction, toward the wall bordering the lower school. They paired up, vaulting onto the wall with leaps, shoves, and pushes, the last ones reaching up to be yanked, feet scrabbling. Then they dropped into the narrow corridor between the upper school and the lower, running westward.

Shevraeth had never been this way, because it was out of bounds. His mind caught up. They were out of bounds anyway, running about at night, no rad or master in sight, long after lights out. How many of the rules were they breaking, and for what? Brushfire? Wasn't that what someone had said? It couldn't mean a plains fire, not in this deluge. But the only related slang he knew was 'brush,' as in 'Sindan's gang had a brush with Forthan's yesterday.' That meant an exchange of insults, maybe shoves or a smack or two.

As Shevraeth splashed along behind Stad's heels, he tried to shrug away the questions. The way the boys ran, tension and excitement rising from them all like a kind of invisible steam, the brushfire had to be something rare, something serious. Worth the risk of being caught breaking this many rules? Another unanswerable question.

But he was not going to turn back. If the others could live through a beating so could he. *I wanted to see Marlovens fighting*, he thought. *This is probably the closest I'll come.*

They ran across a rain-blurred expanse, made a sharp turn, scrambled under a corral fence. Then they swarmed up onto a stone wall, one by one jumping to an adjacent roof. Other boys lined the slippery, overlapping tiles of the roof, the boys lying flat. Lightning flickered somewhere to the north, the weak blue light illuminating a huge gathering of boys. All the upper-school Houses except for the third year seniors and a number of second year seniors crowded on that roof, watching the fight below.

Shevraeth realized they were looking down into the seniors' practice court: forbidden territory.

Someone shoved Shevraeth down, a flat-handed gesture with intent. He slapped full length on the slippery tiles, and stayed where he was as a body dropped next to him, an elbow jammed into his ribs, forcing him up against the boy on his other side.

Below, dim figures struggled. They made long shadows in the courtyard, faintly outlined by the distant castle torches. Shevraeth wiped impatiently at the rain in his face as he tried to make sense of the roil of ghostly figures, then lightning flared again, this time from the south, and he was not the only one who gasped.

It seemed like hundreds of them down there in a battle so fast, so skilled he couldn't make out single moves. Nearly a hundred big boys fighting not just with their hands, here and there glinted the cold blue of steel.

*'Brushfire' anywhere else means war*, he thought numbly.

Lightning flared overhead. In that one glare-bright moment the watchers could see that this fight was not like the shrieking grapple of younger boys, mostly noise and wild swings, it was a grim, voiceless, anger-driven striving by trained warriors to subdue, if not quite to kill. The younger boys—and it was only boys, none of the girls were there—savored the fight in silence, some excited, their avid young faces echoing the blood-lust they saw below in big brothers, cousins, or heroes they'd known all their lives. Some seemed uneasy. A very few, like Shevraeth, were appalled.

Many of the boys were not just intent, they were poised to leap, to join in the battle, given only a single word.

That word did not come.

Someone, not Ponytail House, had had the wit to set up a rough watch perimeter, so when the whisper flashed down the line, almost as fast as the lightning above, "King's coming!" they removed themselves in reverse order, quick as they could. Shevraeth turned his head a little sideways to avoid the splats of water splashing up from Gannan's feet.

*King's coming.*

A thrill of horror coiled, cold and uneasy, inside his gut. He didn't know why the seniors had thrown themselves into this battle that couldn't possibly remain secret, but he knew there would be far worse trouble than gossip in the mess hall the next day.

The colts all thought they reached their barracks without being caught, though Shevraeth was not the only one to feel that crawl between the shoulder blades that you get when you are sure you are being watched. He kept looking around—most of them looked around, braced for trouble—but the observers, far more experienced than they, merely counted the correct number sneaking back in where they belonged, and moved soundlessly on, according to orders.

Inside they dashed one by one through the cleaning frame, which only took the dirt away, not the water. In the dark, lit only by sudden lightning, their drumming heartbeats drowned by the crash of thunder, they all wrestled out of their wet clothes, everyone laying the wet things on their trunks under their bunks in hopes they might dry before morning.

Then into bed, the overwhelming sense of impending disaster so strong that for a time all private boundaries were forgotten, the grudges and personal alliances, until Gannan said, "D'you think we'll have an academy brushfire? All of us get to—"

"Shut up," Evrec ordered.

Silence, except for the roar of hailstones on the roof.

The hail passed as quickly as it had come, leaving the steady, unmusical plunk and splat of drips. In the occasional flares of ever weakening lightning Shevraeth saw reflected gleams in other boys' wide-open eyes. They were alone. Janold was not in his little alcove off the main entrance. This time it was their radlav who had first broken regs, and they all waited, knowing something would happen. It was just a matter of what.

But the drips slowed, and it had been a long, hot, tiring day, everyone striving in the knowledge that testing was nigh. Gradually, one by one, they began falling asleep again, Shevraeth—he without family here, without a stake in quarrels he knew nothing about—one of the first.

∞⟨⟩∞

Evrec, Vandaus, and Baudan were still awake when Janold tiptoed in, his boots in his hands. "Janold," Baudan, the closest, whispered.

The senior paused in the door to his alcove.

Those nearest woke instantly. Janold set his boots down. Most of the boys sat up in bed, pale faces limned in the dim light shining in the window from the distant torches on the walls.

"What happened?" Baudan asked. "I mean, did the king come?"

Janold gave a soft, bitter laugh, one with no humor, only self-mockery. "Oh, yes. Zheirban said you boys were on the roof. That true?"

"We were," Vandaus admitted, when the others hesitated. "But we left again on signal from Mud House. They were there, too, but they set up a perimeter."

Janold sat down slowly on the edge of Baudan's bed. "Zheirban tried to stop them. Forthan tried at first, but they called him out on threat of—" He stopped, lifting his head and peering down the row. "Is the visitor asleep?"

Shevraeth had been lying still with his eyes closed, once again fighting his way out of dreams. He realized he could just continue to lie there, but then he would be listening under false pretenses, the sort of slinking dishonesty the king's cousin Nenthar Debegri favored, and he despised.

So he sat up. "I'm awake. Do you want me to go outside so you can talk?"

"Yes," Nermand muttered, but Janold flipped up the back of his hand, a sharp, hard movement more effective than any curse.

Nermand flushed at the insult that—coming from his own radlav—he couldn't officially resent.

"No, don't go," Janold said to Shevraeth. "You may's well hear it all." He paused while Evrec silently lit a single candle. Then he said, "Truth is we don't come off looking so good, but maybe that's something you need to know. I, curse it, I feel sick." He drew in a deep, shuddering breath, a tremulous hiss they all heard. Janold, tough Janold, who hardly ever cracked a smile, who beat most seniors at archery on horseback and double-stick fighting, who thrashed them with dispassionate and exacting equality when required. His pale hair hung in his eyes, dripping, but he didn't seem to see it, nor feel the soggy stockings making pools on the worn barracks floorboards. He wore a white shirt that stuck to his body, with liberal mud prints all over it. Shevraeth wondered what strange variation in the rules led the seniors to fight in trousers and shirts, leaving off the uniform-tunics. So much unspoken custom that everyone else but he understood.

"It wasn't just Sindan versus Forthan, though that was part. It really is the old ways against the new. Everyone thinks the other side are cowards. They tied Zheirban up after he refused to join and locked him in our storage, but Janred Senelac was hiding on the ceiling beam. Dropped down, cut him free. Jan came and got the rest of us, on Zheirban's command, the idea being to stop it, but we got drawn in . . ." He let the words drift as he stared sightlessly down at his open palms.

"Did the king really come?" Vandaus asked when the silence had gone on so long it seemed unbearable.

Janold's mind returned from its bleak inward review and he said, "Oh, yes. He came. Walked right through the middle."

"With Keriam?"

"With the Guard?"

"Was he armed?"

The whispered questions came from all sides.

Janold shrugged one shoulder impatiently. "He was alone. Empty hands. Walked right through us like a knife through spider webs. Stopped when he reached us. I was there, trying to stop—" Janold sighed again, and looked up at the ceiling, then down at his hands. "The king saw Sindan down. Said to Forthan, *If he dies, you die.*"

"Wha—" Nermand started to rise from his bed.

"Shut. *Up.*" Hauth reached past little Ventdor and shoved Nermand back onto the bed.

Janold didn't hear the whispered exchange, short but fierce. His eyes were distant as he looked back at the disaster.

"Forthan had the knife, see. Sindan's knife. Took it off him in the duel, and—well. He said to the king, *I know.* And then, *Put me up against the wall. I'll go. But not the post.* And the king said, *We both know he's worthless and you, I want you one day to command my army. But you know the rules. You swore to uphold them when you took your command.*"

The whispers broke out again.

"But it was Sindan's fault!"

"Sindan brought the knife, not Ret!"

"It was all Sindan, that horse apple—"

Baudan said, "What's going to happen?"

Janold turned his head. "I don't know. The king saw us there. Didn't even ask what we were doing, just sent everyone back to barracks. Had someone carry Sindan to the Healer, and go with the ones with cuts and broken bones."

Stad said in a low, angry voice, "If they put Forthan up against a post I won't go."

Janold's head jerked round, his face white with anger. "Yes, you will. We'll all be there. If it comes to pass. We broke the rules. That's what Sindan wanted, to break the rule of law, to go back to rule of force, of privilege being above the regs. We're not going to let him win. Even if he dies." He rubbed his hands through his hair, then stood up. "Go to sleep. All of you. If we are given a normal day tomorrow, Ponytail House will be on its best behavior."

He vanished into his alcove and Evrec snuffed the candle.

Nermand muttered, "Forthan's just a coward—"

"Shut up, shit-head." Evrec's venom was so unlike his normal easy tones the others were shocked into silence.

# Thirteen

Breakfast was quiet and tense.

Shevraeth had no more appetite than any of the others, but forced himself to eat. On every side were wary, angry faces, and the few conversations were exchanged in fierce, short whispers. Otherwise the academy sat under a self-imposed gag, because the masters lining the walls—when usually they were not in the mess hall at all—canes at their belts, had not said a word. But their very presence was both threat and rebuke.

*We try to solve our problems ourselves. Aren't we here to learn to command?* Hearing the echo of Senelac's voice, Shevraeth sneaked a peek at the upper level senior tables. There were a number of empty spaces. Most of the rest had bruises visible from across the room.

When they were finished and filing out to the parade ground under the already glare-bright summer sky, a runner appeared and gestured Shevraeth out of line. It was so quietly and deftly done, the others were so busy surreptitiously watching the seniors, scarcely anyone noticed Shevraeth slipping away.

The runner was a young man wearing the black and tan of the Guard. As Shevraeth followed from familiar territory to unfamiliar, he wondered if he was about to be cast out of the academy. He was trying to decide if the prospect made him angry or relieved when they stepped through one of the archways into Guard territory, and through a door at the base of the biggest tower in the castle complex.

Shevraeth followed the silent runner up the oval impressions worn down by countless Marloven feet in the narrow slate-colored steps. The stairwell smelled of torch-resin and ancient stone. Occasional glimpses through narrow slit windows looked out over the academy from the north end. This tower had to be where Commander Keriam had his office and quarters.

Just outside an iron reinforced doorway an armed guard stood at attention; the briefest of signals, no more than a meeting of eyes and a twitch of the head between the guard and the runner, and Shevraeth was waved into a plain room with a desk and on one wall a large, very detailed map of the academy, right down to the number of beds and who slept in them.

The stocky, middle-aged man silhouetted against the window was Commander Keriam.

Shevraeth's hand thumped against his heart.

Keriam flicked up a hand in acknowledgement. He was an older man, his hair grizzled, his square face tired and grim. "We intercepted an outland runner at the outer gates who was apparently seeking you."

Shevraeth repeated, "A runner?"

Keriam lifted something from the desk and tossed it down again, drawing Shevraeth's eyes to a very battered package of heavy paper. He did not need to turn it over to examine the seal: the distinguished handwriting in Sartoran characters was instantly recognizable as his father's.

Shevraeth flushed with surprise and delight. His smile vanished when he met Keriam's assessing gaze. "It's from my father," he said, uncertainly. Surely there was no hidden rule against letters!

Keriam clasped his hands behind his back. "I cannot read that language, but I thought it might be. The timing," he added, "is not fortuitous, but I am willing to accept that it's accidental."

Bewildered, Shevraeth repeated, "Accidental?"

"You did not know that correspondence is strictly forbidden?"

Shevraeth did not even try to hide his surprise. "No. Nothing was ever said. My father did promise to write, but I knew it would take months."

Keriam stared out the window, over the academy. "I have to assume the king said nothing, then, when he made the arrangements for you to be here." He turned his head. "It's not a new rule, it's left from the old days. What happened last night is isolated only because long-standing tradition keeps those boys' families from interfering and making things far worse."

'Last night.' Keriam didn't pretend it wasn't known all over the academy.

Shevraeth said, tentatively, "Is Sindan going to make it?"

Keriam's brows lifted in brief surprise. "It looked much worse than it was. Retren Forthan is far too skilled to have hit a vital organ or life-threatening blood vessel unless he'd intended to, but he didn't lose his head that far. Messy cut along the ribs, shoulder, arm, one over his eye, bled all over but will heal in a week." Keriam gave Shevraeth a wry look as he added, "Forthan will soon be far worse off."

Shevraeth debated, then decided, why not ask? "I don't understand."

Keriam gestured to the window. "The king is over there right now dressing them down. I pulled you out on my own, since I had this to see to." He reached down and flicked the letter still lying on the table. "I also think it's probably better. Despite his young age, the king has his grandfather's gift with . . . creative sarcasm, let us say. You have fit in well, but I don't think the others would like your seeing them get the dressing down they deserve." A faint, very ironic smile was gone again in a moment. "But the reverse would be true if you are excused from watching the punishment, which will probably occur end-week."

Shevraeth looked aghast.

Keriam studied him. He'd dealt with boys for nearly two generations, having seen surprising changes in government, in law, as well as in world events. He could not predict the future, but boys he knew. This foreigner the king had so unaccountably permitted within the citadel of the academy was not sullen, derisive, superior, defensive, or weak. Further, some of his more observant peers had witnessed his silent acts of kindness, nothing ever overt, or referred to. Keriam did not pretend to comprehend Shevraeth's motivation, but he respected it.

He said, "Retren Forthan is probably one of the most esteemed boys in the entire kingdom. It's no exaggeration to say that his name is known, as many people come to see him perform in the winter exhibitions as well as in the summer games, where he nearly always wins. Tdanerend Sindan, from a family distinguished by long service, is probably the most hated, even by many of the other old families who cling to position through what they call tradition, but is really no more than name expectation, coupled with some alliances during the Regent's day that I won't discuss. Never should have been made. Yet we will all gather out there in the parade court at the end of the week, including Tdanerend Sindan, and watch Forthan take a half-century with the cane. At least it's a cane, since there was no death involved."

Shevraeth said in dismay, "I gather putting someone at the wall means to execute him by arrow. So . . . putting someone at the post means to flog him to death?"

"Forthan won't be flogged to death, but he's going to take fifty cuts." And, seeing Shevraeth's reaction of intense revulsion, he added, "We do it to ourselves, not to prisoners, unless there was treachery involved. It is appalling to see. But it seems to be the only way to keep the reins on a people bred and trained for war. They are now learning that it will happen to them, service family—even Jarl's family—or not, if they contravene the regs. It's law, and whatever law meant in former times, it stands now for everyone. Of every rank. Forthan will just be caned, because he's a boy, and because he didn't kill anyone. But he was in a position of command, and he put his hand to a weapon even though he did not bring it to the field, and used it against a subordinate for personal reasons, not military necessity. Sindan was not betraying us to the enemy, or spying, he was just being arrogant and divisive and personally insulting. A good commander should be able to solve such problems without weapons."

Keriam paused. And Shevraeth remained silent, but his brow was troubled, his mouth thin with disgust.

"Fifty cuts is going to put Forthan in considerable pain, enough that he will be excused the field wargame he was supposed to command. The others who took weapons will all get what they call a generation, thirty, whether wounded or not. And the entire school will watch. You as well."

Shevraeth grimaced.

Keriam had glanced once or twice out the window as he spoke; now he seemed to see some sign, though Shevraeth could not make anything out from his perspective. Keriam let out a short breath. "The king is on the way back, and they are dismissed to morning drills."

He reached down and tapped the letter. "Since this letter came all the way across the continent I am reluctant to destroy it, and because of the circumstances bringing you here, I do not feel it right to open and read it, as I would anything sent to one of the other boys. Nor have I been ordered to do so. Go ahead and read it, while I consult on what comes next. But I request you, on your honor, not to make reference to it when you return to barracks."

"Agreed," Shevraeth said.

Keriam walked out, leaving Shevraeth to sit down on the nearest chair and with trembling fingers break the letter's seal. Not one but two pieces of paper fell out. One of them was written in Russav Savona's impatient, slashing hand with its brazen flourishes. Shevraeth grinned, but laid it aside and turned to his father's letter first:

*My dear boy:*

*I had hoped that I would be able to contrive your return for New Year's. Your mother and I both feel that you are far better off where you are, and further that we are justified in explaining away your absence as a taste for the fashions and frivolities of a foreign court.*

Shevraeth looked up, feeling the impulse to laugh. Frivolities. Fashions. Just how much farther could they have gotten from the truth without falling right out of the world?

*No doubt the ironies implied will not escape you. I expect we shall be favored with your descriptions, if we cannot embrace you ourselves. Until I trust this method of correspondence more I will confine myself to generalities, which are more serious even than we once discussed. Observe, learn. Think.*

*Russav Savona pled most passionately to be sent to join you, but the king forbade him to leave. No distance, it seems, is safe enough to allay the fear of possible conspiracy.*

*My courier will hand you a purse that is expected to see you outfitted for the coming year. If it is not enough, you have but to ask.*

*In closing, your mother and I both send with this letter our abiding love—*

Below that their signatures, side by side.

Shevraeth felt his throat tighten. He turned his attention to Savona's letter:

*Danric. Your mother is apparently going to slip this note away, right out from under G.'s nose. I made the mistake of trying to leave to join you. Suffice it to say my own castle at Savona is now my prison, and half my new servants are spies. Write to me if you can. Your mother has convinced me to start living the part in a play. I'm to be the spendthrift wastrel as well as the kingdom's most fickle flirt. What a sacrifice, you say, and yes, I agree. See the tears? R*

He looked up. How was it possible to feel at once that home was so very far away, and yet its problems surrounded him with the strength and immediacy of a runaway herd of horses? He'd just finished reading both letters through a second time when the door opened behind him, and Keriam returned.

"The courier?" Shevraeth asked.

"We're holding him downstairs." Keriam gave his brief, wry smile and added, "Holding as in feeding him and seeing his horse reshod. He's not in prison. But the king is going to send him back. You will not see him. Something else will be arranged, I am to tell you. And I am to give you this." Shevraeth realized he was carrying a courier wallet, which he set on the table. It clinked faintly. "If you like, we can take charge of it here, the same way we do for the others. You send your accounts to this office, as the others do, and we cover them. That includes the pleasure houses and so forth, as you will be in a position to earn liberty days next spring. Unless this is for another purpose?"

Shevraeth had to swallow before he could speak again. "My father says I cannot return home. I am to stay over winter."

Keriam opened his hands. "There are a number of others who are here year round. You will probably like the winter activities."

Shevraeth realized the interview was over. He rose, his fingers half-stretched for the letters, but he remembered that he was not supposed to get them, was probably not even supposed to have seen them, and so he let his hand drop to his side. The impulse to have those papers as keepsakes was strong, but he made an effort to dismiss it. Foolish. Memory, more proximate than paper written on three months ago, was locked safely inside his head.

So he saluted, and Keriam lifted a hand in dismissal.

Shevraeth returned with the waiting runner to the academy, where he found his bunkmates considerably subdued, but the only spoken references they made were to their various determinations to do well in the rank tests, which would establish their place for the week-long summer wargame out on the plains—the one that Retren Forthan had been chosen to command.

# Fourteen

"You're not gonna disgrace us, right, Shevraeth?" Holdan asked.

"About the riding," Hauth said, very quickly. "Riding test." He said it again, and with such emphasis Shevraeth wondered if they somehow meant at the punishment on the parade ground, before the entire academy, that everyone knew was going to happen after breakfast. Only what (Shevraeth thought to himself) would be 'disgrace' at an event that was already disgraceful to anyone who made the remotest claim to civilization?

"Testing. If we do well at riding—" Hauth babbled, his voice a little too high, too sharp.

"—we get more events in the gymkhana—" Holdan put in.

"Quiet, toad!" Hauth hopped up and down. "—and if we're better than Mouse House we get to ride to the game. Not march with the scrubs and the Mice and set up the cook tents."

Shevraeth faced Hauth and Holdan, two boys who usually had nothing to say to him one way or the other. Neither were particularly memorable in their own rankings; Hauth was short, skinny, with freckles and sandy hair. But he was passionate about winning. Holdan, even skinnier, looked like a rodent with his triangular chin and broad forehead and prominent front teeth under his shock of pale hair. "Will ya ride?

I mean better than you did," Holdan asked again, looking around.

Shevraeth said, "I'll ride."

They turned away, shoulders tense, elbows out. In fact everyone in Ponytail House looked tense, or excited, or subdued, and he realized they were trying to hide it. But because they rarely attempted to hide their reactions, there was no smoothness of countenance, no reserve of manner, just the awkwardness of half-suppressed emotion.

Shevraeth had withdrawn behind his court mask the day before, determined that none of them would see how thoroughly revolted he was with the very concept of ritual punishment. He could just barely see the reason behind the immediate canings— action and consequence—but not this cold appointment days after the event, everything carried out with deliberation. Even worse, carried out by those who were supposed to see to one's safety and well-being. He'd spent the day veering between enraged disgust and a conviction that surely the authorities would relent, perhaps with a suitable warning, but would in the end give way to civilized behavior. Because if you want civilized behavior, you model it. Surely, surely, but his mind would chatter back at him, *Is King Galdran civilized when he smiles, hosts parties for those he hates, and secretly makes their heirs disappear?*

Meanwhile the day passed, it ended, night came, he finally slept, and the sun in its remorseless cycle had brought them to this day.

*I need the freedom to put forward my investigations, on behalf of the kingdom,* his father had said before sending him to this academy. *Freedom means I need you well out of the reach of Galdran's arm. Marloven Hess is well beyond his arm.*

His father wanted him here, out of all the places in the world presumably beyond King Galdran's reach. He had to see it out, the bad as well as the good.

Janold emerged from his alcove dressed in his best tunic, scrupulously smooth and neat. The white line of a clean shirt collar was just visible above the high collar, and another white line of clean cuff at his wrists. His gold-topped cane was thrust through his belt at the exact angle he'd wear a knife when he was promoted out of the academy, his hair brushed straight back. He frowned, not speaking, but the others shut up as if he'd shouted a command.

"Get those boots polished," he said, glaring at the expectant faces. "And the sashes smooth. You will do Ret Forthan the honor of appearing your best."

No one spoke. Boots half-heartedly polished got a vigorous going over. Tunics that were short at the wrists, tight across the shoulders, got yanked and tugged into place, each boy checking the other's backs so no wrinkles appeared above the sashes. Trousers neat, the hems straight behind at the heels: they only tucked their trousers into their boots when riding.

Someone brought out a hair brush—for the very first time. Usually the boys fingered their hair straight back after either baths or a dash through the cleaning frame, and that was it for personal grooming.

The brush got passed from hand to hand, each brushing his hair straight back off his forehead. Shevraeth gave his hair a couple of fast swipes and tossed the brush to Stad, whose dark curls would never lie flat, but he did his best, his forehead noticeably paler at his hairline than immediately above his straight black brows.

"All right. Out," Janold said, and waited as they filed past.

As Shevraeth's bunk lay against the wall farthest from the door, he was usually last in line in front of or just behind Faldred, who had the bed next to Evrec opposite Shevraeth. Faldred tended to be slow.

Janold motioned Faldred past, fell in step beside Shevraeth, and then hesitated. Faldred was new, but he was a Marloven. Someone had obviously taken him aside, for he'd fit in with such speed it was like they'd always known him. The foreigner was the only one who showed no reaction at all to what they were about to witness. It probably meant he didn't know what to expect. "Want a word of advice?"

He'd meant to keep his voice low but they were all listening, or at least the ones in earshot; Vandaus, Stad, big, quiet Tulan, and Mondar all turned, their expressions strained.

So Janold looked at the foreigner but spoke loud enough for them all to hear. "We had a lot of half-centuries, even one century, the last two or three years before we got rid of the Regent. Everyone survived just fine."

No one said anything, but now they were all listening.

"Remember two things. One, Forthan will survive it, just like the others. Though it might not seem that way toward the end. And two, his pain isn't yours, so don't try to take it. It won't help him, and you'll wake up feeling pretty stupid if you faint."

"Faint!" Gannan muttered scornfully, and two or three boys in the front whispered. Everyone was listening by now.

Janold ignored them all, including Ventdor's greenish face, the strained lower lip indicative of nausea being fought against.

Shevraeth did not speak during breakfast, which was a hasty meal confined to bread and cheese. He couldn't force anything else down, and felt only marginal comfort in seeing that others, like Stad and Ventdor and even phlegmatic Baudan, ate very little as well.

Then they marched out to the parade ground, where the masters lined the walls—Commander Keriam at the exact center of the back—dressed not in their everyday gray but in their black and tan uniforms, with the marks of the rank they held before they were invited to the academy to train.

The boys lined up not in lines front to back like usual, but side to side, second and third year seniors all across the front. Behind them the rest filed in by year with the smallest boys at the back. Dressed formidably at his best, Zheirban stood facing them, his face blanched except for splotches of color over his cheekbones, his pale eyes savage with anger. To Zheirban, the biggest dishonor was his own, because he had failed to keep control of the upper school.

Most of the boys stared ahead, some shocked, others resigned. Shevraeth braced himself, thinking, why *am* I here? He hadn't seen anything yet, but his inward conviction that he'd die by his own hand before consenting to any such law instituted in Remalna was the only defined emotion he had to hold onto.

*When a king no longer represents the kingdom's interests, only his own . . . his goals could be perceived as harmful to the very kingdom he was sworn to protect. If that happens, then . . . it may fall to others to defend the kingdom,* Shevraeth's father had said just before his son's departure to Marloven Hess.

Vidanric had said in disbelief, *So you are telling me that you and the other nobles might have to defend Remalna against the king? I don't understand. Why would he want the entire kingdom as an enemy?*

*You have to reframe the question to begin to comprehend it. Galdran does not want us as enemies. He wants us to fall in with his goals. What those goals are, we don't know, beyond building a great army at the cost of other things. We suspect that he's connived at murder to begin attaining his goals. Nothing is going to happen for a while, except that we become more careful, and more watchful. And you go away for training. Remember, my son, in Marloven Hess you will not just hone your military skills—and despite their internal problems the Marlovens are still the best in the southern half of the world— you are to learn as much of statecraft as you can, by observing a once great kingdom in the midst of change.*

*Statecraft*, Shevraeth thought bitterly, his fists gripped tightly at his sides.

Forthan left the line of seniors, and removed his belt, his wand, and finally his tunic, handing them to another boy. This deliberate ritual made it clear at last to Shevraeth that they wouldn't disgrace their uniforms, even if they disgraced themselves. He walked to the wooden post that someone had set up. Shevraeth lost the relative comfort of memory, and the moral superiority of disgust. He was locked in the now as Retren Forthan cooperated in the process of his hands being made fast: consent to the unthinkable.

Galdran did not ask for consent when he murdered heirs he didn't think would be loyal to him personally. Even when they were loyal to the kingdom.

Try as he might, Shevraeth could not lose his mind in questions of Remalna's current problems, its past, or its future. Little things—the sound of Stad's breathing directly to his right—kept forcing his attention back to the here and now.

*This is as bad as it gets. I'll survive it. Janold was right, it's not me there.*

But it did get worse, from the first sound of the wooden cane hitting human flesh, a sound loud in that utterly silent courtyard, all bounded by stone, so noise was mercilessly thrown back at those gathered inside. For there were no trumpets or drums, there was no counting out loud, only the master (and he wore black from head to toe, including over his face, so his identity vanished behind symbolism) with his long yew cane striking the boy across the shoulder-blades.

Three. Four. Five.

Shevraeth shut his eyes, but then the sound seemed louder. Memory, where is memory when you need it? Not warnings, good things—rides, laughter, Russav's sarcasm when he was teased by Tamara Chamadis—Eight, nine, *why* couldn't he think of something else?

So he opened his eyes and glanced at the extreme edge of his vision down his own barracks line. Revealed on those profiles was a range of naked emotion: grief, shock, anger, terror. Nermand's eyes were closed, his mouth compressed. But in Gannan's steady gaze, his parted lips, Shevraeth witnessed the avidity of excitement, of bloodlust, and his guts wrenched. He had to mutter the Waste Spell as a surge of burning nastiness rose in his throat.

Twenty. Twenty-one.

*Not even half-way! I don't want to count. Think of home, what is Russav doing now, let's see, the time here is morning— was that a sound? He did, he made a sound! Think! Don't listen, if it's first bells of the morning here, it's got to be midafternoon bells in Remalna—*

It worsened when Forthan broke and gasped, a high shuddering gasp that caused Shevraeth's gut to tighten into a cold mass of agony. The agony worsened when Shevraeth glanced up just once and saw the shocking brightness of blood down that white shirt, and not just there, but splattered on the dust.

It worsened yet again when three boys, one in Mud House, and two small ones, slipped soundlessly to the ground and were left to lie there on the stones.

And worsened when Forthan fainted, and they woke him up to finish the last five strokes.

Shevraeth felt lights flickering around the edge of his vision, but kept repeating Janold's words over and over, until he realized he was whispering, but at least he was whispering in his home language, and anyway no one gave him so much as a glance as Forthan was carried away, his legs worming as he tried to stand but couldn't, and the next senior marched out of line.

They had gotten the longest one over first. Shevraeth was not the only one who sweated coldly in anguish for those awaiting their turn. After they were gone the horror gradually lessened, though some wept silent, burning tears. Surreptitious tears, left on their faces to dry, for no one moved except those who had slipped for a time out of the demands of the physical plane, to wake up lying on the stones, shaky and miserable. No one paid them any heed. It was enough of a punishment to wake up there on the stones, knowing one had passed out right in front of everyone.

When the last senior was taken away, still no words were spoken. Zheirban dismissed them in rows—neat rows, sharply turning, walking swiftly—to their first rank testing, his voice so like the crack of that yew cane the smaller boys jumped, and one of them began to grizzle as they were led away; his mate whispering "Shut up! They'll think we're babies," the sibilants echoing around that dead-quiet court.

As soon as Ponytail House reached the relative safety of the stone corridor some of Shevraeth's bunkmates who resented Shevraeth's ability to remain cool and expressionless looked into his face and saw his sightless gaze, his clenched jaw and whitened mouth, and those who sought vindication in his inability to hide his distress found it, the rest saw only a mirror to their own emotions. For Shevraeth had lost, at least that morning, the court mask that he'd been trained to hide his emotions behind since childhood.

By now all but the most willfully stupid knew that he suffered the same emotions they did, he was just better at hiding them.

They also saw that Gannan, alone, had enjoyed the morning. Even Nermand had trouble with that.

By the time Shevraeth reached the riding court, the sense of sick shock had tightened inexorably to rage. He trembled with the effort it took not to run, to get as far from these people as he could, not to shout his utter rejection of them and their so-called regulations. Their laughable notion of honor.

All these smoldering emotions snuffed into nothing when he entered the riding court and there, standing among the waiting masters, was Senelac, her eyes red-rimmed.

Then he remembered that her brother had been one of the very last. The impulse to speak words of commiseration to Senelac, who he'd been seeing nearly every day for months—talking, laughing, sharing tea or cocoa after his lessons—started him a step or two in her direction until her eyes, ranging over the boys, met his, and the wrath he saw in her wide, blinkless gaze, her tense brow, knocked him back as if she'd slapped him.

Wrath. He had no idea why, or even what her private relations were like with her family, for she never spoke of them. But now, it was clear, she wanted no pity, least of all his.

He did not understand why he was seized with an intense desire equal to his previous disgust to prove himself, to ride like he'd never ridden yet. The impulse was there, a fire in every nerve and muscle, and so ride he did, his hands a smooth line of communication from elbow to halter as he sent his familiar mount not just around the court but over the obstacle run, at the invitation of the watching masters.

It wasn't a faultless ride—he knew enough now to recognize his weaknesses—but it was good, in fact far better than most of his bunkmates who were overconfident in their abilities or were still mentally back in that parade court where the blood was being scrubbed from the stones by the remaining seniors.

At the end of the test, after he dismounted, he looked Senelac's way. She did not smile, not once that day, but she gave him a tiny chin-lift of approval that flamed along his nerves.

# Fifteen

The rest of the day that small triumph carried him along, and he acquitted himself adequately. He knew he was not one of the best, but he was far from being the worst, except at archery.

When at last they returned to their barracks after the evening meal, the sight of the largely empty senior tables did not smite Ponytail House into silence. Most of the boys had recovered their wits and their readiness to find entertainment in the smallest thing. Or maybe it was a sense of release, but the jokes, stupid as they were, kept volleying back and forth, and they were not the only ones. A general feeling of strained hilarity pervaded the mess hall.

Back in the barracks, they all dashed through the cleaning frame, carrying away the last of the sharp smell of sweat from the day's emotional obstacle course. They fell to speculating about their ranking in the testing, which would determine their assignment for the big summer wargame.

Shevraeth had not spoken once that day. He collapsed onto his bed, thinking of taking out one of his endless letters, but when he felt for the top of his trunk, his hand encountered two square shapes: a book, and the smooth cold of metal.

The others talked in small groups, or played games, or just lay, staring upward. No one was looking his way. He slid off his bed and knelt at the side of his trunk, which had not been opened. The items had been set on top of it, unnoticed by anyone unless they crouched there and peered under the bed.

The book was a private memoir, written by one of the Montredaun-An kings. Shevraeth opened it with careful hands, feeling a cold thrill when he saw the faded ink, the old paper, and when he looked for but did not see the sigil indicating a copy. This, then, was the real thing, written by that long-dead king's own hand.

Shevraeth laid the book carefully on his knee, and turned to the second item, which was a gold case, gleaming with muted but rich highlights. It looked like a magical scroll case, only it wasn't round. Puzzled, Shevraeth clicked it open to find a square of paper inside. It was written in a neat hand, the same hand that had lettered the cities and counties of his own kingdom on the map up in the king's study. The note was a brief instruction for sending letters by magic, adding that another letter-case had been transferred by magic spell to his father.

No rules, no warnings, no admonitions, just the instructions. And it was signed with two small letters: *M-A.*

Shevraeth frowned, trying to think who might have those initials, but he was hampered by knowing so few first names. Then he studied the little paper again, and this time noticed the marking between the two letters indicating two joined names.

He looked up, not sure what to think, except that M-A could only be Senrid Montredaun-An.

                          ⳾ℭℛℰↃ⳾

*Father:*

    *I gather you received one of these, too.*

    *Today we had to line up and witness a ritual punishment. I will not detail it. I want to write it even less than you want to read it. Its result was to give me an aversion to this place strong enough to have nearly caused me to bolt.*

*Had you been a day's ride away, and not four months, I probably would have.*

*But three things stopped me. One, people get over terrible things faster than I thought possible. Maybe faster than is right. In the morning I hated not just this place and everything about it, but everyone in it. By noon I was just like the others, riding in triumph at having impressed the masters conducting the tests with little things I'd learned. Maybe that means something is wrong with me—or maybe I'm not as civilized as I liked to think.*

*The second thing I discovered is harder to describe, but arises out of the book I was lent. When I opened it, I discovered a ribbon marking a certain page, which dealt with an affair not dissimilar to today's.*

*This king, whose reputation is formidable enough that we've heard his name at our continent-wide remove, had written afterward, in archaic language I don't translate well:*

**When people carry out a role in crown rituals, they are signifying their agreement with how power is not only defined, but shared. If that ritual is described by law, and carried out as described, then each might know what to expect given a choice of behaviors. If the outcome of the ritual is altered by royal whim, then the outcome of a choice becomes less predictable. In which case, why choose the right action?**

*I think what this means is, first, though the ritual might be monstrous in our eyes, the reasoning is sometimes not monstrous, and that kingdoms, kings, and citizens are not so simple to dismiss as wholly evil—or to praise as wholly good. At least, I hated every single thing about what they did today. I will never agree that such a rule would be beneficial to any civilized kingdom, but at the same time, I cannot take comfort in the civilization of Remalna if our king is killing people on whim, and there is no recourse. It's not so easy to impose one's sense of what is right onto others, especially without trying to understand what they consider right. Because Forthan—who caught the worst of it, though he's not a villain—went along with the horror after accepting blame for a lack of leadership. Can you imagine Galdran ever accepting blame for any mistake? I sure can't.*

*So, the side with power as well as the side who has sworn to obey that power must keep the rules just as do the governed. Or there can be no mutual good. Yes? No?*

*That brings me to the third thing. Though I think their rules barbaric, I don't believe our letters are being secretly read. When you sent yours, no one had opened the seals. I don't know if they don't touch correspondence, or if such decisions are left to the king in cases like my being here, but there it is. Yet Russav's letter to me made it plain he had to sneak his note to Mother, because of Galdran's spies. So—and this really sticks in my throat—maybe in the Marlovens' eyes, we Remalnans are not civilized. Anyway, I don't think they'll be nosing into these . . . and if they do, well, it's not like I know anyone's state secrets in whatever country I'm in.*

*All right, a bit more then I'll have done. It is such a relief to know that I can send this accumulated pile of added-to letters at last. I hope you can get Russav's share to him. Read*

*them or not as you will. As you can see there*
*remains little space at the end of this paper, and I*
*do not want to begin a new sheet. I do not know*
*how long the magic lasts on these things. So for*
*now this is all. My love to you and Mother, you*
*are always in my heart—*
      *Vidanric*

He slid the papers inside the gold case, whispered the words given in the instruction sheet, and felt a faint tingle through his fingers.

When he looked inside, the papers were gone.

ॐ෬෬෬෨ର

The box was still empty the next morning, when Janold came in with a paper in his hand, and read, to everyone's intense interest, a series of numbers after each name.

Shevraeth could not make sense of his. *Four, two to eight; five, four to eight; three, zero to eight; seven, seven to ten* and so forth meant nothing, until he saw by the reactions of the others that these scores of his were not to be regarded as mean, or unrespectable.

Then, judging by reactions and comments of the others, he decoded them enough to comprehend that the first number indicated his standing in a given form—riding, sword, archery, knife, and so on—and the second range of numbers indicated his improvement, as scored not against the others but against himself. 'Eight' was considered in the range of high achievement for first year colts. His single ten, in knife throwing, was considered first-year senior level.

At the end, Janold put the paper down and gave a nod. "So for this year's summer game Ponytail House has been assigned horse pickets."

A shout of approval rose.

Janold grinned. "Mouse House got cook tent."

Laughter, taunts and threats.

On the way to mess, Vandaus said, "Shevraeth, has anyone explained the big game to you?"

"You mean the camp or the gymkhana?"

Vandaus flicked a hand. "Gymkhana is horse competition. Won't be much this year, with the ranking seniors either gated or bunked. That is, we'll win more events, because there aren't many seniors to carry off the best scores, but no one will come watch. Except us."

Vandaus and Stad walked on either side of him. Stad said, "The big summer game is a battle involving the entire academy. We're in two armies, see. Some years it's all mixed, others not. This year it's north Houses against south."

"Armies," Shevraeth repeated. "Objective same as before, prisoners, territory, and flags?"

Two flicked hands indicated assent.

Vandaus said, "We first and second years do setup and maintenance. During the week the little boys get the grunt chores, just like we did when we were little. If there was a real war, see, we all would be running errands, doing the chores. There aren't any servants on the field of battle, never have been. Our ancestors far enough back rode the plains, didn't even have houses. So the boys are runners, and maybe will get to have a sortie or two of their own, depending on the commanders."

"Who are the commanders?"

A quick exchange of looks, and they paused just inside the corridor, out of sight of the others.

Stad said, lowering his voice, "Ordinarily it would have been Forthan versus Zheirban. This year it'll be Zheirban versus someone else, maybe even the top ranking second year senior. They probably won't tell us until the day. Third year seniors being still in Norsunder, all of 'em except our House radlavs." He pointed with his chin toward Janold, who walked a few paces ahead. "And they had their own defaulters to work off, for having broken bounds to go watch that brushfire."

Shevraeth said, "What I want to know is, how do the horses figure in? So far in these games we've been running about. But I understand our performance in the riding test gained us something?"

"Yes! That's the fun of it. Mouse House will be mostly overseeing the scrubs at chores, and doing all the cooking for the entire academy. This year we'll be guarding the picket line as well as tending horses with the second year colts, who usually tend weapons and gear. Everybody'll run sorties against us to capture horses. So we'll get some fun."

Stad grinned in anticipation.

"Seniors can fight on horseback, with the wooden swords. We chalk the edges, so a hit shows on their tunics."

Stad's smile disappeared, and both boys looked around. "This year, though, you can bet the masters will be there, all of them. And one single duel, one break of the rules, and—"

"Dust-storm," Andaun said gloomily.

"Well, they won't."

Four heads turned with the quickness of guilt. Shevraeth did not react with guilt, but he was startled to see Janold standing behind them, his eyes narrowed, expression about as giving as a stone wall.

"You'll see. After you get about your business." Tap, tap, the wand against the palm.

They ran.

∞ ⟨ℜℰ⟩ ∞

The gymkhana, already half-ruined by the lack of participation from the gated seniors, was thoroughly ruined by a thunderstorm. The mud was only fun for a while, the rest of the competition was mostly grim endurance. But a sense of competition seldom is entirely lost, and the lower Houses competed just as determinedly as ever. Ponytail House acquitted themselves well enough.

And so the year's events were mostly over with except for the big game. On the morning of their departure, the others woke well before dawn, jokes, kicks, punches, fake wrestling all expressing the hilarity of anticipation, of the relaxation of the usual monotony of regular schedule, the way words never could.

Shevraeth did not share their elation, but he was used to his emotions running orthogonal to the others'. His chief emotion was a sharp disappointment that swiftly turned to resignation when he surreptitiously checked his mysterious golden case and found it again empty.

He had to laugh at himself as he finished dressing. Months and months of accustomed silence, then a letter. Now that anticipation of communication had changed from waiting through months to waiting a day, he was annoyed when the day passed without another letter.

He had not been commanded, but he regarded the secrecy of the case as a matter of trust—of honor—all the more to be heeded just because he had not been admonished. Keriam had told him why the others were not permitted communication. So he decided on his own that he would not bring the golden box on the summer game, severe though the temptation was. He suspected any sort of secret was impossible to keep while living in a tent with a lot of others.

The sun was just bluing the eastern sky when Ponytail House reported to the stable to be handed off the horses chosen for this exercise. The girls were already there, their faces glum. Girls were only newly allowed back in the academy at all, after a half generation of being shut out. Command had decided that, as yet, girls were not going on the field games.

And so they showed in their short answers, their many insults slung between instructions, how disgusted they were that things were not changing fast enough for *them*.

The boys all knew better than to give them any trouble.

Instead, they and the girls together saw to the organization of the field gear for the animals, and got everything ready short of actual saddling, which would follow breakfast, their last meal in the academy before departure to the game site.

As soon as that was over (the fastest meal of the year) back they ran to the stable, and so they were ready to ride, their Ponytail House banner (gripped in Stalgred's hands) limp in the weak morning breeze, when the seniors came riding out of their own compound.

The sight of them thunderstruck Shevraeth with another lesson about violence, pain, glory, and the warp and weft of the human spirit:

At the head of the North House seniors was Zheirban, as expected. But riding at his side was Retren Forthan.

He was thin, his face so blanched it was nearly green, but he sat straight; he rode at the head of the South House, obviously intending to spend a week sleeping on the dirt in the field, exchanging stinging blows with willow swords.

And the younger boys greeted him as they'd greet a hero.

A spontaneous cheer echoed up the stone walls, a heartfelt roar Forthan only acknowledged with two inadvertent patches of color high on his cheeks. Shevraeth was amazed at his own reaction, for he was yelling too.

# Sixteen

"Ah, my dear," said Princess Elestra of Renselaeus, as relieved as she was overjoyed to see her husband safely home from the court at Athanarel Palace in Remalna-city.

Prince Alaerec bent his head and saluted his wife with a kiss, but his joy at their reunion was diminished by the tension in her hands as she embraced him.

They could not speak until they were alone. His heart beat faster: he was the only one who could have court news, which had to mean that the mysterious gold case they had been so unaccountably sent from faraway Marloven Hess had actually brought return letters by magical transfer all the way across the continent.

She slid her arm through his, and with the strength of many years' practice helped him walk down the corridor, his painful gait much eased.

As soon as they were alone in their own chambers she helped him into one of the deep, cushioned chairs they'd had specially made, as he could not sit on floor cushions. Age made walking difficult even with her help; he caught his breath as she took from inside her gown a number of small-folded, exceedingly rumpled sheets of paper.

"Danric has been writing from the beginning. He sent them one after another, not half a day after you left. There are some here for young Russav." She laid her hands on a locked box of carved wood lying on his desk.

"Those you will have to take to Remalna-city," the Prince said.

"Me?" Princess Elestra widened her eyes.

The Prince gave her a grim smile. "I rather think my bad hip is going to take a severe turn for the worse, as is your mind, my very dearest dear. When next we are summoned back to court, I think it better if you begin hosting parties, the more frivolous the better. A distraction has become desperately necessary, and it is we who must provide it."

She put her head to one side. "A jester, or a gambler? Would distraction serve, or competition?"

"I hardly know. I had not considered that." He kissed her hands. "I leave it to your discretion. If you must gamble, make the stakes high."

"Royally high, yes." She smiled with irony as she ruffled her fingers through her wavy gray-brown hair, dislodging her careful coif. The result, with her large eyes so wide, making her look a little eccentric, even vacant. "And manage to lose just more than I win, to keep the sense of competition keen."

"Ah, yes. My grandmother wrote something like that during her days at Everon's court. Am I right?"

"I was just rereading her memoir recently, which is where I got the notion. But that aside. If you wish, I shall take these letters to Russav. But before we talk more you must read Danric's letters to us."

Now he knew that she was disturbed by whatever their son had written to them, and so he sat right down in his chair, not even changing from his dusty riding clothes, and took up the first rumpled paper. His heart constricted at the sight of his son's dear, familiar hand.

Elestra sat nearby, waiting in silence until he was done. It was not a short wait, but she was a patient woman.

When he set aside the last paper and met her expectant, sad gaze, he winced. "I was wrong. Is that what you are thinking? The risk of leaving him there is greater than that of bringing him home?"

Elestra rose and paced before the window, her tiny body in its exquisite gown silhouetted against the mighty waterfall, silver-gilt in the sunlight. "First tell me the gist of your court news."

"It's Arthal," the Prince said, referring to King Galdran's sister Arthal, Marquise of Merindar. "Stirring them. So softly, so rarely, I nearly missed it. Increasing the anger toward Galdran even more than he does on his own. Once is not random, not with Arthal. And twice is a warning to take heed."

"Oh, definitely gambling, then." Elestra smiled, already full of ideas for her court strategy.

He lifted his hand in acknowledgement. "Meanwhile I have no proof of any of our surmises; I've been forestalled at every turn. That is not like Galdran, the very meticulous care, the thinking ahead of me at every path. That is Arthal."

Elestra pressed her fingers to her lips.

Alaerec said bluntly, "She speaks of going to visit the court at Sles Adran ostensibly to see their son, probably to seek suitors for Fialma. But before she leaves, I really believe she is trying to drive Galdran mad with fear and rage."

"Which is the greater danger?" Elestra murmured.

"I don't know. What I fear is that he's going to push those of us in court to fighting one another. And when he's gotten us to half destroy one another, she could then return from abroad to the kingdom's rescue."

"You think the fighting is imminent?"

"Not yet. No one thinks of actually taking up arms—not even Galdran. They only see the increase in lawlessness, the frequency of road theft and burglary in the towns and so forth, without comprehending that most of those unfortunates have been driven from homes by the increase in taxes. He sees the kingdom's restless element as a direct flouting of his royal will. And so he talks of more stringent laws, and more extreme measures against lawbreakers. Always, always hiring more guards to enforce his will. Which of course means higher taxes to pay for them. All talk, as yet, but no actions taken."

She nodded. "What you say strengthens my resolve, that though I miss him terribly, Danric has to stay where he is."

"You recognize that he is changing." The Prince's manner was one of question.

She turned away, wringing her hands, clapping them together, and wringing them again, rare signs of anguish. He felt the same anguish, on his son's part and on hers.

When she turned again, her eyes gleamed with tears. "Change is inevitable for us all. We agreed on that. But if he returns . . ."

The Prince sighed. "I strongly believe we dare not bring him home while Flauvic Merindar is kept out of the kingdom, at the court of Sles Adran. If Arthal wants her own son out of Galdran's way when she wishes to see him heir, then I believe it wise to emulate her in this one thing."

There was a long, painful silence, then Elestra said softly, "Then we are agreed. Vidanric must remain where he is. And we must trust that he keeps his moral balance."

The Prince bowed, his gaze on the letters in his hands. "We have been granted this means of staying in contact. We must exert ourselves to communicate with him, not to remonstrate or scold, but to provide . . ."

"Moral balance?" she asked, her smile wry. "When we talk of lying to the king by implication?"

The Prince shook his head sadly. "I don't see any easy way to save the kingdom, to save ourselves, to save our son. Except by doing what we are doing now."

🙰❧❦☙🙴

*. . . . and I have to admit that the sight of the seniors riding with both grace and precision, their wooden swords clashing, would fire the laziest heart. No, it's more honest to say the most*

*civilized heart. At least it did mine. Does that mean my heart, if not the generality of human hearts, is not truly civilized? That ferocity is more inspiring to us than tranquility, or is it just that this war gaming is more fun? For always in the back of my head is the knowledge that no one was going to die on that plain, that the masters were all there in force to see that grudges did not make the lightning-strike change to real fighting with intent to kill. They are certainly all capable of it.*

*And so, these last weeks after the game all I could think was, in two years, if I am still here, I will be the one riding under those snapping banners on the back of the best-trained horses in the world, and I will be fighting in that style, or racing across the plain in a charge. And I have to admit I can hardly wait.*

*Thus my first year is all but done, and I survived. So did the academy. My House even got two more scarfles—and after the unending plainness of the regular food, I've come to regard those honey-buns as high treats of the most exquisite rarity. As for survival, my riding boots didn't. My poor mother would probably faint if she saw the holes in them, and the corresponding ones in my stockings. But at least my feet stayed cool over the heat of the last month, with this added ventilation. As soon as the other boys are gone, I'm digging my civilized shoes out.*

*As for now, because the seniors are still in Norsunder, there were no celebrations here except in the barracks. Instead, everywhere there is the noise of leave-taking, of winter-plans and resolves against next spring, as the majority of them prepare to go home. The rest of us will apparently be moved—*

Through the tapestry Russav Savona heard voices. Alarm gripped his neck when he picked out among them the familiar low, angry rumble of the king's voice. The king never scratched or tapped outside tapestries, despite that being one of the first rules of etiquette any child learns, from low to high degree. Savona had heard the older people whispering about how Galdran reserved as royal right unwarned entry because he looked everywhere for signs of conspiracy.

*And here I am reading a secret letter that could get Danric's entire family killed.*

Regret, bitter and heated, surged through Savona as he pitched Danric's half-read letter into the heart of the fire. It flared instantly, the black letters for an instant red and then golden, as Savona glanced in relief at the open windows; the breeze from the ocean was steady and cool. Just as the king's hand thrust aside his tapestry, the letter curled away into ashes and vanished beneath the steady flames of the Fire Stick.

Savona whirled away from the fire, desperate to find something else to be doing. Relief! The old mirror his mother had had placed into the wall. When the king lifted the tapestry and stepped in, Savona postured at the mirror, turning this way and that as he admired himself from head to toe. Well aware of the king at the door, though pretending to be absorbed in his own image, he stared complacently at his long, curling black hair and the fit of his tunic. Savona was the handsomest of all the younger generation: at sixteen he looked twenty, so splendidly was he made.

His black eyes were keen and observant above that slashing smile.

"Boy." The king called them all that, as often as not.

Savona mimed well-bred surprise, but if the king took it as a hint that he ought to have scratched, he ignored it.

Savona bowed, the low formal bow that Galdran Merindar liked not just in the throne room, but at all times.

Galdran's restless gaze moved from the fireplace to the table, where no pen and ink lay ready, to the walls, the windows, and finally the furnishings, which had not been altered since the days of the dead duke and duchess—Galdran had whiffed the scent of burning paper, or thought he did, but nothing was to be seen in the fireplace, and the table was bare of ink or paper or courier wallet.

And Savona seemed to be entirely involved in studying his own face in one of the framed looking glasses that had been built into each wall. Savona's mother had loved to see herself reflected wherever she turned: when she sat on the big velvet cushions along the platforms, and at the low tables on which one could still find fresh flowers, hot-house flowers in winter and early spring.

"My nephew has an idea," Galdran said, grinning. "How would you like to ride under his command, and teach some of this rabble to behave?"

"Rabble?" Savona remembered what Princess Elestra had told him: *Look past the smile to the eyes.* He saw anger. Judgment. Question, even. Certainly no humor, despite the toothy grin.

"Cursed populace, disobedient. My sister hints I'm too lenient. She thinks my nobles all sit around at their ease eating and drinking at my expense, and taking advantage of my good will and hospitality."

What could be said to that? Savona just bowed, hand at his heart in the mode of *rue*.

Galdran sighed. "My nobles got their titles by governing their territories. It's time for you to do that again, under my nephew's command. But first you have to learn to follow orders."

Savona's very first reaction was joy—not at the prospect of riding under the command of Nenthar Debegri, but at the prospect of getting away from the deadly atmosphere of court. Maybe he'd even get the sort of training that Danric was, only without the canings and beatings by Marloven bullies.

Was he showing too much eagerness? The King still grinned, but his eyes had tightened to suspicion.

"Of course, your majesty" Savona said, bowing low. "As long as I get to wear my good clothes." He dusted his sleeves. "Commanding would be fun. But not if we have to get dirty."

"If Nenthar tells you to get dirty, you will get dirty," the king retorted, but that narrow look of suspicion had eased. "Command must start at the top, and it's not effective unless the lower ranking commanders know how to obey orders."

Savona felt like a liar and a cheat, but he remembered his promise to Danric's father and mother. *Play a role,* they'd said. *You don't have to be a coward, or a villain. Just be a clown Even suspicious kings do not feel threatened by clowns.* "I do so hate to get dirty. Can't I just stay on horseback? I like riding, and I'd like commanding, but a duke shouldn't have to do sweaty, dirty work."

The king was already bored, but that was far better than wariness and suspicion. He waved a hand. "We'll see, we'll see. There's time enough to discover what Nenthar has in mind for drills and the like. Remember, you are not just here to be decorative."

Savona bowed again.

"I told Nenthar if he does well with command I will give him a barony, and all the rest of you will have suitable military ranks besides your birth rank. You would like that, would you not?"

Savona bowed again; he stiffened his fingers against any betraying flourish that might hint of irony.

"Good. We will discuss this matter further when I have seen what you all look like out in the field."

The king strode away down the hall, followed by the two honor guards he always took with him. That left Savona feeling angry, disgusted with himself, with the king, with the world.

That feeling persisted until early evening, when they all attended a card party held at Lord Grumareth's rooms. Lightning flickered in the distance, just before they were going to cross the Residence court to supper and music.

Princess Elestra gave a faint shriek. "My *hair,*" she wailed. "I can*not* abide rain. What will it do to my hair? Send for a canopy!"

A bustle of servants brought rain canopies and they all began to progress, Savona with the boys behind Arthal, the Marquise of Merindar, who always insisted on rank precedence.

The Marquise, a large fair woman with a high brow and a smooth, serene demeanor, stepped next to her brother, who said something in a low voice. The Marquise laughed, and answered mockingly, ". . . as empty as her skull. Just contemplate someone that old and wrinkled actually thinking any of us have the least concern with her looks? 'My *hair!*' The rallying cry of the fools."

Savona thought, *It worked.*

His bad mood was gone. Deception was a weapon, all the more effective for not being perceived. He resolved that he would use "My hair!" as a cry at least once that week, if the rain cooperated.

When Nenthar Debegri gathered the boys in the court to see what they could do by way of military drill, Savona kept up a running stream of sulky complaints about his clothes, the dirt, the boredom, and he managed to drop his sword four times.

At the end of a month, as summer vanished at last into the first cold rains of autumn, Savona realized most of the smarter boys were following his lead. On a bitter, rainy morning the king appeared on the balcony overlooking their court, and watched.

The drill was spectacularly dismal. Savona managed to get his horse to thump into every single one of the others at least once, upsetting the entire exercise. His quick, black-eyed cousin Deric and their friend Geral complained, called out conflicting orders to which no one listened, as Savona exclaimed in horror that his gloves were getting grimy from the dirt and wet. Nenthar Debegri lost his temper and screamed invective instead of orders. He only shut up when King Galdran shouted "Hold!" from the balcony.

"You boys practice at home," the king roared, as everyone bowed from horseback. Savona let his hat fall off. "You'll take it up again in group next spring. Go on, take horse. Go home. It's harvest-time. You all have land to oversee."

That meant taxes and tithes in food and supplies to pay for the king's new garrisons.

The next morning Russav Savona was riding home to his duchy amid the spies the king had set about him. He kept a pout on his face, but inside he laughed in triumph. Just before his departure he had slipped a letter into Princess Elestra's hands.

∞⃝☙⃝∞

*. . . and you should have seen us. Besides me there were Geral and Alcanad and even Olervec, though with him it might have been real, all whining, dropping swords, exclaiming in horror if dust got on their clothes. Deric fell off his horse more times than I did—I had to pay him a staggering sum as we'd had a wager going. Your Marloven barbarians would have died laughing.*

*The result was, the king ordered us all home for the winter, and so between tonight and the morning I shall contrive a way to slip this letter into your mother's hands. If I don't, I guess you won't be seeing these words, hmm?*

*Anyway, I've tried to decide just how excruciating a winter to give Galdran's spies, and have discovered the perfect ruse. I am going to take up painting fans. Want a wager? By the time you come home, no fashionable young lord will be seen without his fans to match his outfit. I will get the girls to start teaching me more of the fan-flirtation modes. My master plan is to have all of us chattering about the new fashions in shoes while our fans semaphore the latest news from the borders, and all of it directly under Galdran's suspicious eyes.*

*Noises outside. Probably one of the spies. I must not be seen writing, except orders for fans and paints. Russav.*

# Seventeen

*My darling boy. We have agreed that we shall restrict ourselves to once a week for letters. This is partly to protect you, for we remember what you said about the fact that you were not supposed to be exchanging letters from home.*

*But I will admit, just this once, that were I to write to you daily, I would fall into a melancholy tendency to ask what kind acts have you done of late? Before I leave the subject, know only that the same rule applies for each of us when we are in court, and no challenge could be more difficult.*

*I will not bore you with the tedium of my visit to court. I will leave it at the word 'parties,' and you will probably remember that one of the very first lessons in etiquette that I taught you was that it is bad manners to bore on about parties you have been to, but which your auditors have not.*

*At home, there will be no parties, not a one, for an entire quiet winter. Instead, I will begin a course of reading, and discuss it with you, and your father joins me in hoping that you will commence a similar course of reading, and discuss with us what you have read.*

*And now to fold into this missive the letter that Russav slipped into my hand just before his departure, as he kissed my fingers most properly.*

*I shall await impatiently yours by the end of the week.*

*All my love,*
*Mother*

Shevraeth read the letter through twice, and then stooped to lay it on the flames. He stood watching the paper curl, sending up the sharp smell of burning rag, and wondered what in his letters had so worried her that she would think it necessary to remind him of his promise.

He walked to the window of the senior rec room and leaned his arms on the stone window sill, looking out at the softly falling snow. *Shall I enumerate my acts of kindness?* he thought. *No, it's petty. What I have to do is think back over what I wrote, and try to discover what must have alarmed her.*

The ring of heels on warped wooden flooring caused him to glance at the fire. The others were returning from breakfast to get ready for the day. His letter had been reduced to ash, and so he went back to staring out the window onto the spacious courtyard outside the senior barracks—their winter home.

Shevraeth had seen why at once. The buildings were the oldest, mostly stone, more spacious than any, and with this recreation room adjacent to the dormitory, something none of lower school barracks buildings had. Once he'd gotten accustomed to the faint tang of centuries of mildew and sweat (despite ritual cleanings by generations of boy hands) he decided the place was comfortable: they had a good fireplace, the mess hall was nearby, and so were all the various practice courts.

He'd returned from breakfast early, partly to check his magical letter box, but also because he'd wanted to read before the day's drills.

Most of the others passed on by, some with casual flicks of the hand. Boys of all ages stayed over, for various reasons. Shevraeth had discovered within a day that former rivalries were entirely suspended over the winter, and so were the privileges of age. The boys all wore sturdy wool tunics, whatever age they were. And best of all, the notorious bullies were all gone.

Shevraeth had not been surprised to find himself assigned to sword, archery, and riding practice. Not two weeks had gone by and he was already used to the rhythm of the days.

He was mildly curious to be approached by a tall, familiar figure with light brown hair and a sober expression in his light eyes: Retren Forthan.

He spoke as if they had known one another for years, though they had never exchanged a single word. "King sent me to you."

Shevraeth opened his hand in invitation to speak.

Forthan looked around the room, and then said in a low voice, "He said to ask. If you'd tutor me."

"In?" Shevraeth asked, mentally running over impossible-sounding topics: Fashion? Sartoran ballads? Dancing?

"Reading," Forthan said in that same low voice, his gaze on his weapon-roughened hands.

Surprise bloomed behind Shevraeth's eyes but he was far too experienced to show it. "When and where you like."

"King wants me really reading before we begin the next season," Forthan said, still to his hands. "I reckon, every day. In case it, well, takes time."

Shevraeth considered his schedule, and then figured Forthan's had to be far busier, as he was not only serving as a trainer for some of the younger boys, he was also in charge of organizing the exhibition drills and games that the older boys would perform to entertain the Jarls when they arrived for the Marloven New Year ritual called Convocation.

Well, sleeping in of a morning did not seem to be part of the Marloven habit of life, he thought wryly, bidding good-bye his briefly enjoyed luxury of rising just before breakfast mess.

"We'll meet at first morning bell, then? Library, up at the palace? The king did give me permission to use it, and no one ever seems to be there. Certainly not at that time."

Forthan's relief was obvious. "Tomorrow?"

"Tomorrow."

The next day, early as Shevraeth was, Forthan had preceded him, and Shevraeth found him prowling along the shelves of books and scrolls. When he saw Shevraeth, he turned around, and indicated a table with a lamp already lit, and paper and pens waiting.

They each took a seat, and Shevraeth said, "You do not have to answer, but I assumed that there was already some reading required for the seniors."

"Not until Senrid-Harvaldar came to the throne," Forthan said in a low, embarrassed voice. "No need before. No need at home." His gaze shifted. "I've gotten by. I can parse out my name, and other names. I do know most of the alphabet. But Jan Senelac has been doing my reading for me on the sneak. I hate sneaking, and the king wants me reading." He turned his palm up, the Marloven equivalent of a shrug. "So he sent me to you."

Because I won't talk, Shevraeth thought. Or because it's some kind of test. Maybe both.

Out loud he said, "Then we'll get started. Your knowing some of the alphabet already puts you in the saddle, so to speak. We'll get you familiar with the rest, and start on consonant groupings. You'll find words a lot easier to read when you learn these, and it's just like drill . . ."

Shevraeth did not know if the Marlovens had a specific order for groupings, the way they were taught at home, based on Sartoran roots. He decided it didn't really matter.

And as the weeks sped by, New Year's drawing ever closer, he knew he was right. They met every day, the famous senior commander and the visitor from a faraway land, working through simple texts at first and then more complicated ones, historical texts written in small, sometimes crabbed handwritings, by the kings and real war commanders actually involved in major events.

Forthan's interests were narrow in range, confined to battles, strategy, tactics, logistics. He was quiet, serious, focused, indistinguishable from other Marloven boys just on the verge of manhood when sitting in his chair with a pen gripped in his big hand. There was no sign of the formidable warrior until he was outside, in the field, or standing in the fighting salle with a sword in hand, then his demeanor changed to the mode of command.

They never discussed anything but their readings. Forthan was diffident about all subjects outside of war, perplexed by social customs not his own, by history that did not impinge on the Marlovens. Shevraeth learned not to refer to it. Forthan didn't care, unless it related to the matters at hand. His life lay before him, a clear path. Unless he disgraced himself or died in some other manner he would command a Marloven army. That was the summit of his ambition. Yet he never talked of conquering, of killing, he never bragged or scoffed. He was, Shevraeth thought one day as he trudged back to the senior barracks through a thick snow fall, both easy and difficult to understand. *The difficulty comes in me not being able to figure out the warrior habit of mind. I can't imagine ever wanting to lead an army.*

৵ৎ৪৫৩৵

At the same time he was walking back to get ready for breakfast, from above Retren Forthan and Senrid-Harvaldar watched his solitary figure tracking blue prints through the fresh-fallen snow.

Forthan waited for Senrid to speak. He did not know why he'd been summoned. The king had always been about as hard to decode as letters, even when he was five years old, and

Forthan ten, new from the farm where his parents had discussed with him the hard facts: that they would not survive the Regent's increasingly brutal taxes unless they took the bounty for giving up a son to the growing demands of the army. He had agreed, and a cousin had taken his place as heir to the farm. That was life.

'Giving up' it had been in those days, that now seemed a long-ago nightmare. The nightmare had begun with relinquishing your name and taking a number, the Regent's desperate plan to control the worsening corruption and in-fighting. His idea had been that if you had a number, not a name, then your loyalty would cease to be to your family and you would be loyal only to the Regent.

Of course the only ones forced to give up their names were those from families not attached to historic rank.

Ret Forthan, under his modest number, had earned point after point until he was discovered by Keriam while riding the kingdom on inspection, and he was brought to the academy despite his lack of family. Previously you got in by birth, though all pretended it was merit. But it had been the merit of a glorious past, not through present efforts.

Their rare glimpses of the king, who was not permitted to train, had been discussed in whispers, Forthan remembered, as Senrid stared sightlessly out into the fallen snow. What he did, what he said. His trying to get training all by himself, when most small boys were still chasing around with sticks and trying to scamp chores.

Training. Forthan remembered stealing up to the castle with Ndarga when the king was barely ten. After the Regent put him up against the post in front of all the army and Guard commanders as well as the entire academy. Crime? Sneaking down to a training session—"Flouting orders. A king has to learn to obey orders before he can issue them," the Regent had announced before the entire assembly.

The upper school had all known that the real crime had been committed by them, and not the king, when they made the costly mistake of trying to talk the Regent into letting the king join the academy. But the king had paid the price.

You did. Not. Argue with the Regent.

Life under the Regent meant rewards for treachery, sneaking, lying, and bullying, so long as it was in his favor, and punishments for wanting justice according to King Indevan's laws.

And so they'd been forced to line up and watch injustice carried out according to a distortion of the law. They couldn't take the pain away, so afterward they did what they could, and Forthan's nerves chilled as he looked back over that horrifying week: night after night they risked a century apiece for breaking bounds as they hopped the wall, ignored by the guards in silent collusion, to talk the king through his recovery, fading away again before dawn. Every day for a week, though for the first three or four nights Senrid lay on his stomach with his face turned to the wall, without speaking. He never did speak that week, but the fifth day they got him to eat, and felt it as a victory.

Forthan didn't understand the king, whose words were even more oblique than the foreigner's, but he could always sense someone he'd trust at his back. So far, he'd been right. The king was someone he could trust.

"What do you think?" Senrid asked finally.

"About reading?"

Senrid lifted a shoulder impatiently. "I know you can read now. And I want you reading the real field reports in the archive, not the bran gas others wrote afterwards as records, or if you do, compare them. That's what I've been doing, and I think there's a lesson in it, how people will resee events, and put themselves in as the heroes. It's as much bran gas as predicting new eras of peace and golden ages."

Forthan thought, *What's behind all that?*

"What do you think of my experiment—having the foreigner here?"

"I like Shevraeth. He'd make a good rad, one I'd have under me. No swank. I don't even think he knows how good a rad he'd make."

Senrid said, "Keriam wants to give him more responsibility." He turned, almost a jerk, and started pacing along the windows, a restless habit that Forthan had seen before. Meant something was disturbing him. On his way back he said, "After Convocation. Shift your things over to the Guard."

Forthan struck his fist over his chest. He'd expected the order, but it was good to have it come at last. Except why was Senrid angry?

"Problem with the academy?" he asked.

Senrid turned around fast. "Problem with the kingdom. With the world. I don't see my way clear enough. I need more time to learn, to find out what I should change and how, but there *isn't* time." His fist pounded lightly on the table next to him. "I told Liere and the others in the north, when Siamis left his sword behind it wasn't a surrender. Despite what they wanted to believe about new eras of peace, and alliance, and good magic prevailing." His mouth twisted. "I told them you don't leave behind a four thousand year old sword that's been kept outside of time, except as a warning. Liere was the only one who believed me. Sent me a message just a few days ago, telling me I was right."

Forthan felt sick. "Siamis is back?"

"Not yet. But he, or one of them, walked into that palace up north, ripped through all their magical wards like so many spider webs, and took the sword. Left everything else. Don't you see it's the back of the hand?" Senrid flipped his hand up in the age-old gesture of contempt.

Forthan didn't doubt it. "So it means war? In the north?"

Senrid whirled around and started his pacing again. "I don't know—who is there to talk to? *They* don't know. The smartest ones are my age, but like me they're just learning. The older ones still seem to be asleep, or living in the past, in the time before Siamis came out into the world from wherever he'd been hidden. They don't seem to see it, that Old Sartorans don't think like us, not when the world they were born in was four thousand years ago. Time doesn't mean the same thing. Their view of the world isn't the same. Nothing is the same. We don't know what to expect, except trouble."

Whirl, pace.

"There's a new one, a renegade Chwahir, who's been forcing his way up command in Norsunder's temporal forces. He's apparently brilliant—and mad." Senrid looked grim. "And one of these days he's going to be coming out of Norsunder looking for well-trained armies."

*Like us.*

Neither said the words, but they were thinking them. And could see it in the other's face.

Forthan felt cold grip his neck. "What do we do?"

Senrid looked out the window again. "I don't know."

# Eighteen

N ew Year's Firstday came and went, uneventful except when Shevraeth accompanied the rest of the winter stay-overs to the castle to watch the exhibitions. Forthan and his chosen troop performed riding, archery, fighting on horseback and on foot, spear tossing, and then a kind of organized target-game on a snow-dusted parade ground. Their audience was made up of city folk and Jarls, all crammed together in stands that had to be centuries old.

The first exhibition was held at night, lit by the ubiquitous torchlight. The second year seniors rode past one another in lines, lance in hand, tagging (or *tigging*, as they called it) their partners' lances each time they passed.

The lances looked spectacular when handled well, but Shevraeth had enough training by now to suspect they were tough to learn. At least that was for the seniors to worry about. He might very well be gone by then. Odd. Though he wanted to see home again, he didn't feel the unalloyed relief he would have felt last spring at the prospect of being sent away.

After that Forthan and a small group of third year seniors rode around and around in circles, breath clouding, horses' hooves kicking up frost-bursts of white as the seniors worked through choreographed fights with real, lethally sharpened curve-tipped swords.

The audience roared approval. Shevraeth looked out at
the ruddy-crowned silhouettes of Marloven Jarls, countryside
captains, and city people. Mostly male voices, from the sound,
but not all.

After the exhibition, Shevraeth found his way to the
library, which was marginally warmer than the outside. He
picked out a handful of promising histories and sat down to read
a little of each, to determine which—if any—he'd take back to
the senior rec room to read and report on to his parents.

All that week, as he passed to and fro from the library, he
figured there was plenty of statecraft happening in those vast
rooms on the first floor from which deep voices emanated,
occasionally punctuated by Senrid's higher voice. If so,
Shevraeth wasn't getting a sniff of it.

He was not the only one who knew nothing of Senrid's
concerns over events in the northern lands: most of the Jarls did
not know, and wouldn't have cared if they had. Whatever
happened beyond the borders was of little interest unless there
was an army lining up.

After New Year's Week was over the Jarls departed at
the heads of their entourages—a tenth of the size deemed
appropriate, or practical, in their great-fathers' day—their
banners snapping in the icy wind as they rode into the snow-
covered plains under the gray sky.

Then the boys who'd done the exhibitions brought food
and drink from the city to the senior barracks for a going-away
party. Everyone knew that Forthan was moving out. That night,
in fact. His few belongings had already been shifted over to the
Guard barracks, where, for a time, he'd be patrolling the city and
continuing his training.

ಬಿCRෂౕCB

In Remalna, Russav Savona had been permitted by the king to
spend New Year's with Shevraeth's parents. This is how the
four of them were able to write letters back and forth via the

golden cases, Shevraeth and Russav mainly exchanging jokes, and Shevraeth and his parents talking about reading, and events at home.

The first few days, Shevraeth had scrupulously hid when reading the letters, burning them as quickly as he read them. The many notes caused him some consternation until he discovered that the no-communication rule was suspended over winter, when two or three boys received runners from home, all carrying messages.

And so he enjoyed his correspondence with his parents, who gave him amusingly worded glimpses into the outer world—what they knew of events.

Not even his father was yet aware that Siamis, the Old Sartoran sorcerer who'd put the entire world under enchantment for an entire year, was again at large.

ಬಿ☙ℭℜℬ☙ಛ

After Forthan moved to the Guard barracks, it was right back to the winter schedule. Forthan was glimpsed occasionally going about Guard duty. The days slipped by, some bitter cold, memorable only for the ferocity of the wind howling unhindered across the plains as storm after storm passed, Shevraeth and the others were either busy in the warm rec room, or else keeping up their practice as best they could.

Gradually the scent of the wind changed. It had gone from the bone-aching smell of old ice to a whiff of mud and sodden grass when one of the new seniors appeared abruptly, dumped his gear onto a bunk, and said to Shevraeth as though they had known one another all their lives, "Forthan said to get you riding to halter. If you're agreed, we can begin tomorrow, now that there's some ground to fall on."

"Riding to halter?" Shevraeth repeated, now somewhat used to these abrupt meetings without a scrap of the politesse it was unthinkable to omit at home.

"Sword." The fellow waved a finger. "On horseback."

"I thought we were to be trained first time this next year. My group, I mean."

The fellow was blond, like most of them, with a long, square-chinned face, otherwise unremarkable. He grinned. "Yep. But they all practice at home. Though they're not supposed to. Forthan said, better to dump on your butt here," he jerked a thumb at the seniors' private practice court, "than before your House. And learn it right the first time. If you've a mind."

"Thank you," Shevraeth said. "I'd like that."

A shrug was his only answer. "I always come early—my dad being on spring training duty over at guard-side." The fellow paused, then pointed down at Shevraeth's fine brownweave court shoes. "Better visit supply, get some boots made." He was gone on the last word.

This training opportunity, Shevraeth realized as he trudged over to the supply building where the academy boot-maker worked, was Forthan's way of paying Shevraeth back for the lessons—as usual, no word, no way of thanking him.

The boots were ready the next morning; they were stiff, the high heels making him stand differently. But they were comfortable at once in a way his old ones never had been, with enough wiggle room for growth in the squared toes. Getting used to how the heels made his walk change, he made his way across the academy to the seniors' huge court.

And by the next day's end he'd discovered the hard way that riding well and fighting from horseback well were two different skills, only connected by some similar commands, and by the grip of the legs on the horse.

The very first bout, in fact the very first hard strike that he blocked, he had about a heartbeat to congratulate himself for having met blade to blade before his partner ripped his blade down, twisted, and Shevraeth lost his balance and tumbled right out of the saddle, squawking and clutching desperately as the horse snorted and danced away, then looked back at him reproachfully, ears flat.

Khaniver—his partner—grinned.

Shevraeth climbed grimly back onto his mount, ignoring the shaking of his legs and ringing of his ears. At least he knew how to fall, though falling into the frigid, slimy mud of new melt was no experience he wanted to repeat.

But repeat it he did. Several times. Though each day brought fewer errors and at last he managed to stay in the saddle. He considered that a mighty victory.

ஐ☙✦❧ౡ

Grass shoots fuzzed the fields when he received a summons to Keriam's office.

Shevraeth made his way along the stone corridors, hunching his ears into his coat. The wind was still bitter, making a low, almost shuddering howl across the vast plains.

He was too cold to think, and so he wasn't particularly worried, or even curious, at the summons. He was just grateful for the warmth of the office, and Keriam's familiar grizzle-haired, stocky bulk behind the desk, neat in the black-and-tan uniform.

Shevraeth saluted, an automatic gesture by now, and Keriam waved him to the waiting chair, which meant he wasn't in trouble. Not that he'd expected any—but there was always the chance he'd tripped over some invisible rule without realizing.

"What do you know about homesickness?" Keriam asked.

Shevraeth stared in surprise.

Keriam watched that surprise. That much had been deliberate, the better to gauge the foreign boy's reactions. Instead of recognition followed by scorn, by derision, even by affront or anger, Shevraeth's expression became pensive, and he said, "Is this a personal question?"

Keriam waved a hand, pleased he'd called his man right. But he would not make the foreigner self-conscious by pointing that out. "I'm talking about our new ten-year-olds. Many of them—sometimes most of them—are happy as pups the first night or so, and then when the newness wears off, they, well, they get homesick."

Shevraeth would never have imagined such a conversation here, of all places. "So you are asking what I would do?"

Keriam opened his hands. "The Regent, you have to understand, gave out explicit regs concerning homesickness, oh, twelve years ago. We were to beat the weakness out of them." He saw the quick contraction of disgust in Shevraeth's face, followed immediately by that peculiar blandness he seemed able to draw on like a cloak of invisibility. And Keriam rejoiced, convinced he'd been right.

Shevraeth looked inward, remembering long ago, when Russav Savona first came to them. He'd been, what five? His parents recently dead, both of them, and the grown-ups would not tell the boys where, when, or how, even. Savona had fought and kicked and thrown things for what seemed days and days. Shevraeth remembered hearing his howls of rage turn into tears every single time, until at last Savona consented to let Shevraeth's own mother come to him, and then stroke his head, and finally he climbed into her lap.

Shevraeth remembered his own feelings, watching another boy in his mother's lap. How at first he'd wanted to push Savona off, until he saw his own mother's quiet tears, and then his feelings changed, and he thought, *There is enough lap for two. My turn will come.* And of course it had. Little as she was, his mother somehow managed to have lap enough for two.

He looked up. "If they cannot have comfort, the sort of comfort you get at home, then the next thing is being busy." *We'll keep Russav busy, Danric, dear. Every day something new, something fun. And if you can make him laugh before you go to sleep at night, well, then, you can order whatever you like for dinner the next night, and we will not complain. Even if it is nut-and-chocolate cake every day.*

He nodded. "Fun, busy, make them so tired they fall into bed. But if they wake in the night, I see nothing wrong with whatever sympathy one can give." He looked away from memory. "Do you have a different view?"

"I don't have any view as yet. I can tell you that I've always placed the most sympathetic rads down in the small boys' school. You might have noticed that while some come, as you did, into the upper school their first year, for many reasons we hold to tradition and most boys come in at ten. Under the Regent that end of school was expanded because he felt that the younger they came in the more amenable they were to his . . . ideas of training. My rads were picked to . . . complement that training. Specifically I told them to circumvent what I thought were . . . counter-effective orders."

Shevraeth was beginning to understand his Marlovens by now, and realized that Keriam, and his rads, had actually been in some danger of discovery by Senrid's uncle Tdanerend, the Regent, in their effort to infuse the Regent's rules with some humanity. "Does the king have a new rule?"

"He doesn't have any rule, as yet, so you will find boys of all ages in some classes. Some seniors staying five or six years instead of three. Or only two. And not necessarily for reasons of skills either superlative or wanting. He says he doesn't know enough to figure out what's best for both kingdom and individuals, so we keep experimenting. I like your strategy. I like it well enough to put you in as a radlav this year."

"What?" Shevraeth exclaimed, not even trying to hide his dismay.

Keriam grinned. "I know. We get very few volunteers for the lower school, so I've made sure there are perquisites. You'll belong to a House, of course, for regular drill and games, but you and another of your class are assigned as radlavs under a senior down in the Puppy Pit, which is the current name for the lower school. Upper school gets one radlav per House, but the smaller boys need more guidance—and the guidance needs more time away from duty. You get your own room down there, and you trade off with nights of liberty. Not just the week's end liberty your House gets, but every other night, once the first two or three weeks are over. We keep you all on duty until they adjust."

Shevraeth said, "I won't beat them."

Keriam turned his palms up. "Use whatever means you have that work. I do advise you to wear the wand, or they will try you, but you may suit yourself about actually using it. They come knowing about what they call dustings. Most get the same at home, for their fathers were usually through here in their day. Here, too, the king has said that if we can find a way to get them into a semblance of order without beating them, he's open to ideas."

Shevraeth listened in amazement, then said cautiously, "I know the rules, but . . . what about scarfles?"

Keriam gave his brief smile. "What about them?"

"Well, I know that eating in the Houses is forbidden, yet the rads break the rules when they bring in the pastries. I gather that's a reward that is not to be counted on or asked for."

"Yes. Go on."

"So when does one provide one? And, ah, does it depend on one's money from home, or—"

Keriam flicked his hand up. "School pays. You just tell whoever is making yours to send the bill to me. But I suggest you let Lennac decide those." He hesitated, then said, "In case he leaves it to you, only give them out for a genuine reward—and, rarely, a consolation. If you find yourself providing food for popularity or bribery, well, let's say these were problems of the past."

Shevraeth hadn't considered that aspect.

Keriam pointed with his pen. "Be sure to visit supply before we make the shift-over for spring. You've outgrown those garments you brought from your homeland—you probably have outgrown your academy togs as well."

Shevraeth looked down, and for the first time noticed his wrist bones protruding from the exquisite edging on his fine woolen coat cuffs. "Oh."

# Nineteen

And it seemed, afterward, an eye-blink later when he stood beside Marec, who had grown a full hand over winter, though he still had the same red-blond curls sticking up all over his head, and Lennac, a tall, tough, pale-haired senior who was the chief aran radlav—the House rad. Shevraeth and Marec were technically aran radlavs as well, and everyone knew it, but they would be just *called* Radlav at inspection and assembly. More of those invisible rules.

Facing them were two lines of small boys, some of them twitching, others very still, all of them more or less apprehensive, as Lennac read out their names and then pointed to the beds.

Shevraeth's foremost emotion was the impulse to laugh at those apprehensive looks, the inexpert attempts by some of the boys to smooth their bunks or fold their clothing. You could tell instantly who had servants at home. He demonstrated the regulation folds, watched intently by mostly blue eyes that sometimes strayed reflectively to the polished wood wand stuck through his sash—for he was not a senior, and so he did not wear a belt.

They were ready for their first inspection bare moments before Kethadrend Tlen, the new Danas Valdlav, marched through. His cold blue gaze brushed with seeming indifference past his pale-faced small brother as he glanced at bunk and chest and clothes, and then passed on.

Tlen. One of three names Shevraeth recognized from the records he had been reading all winter, leading him to realize at last why there were two sets of archives at Athanarel Palace in Remalna-city. The greater proportion of them told what happened. The small archive contained the records that told why.

Of the puppies, Tlen was immediately recognizable, as was Sindan; Torac and Sereth were less so, and he had his suspicions about others. But curiously enough, famous last names did not necessarily correspond with evidence of servants at home.

"Good enough," Lennac said. "Now, remember. If we pass the week with no defaulters, then we go to Lastday inspection. Line up outside, and let's get some grub."

Whooping and screeching, the boys released themselves from their unnatural straightness, stampeding outside to the court they shared with the three other barracks. At once the boys glared at the boys from the other houses, already primed for rivalry, and a few high voices had begun on tentative insults before Marec pulled out his wand, slapping it once against his boot-top.

Instant silence.

Shevraeth smothered a laugh, feeling more and more false—no, not that. False implied a lie. He felt unreal, yes, that was it, as he walked along at the rear of the straight lines. What *was* he doing here? His life had become curiously unmoored. The Vidanric Renselaeus he had lost a year ago, come to terms with over the course of the summer, lost again in the parade court while Forthan's blood splashed the stones, had once again discovered a new identity when he plunged into the midst of these small boys surreptitiously nudging one another. They were in so many ways unlike the boys he'd known at home, and yet alike in others.

Once again, the first day's mess was conducted under the silence rule. After they ate, dealt with call-over, inspection, and then dismissal to their classes he noticed with relief how easy it was to go to his own classes, take up the now-familiar drills, to jettison his running stream of thoughts as his body took over. He did not have to think while shooting arrows, or throwing knives, or even while practicing, over and over, the ritualized strike patterns that eventually he was supposed to use from horseback, a Marloven cavalry blade with its wicked curve gripped in his hand.

Two, three, four days thus slipped by, the new beats of his day just beginning to assemble into a rhythm.

On the fifth night, he and Marec were just going to their little rooms. Shevraeth's room was barely big enough to fit a bunk—his trunk beneath it—but he was alone, and there was even a window. Marec's room was adjacent, again no larger than a broom closet at home, but between the rooms they had their own cleaning frame. Austere living space indeed, but enough for some privacy from all the sounds of sleeping bodies, and most precious of all, fresh air. Things once accepted without thought, and now appreciated.

Marec clapped the lights out. Shevraeth cast a glance back down the short hall leading to the dorm—no more than three paces long. The dorm seemed quiet, except for the expected squeaking of wooden frames, and a soft snicker, followed by multiple shushes.

He remembered his conversation with Keriam, and realized with a rush of gratitude that homesickness was not, at least so far, going to be a problem. The first night they'd had to patrol constantly to stop the whispers and muffled giggles. The second night some fell asleep within moments of crawling into bed, and Shevraeth had passed two or three beds from which came the revealing sound of suppressed, shuddery breathing, the kind that means the sufferer does not want attention, and so his step did not falter.

None since.

The reverie broke. A noise? Yes. There was another. Twice, now, too soft to identify, but just loud enough to disturb his thoughts.

Shevraeth moved to his door in his stockings. His candle cast a silhouette along the floor. He retreated, blew out the candle, and waited.

Nothing.

So he undressed, fell into bed, and dreams closed in immediately, breaking when once again noise interfered, followed by the distinctive squeaks of half-smothered boyish giggles.

He reached for his tunic and trousers, but pulled his hand back when Marec appeared in the hallway just outside of Shevraeth's room. A sliver of moonlight slanted through Shevraeth's tiny window, illuminating Marec fully dressed, hand resting on his wand.

*R-r-r-r-uk*! A sound like the tearing of canvas was followed immediately by a *brap*.

Shevraeth identified the noise at last. A farting contest.

Disgust and a brief spurt of amusement at the predictability of small boys flared through him. Marec raised a hand in silent enquiry, and Shevraeth gratefully left him to deal with the problem.

Marec stalked through the open doorway into the dorm room, clapped his hands, and the sudden light from the glowglobe painted a white square on the wooden hallway wall. Voices rose, shrill, some defensive, others shaking with residual laughter, soon snuffed by yelps and yips as Marec, from the sound, dealt every boy in the room a stinging whack across the shoulder-blades. He never spoke once.

Shevraeth lay back down. What was it with boys and the forbidden? He remembered his own very brief but very intense interest in what the human body produced, and how it compared with animal waste. How difficult it was not to use the Waste Spell just that once, his interest very swiftly followed by disgust, and then consternation when the stable wands did not work, and he'd had to bury it, bathing about eight times afterward.

He remembered melting helplessly with laughter when Savona deliberately farted after one of Galdran's sudden visits into the Renselaeus rooms at Athanarel, unannounced, as always, and how stern his mother had been about fouling the air. "Use your wit to register your disgust, not your body," she had said, with no hint of amusement whatsoever. "Animals don't know any better. You do. I will not tolerate that again."

Severely chastened, the boys had retreated, and Savona had afterward posited the theory that girls didn't fart, didn't even know how—a theory they believed until they were around these boys' age. Savona had dared Shevraeth to ask Renna, whose parents brought her to court frequently. She'd said cheerfully, *Of course we can, but we don't. Doing it on purpose just for fun is a disgusting boy trick.*

*Hah!* Savona had said triumphantly.

And Renna had gone on to squelch him, adding, *But when we were little, you should've heard Tamara after her grandmother yelled at her. Worse than a bran-stuffed horse.*

How Savona had teased Tamara, getting them all to call her Bran-ara . . .

Shevraeth fell asleep on the memories, which slid into dreams of childhood at Athanarel, so pleasant, so fun when Galdran's threatening presence was not imminent, the snowball fights, the ice sleighs, running through the gardens, running, running . . .

❧☙

The week-mark passed uneventfully.

This year Shevraeth saw the sense behind the mess gag during the first week. The boys were more orderly under the strict rules, whatever their lives were like at home. They experienced the truth of the academy promise that obeying simple rules netted prompt rewards.

Naturally that did not change them into new people, despite the new environment. Within a few days after the gag was lifted, the more venturesome ten-year-olds broke out in bread-pill flicking and foot-shove battles, which Lennac dealt with by breezes and defaulters, which meant sweeping floor and court each morning before the others were wakened. Shevraeth was surprised to discover that the lead trouble-makers were not the ones he'd expected. Sindan, cousin to Hotears Sindan (gone and unlamented by anybody) was a stolid, quiet boy whose primary interest appeared to be in food and dogs, in that order.

The second week passed, and the third. Shevraeth and Marec were at last told they could begin swapping off nights, as Keriam had promised. But the very first night was Shevraeth's alone.

He expected trouble. He'd already seen the furtive signals and signs promising it, and had wondered what it was in boys—was it in girls, too?—that made them test limits. They had had two weeks to learn something of the rads who were learning something of them. In their ten-year-old view, observations were simple. While Lennac handed out impartial breezes, and Marec had given them single whacks, Shevraeth's wand had never left his sash.

*Does that equate with cowardice in their eyes?* he wondered, as he made the last walk up and down the silent dormitory before clapping out the light.

Of course it did. Well, not cowardice, precisely. The boys already had assessed, with the dispassionate, not to say merciless, eye of the young, the performances of their rads in comparison with the other older boys. Shevraeth the Foreigner wasn't much with the sword, he was all right riding, but he was hot with the throwing knives. Still, he had never pulled his wand on anyone. What did that mean?

As soon as he was gone, and they saw the reflected light from his room go out, a boy named Mondar started the farting contest. From the other side of the dorm, Nessan responded, and the rest buried their faces in their pillows, shaking with laughter,

Sand shaking so hard his bunk squeaked on the floor, causing a volley of hissing curses.

Silence.

Then, *fw-e-e-e-t*, Tevac cut a long one, sending them into helpless spasms of laughter—

Light.

There stood Shevraeth. He looked around the dormitory, studying the red faces, some gazes averted, one or two challenging—and again, they were not the ones he might have expected.

"It stinks in here," he said in his pleasant voice, with the faint accent. "That means the barracks is unclean. So tomorrow's rec period will be spent in scrubbing the walls, the bunks, the floor. The next day's rec will be spent scrubbing all the windows, inside and out. And the following rec time will be spent scrubbing the entire court. Oh, no rec time? Then you will rise before dawn, and the scrubbing will be inspected before morning mess. Scrubbing, yes, not sweeping, you heard correctly. If it is not done to my satisfaction, then you will spend the rest of the day until you get it right. Now go to sleep. Unless you would like me to add some more chores?"

Silence.

He clapped the lights out.

Silence.

Then, a small voice, "Tevac, you idiot."

A desperate hiss of "Shut up!"s followed.

Next day, a rainstorm came through. But in spite of the bitter wind, the entire barracks was up before dawn, their stern-faced rad Shevraeth with them.

The barracks soon smelled of damp wood and wet wool, the latter reminding Shevraeth of young dogs in the rain. He was smiling inwardly, though outwardly maintaining the necessary blank face and exacting eye, when Lennac and Marec arrived from their liberty nights.

Lennac looked around, hiding his surprise, but he turned his attention to inspecting the job being done. All three of the rads made certain that every drop of water was scoured away, the two rows of bunks were re-aligned neatly—headboards to the walls, foot making an aisle down the middle—that everything, in short, was better than it had been, before dismissing the sodden, weary boys to get ready for inspection before morning mess.

While they were dressing, the three closed themselves in Shevraeth's room.

"What happened?" Lennac asked.

Shevraeth gave a succinct report. Both the older boys grinned, Marec's shoulders shaking. "Second time in a second week, eh? This group is going to be hot at hand."

Lennac laughed. "Just what m'father warned me about. Said they'd break out with something or other, and the earlier the better for us, if we come down hard all at once. Good. We'll ride 'em all week. But why not just breeze 'em?"

Shevraeth said, "I would rather not."

Lennac pursed his lips. Marec said quickly, "They don't, where he comes from." His tone was defensive.

Lennac waggled a hand. "I don't like it either, but it's part of life. If you can get 'em to obey without it, and not dishonor us before the others, I don't care. But how did you think of this?" He jerked his thumb out toward the barracks. "It's great."

"It's in your own records," Shevraeth said.

The other two looked surprised.

"I spent the winter here. Read as much about the academy as I could find. There isn't very much," he added. "Some records have details of several years, by a single hand, naming boys, wins, games, and sometimes the schedules, some of which I recognize and some of which has changed. Other times are silent. There was a century of silence around the time of my own ancestor."

Lennac sat back. "Ah! So that explains why you are here."

*No it doesn't*, Shevraeth thought, but he said nothing.

"Who's your ancestor?" Marec asked. "You never said anything last year. Some of the others thought you might be related to the king."

"I am, though very distantly. My ancestor was sister to one of your kings of three centuries back, by name of Ivandred Montredaun—"

The reaction in the other two was so sudden, so sharp, Shevraeth bit off the rest of the name. "What is it?"

Lennac and Marec exchanged quick looks, then Marec slouched against the door, his face averted.

"We never name him," Lennac said in a low voice. "After we're told the story. Ever. Until we have to tell it to our own children."

Shevraeth sighed. "So that's why I couldn't find anything about him. In our records, we only know that he started wars. And won them. Then vanished." *Starting wars does not seem to be confined to this particular one of your kings, so . . . why is there a problem?*

Lennac said, "He rode into Norsunder under the Banner of the Damned."

*The Banner of the Damned.* What was *that*? "I will abide by your custom, then," Sheraeth said. "Though I don't know any of the circumstances. But it seems strange, to eradicate someone from history, and yet not eradicate him."

"We all know," Marec said, unsmiling, "because Norsunder is beyond time. That means he could ride out again, at the head of the First Lancers. Any day, any time, and where do you think he will come first?"

# Twenty

*Russav:*

*I have come to the conclusion that commanding an entire army cannot be more difficult than holding the reins of eighteen ten-year-olds.*

*Yes. You laugh. I can hear you laughing, and I can only hope that one day you too will find yourself in a similar position. It will be good for you. I am convinced, in fact, that it will be beneficial to your moral development. Ten year old boys here are little different than we were at that age. They all share one skill. They can turn order into chaos between one heartbeat and the next. These boys live for practical jokes, or "stings," and the most valued of these stings— which never err on the side of subtlety—are those that catch radlavs by surprise.*

*You will have an opportunity to practice patience. Everyone tells us patience is a virtue. When you have heard for the five hundredth repetition the same jokes that you did not find funny the first time, or had to keep your gaze sternly on the table lest the same two boys endeavor to begin yet another bread-pill flinging contest, or any of the other crazed plots that ten year olds think original and funny, you must maintain your court mask as though you never heard a word. No anger or laughter. One lapse, and they do not forget.*

*Amazing, how a small society will take on the tone of its leadership. And the 2 leaders of our pack of scrubs could conquer the vast Land of the Chwahir. All by themselves, just by their indefatigable and stolid resistance to civilization. Tevac could rule the universe, if he put his invention to anything useful, instead of circumventing rules and inventing stings. His faithful lieutenant, the huge yellow-haired Mondar, I think is actually a horse in human guise. Not very human, either. Unlike his older brother—who is quite ordinary, if on the quiet side—he's stronger than most men, tireless after extra chores that would defeat half the seniors, and incapable of any subtlety whatever...*

Shevraeth scanned the boys' faces before he spoke.

All of them were tolerably easy to read: wary, apprehensive, scowling, worried, and one or two challenging and resentful.

He had learned so far that small boys felt they had won something if they made rads angry. Even if they got punished, in their worldview they had still won.

So he had not been surprised to overhear a brag— *Shevraeth's never breezed us*—a few days before. He'd been considering whether a couple of them had meant for him to overhear as he walked rapidly back from target practice, and discovered four crimson-faced boys, who had obviously run in the hot summer air all the way from the stable, in the act of shoving horse droppings into rival boys' bunks. He knew it was no happenstance that they'd picked his day watch in which to execute their sting.

Never one to put off trouble, he'd ordered them to line up.

Now he kept his face bland, his voice pleasant and light. "It's true, Mondar, none of you have gotten a breeze from me. And it's no accident."

Furtive looks, nudges, and one grin convinced him that yes, he'd been meant to overhear.

"And you probably won't get a breeze from me. I say probably, because who knows what will happen in the future?" He smiled.

The grins faded to speculation, and a couple of the scowls turned to apprehension as feet shuffled, bony shoulders twitched, tousled heads turned to examine sky, the stone flags of the court, shoes.

"In the meantime, I can promise you this."

He whacked the wand against his boot. Snap! Their attention was back.

"I prefer not to use violence against human beings. Supposedly we all have the wit to learn to make constructive choices. I believe, and will exert myself to convince you, that actions always have consequences."

He put the wand back in his sash. The scrubs were puzzled by his speech patterns, a couple of them irritated by them though they could not have defined why they found his style of talk so intimidating. It strayed outside experience.

"The consequences you are accustomed to are your breezes. A little pain, and you go right on. But consequences in the real world do not end there. They go on, and on, and on, like the ripples in a pond when you skip a rock."

Pause again.

"Like what?" Tevac asked, brows aslant. "I mean, with us?"

"I am glad you asked. Like, just for example, if you continue putting disgusting things in one another's shoes, or beds, then I am going to think you really don't understand the consequences of making messes that someone else has to clean up. So on Lastday, when the other houses are at the game, you will collect all the dress boots owned by the seniors and you will clean and polish them. Inside and out. If you still feel you must throw bread pills at meals, during your rec period you will march to the mess hall, and clean the entire floor."

"You *idiot*, Tevac," someone muttered.

"I want you," Shevraeth said, feeling a quiver of laughter in his stomach, "to consider the consequences next time you contemplate an action. If you just stop and consider, then there's no need for this." He flicked the wand in his sash with dismissive fingers. "There will be an inspection before mess," he added, "since you seem to have little to do right now."

Inspection meant yet another thorough cleaning of the barracks. He left, and this time pretended not to hear the mutters, sighs, and threats, because they were all aimed at Tevac.

Marec was waiting in Shevraeth's tiny room. Shevraeth shut the door, and Marec dropped down onto the bed, snickering hoarsely in an effort to keep from being overheard by the boys. "You were terrifying."

Shevraeth looked at him in surprise. "I was? I meant to be reasonable."

"Sometimes reasonable is frightening," Marec said, still snickering. "Go on. Start your rec watch before it rains. I'll run the inspection."

The windows let in the strange, orangish glare that precedes a sunset thunderstorm. So Shevraeth flung the wand down on his bed—he refused to go into the city with that thing—and passed through the cleaning frame.

As he walked toward the old mossy tunnel that led from the academy into the castle, he considered how things could change both outwardly and inwardly, and without any fanfaronade whatsoever. Last year he'd been *told* that the practice courts were for free practice between lessons. What that had *meant*—last year—was that Sindan and the seniors had had certain ones marked off for their quarrels. So no one below senior level dared go there for extra practice, and had to make do with their own small courts, or the alleyways between buildings.

This year, outside the senior wall was reserved for violent resolution of private quarrels (now strictly supervised by other boys), but the practice courts were just that.

Shevraeth learned it from Marec by the end of the second week. He was in the habit of rising before dawn now, though he no longer had private riding lessons. On the mornings when he didn't have wakeup duty, he thought: why not get in extra practice, since he was used to getting up early?

After he and Stad encountered one another more than once in the early morning, they met by design. Stad was by far the better in everything except knife throwing. There he and Shevraeth were nearly even. At their morning practices together they'd shoot against one another unless the wind was bad, and then do some double-stick practice, or contact fighting.

Shevraeth liked the extra practice—but what with those and being a rad, there hadn't been time for reading.

So on this, his first free day, he did not go to the library as he had on his half-watch rec periods previously. He still had a half-read book in his cubbyhole of a room. Instead he kept right on going straight into the city, with no goal or plan. Just thinking.

*Terrifying?* Marec had to have been making fun of him. He could not see how it was possible for him to be frightening to anyone in this strange kingdom where he'd felt more fear during those first months than at any other time in his life. Even when King Galdran was ranting.

"I am no threat to anyone," he muttered, scarcely aware he was talking, as he turned down a street at random, and strolled along, looking at the rows of stone buildings, small windows low down, broader windows higher. "Not even boys of ten."

Not that he wanted to be threatening to small boys. Except . . . was that the only way you maintained authority over them?

He grimaced. This whole idea of authority over others— that they had to do what you said, or they'd be in trouble, even if what you said was stupid—unsettled him. His mother had taught him that civilization was achieved when everyone chose to do the right thing, even if no one there was watching. Of course, he'd discovered when he was older, that 'the right thing' wasn't always the same thing for different people. Was that where governing by fear, and not by sense, happened? He liked to think he had more sense than ten-year-old boys, but they only seemed to obey him if he threatened them. *Why?*

Well, he didn't have to think about it now. For the first time he was in the city, but to his eyes it may as well have been an extension of the castle. The first thing you noticed was that this city would be tough to attack. Yet the Marlovens had managed to make it somewhat pleasant, at least to an eye now grown accustomed to ubiquitous stone. The color of that stone was not the light gray granite so common everywhere else, but a light, warm sandy-peach color. The even stone squares of the clean streets contrasted with leafing pepper trees planted at intervals.

One saw no artistic carving, nor heard much in the way of musical instruments, two common things in Remalna-city. But Marlovens did sing ballads, most in variations on a galloping rhythm.

"Hey! Shevraeth!"

A familiar voice—a girl's voice. There was Senelac in the company of two other girls, all three in their uniforms, just as he was. He recognized the two from the stables, though neither had ever spoken to him.

"Going for your foreigner pastries?" Senelac flashed a white-toothed grin, her brown face framed by dark, curling short hair.

"Foreigner pastries?" he asked. "Where?"

All three girls exclaimed, "You didn't know?"

Shevraeth turned out his hands.

"Come on. You can tell us if their sweet-rolls are really like the ones in Old Sartor, or if they're lying."

"I wouldn't know what Old Sartor's food is like," he said as he joined the girls. "Or even new, Sartor having so recently rejoined the world."

Senelac waved a hand. "To us it's all the same, that cosseted eastern stuff, with all their fans and lace and strange foods that don't look like anything you'd recognize."

He could hear her joking tone, but he sensed the curiosity the girls were trying to hide. What he didn't sense was their interest in *him*.

Two, three blocks, as the wind moaned round stone corners and blew at hair and clothes; big warm raindrops began to splotch their tunics just as they ran across a street, dashing round a cart laden with cabbages, and through a door.

The shop was a narrow long room much like those at home, a counter down one side, behind which were wooden shelves with glass-fronted bread-boxes, not much different from those at home. Inside all those boxes were cakes and pastries, many of which were indeed familiar.

The aromas of baking pastry were so enticing that he didn't mind the extra heat emanating from the back room behind its billowing heavy curtain.

Small tables lined the opposite wall; two of them were occupied but the last, nearest the back, was free. The four made for it, despite the heat, and sat down as lightning flared outside. A sudden downpour hissed. They laughed at their narrow escape from the deluge and watched the rain sheeting with satisfaction. The sinking sun had not quite been blocked yet, its slanting rays touching the raindrops to silver. The downpour intensified, droplets bouncing back up in a steamy haze.

A girl their own age, dressed in a yellow tunic and green trousers, came up. "Hey, Fenis. Maddar. Shem. Who's this?"

"Shevraeth the Foreigner," Senelac said, and Shevraeth realized he had no idea which name was hers—or if it was a real name or a nickname. "This here is Henad."

"Oh," Henad said, studying Shevraeth with interest.

Senelac turned to him, still grinning. "So. You pick for us. What do you recognize over there?" She waved her hand at the fresh baked goods in the glass-sided boxes. "What is good where you come from?"

Shevraeth moved along the counter, studying the pastries.

From behind came a whisper, "Make him talk. I love the way he talks."

The impulse to keep going right through the door was strong. He squashed it, and ordered four familiar pastries, one with custard, another with berries, a five layer cake made with thin layers of spiced pastry laced with ground nuts and fitted between thin layers of sweet buttercream. The fourth was a dark little cake iced with hardened chocolate, his mother's favorite.

"Who's paying?" Henad asked.

"Who has the most money left this quarter?" Senelac asked her friends.

"Put it on mine," Shevraeth said, and the others looked startled. He added uncertainly, "At least, Commander Keriam gave me to understand that this was customary. And if so, I have never used any. There ought to be plenty left from the ordinary expenses we incur."

"If you gave him money to hold, then that's the way to do it." Shem smiled when he turned her way.

He nodded, and they thanked him for their share. When Hened brought the pastries, he waited for them to choose, knowing he'd like whatever was left. They all avoided the chocolate one, and he wondered why.

Hened said to him, "I can't get them to try chocolate. I know they'd like it. We have some customers who come from outside the city and stop here first, just for these."

"It looks like it sat outside for a year." One of the girls, the one with very fair hair, wrinkled her nose. "I want to see buttercream. Then I know it's real pastry."

The girls exclaimed their enjoyment.

Senelac was amused by the way her two friends sat facing the foreigner, directing their comments to him, and listening to his every word. She could see they found him attractive. He was much harder to read. As always.

He was discovering how nice it was to sit with three girls. Three pretty ones, he realized, though a year ago he wouldn't have thought about it. He began comparing them to the girls at home, with their elaborate hair and clothes, all dressed with gems and ribbons and velvet in winter and flowers in summer. These girls wore the same clothes he did, but he caught himself looking at the tunics for hints of the shape beneath, and forced his eyes back to his pastry. The girls' voices, even their smell, were just so . . . *pleasant.*

The talk was nothing much—they asked about the Puppy Pit and he made a few jokes about bread-pill fights and inspections, discovering (as usual) they'd already heard about such things. Further, apparently young girls weren't all that different. They too had scarfles, only more elaborate, including midnight picnics.

Then they talked about the horses, most of whose names he now knew. He became aware of everyone working to keep the talk in safe channels, much like one would at a court, but without the tricks of reference to old poems or songs or plays. No one introduced anything deep or meaningful or even all that interesting. It was just chatter, yet no one seemed bored, or impatient.

He found his gaze straying again—not to pale blond Maddar, or red-haired Shem. He kept wishing that Senelac would lean close, or that he could move near. What did she look like under that old smock, and did her dark, curling hair really smell like sage, or was he just imagining?

There was only one bad moment, a brief one, and afterward he was glad that he had not been the cause, however inadvertent. In fact, he did not even know which word it was of Maddar's, when they were talking about old riding games among their grandmothers during their academy days. A place name, he was fairly certain. Darchelde, was that it? Whatever it was, it wiped the smiles from all their faces as if flicked away by an invisible cloth.

But then Senelac started talking with a determined air about her grandmother's cherished academy medal, awarded by the old king. The others commented, a little self-conscious at first. Then gradually relaxed.

A bell rang, and despite the rain it was time to go. Henad bade them all good-bye, and the girls took off on a footrace, laughing as they sprinted, their entrance to the academy being farther up through the labyrinth of the castle.

*Fenis.* Shevraeth smiled reflectively all the way back to the Puppy Pit.

⊰ෲ𝕊ℭ⊱

Up ahead, Shem said, "Why do they always like you best, Senelac?"

She laughed. "I guess it's my staggering beauty."

Maddar hooted, then turned to Shem. "How could you tell he liked her? He was so nice and smiling, just like a traveling player on a platform. Was any of that real?"

"Are *you* blind! He kept sneaking peeks at Fenis. You were too busy stuffing your face."

"Oh, feed it to the horses," Maddar said in disgust, on the others' laughter. "Got any interest in him, Fen?"

"He reminds me of the king," Senelac said, as they rounded the last corner.

"Whee-ew," Shem exclaimed, slinging rain off her braids.

"Bad or good?" Maddar asked, brows aslant.

Senelac tipped her hands back and forth. The other two laughed appreciatively as they splashed through a puddle.

And then they were home.

※⟨ℛℰ⟩⁂

It took him four days to discover that her name, or nickname, was for a wild herb of the plains.

# Twenty-one

Lastday, the scrubs marched out to the game field, the boys, after several days of painfully good behavior, now letting loose pent-up feelings with shoving fights, shrill laughter, wild insults shouted up at the Houses ahead, who were the enemy for the day. In between these fits of wildness they sang snatches of marching songs in loud, tuneless enthusiasm.

Shevraeth walked at the back, and fought against yawns. He expected a long, boring afternoon. He now understood the reasoning behind the games, and played as hard as he could when he was with his own class, but he still just didn't really care about winning flags. What he kept trying, every single week, was to comprehend the whole while he ran about in the game, never with much success.

He was sure it would be just the same today. As a rad he was expected to guard a boundary. He would not even get to run. He knew he'd be bored half to sleep, and so he deliberately chose the most uncomfortable of the boundaries atop the jumble of rocks dotting the little hillock at the north border, beneath a spreading tree.

Lennac chose the stream, and Marec was left with the better position, the grassy hill at the south, adjacent the road.

Shevraeth leaned against a rock, wishing the three of them could be near enough to chat. No, the time had to be endured alone, so they'd do their job.

Each of the three Houses separated, dividing into the ridings their senior rads had appointed earlier. Then Marec blew the horn, and the game began.

Shevraeth watched, at first idly, as the groups of boys jockeyed for position; he soon spotted the riding captains of the other two sides, and was mentally comparing them to their own boys when he realized what he was doing.

He frowned, straightening up. How strange. How very strange—he was gauging not just the ridings' strengths, but what sort of offense it looked like they'd been ordered to try by their rads. And how those tries would match against the orders that Lennac had given them for defense as well as offense.

He assessed the boys as individuals, as leaders . . . their movements as ridings . . . the ridings' success or lack.

He'd got it. He was not just observing but understanding the entire battle.

When had that happened? Was it because for the first time he stood completely outside the contest, as Senrid had suggested last year?

It was almost dizzying, this insight. Shevraeth stepped forward and leaned his elbows on a low branch of the tree, and now he could not only see the shape of the whole battle, but he found he could predict the next immediate movement of the three leaders. *To the rocks, and realize that's a dead end—you, yes, flank 'em, that's it. And Torac decoying the enemy, so they don't notice. . . I think you've got it, Lasda. If you just keep them together, and Torac keeps their attention—*

"You see it now?"

The light voice startled him. He sidestepped, a hand half-rising in a defensive gesture, then he recognized Senrid-Harvaldar, and his hand dropped.

If Senrid noticed, he gave no sign. His gaze was on the small boys running about below. "That one, the one with the ears. He's running 'em all in your House, don't you think?"

Senrid's assessment had taken about three breaths, Shevraeth realized, his own triumph souring into self-mockery.

But of course Senrid had been observing these games ever since he was small, because he'd been forbidden to participate.

"I remember now. His name is Lasda."

"Yes, I see it." Shevraeth leaned on the branch. "I guess I needed to play a number of those games as a participant, a marker on the board, before I could comprehend the whole."

Senrid flicked his fingers out in the open-hand gesture of assent. He was shorter than Shevraeth remembered, the top of his blond head just clearing Shevraeth's shoulder. Shevraeth realized that he'd grown but the king had not. In fact, Senrid was exactly as round-faced as last year, no whit of difference.

Senrid stood under this scrutiny without speaking. He had no plans to discuss why he'd taken the spell to halt aging. Sometimes he wasn't sure he could explain it to himself. "I have something for you." He pulled out a metallic token that had been affixed to a gold chain.

Shevraeth took it, looking a question.

Senrid said, hating the necessity, "It's a transfer token." His guts tightened, but he forced his tone to stay even. "There's evidence that Siamis might return."

Shevraeth's light eyes widened, then narrowed speculatively. "And you expect to be his initial target?"

"Not his." Senrid turned his attention down to the shrieking boys on the field. How he hated giving voice to his fears, though he knew it was stupid to dread that speaking the words would turn probability to certainty. The certainty had already happened. His voice was flat, devoid of expression. "It's not Siamis that worries me. At least, he's a big threat, bigger than I can handle. But there's a worse one."

"There is?" Shevraeth's heartbeat quickened.

Senrid flicked his hand out. "Siamis was betrayed to Norsunder when he was just a few years younger than us. Records say he was betrayed by his uncle, Detlev Reverael ne-Hindraeldrei, at least that seems to be the way to say it, in the old tongue. He was, we are told, a *dyranarya.*"

"What is that?"

Senrid's shoulder lifted, a sharp movement. "No one's exactly sure. Except that they controlled people by thought. And he and I have tangled before. He promised me we would meet again. From all I can gather he keeps his word. When it suits his purpose."

Below, unheeding, the small boys screeched and jumped and shouted, as the last struggle for the flags commenced. Around them the shadows had lengthened, leafing tree-branches segmenting the field, light and shadow.

Shevraeth tried to think of something to say, then realized nothing was adequate. So he just held up the golden token. "I take it I am to wear this?"

Senrid turned his head. "Day and night."

Below, Tlen led a wedge of boys running up the hill among the rocks. When they saw Senrid and Shevraeth their round pink mouths opened, and their hands thumped their chests in salute to their king. Then they veered, sudden as birds, and fled downhill again, yelling wildly as they plunged right into the midst of a clump of the enemy. The yells were sharper, higher, more exaggerated: they were conscious of being watched.

"It seems unfair that the only living Old Sartorans would be those one would exert oneself never to meet." Shevraeth flung the chain over his head and slipped the token inside his tunic. The metal token thunked against his chest, cold and ungiving.

Senrid grinned again, that quick, toothy grin. "Oh, there is also Lilith the Guardian, but she is even more rarely met. And as dangerous, in her own way."

Shevraeth had heard of her—of course. In old, old ballads. "She's real? I mean, not in the historic sense, but lives?"

"She too has recourse to someplace outside of time. Because she does live. I've seen her."

Shevraeth whistled. "And you can read Old Sartoran."

"Only marginally. If that. Liere and I have been trying to study it. But with all the success of a couple of puppies trying to learn the famed Colendi flower symbols, their ribbon symbols, their fans and the rest of it."

Shevraeth laughed. "I wonder which one is the more obscure, Old Sartoran—about which my father had some pungent things to say, when he told my tutor to confine his exertions to modern history—or Colend's court customs."

Senrid made a sudden movement. "I'm beginning to think that the Old Sartorans didn't deliberately set out to be obscure, it's just that they had to employ metaphor to describe things for which they otherwise had no terms. They were, we believe, a lot closer to the non-human beings in this world— were until we humans almost managed to destroy ourselves along with everything else. So, if that's true, then human language wouldn't suffice, would it? I mean, how would you describe red to a blind man?"

Shevraeth nodded, as below a sudden cry of triumph rose, shrill as the cries of gulls over the Remalnan marshes. One riding of boys scrambled to lift up one of their number who waved a flag triumphantly. As they paraded around, dancing and crowing and hooting insults as the losing Houses, he said, "But I understand there are few records of those first days."

"Very few, very rare, at least that I know of. And most of those are copies, whose texts could have been tampered with."

Shevraeth said, "So there is no way, really, to translate metaphor into meaning?"

Senrid's teeth showed in that brief, startlingly unpleasant grin. "Oh yes there is. Fall into the hands of Siamis, or worse, Detlev. They'd probably be glad to discourse on the verities of their day, right before they rip your identity from out of your skull, and all without moving their hands. See that you keep that thing always by you. If I do have to act, there probably will be no time for warning."

He jerked round, walking rapidly down the backside of the hill to where a horse waited at the stream a little distance away.

Then Lennac called "Shevraeth?"—unaware of the king having been there, Shevraeth realized—and it was time to go, Lennac saying, "You and Marec get them unpacked, clean, and sorted out. They've earned their first scarfle, don't you think?"

## Twenty-two

Russav Savona did not write back immediately.

Shevraeth knew that his parents and Russav would not take a communications device when summoned back to court by King Galdran. There were no resident mages in Remalna by law. If the king knew about the golden cases, he would forbid them to anyone but himself. They'd explained how their rooms were searched sporadically by the king's spies while they were on protracted outings, and so they did not dare leave any kind of communication anywhere in Athanarel Palace.

Answers would have to wait upon his mother's making excuses to go home to Renselaeus, where she could read Shevraeth's letters in safety. Russav would have to wait until she returned. Then he'd have to find an opportunity to slip his letters into her hand—and after that find an opportunity to collect any answers.

The fact that he wouldn't get an answer any time soon was Shevraeth's excuse not to write anything about Senelac, but in truth he wasn't sure what to write. He found himself thinking about her, and missing the daily riding lessons of the year before. Wishing he had any excuse to see her again.

Another thing he kept thinking about was that strange reaction from the girls when one of them mentioned Darchelde.

On his next rec period he returned to the Residence library, and found Darchelde on the big map. It seemed to be a wooded area near the southeastern border of the kingdom.

A persistent tug of memory caused him, over the succeeding days whenever he had liberty, to delve back through some of the histories in a more methodical manner. No mention . . . no mention . . . no mention . . . he was beginning to think that Darchelde was another of those oddities erased and yet not erased from history, like Ivandred Montredaun-An.

Ivandred! On impulse he went searching deliberately for the single brief, dry mention of Ivandred Montredaun-An that he'd found on one of his early forays.

He'd read it without interest, for it gave the barest facts of Ivandred's rule. Now, knowing a bit more, he realized the facts were not dry at all, but freighted with hidden meaning, sparse as they were between 4408, when Ivandred came to the throne and 4418 when, as it stated so blankly, *He left the kingdom.*

Left the kingdom not over a physical border, but riding at the gallop at the head of his cherished First Lancers, unbeatable warriors according to the records, the gold-and-black fox banner snapping in the wind as they rode straight into a rift shimmering between ground and sky. A rift that opened onto the blackness of Norsunder.

*The banner of the damned.*

There were no drawings of that fox banner anywhere in the library, but Shevraeth suspected he had already seen it, in Remalna's royal palace, before he embarked on his long journey. His father had taken him to the dusty archives that Galdran had no interest in, and had opened one of the Calahanras records, showing him sketches made by a living hand 320 years ago. These had been drawn during the visit Ivandred made to Remalna, escorting his sister Tharaez—or Therais, as the Marlovens had pronounced it. Not *Ther-RAY-ez*, but *THAR-ray-is*, the ending a soft almost unvoiced sound—like the 'ya' of Hesea in the kingdom's name in those days. One of the courtiers had made sketches of the visitors. There was one of Ivandred, just a profile, not very good, indicating a tall blond man. Several sketches followed that Shevraeth realized now were attempts to capture the grace of the Marloven horses, bred on the plains of Nelkereth. Last was a sketch of a slightly sinister, curiously raptorish fox face, its mane like flames. It was gold, set against a black background: the Montredaun-An fox banner.

Ivandred, Norsunder—and Darchelde, which he realized now had been the ancestral Montredaun-An home.

Interesting, somewhat menacing stuff, as was so much Marloven history, but Shevraeth did not think that the Ivandred years were the reason the girls had reacted as they had. What had Maddar been saying? He couldn't recall it, but instinct insisted the reference was far more recent.

One mystery solved, just to reveal another mystery.

At least there wasn't any mystery about the new training. His gratitude to Forthan for his thoughtfulness intensified when his own House began the mounted hand-to-hand fighting part of their cavalry drill. Shevraeth, now used to the basics, had said nothing; he did not know most of his Housemates yet, as he bunked in the Puppy Pit, but he was very aware of the sidled glances, the covert signs of expectation when the first drills began. But he did not fall off his saddle, or drop his willow sword. Khaniver had used real steel with him the last few days before the official beginning of the year. He knew how to grip the horse with his legs to balance for sword blocks and strikes, and how to lock his heels down into the stirrups to brace. And he knew the ring of steel down through muscle and bones, and how to brace against it while on the move. He wasn't fast—not enough time for that—but he was one of the few who kept hold of his weapon. Two boys even fell out of the saddle.

❧✦❧

*Russav: It's been a month now, and we're near our first overnight with the Puppies. Not,*

*you need to understand, that they call it an
'overnight.' As anyone will immediately grasp,
there are overnights and non-overnights that last
over a night. The first, you of course will have
guessed, are the wargames that go into the night.
But the second ones are the scouting forays. The
small boys are not permitted to wargame till
midnight until they are older. Their first year is
mostly scouting, which means tracking and map
reading and making. So there is no fighting at
night. Each class of older boys has to do one
tracking and scouting camp for the scrubs,
planning and executing it being their own lesson.
My class had their lesson last year when I was
recovering from Sindan's loving attentions.*

*The boys may consider these to be mere
chores, but I confess to you I greeted the news
with (hidden) relief. I trust that means we rads
get some sleep. But boys being what they are, I
suspect we won't.*

*Meanwhile, I've made another discovery.
Useless as it is—can you imagine Nenthar on
horseback, actually attacking someone, instead of
hiding behind a rock and sending his bully-boys
in? No, how about Galdran? Now there's an
image! Galdran on horseback, swinging a
sword!—well, absurd as it all is, I really enjoy
horseback fighting. I've probably lost my
pretence of civilization at last. Maybe I never was
civilized, but riding about on a grassy plain
whacking and stabbing at my fellow man with a
willow blade from the back of a high-bred horse
is more fun even than horse racing.*

*But as usual, my pleasure was short lived.
I know now what the true purpose of this kingdom
serves in my life, and that is to crush me*

*thoroughly whenever there is the least danger of
my feeling the tiniest modicum of complacence.*

  *What now, you ask? I will tell you. They
began us on lance drills. Just drill. We don't
pretend to actually use them even for fake
charges until next year. The first drill is to grip
the thing and describe a circle. Simple-sounding,
eh? If you'd seen those attempts at a circle, you
would have thought we were more drunk than
Grumareth on a good gambling day, and about as
graceless . . . and in case we thought it wasn't as
bad as it seemed, one look at the masters' faces
as they obviously tried not to laugh . . .*

L ances.
  Russav Savona stared out his window, not seeing the
brilliant fuzz of light green all through the garden behind
Athanarel Palace. He read the letter again, paying close attention
so he would remember it all when he had a chance to answer it.
Then he put it on the fire and stood there until it was consumed.

  Midway through the night, he was just returning from
one of the king's interminable card parties when Shevraeth's
reference to drunken Grumareth brought the letter back to mind.

  He'd been drinking himself, matching the adults glass for
glass just to prove he could do it and keep his wits. Abruptly he
took the lantern from the hand of the servant lighting his way
back to his rooms. "I'll light my own way." And because this
man was one of the king's spies, he added in his best drawl, "I
was just put in mind of a theatrical, and I want to see if we have
the props in storage."

  The man bowed.

  Savona yawned beyond his fan. The spy betrayed
disgust, but no surprise. More vagaries of the nobles to gossip
about, then, and thus no alarm to report to the king.

  Good.

They parted, and Savona's sense of his own cleverness lasted until he reached the old storage area out behind the guard barracks.

He'd nearly reached the big barns when he was challenged by a roaming sentry. He just lifted the lantern up so the light shone on his face, and the guard, who was his own age, gave him a polite bow. But his eyes were curious as he said, "Is there anything you need, your grace?"

"Yes. A way into the storage shed. The big one, where all the old armor and so forth is kept."

"Old armor?" the sentry asked.

Savona had already thought out his answer on the walk. He staggered slightly—*drunk as Grumareth*—and then said, "M'dad showed me the old stuff before he died. I was very small, but I carry a memory of fabulous armor, rusting in ancient glory, and a rack of astonishing old weapons we hardly touch now. I'm thinking of a sort of theatrical, d'you see, for the king's pleasure."

"Oh. I know what you want," said the sentry.

"I hope it's still there." Savona gestured drunkenly with his fan as the sentry lifted the bar to the broad door and led the way in by the light of Savona's lantern.

The sentry paused by the door to hang the lantern on an old hook, and took down another lantern, its candle wicked and ready. He lit it and carried them both inside, past racks of horse gear and halberds and spears, from practice gear to the fancier weapons used at ceremonials.

At the very back wall they found the rack of lances that Savona had remembered. And despite the fact that he was much bigger and taller than he'd been at four, they were just as large as he'd remembered.

Laughing immoderately, he affected a stagger and a sway as he moved forward to lift one down, saying, ". . . and my idea is a wager. We dress like one of the old kings, and recite whatever ballad is most pompous, see, and most obscure, and see who can guess whom it belongs to . . ." Chattering on inanely he hefted the lance.

He could lift it, he was glad to find—but holding it steady very soon had his arms shaking. When he tried holding it with his right arm, his wrist bent. As for describing a circle—he made it halfway up in an arc, a white pain shot through his shoulder, and his knee came up to balance his arm.

He laughed, the sentry laughed rather perfunctorily, and Savona replaced the lance. To bolt the impression, he said, "M' tutor once made me memorize a two hundred line snore about an old king, and I swore I'd make money off it some day in some wager. Make m'effort worthwhile. Want to hear it?"

"No thank you, your grace," was the polite-but-hasty reply.

Savona thanked the sentry, then started quoting anyway, mixing together lines from several ancient poems he'd half-learned when being made to practice his handwriting as a boy. He poked about, making a pretence of locating various bits of ceremonial armor, and there was no mistaking the uncomplicated relief, and disgust, in the sentry when Savona finally pronounced he'd found what he needed, and they left.

On the way back, his thoughts proceeded thus:

Of course Danric's Marlovan lances had to be something small, light, practical.

No, lances were lances.

Danric was lifting those things as a matter of course.

Danric, his oldest and best friend, little weedy Danric, was training with a weapon Savona could hardly lift. And having a rotten time doing it, too. So why did Savona feel so . . . sour?

He entered his rooms and sank down onto a pillow in the dark.

*The truth. Danric is telling me the truth. I can do myself the same courtesy.*

The truth was, Danric had always been his shadow, just a little slower, a little weaker, a light-built little boy who'd needed his friend's protection when they were small. And Savona had been glad to give it to him, for weren't they like brothers?

But now, it seemed, his little brother was training with lances.

Savona grimaced. *It isn't you who is in danger of becoming complacent, it's I. A lazy, drunken sot of Grumareth's sort, only a few decades younger, so the effects don't show. Yet. I think I'm so clever, but who is fooled?*

He did not answer the question, just sat there staring into the dark pit of the unlit hearth, until dawn gradually grayed the sky.

# Twenty-three

The scrubs' first scouting foray dawned clear and breezy. Despite the boys' scoffing and complaining, they were excited, full of insults, jokes, pushes and shoves as they packed their overnight gear and then lined up for inspection. Shevraeth was growing more exasperated and Marec and Lennac had handed out half a dozen whacks with their wands before they were able to dismiss the boys to breakfast. It was like releasing a human arrow from an over-strung bow. The boys charged to mess, the sooner to be done with eating.

This year's colts had departed before dawn to the chosen field, where they were busy planting clues and picking hiding places as the scrubs finished breakfast, attended morning training drills, then at midday gathered their gear, and lined up to march beyond the walls.

They spotted the flag marking the campsite in the very late afternoon, just as the weary colts were returning from their duties. They'd rise before dawn the next morning to hide so that the scrubs could track them, mapping their trail.

Shevraeth helped scrubs set up tents. He left them arguing about who was going to sleep where and took a look around the camp. A clump of colts turned away quickly, but not before he saw one sneering, and another with exaggerated disgust.

He couldn't be breaking a rule to help the smaller boys. No, Lennac was at the other end of the row, lending his strength to the determined but ineffective efforts of two small scrubs laboring valiantly to get the pegs of the last tent deep in the dry, clay-hard soil.

Shevraeth turned away from the unknown colts, thinking sympathetically that after a long day such as these boys had obviously had, his mood would be equally vile.

And so he thought no more about it as both camps dealt out the heavy bread and sharp cheese common on scrub overnights—which avoided the mess of cooking—then went about cleaning up and readying for morning as the last of the sun faded in the west.

Afterwards the rads drew straws for perimeter patrol while the camp settled down. Shevraeth was glad to discover he had the first watch. Lennac sighed when he drew the longest straw, meaning the watch everyone hated most, from midnight until first bell.

At first Shevraeth's job was easy as the boys settled around the campfire, singing songs, often accompanied by the hand drums, and then others told stories with typical crude humor, sending the scrubs into gasping fits of laughter. When one of the two masters, silent until now, came forward and gave the order to rack up, there was some unnecessary running about, some fast practical jokes, heralded by muffled laughter and whispers. Marec (who also had early duty) and Shevraeth both had to chase their errant scrubs to their tents as they tried hard to be the last ones in.

When he'd seen Mondar and Tevac inside their respective tents (no one would let them bunk together) he turned away. He was weary, looking forward to just sitting down. But as he began to pass between the colt tents he heard whispers and snickers, and something about their tone made him wary.

He plunged between two tents. Lanky colts silhouetted against the fire as one boy said in a hoarse whisper that Shevraeth knew immediately was meant to be overheard: "Of course their army—if they have one—is drawn from farmers and servants. Who else would think of cleaning shoes?"

Then Marec appeared from the other side of the fire. He stepped in the middle of them, the firelight making his wispy curls glow reddish. "Tents, tents. Didn't you hear the order? Would you like me to repeat it, keeping time with the beat?"

Honking fourteen and fifteen year old voices responded, "We're going, we're going."

Marec stood there watching until they vanished inside their tents.

By then Shevraeth had joined him. "I take it that was aimed at me?"

Marec faced the fire and grimaced. "Marlovair is that way. He can't seem to get up in the morning without contemplating his family's greatness. Not his own, you understand—"

Lennac's voice snapped from the other side of the tents. "Mondar! Tevac! You're supposed to be in your tents—what's that in your hand?"

"Nothing!"

"Nothing!"

Lennac appeared, driving the two errant scrubs before him. He gave them both a whack for lying and demanded they open their hands; the boys, who had not reacted to the whack across their shoulders, now slumped, Tevac babbling excuses right to the end.

But there was nowhere to run. They were now surrounded by all three of their rads, after having been silently shadowed by Lennac, who had been expecting the two to execute a sneak.

They reluctantly relinquished itch weed, hoarded what would seem forever to a small boy, against their first overnight.

The rads made certain that the boys' hands (and pockets) were emptied into the fire, which sent a brief spurt of burnt herb scent through the summer air—causing violent sneezes in everyone who sniffed it—and then the two were marched back to their tents and thrust ungently inside.

Marec and Shevraeth rounded the great fire pit. Marec said in a low voice, "Their first target seems to have been Marlovair's and his cronies' tents. Would have done them good. But no doubt we were next on the list."

"Do you think I'm going to have trouble with this Marlovair, who I don't even know by sight?"

Marec sighed, turning his eyes skyward to the glittering stars. Then he shrugged. "Probably."

Lennac and the colts' rad appeared then, having done a fast circuit. "All in," Lennac reported.

"All in," the colts' rad said.

The master in charge opened his palm, ruddy against the firelight. One of the boys blew the trumpet for lights out, meaning anyone leaving a tent was out of bounds.

Marec waved a hand. "On my way." Lennac went back to the tent to catch a nap before midnight.

Shevraeth had inner perimeter. He was alone with his thoughts for the next stretch, walking around the camp in the soft air, glancing between the tents at the slowly diminishing fire, as the noise gradually died down. To the east a clump of trees growing beside the stream blocked the stars. South the hills rose gently, rock and greenery inevitably hiding the markers the older boys had laid down, for to the north the land stretched away flat under the star-studded bowl of the sky. He caught Marec's silhouette against the horizon, pacing the outer perimeter.

It was not unpleasant duty, for Shevraeth enjoyed the walk in the cool evening air. He did not waste much time thinking about this unknown Marlovair and whatever it was that he resented about Shevraeth the Outlander. Instead he reviewed his reading, and mentally composed letters to his parents and to Savona.

When midnight came at last, the rad who was his replacement joined him with a brief, "Watch change." He said,

"You have the post," and left. He discovered as he walked toward his tent that he was quite tired.

He felt his way into the tent he shared with Marec, found his bedroll right where he'd chucked it on arrival. Marec was there, having been replaced by Lennac.

By now Shevraeth knew how to tamp down the grass to make a kind of mattress under him, and how to lay out the bedroll so his head wasn't lower than his feet, or over holes, or at a slant. He stretched out, listening. Marec was not asleep, judging from the sound of his breathing, so Shevraeth permitted himself a long, slow sigh of relaxation as he turned his attention to the quiet noises of a nighttime camp.

He was just beginning to drowse when it occurred to him that the noises he heard were not the regular ones of night. Stream rushing, trees rustling, insects chirring, the flit of wings and mournful calls of night birds on the wing, the occasional clop of horse hooves . . . those were expected. Not expected but soft, then progressively louder and more frequent were the all-too-familiar sounds of another farting contest, followed by muffled giggles. He was sure he heard Tevac's characteristic snicker, and from another tent, Lasda's shrill hee hee hee.

Shevraeth sighed.

Marec, lying awake in his bedroll, chuckled. "Bide fast."

Shevraeth murmured softly, "I don't suppose it works to remind 'em they need their rest to be alert tomorrow?"

"Wager it takes care of itself," Marec returned, laughter making his whisper husky. "Remember, the colts have been up before dawn, and have to rise again at dawn next watch—"

He hadn't even finished his sentence before they heard the rustlings of several footsteps in the tall grass. Marec gestured to the tent flap, and they wriggled forward on their elbows and peered out to see four of what had to be colts walking in duo, something heavy carried between each pair.

Puzzled, Shevraeth watched as the pairs separated, one of each yanking up tent flaps and the other boy with business-like speed tossing in what Shevraeth saw briefly in the faint glow of the dying fire was a pail of water. *Full* pail.

Wails and squawks issued forth from the two tents as the older boys scurried back to their own tents, pails jingling.

The master and rads on duty seemed totally unaware of anyone breaking bounds.

"Happens nearly every year," Marec whispered, his voice now shaking with pent-up laughter. "Happened to me. Lasda and Tevac will be throwing the water in three years."

"And our boys cannot complain, right?" Shevraeth whispered back, thinking of the small boys with soggy clothes and bedrolls.

"Not unless they want to admit to the master what they were doing inside their tents after lights out."

"Summary justice," Shevraeth said, his insides quaking as he tried not to laugh out loud. "Will they get a scarfle when we return?"

Marec looked over. "Would you, if you were Lennac?"

Shevraeth considered. "No."

Marec lifted a hand, a silhouette against the ruddy glow through the crack in their tent door. "Exactly."

# Twenty-four

The tracking and map-making went without mishap.

They ate the last of their food at midday, broke camp, and began the long journey back.

They'd just reached the barracks, and the weary, dirty, happy scrubs were busy putting themselves and their bedrolls through the cleaning frame—loudly criticizing the older boys, and the masters, and the score, and one another, with happy abandon, unaware or unconcerned that nobody was really listening—when a runner appeared in the doorway.

He and Marec spoke. Marec flushed. Then both glanced Shevraeth's way. *Now what?* he thought.

The runner vanished and Marec jerked his chin toward his room.

Shevraeth left the boys to sort themselves out and joined Marec. "Lennac will be here shortly, soon's he reports in. You and I are to join command class." Marec grinned, a beaming grin of pride, his skin nearly as red as his hair.

There was no corresponding joy in Shevraeth, whose inward chill was like the feeling you get when you step out on smooth snow, the ground suddenly gives way under you and you sink into a hole you hadn't known was there.

He remembered Baudan's explanation of command class last year. He'd heard it mentioned from time to time since, but he'd ignored it, comfortable in his assumption that it would be confined to Marlovens.

He realized he hadn't spoken for too long when Marec's brows twitched together. "Is that a problem?" he asked.

Shevraeth hesitated. He knew he was supposed to be honored to be chosen—unless, of course, his father had paid for that. No. Wrong path. If Baudan was right about its purpose, Commander Keriam—and through him, Senrid—wouldn't make their command class a matter of money or influence. It might have been in the Regent's day, but wouldn't be now. The problem, if there was one, was the class's intent.

So the question was . . . ought he to go?

The very idea of discussing command—specifically running battles, the most efficient method of killing other human beings, whether warriors or not—was so morally repellent he got angry every time he thought about it. And was that not the definition of command?

But he was *here*. Of course he could explain away what he'd learned so far as self-defense, or how to organize small groups. All things he could use at home. So he'd avoided thinking about intent outside of defense. But the time had come to face the dilemma after all.

Marec was just a fellow student, not the authority in charge. And so Shevraeth said only, "I take it the first class is to commence immediately?"

Marec's face cleared in relief, and Shevraeth wondered what he'd betrayed in his own expression. Was he losing control of the court mask? That was another horrible thought. It was sometimes the only personal defense he had.

"Now." Marec jerked his thumb toward the door. "Keriam teaches it himself, did you know that? The king apparently sits in a lot, or did. I once heard Forthan talking to Ndarga when I was a scrub, and they didn't know I was pitching hay right outside the stalls. Anyway Keriam's been gone until yesterday, which is why the class is starting so late this season."

"I didn't know any of that." Shevraeth remembered Senrid's tension during their recent conversation. *It's not Siamis that worries me. At least, he's a big threat, bigger than I can handle. But there's a worse one.* Controlling the instinct to finger the token hanging inside his shirt, Shevraeth thought, *I am very glad I am not a king.*

"I hadn't either." Marec flicked his hands open. "As for the Commander, the king sends him out on missions from time to time, but we almost never hear about them afterward." He grinned. "That same year, Ndarga told us one night someone in his class had dared someone else to ask, but all Keriam said was 'I went places and saw people.' And nobody quite had the brass to ask him for more detail."

Lennac appeared then, and waved at them to go. Apparently one's House rad had to be inside the secret.

They didn't talk much on the walk to Keriam's office; just before they reached the archway opening into Guard territory they spied a group of their own House on the way back from archery.

Mondar was one of them. He held out his bow to stop Shevraeth and Marec, as Vandaus and Gannan lingered, listening in. Mondar said, "Is it true my brother really brought itch weed on the track-and-scout?"

Marec grinned. "Saw every leaf and twig burned myself."

Mondar sighed, staring upward. "What gets into his brain? When I catch him out . . ."

The rest of his words were inaudible under the sound of Vandaus's and Gannan's laughter.

They walked on, and Shevraeth thought: *I guess reporting your brother's stupidity is not akin to falling off a horse.* And, *They didn't ask where we were going.*

They reached the Guard side of the castle, and Keriam's tower, from which he could see both the king's garrison and the academy. They started the long trudge up the spiral staircase with those worn ovals. About a dozen steps ahead a lanky figure with curling dark hair turned at the sound of their step, and there was Stad's familiar cleft chin and dark-eyed smile. "Marec. Shevraeth!"

"No, they can't be letting *you* in," Marec exclaimed. "Must be desperate."

"Been desperate two years." That was a new voice—as they caught up with Stad, they discovered Evrec a few steps above. He grinned and lifted a lazy hand. "So they invited you two slackers?"

Marec searched high and low, miming looking for someone. "No, I'm just a spy. Pretend you don't see me," he whispered, and Stad choked on laughter as Evrec pushed open Keriam's door.

They passed inside the office, which was much the same except for the addition of a black slate-board set up against one wall, and three benches opposite the big desk. On the opposite wall someone had put up a huge map of the kingdom, with the neat printing that Shevraeth recognized as Senrid's hand.

Already seated shoulder to shoulder was a group of seniors on the back row, some of them glowering. And near the end of the first row, a slate and chalk on her lap, was Senelac.

At that moment she looked up, and her brows lifted slightly when she saw Shevraeth. He felt prickly heat all over his body, but said nothing as he dropped down onto the third bench between Marec and Stad.

Senelac whipped round and faced front. She took a deep breath to fight the blush scorching her skin. Then she let her chalk fall off the slate just so she could bend, pick it up, and glance back.

There he was between Marec and Stad, looking down at the slate, his expression remote. She mocked herself for the silly subterfuge, at least for about a heartbeat. She really wanted to laugh. He wasn't paying her the least bit of attention, and here she was, acting just like the sort of girl she utterly despised.

"We're all here," Commander Keriam said, gathering their attention with his gaze. As expected, some of the seniors glared covertly at Fenis Senelac as if a tree had suddenly grown in the office. No, a tree would not be nearly so offensive as a female in these hitherto male precincts of power. He said in his most bland voice, "You are all here by invitation of the king. More might be added. Some might be subtracted. Any questions about selection for this class, the king requires you to go directly to him."

Pause, silence. Senelac had been red-faced, now she was pale, sitting unnaturally straight. Aware—and Keriam knew she was aware—of the resentment of the seniors in the back row, whose shifting feet and rumbling mutters made their feelings clear.

The second year colts reacted as expected: Stad, until today the youngest, seemed glad to have his three classmates with him. Of those three, the foreigner regarded him with a steady, wary gaze.

"The second question in your minds is probably where some of your fellows are, like the Valdlavs, and yes, there is a senior command class. Some of you might end up attending class over with the King's Guard for a time. Or not."

The shuffling halted.

"So let us begin."

He paused, letting the silence snuff the last distracted rustles and whispers.

"The first thing you must remember is that an army is the opposite of a crowd. Many of our civilian kingdoms do not understand that distinction. They conceive themselves as peaceful people, morally superior to military concerns—and thus when they find themselves driven to protect themselves they are either slaughtered or they slaughter, because they have no organization as opposed to discipline, they have no command but shared mood. They do not understand that uncontrolled groups of people are nothing more than crowds, which can become as lethal, at lightning speed, as any Norsundrian military unit. They trample as many as they kill. Your history class will have furnished you with corroborative details."

The Marloven boys, of course, just waited for the point, because that was old ground for them. But the foreigner sat up straight, his gaze narrowed, the wariness gone. *Score one to the king—not that I had any doubts.*

Keriam continued. "There are two things we will focus on in this class. One, how to command, and two, how to be a commander. You will learn that the commander who by whatever means makes himself the enemy of his own force creates a war within his ranks as well as the one outside, and thus does the opponents' work for them. Example, our own recent history."

Shuffling, looks, one muffled snicker. Keriam waited for absolute silence again.

"You will learn that a commander must not only know what is going on, but what to do about it, and to that end we will be studying battles of the past from both sides, and I will set you a problem at the end of each session. You may work it out on your slates or not as you choose, but when you come in your slate must be empty, ready for the lesson, and your answer must be in your head. A commander will not go to the field with a handy book of tactics to riffle through as both sides wait for him to decide what to do."

A minor chuckle.

"So, yes, you can work with others if you wish, you just present your solutions with both or all names." He paused, and said, "Through our history you will have gathered by now that the purpose of an army has changed many times. Today, we say that its purpose is to deliver victory by the fastest and most economical method possible. By 'economy' I mean preservation of life as well as land and property." He looked up, scanned his students, then said, "Questions?"

Shevraeth pressed his lips tight, at first unwilling to speak. But Keriam's gaze stayed on him as if he were waiting, and once again he wondered what he was betraying. Stad elbowed him, and so he said, "Is the victory a defensive one or offensive?"

Senelac could peek now because everybody else was staring at the foreigner. At first glance he was so very much like them all—and yet not. He was already as tall as a senior, though he didn't seem to know it yet, or how beautifully proportioned he was getting to be. His posture was so straight, with a perfect line to his shoulders, his features were refined in the subtle way the king's were, though they didn't resemble one another in any obvious way. Stad on the one side was considered by most of the girls as next year's Handsomest Senior, Marec had his own engaging charm, with his lopsided smile and flyaway red curls, and Evrec's deceptively casual lounge and lazy way of speaking made him attractive as well. But her insides didn't heat up at the mere sight of them, or the sound of their voices. Why this foreigner? Argh.

She faced front again, determined to get a grip on herself.

"Both," Keriam replied, after a pause for thought. "Your underlying question seems to be whether or not we are training future conquerors, and to that I will say no. Or you would not be here."

He paused again to gauge their reactions. The students stirred, and a few seniors muffled snorts of laughter.

"We have no intention of attacking our neighbors, but it is conceivable that . . . someone . . . might soon attack us."

Another murmur, this time with the whispered word *Norsunder*.

"If some force rides across the border to lay siege to Choreid Dhelerei, we might mount an attack before they get their siege organized. Still technically defense, but we initiate the encounter, so the tactics might be offense. Is that clear?"

Shevraeth began to nod then signified assent with the open-handed gesture used by the Marlovens. And as the commander Keriam looked down at the papers on his desk, Shevraeth could not resist sneaking another peak at Senelac. All he could see was her back, for of course her attention was quite properly on the commander.

Keriam said, "Now. One of the reasons we began the history classes is to clear away some of the fog of emotion that accretes around famous events of the past, especially when records are sparse. The songs are exciting, some stirring, and they are important to us as a people, but they don't always tell the truth. Take our most famous Marlovan, Indevan Harskialdna Sigun. What is his most lasting accomplishment and when?"

No one spoke.

"Come along," Keriam said, palm-heel striking lightly on the table. "If you're wrong you won't be taken out and shot."

A muffled laugh, and Senelac said, "The Battle of Andahi Pass in 3914."

Shevraeth, who had no historical reference for whoever-this-was, sustained another flare of warmth at the sound of Senelac's voice. The sight of her slender neck, the smooth curve of her shoulders inward to her waist and then outward again at her hips—an entrancing curve, unlike the broad, angular backs of the fellows in the rest of the front row—kindled a brighter flare of that internal heat. The urge to laugh at himself forced him to look away, but the mental image stubbornly remained, and he was thrown back to his mother's talks on what she'd called the book of life. He wondered when the mysterious page his parents had so patiently explained to his squirmingly bored younger self had turned inside him. On this new page, though Stad next to him had exactly the same dark, curly head as Senelac—if they weren't immediately related, they probably had to be back in their families somewhere—on this new page he had no interest whatever in Stad's dark curly head, but *her* curls he wanted to touch, just to see if they were as soft as they looked—

Pay attention!

Keriam was speaking. ". . . are still some who claim the Battle for Andahi Pass his most lasting achievement, yet the Battle for the Strait in 3921 accomplished more for the world, though you will see almost no reference to it in our records. There are ballads that claim as his victories battles he never fought; outside the kingdom there are ballads that claim his land of birth was Khanerenth, Tser Mearsies, Bren, and others. In Ymar he figures as a pirate and a villain. The ballads reflect more on those who wrote them and perpetuated them than they do on Indevan himself, who remains a somewhat mysterious figure as apparently he left no written records. And whatever the king at the time wrote about him never survived the end of that family's reign."

The seniors' minds wandered. They all knew what was coming next, as they'd been forced to read it. *He's talking to the foreigner,* one semaphored to another, who rolled his eyes in disgust.

"The single record we have from his time is the one written by our king's own ancestor, which, difficult as it is nowadays to read, we require our seniors to study."

Shevraeth wondered if the record was in the library.

"As useful, just fewer in number, are the letters written by both the king's and Indevan's wives to the queen over the mountains, and archived by the Elsarions. We are given to understand that those letters are largely personal and not military, even though the queen and the princess were in fact well trained in military defense, as were all women of rank of that time."

Another murmur—and both Senelac and Shevraeth firmly determined to keep their minds on the lesson.

Keriam lifted a hand. "Those letters exist, I say, unless those, too, have been destroyed in the course of Enaeran's current problems."

No one said anything—they'd heard about the civil war over the mountains—so he continued. "Some ballads call Indevan Harskialdna a great cavalry commander, when most of his battles were actually fought at sea."

A quiet chuckle met this.

"Then, the academy had traditionally boasted of him as one of its best products when he was actually only here two years. And not as a senior, but as a scrub. Some of the king's ancestors trumpeted him as their progenitor, though in fact he was not a Montredavan-An, as the name was pronounced in those days. There are claims he was a pirate, when he fought pirates, that he was not educated except in war, which again we are assured was not true, he apparently had an excellent education, young as he was—supposedly he and the king, when boys right here at the academy, used to pitch hay to the cadences of Old Sartoran narrative ballads."

Another chuckle as Keriam turned a paper over. "So, to resume, we will break down types of battles: those on ground that permit retreat, and ground that cannot be relinquished. Plains battles, mountain, and even sea, because though at present we have no coastline, as Indevan himself is reported to have said, sea fighting can sometimes be seen as a metaphor for land battles, and the opposite also holds true. We will discuss types of commanders, and styles of command, and how that aspect influenced wins and losses."

Keriam paused and surveyed his charges. This time the foreigner and young Senelac did not sneak peeks at one another. Their attention was wholly on him. He made a dumb-show of consulting his papers until the impulse to smile was thoroughly squelched, and said, "So we will begin with what you do know, and proceed from there. Now, what are the traditional cavalry strategies, Marec?"

"Outflank, break the line, or both."

"Good. So let's look at some specifics . . ."

At the end of the session Shevraeth used his sleeve to erase the chalk from his slate then rose to stash it in the pile, dropping the chunk of chalk into the wide, flat bowl next to the slates. There were plenty of slates and chalks at the barracks, mostly used for practice by the scrubs whose reading and writing had been neglected.

As they filed out the others chatted. Shevraeth's mind was pulling him in three directions. First, the assignment to work on, second, Senelac—he could feel her presence somewhere behind him—third, somewhat surprising, Commander Keriam had issued no orders about the level of secrecy of the class.

Catching sight of Stad just ahead, he remembered Stad had actually been in command class as a colt. But no one had known.

Interesting. What would you get if you blabbed? Maybe a moment of envy, gratifying if you craved envy, and then a long, cold slime-patch of resentment from those who wanted, or thought they wanted, a future in commanding wars.

Shevraeth's mood was sober, his unseeing gaze on the toes of his boots as he shuffled down the worn stone steps behind the others. *I do not want to command a war. But my father did not want to be attacked by pirates when he was young. And I'm sure Savona's parents did not want to be killed in a mysterious accident—along with far too many people in court.*

⊷ C₂₈₀ ⋈

Ndand Maddar covertly watched her best friend through dinner. Fen acted business-like, as usual—too much, Ndand thought. Something was wrong. Probably with that stupid command class that Senelac had confided, in strict secrecy, she'd been invited to. Though the girls had been rigidly forbidden to interact with the boys (and vice versa) in the mess hall, she had gotten good at scanning the senior tables while getting another rye bun or refreshing the water pitcher. Experience decreed that if there had been some sort of disaster the boys would be yakking it up and slewing round to stare at the girls and make loud comments until one of their stone-headed rads would finally notice and give them a (long overdue, in her opinion) breeze.

But the boys' tables behaved exactly like usual: loud, boisterous, and full of their typical braying laughter. Like there had been no command class. Which would argue that things went fine, because one thing she knew about boys was, they were definitely not subtle.

Well, maybe that strange one from the other side of the continent—

Oh.

Maddar said nothing immediately. After dinner there were the horses to bed down for the night, and their own evening chores. Once or twice she glimpsed Senelac's dark hair in the midst of a mob of yellow heads, and then, quite suddenly, she was gone.

Maddar made her way through the others and leaped up the stairs to their rooms over the big stable. And there she found a streak of yellow light under Senelac's door.

She tapped softly, the triple knock they privately used.

Then waited, counting heartbeats, until she heard a reluctant, "That you, Mad?"

She slipped inside and leaned her shoulders against the inside of the door as she surveyed her friend. Fenis lay on the narrow bunk, arms crossed behind her head, two books and a scroll lying on the floor below her, and a slate board on her upraised knees. "Headache," Senelac began.

"Shovel that in someone else's stall," Maddar said rudely. "Unless you mean a two-footed headache. Fath again?"

Senelac impatiently brushed a curl off her forehead. "She's busy with the foals. For once actually doing her job."

"I'm going to faint."

Senelac gave a brief smile.

"The command class—"

"It was fine. Except I still don't know why I'm there. Maybe as an object lesson in King's Will to the others. Not sure how I feel about that—"

"—but it doesn't matter, because everything we do clears the way for our daughters. I know the chant. So, give me specifics."

"Oh, the class was fine. The seniors were divided between trying not to glare at the foreigner, and trying not to glare at me. Even if I committed the treasonous crime of being born female, at least I'm Marloven."

"So the class is full of dire secrets, I take it."

Senelac snorted. "History and battle plans, exactly like the king told me. I'll ride this obstacle course because he asked me to. And it is interesting, even if I'll never in my life command anything but snot-nosed boys and girls in the riding ring. But my daughter might." She paused, frowning, then smiled, her voice lifting a little. "I think I like that. Not any real battles, but her at the head of a riding—a wing—on patrol. Yes, I like that, because any daughter of mine is bound to have twice the sense that a son of someone like Sindan will ever have. Just to name one."

"So . . . ?"

Senelac glanced up, her dark eyes narrowed with ironic humor. "You're going to worry at it, aren't you?"

"Like a dog with a knotted rope."

Senelac sighed. "But we've been over it. The foreigner— why is it he just has to walk into a room, and I turn into . . ." She groped, then dropped her hand onto her middle.

"Ndand Fath?"

Senelac grimaced. "No. I'm not *malicious*. Just, well, you know."

"Yeah. I know." Maddar looked out the window, taking time before she spoke. Yes, she knew. All last year Senelac had talked about that wooden-faced foreigner, who was just a skinny weed of fifteen, while Retren Forthan, easily the most romantic figure in the entire academy—and about the most shy of all the seniors—had looked after Senelac hopelessly.

Maddar had to admit that Fen Senelac never gave anyone the least sign of flirtation. She just hadn't *noticed* Ret, except in the way the boys did—unstinting admiration for his skills, his courage, his flair in leadership. While Maddar herself would have stood on her head and hooted like an owl if she'd thought it would catch his attention for a single heartbeat.

She sighed. Life was *not* fair. "So why don't you just talk to him? It looked to me at the bakery like he's finally woken up and noticed there are girls in the world. And he was most definitely interested in you."

"But what does that mean, in his culture? That's the thing that slays me. Here, we all know what words and signs mean. What do they mean to outsiders? Especially ones that, when they finish, will go home again and never think twice about us?"

"How can you know that?" Maddar exclaimed, exasperated. "He might speak a different language, but I will wager the Nelkereth Plains he comes equipped with the same emotions we have. Why, he looks exactly like one of us now, moves like us, except when he's doing his wood fence imitation, or doing that weird fluttering thing with his hands, like a cymbal dancer—"

"I think that's courtly gesture. My grandmother, who went along as escort when King Indevan fetched his wife down south, said to watch out for it."

"Why? Never mind, I don't want to know. I don't even care. But if you've got a heart-burning for him, either feed the fire or put it out. *Talk* to him. And if you like talking, go ahead and kiss him."

Senelac sighed. "Maybe you're right."

"Just keep it out of the academy," Maddar warned.

Senelac flicked the map lying below her on the plain boards of her floor. "As if I'd forget."

# Twenty-five

So when Shevraeth finished his lance drill the next morning on what was already a hot morning, and rode wearily in for the brief respite of the midday meal before a full afternoon of duty and practice sessions, he was surprised to see Senelac among the girls standing there to take their mounts. Except for command class and the bakery, he hadn't seen much of her so far this season.

He did not know that she had quietly made it her business to discover his entire schedule, and so she whisked herself out of range when he might see her—but somehow, almost every day, she'd found some way to just pass where he was shooting, or riding, contact fighting, or throwing knife or javelin, just to see him at it.

He dismounted, trying hard not to let his face heat up, and said with what he thought was a casual, cool voice, "Morning, Senelac. How's—" He remembered that the command class was supposed to be secret, but a quick look around showed nobody facing their way, and those closest were all talking to the girls or to one another. "—the assignment," he finished under his breath, flushing to the ears.

"Research instead of experience," she said.

He laughed, the quick, soft laugh she found so dazzling, so different from the loud brays typical of the other boys. Then he made one of those court gestures. Cymbal dancer—huh! It was amazingly graceful, complicated, and intriguingly oblique.

"Same here," he admitted.

And it was out before she could call it back, "Want a study partner?"

His brows went up, his lips parted. She tried not to stare at his mouth, which was so entrancing a curve—

Stop that!

She half-turned away, furious with herself, when he said, again in the low voice, "Bakery? I have liberty tomorrow."

"I'll meet you there. Take you somewhere less popular with the academy," she murmured, and then she did turn away, leaving him staring after her somewhat bemused, wondering if he'd somehow offended her.

He was still puzzling over her reaction the next day when they met one another in the street outside the bakery, both of them carrying their slates. She had her map as well, rolled up neatly.

She glanced up into his face, thinking *He's so tall—are all his people like that?* and he thought *She isn't growing as fast as I am* because he didn't realize yet that Marlovens tended to be on the short side—and she, being older than him, had already reached her full growth.

She said abruptly, "This way." She turned her back on him, leaving him to follow or not, and walked rapidly back up the street past an inn, a glazier's, a saddle-maker sharing a shop (as was common here) with a cobbler, and then led the way up a short side street toward the east wall. The street zigged and zagged, the buildings varying slightly in design, then around a corner and into an eatery that smelled delicious. He noted again that there were no written street signs, just some obscure swinging boards that could have been mistaken for local buildings' names.

He breathed in. "Why don't we get to eat like that?" he murmured.

He hadn't meant to be overheard in the noisy crowded room, but Senelac seemed to have quick ears. She flicked a dark-eyed look over her shoulder and said, "Because it's coastal cookery. Rualese. We got trade going with them again, just this last year. They trade big in spices from over on Toar." A flick of her hand indicated the continent on the other side of the western sea.

The eatery offered rough wood tables and benches, but people obviously didn't come for the furnishings. All the members of two families were busy delivering to the tables full plates, the most common dish apparently some kind of fish grilled in caramelized onions and spiced wine sauce, with small potatoes and carrots. Bowls of what appeared to be pudding with fresh berries or honey on it. A boy and a girl his own age hefted sweating jugs of what smelled like dark rootbrew and ale. Others lugged back stacks of dirty plates, cups, bowls.

The two found a tiny table in a corner just as four people got up to leave. They sat down, Senelac piled together their dishes, and handed them to a young girl who showed up a moment later to take them away.

"Did I do something wrong?" Shevraeth asked.

Senelac sat back in surprise, then leaned forward again, color ridging her cheekbones. "No. It's just—I, ah, am somewhat ambivalent about this class. I mean, I know I'll never lead any war party."

He laughed. "Nor will I."

She frowned. "Then why are you here?"

He spread his hands. "Because my father thought it better that I learn, in case things at home get worse. Let me rephrase. I hope never to lead a war party at home. But meanwhile, I've never even commanded one of the afternoon games."

"That will come next year, is my guess."

He leaned on an elbow, just enjoying the excuse to look at her face. "Why do you say that?"

"Because last year you were the foreigner to everyone. Now you only are to those who want the old ways, bad or good.

Last year, to put you in command would be to make things harder for you. This year you're a rad, and not really a part of whatever competition your House has going. Next year, except for the old ways sticklers, they'll think of you as one of us. And a former rad. Won't be the same problems."

"Except," he said wryly, "if I'm a bad commander."

"I said, same problems. Not that there won't be problems." She grinned, nerving herself to meet his gaze. His eyes, when you looked at them straight on, were larger than you'd expect, and though from a distance his coloring was unremarkable, up close gray eyes were curiously compelling. "As for being a bad commander, well, then you'll deserve what you get."

"That is true. So, if I haven't done anything wrong, why are we squeezed in here? Not that I mind," he added quickly. "If the food is as good as it smells."

"Because the rules on us girls are strict. We're on trial, so to speak. Isn't fair, but there it is."

She could drown in those eyes. She looked away, scanning the room for any sign of gossips. They were not out of bounds, they could meet here quite properly, but she loathed the idea of talk spreading all over the academy pairing her with the foreigner.

"In your histories there are references to women in the military," he said, still leaning on one hand, watching her face. That gaze, it really was scorching.

She shrugged, firmly resisting the urge to fuss with her map or tap her fingers or finger her hair. "Off and on over the centuries. As defenders. Then as runners and guards for women of rank. Then as archers on the flanks of light cavalry. My grandmother was one." She gripped her fingers together in her lap. "But the Regent hated women, and with one stroke of the pen sent us back to raising horses and waiting on men." She grimaced. "We still had bows in our hands, but not where any of his people could see."

"Ah. And so, because there are so few of you, what, the academy authorities don't want you becoming the focus of rivalries among the older boys?"

Her forehead cleared at his immediate comprehension. "Our armsmistress—who was one of those archers I mentioned, back in the old days of our king's grandfather—told us to keep our . . ." She would *not* say flirts! "Our friendships with boys here in the city, at liberty times. In the academy, we stick to business. If we all obey the rules, then the boys will, too, because they know what to expect."

"So that explains why the girls don't ever talk to anyone at mess?"

She nodded, grinning. "Well, we talk to one another."

He laughed. "Right. But you otherwise have the same rules—last names only, same rank structure?"

"More or less. Obviously we're not part of the army, though that will change, we're told. And last names, yes. Easier, for one thing: nearly half of us sixteen down to about ten are named Ndand because the Regent made it really, really clear that he expected loyal families to name daughters after his daughter."

"The Regent had a daughter? First I ever heard of that."

"She vanished." Senelac winced. "The king insists it's to somewhere good. But not here in the kingdom. In any case, none of us really knew her. The Regent tried mind control spells on her, in his plans to control the king."

Shevraeth was appalled—and saw his own emotion reflected in her face.

"Anyway." She made a quick, self-conscious look around. "Most of the girls are Ndand, so they have nicknames just among us, but you boys use our last names, same as for each other."

"But I heard your friend call you Fenis," he said tentatively, tasting the word.

She felt an inward shiver at the sound of her name on his lips, in his voice. To hide her reaction, she said, more sharply than she'd intended, "We're here to work, aren't we?"

A gangling teen-aged boy appeared, plates on either arm. Shevraeth looked up, glad to have a distraction while he tried to figure out what he'd done wrong in just saying her name. He realized the boy was offering one of two choices, and he pointed at the nearest one without noticing what was on the plate.

She chose the other. The boy slid the plates expertly onto their table, and went to the next waiting group. Shevraeth discovered that he'd chosen fish cakes and asparagus as well as the little potatoes. Senelac had the savory-smelling fish with onions and wine sauce.

They busied themselves with their food, which was delicious, but at first they scarcely knew what they were eating. He regretted his lack of finesse, and she wished she could take back her words.

But you can't take back words. So the next best thing was to pretend she hadn't spoken that last nasty, snotty bit. But what to say? The subject had been Ndand . . . With her spoon suspended midway in the air, she grinned. "Another reason not to use first names is that there are some real problems. Like, Ndand Maddar really hates Ndand Fath, who flirted horribly with her twin brothers last year, who were third year seniors. Identical twin brothers. Share everything. Even after years together, some still couldn't tell them apart. But what does Fath do? Flirt with just one and ignore the other, then switch on them—flirting with Keth and ignoring Havid—just to see what they would do. She thought it immensely funny."

Shevraeth's lips curled with faint distaste.

He could see Fialma Merindar finding that quite entertaining. No, Fialma liked physical cruelty best. Tamara Chamadis, yes, she'd probably enjoy that, only she'd be more likely to flirt with both at the same time.

Senelac wrenched her gaze away from his lips, and twirled her spoon in a circle. "So last names are best." She returned to eating, not speaking until she was done, then she smiled. "I have the map, but I just realized I forgot my chalk. Give me yours, and I'll sketch out the terrain."

⌘

*. . . I've met this girl—*

No, that wasn't quite right. Shevraeth neatly lined the words out.

*Last year one of the girls—*

That just sounded stupid.

*There's this girl—*

He'd heard people begin like that before, and watched the auditor's eyes shift focus as the talker went on and on with increasingly trite terms. He wouldn't do that to Savona. Or to Senelac . . . especially as he didn't really know what his own feelings were. Other than that he really, really liked being around her. Looking at her. Listening to her. Sniffing that elusive scent that reminded him of sage. Was it really scent, or just her?

Shevraeth grimaced, then tore up the expensive paper into tiny, tiny shreds. He threw down his pen. Then glanced at his slate, which was wiped clean. But he had the solution in his mind, along with the images of Senelac's capable brown hand sketching out the terrain before they worked on where they'd put their forces.

He had no idea if their solution was any good or not; he realized he'd forgotten to get his chalk back. None of that mattered, really. He just knew he could hardly wait for command class so he could see her again.

And on her side of the austere compound, she lay in her bunk over the stable, listening to the wind through the open windows, and the sounds of the horses below her. And when Maddar passed by her open door, she saw Senelac lying there on her bunk, tossing a piece of chalk on her palm, her black eyes wide and unseeing in the light of a single candle.

# Twenty-six

"Well, that was embarrassing," Shevraeth commented as he and Marec left Commander Keriam's chamber after command class a couple of weeks later.

"Which embarrassment would that be?" Marec retorted, his grin more grimace than smile.

"I think the word 'that' about covers us all. At least, us new ones. Though he did seem to have a few, ah, vivid remarks reserved for the seniors when they found our solutions funny."

Marec squawked a laugh, then sneaked a guilty look behind him. But the seniors were all trooping off toward their end of the academy, leaving Marec and Shevraeth alone on the path to the Puppy Pit. Stad and Evrec were not there, as the second year boys were gone on an overnight, but they'd turned in their solutions early.

Shevraeth and Marec passed a troop of guards muttering and glancing skyward as they headed for the stairs leading to the wall and sentry duty.

The boys shot through the archway leading to the academy, where an errant hot breeze blowing along the walls' narrow stone canyons brought the distinctive whiff of warm stables.

"I think, on consideration," Shevraeth said after they'd passed by the colts' court, "Stad's came off the best."

"Uhn. Told me yesterday that Lennac gave him some pointers last year," Marec replied. "Don't know for certain, but I suspect Lennac is in the senior command class. Always been good."

Shevraeth sighed. "Experience seems to be one of the missing elements. Experience is not just seeing what's happening. That I've come to understand. A little, anyway. But directing events."

Marec frowned down at the stone pathway.

Shevraeth said, "If you have something to say . . ."

"Why are you studying with that girl?" Marec didn't look angry. Offended was more like it, and Shevraeth wondered what unspoken rule he'd broken this time.

"She asked," Shevraeth said, after the slightest hesitation.

"If you wanted a study partner, you could have asked me."

Shevraeth opened his hand. "I didn't know I wanted one, but when she asked it seemed a good idea. She knows the terrain—she even had a map. I would have had to make the time to go to the library on my next liberty, which was yesterday, and get and copy a map, and how long would I have had to work on a solution myself, when I haven't the remotest idea where to begin?"

"Maps all over the academy. Can ask to borrow one and no one thinks anything of it." Marec scowled. "Hold hard. Most don't. Some are incurable noses, but you know who by now."

"Marec, I am still trying to comprehend the invisible rules here. Ones you grew up with. Senelac offered, so I figured there was no hidden problem. I am not being jocose."

*Jocose.* Marec suppressed a snort, but his sense of humor vanished when Shevraeth added, "You might remember the last time I didn't take your invisible rules seriously I nearly got my ribs kicked in."

Marec half-raised a hand, the signal of a hit in sword-fighting. "That was Sindan. Ought to know by now I wouldn't kick your ribs in if you wanted to study with me. I mean, we're there together in the Puppy Pit."

Shevraeth hesitated again. "I made plans for our next study session. It would be rude to turn her off. But there's no rule against you and I studying together as well, is there?"

"No."

"So what do you suggest?"

Marec ran a hand through his red hair so it stuck up in red fluffs, then he laughed. "We have a whole barracks full of scrubs. Lennac's been running his ideas on 'em, why can't we?"

Shevraeth whistled. "Now that is what I call a brilliant idea. Would that be command thinking?"

Marec gave his squawking laugh. Then he said, somewhat tentatively, "You don't really need to resort to the girl."

Shevraeth sent him an appraising look. "Is this a specific or general observation?"

"Specific or—oh. You mean, on Senelac. No, I don't know anything about her at all, except she's hot with the horses. Senelac family is hot at whatever they do, but, see, girls don't command. So why ask someone even more blind than you are, when you want to see something?"

"Because she knows your history. Seems to have good ideas. The king has to have invited her for some reason."

"As a swat-down to the big mouths yapping on and on about the good old days, if you ask me." A quick, pensive look. "Do girls command where you live?"

"Nobody commands. Except the king. Which is why I am here." Shevraeth ducked through their archway, then stopped, well out of earshot of the scrub barracks. "Our royal family has disapproved of martial ability, except for dueling, for generations. It's a matter of royal policy, you might say."

Marec made his characteristic half-smile, half-grimace, as he struggled with new ideas, one of which was that Shevraeth did not always say everything he meant. But still, the idea seemed pretty clear they had a tyrant on their throne. Meaning the recent problems here with the Regent were not isolated Marloven problems, but others had them as well.

"All right," he said, and started toward the barracks. "Let's run these puppies and see what we can discover."

⊱⌘⊰

And so another month passed swiftly, without anyone paying any more attention to the passage of time than to the steady lengthening of days. Drills were ever more complicated and demanding—not that they noticed, because it had always been that way. Marec and Shevraeth, with Lennac's good will, took over planning the scrub outings. They watched the boys' games and discussed the results, comparing notes with Stad, who had no convenient scrubs, so he continued using whoever showed up for extra practices and was willing to try out his ideas: Stad, Shevraeth realized after a few comments about past experience, had been commanding little groups of boys before he even knew what command was. He'd apparently been 'trying ideas' since he was small—not that he talked about his home or family.

It was Evrec, with meaningful rolls of the eyes, who told Shevraeth a little of Stad's background as they walked to the baths to cool off on a withering hot day, when both happened to have rec time during the same watch.

"His people raise horses." Evrec splashed into the water. "But he's got high ranking cousins. When they found out how good he was at games, well, he ended up here."

He went on to explain how, with their rad's permission, he and Stad had a competition going—trying to win House contests by using their ideas on all their overnights. Shevraeth almost wished he was sleeping at the second year colts' barracks with his class, but on the other hand he liked having his tiny room to himself, and the scrubs had more or less settled down at last. As much as ten year olds ever settle down.

"Marec and I don't come up with original ideas," Shevraeth admitted as he floated on the cool water, staring at light patterns on the stones overhead. The newer wall to the right, and the faint sounds of girl voices from beyond, testified to change. "We've been using what we hear. Trying them out for ourselves."

Evrec wondered if he should say that that was he'd done as well, just a year or two before, then decided it sounded like bragging.

Shevraeth went on in his light voice, "I very much fear that field command is never going to be my undiscovered talent."

"They all tell us study and trial and error and logic are better than brilliant ideas."

"Your king seems like the brilliant type."

Evrec grinned. "Maybe, but he's also dog-stubborn at trial, error, logic, and study." Then he shifted to what was far more interesting, "So do you and Marec actually study with Senelac?"

"Yes. Well, we just started a week ago."

"How's that working?"

Shevraeth hesitated, then gave a courtier's answer, "Senelac can name, as backup, every relevant battle and its dates."

Evrec laughed. "Her brother Jan probably saw to that before she could read. The Senelacs are an old, old service family."

"But not one of high rank?" Shevraeth asked.

"Oh, they had rank, too, but lost it along with the northern lands. Jan told us their family has a saying: Senelacs are good captains but bad governors."

The bell rang, ending their free time.

The next command class fell into what was developing as a pattern. Shevraeth's solutions were never chosen as the best for any session, but they were seldom the worst—an epithet

Keriam saved for plans depending on the wildness of chance, or for heroic charges or spectacular sneak attacks that could so easily go wrong with a change in weather, a horse stumbling, or even with the mood of the men. He also reserved his disparagement for plans that ran against nature, such as expecting cavalry to make uphill charges, or mad dashes across far too much uneven ground.

At the end of class he regarded the seniors with grave displeasure. "Yes, you can name a battle where just such a charge won, but to each of those—and there were reasons they won—I can name as many losses as there are stones in the court. Don't let me see that again."

The second year boys and Senelac sat very still.

Keriam threw his chalk down. "You still don't seem to understand me when I keep telling you that, so far, the supposed enemy commanders in our battle problems are neutral. We're trying to concentrate on the basics of strategy and tactics, though it seems we'll be at it a while yet."

Silence met these words, except for a scrape of feet from one end of the seniors' bench.

Keriam said, "In real life there was no such thing as commanders coming to battle with neutral emotions—however much the later songs and stories might make our heroes seem above mere human concerns. Dismissed."

As soon as the seniors were out of earshot (their emotions registered in the loudness of their clatter going down the stairs), Stad said to his classmates in an undervoice, "That's six to us and four to the seniors, all told. Where do they get those crazy ideas?"

Senelac was walking right beside Shevraeth, but Stad's question was not addressed to her. Stad wasn't shutting her out deliberately, he just didn't see her.

So she didn't tell him which ballad the seniors had mined for that spectacular overhill charge that Keriam had just thoroughly burned.

"Overhill charge." Evrec laughed. "They forgot to add to their solution finding a mage, and getting wings attached to their horses."

Marec said doubtfully, "Maybe it's time to try to figure out solutions with different intents in the commanders. Pick the best of ours to present."

As the others agreed, Shevraeth turned Senelac's way. He was waiting for her answer, though she was still invisible to the others.

Appreciation was almost as warm as attraction. She lifted a shoulder, laughing at herself inwardly. Was she visible to Shevraeth for her brains or for her amazing and oh so fascinating looks? Better not to answer that even for herself.

She was wrong when she assumed she was invisible to Stad. She just wasn't relevant. If girls were going to be part of the competition for command, he'd pay attention. Until then, they were extraneous to his goals. But he did observe the others.

So as Shevraeth and Marec continued to meet with Senelac, the underlying attraction between the foreigner and Senelac was something Stad comprehended far before Marec did. But Stad considered Shevraeth a friend, so he kept silent about the long looks that arrowed back and forth whenever he saw Senelac and Shevraeth together.

As for Shevraeth, he felt another page turn.

Last year he hadn't really noticed the girls beyond the anomaly of their presence. But now with just a glance he could pretty well peg which of the older boys and girls were secretly twoing, just by the way they'd covertly watch one another across the width of the mess hall. He could also spot who had quarreled—there he'd see either glares or backs turned—and of course who was talking just a little too loud, looking in the wrong direction just once too often.

And he could spot the ones who just wanted to attract attention.

Like Ndand Fath's hip-swinging walk into the mess. Though everyone but the seniors wore the same shapeless clothes, he couldn't tell you how she managed to get her tunics and trousers to outline her shape, but she did. And though he (and many seniors) found her gyrations highly entertaining, the corresponding disgust in the girls as she lifted her hands to fling back her artfully arranged hair, or smoothed her hand down the front of her smock, pulling it tight to her very nice body, made it clear they had no appreciation whatsoever for Fath's little tricks.

Shevraeth ventured a joke, just once, when Senelac and he were sitting under the shade of a huge tree between two of the short streets. Marec had scrub duty, and they'd finished their work early. "I wonder if flirting Ndand Fath's way could be considered command? She sure gets notice."

"She sure rides close to the limits of the rules," Senelac said with a tight mouth and a narrow glance. "And she doesn't really care what happens to the rest of us if she gets caught too many times."

Shevraeth remembered what Senelac had said about the rules—about having girls as an experiment. He grimaced. He should have seen the reason the other girls resented Fath so much. He regarded Senelac in silent appreciation, thinking that, if she wanted to flirt, she'd get plenty of her own attention, even if she wasn't as pretty as Fath. She was far more interesting.

"If she doesn't care, why is she here?" he asked, no longer teasing.

She sensed his shift in mood, and her own tension faded. "Because she's rich, comes from a family of influence. She is not here to train for service, she is here to catch the attention of a suitable fellow—someone of status—for marriage."

"Like court—" He began, then shut up.

"Court?" she repeated, and when he hesitated, she said impatiently, "I'm not so ignorant I don't know what courts are. It's the toffs around a king or queen, am I right? You're one of those? Oh, but then you would be, if you're really related to the king." Her eyes narrowed. "Which makes me wonder, for the first time, why you are here. I assumed you were going to be a trainer when you go back."

"I probably will be," he said slowly, and—again—tried to guess just what his father expected him to do with the knowledge he was gaining.

They both shut up then, she with a troubled air, and he wondering why she didn't ask any more questions. It was like she didn't really want to know anything about his other life.

That was enough of a realization to make him thoughtful. But it wasn't enough to make him wary.

# Twenty-seven

Shevraeth and Marec were sitting on a wall one still, oppressive summer night, their slate between them. To represent their forces they'd laid various sizes of pebbles on the slate. As they worked on their latest battle problem they pushed the pebbles back and forth, arguing agreeably in low mutters.

They were peripherally aware of footsteps on the flagstones below. People had been crossing back and forth. But these approached.

They mentally backed out of the imaginary field where forces charged and retreated, attacked and defended, all without shedding a single drop of blood. The mighty forces dwindled into little stones, the battlefield shrank to a slate as they peered down against the torchlight, which shone on Lennac's pale head as he flung back sweat-damp hair from his eyes. Unconsciously the two on the wall also flung their hair back. It was time for a haircut, but they'd been too busy to notice.

"There you are," Lennac observed. "Hal was looking for you."

Haldred Pereth was the senior in charge of the barracks Marec and Shevraeth technically belonged to.

"We chalked up for some duty?" Marec asked, hand poised to sweep up his markers.

The planes of Lennac's face shifted in the ruddy, flickering light as he grinned. "In a sense. Keriam wants all first and second year colts out for a combined two day run," he said. "He wants a couple of second years as enemy commanders, and I convinced Hal that you two are it. Stad and Evrec have had more than their share of chances, and everyone else in the barracks has had at least one turn."

Marec whistled.

Shevraeth murmured, "I thought—"

His mind caught up with his mouth, which he shut.

The other two waited, then Lennac said, "Thought what?"

Shevraeth sifted possible responses, then settled for, "I thought there wouldn't be any command. For me, I mean. Until next year."

"Who told you that?" Marec asked at the same time Lennac said with a lazy wave, "Might have been true last year. This year, well, you thought wrong." He flicked an ironic salute and walked off.

When his footsteps had faded away again, Marec let out a long breath.

"So what next?" Shevraeth asked, thinking, *A year ago I wouldn't even have known what to ask.* "Do we pick the armies, or do they? Boundaries? Site?"

"Everything, or he would have said." Marec vigorously scratched his scalp, then whistled again. "Everything! I wonder what lies behind that? It really is a year sooner than we could have expected. Maybe it's just Stad and Evrec bustling things along."

Shevraeth remembered Senrid's anxious words at the end of their last conversation, and thought, *Either that or they're pushing the schedule up, trying to get everyone to learn faster.* But he had no proof, so again he kept it to himself. "What do we know about the first year colts?" Yet another thought, this one a spasm of disgust. "Besides Marlovair being in their class, and apparently he hates foreigners."

Marec sat back. "You'll probably have to deal with that."

Shevraeth crossed his arms. "If he's stupid enough to try to scrag me, this time it won't be my ribs getting kicked in. But I'd really rather not." He wondered if that sounded arrogant, and he added, "It's too hot for all that effort."

Marec snickered.

"So should you take him, or should he be in my group? Get it over with the faster, whatever idiocy he'll inevitably try?"

"I don't want him. He's mouthy, and swanks his family's great past, and he thinks it high sport to turf the rules. I'd as soon not have his trouble *and* command to think about in this weather. But I'll take him if you don't want him. My father's just a captain of foot. I'm invisible to the rankers with swank about their ancient shields. You're a target."

For a moment Shevraeth considered dumping the problem onto Marec.

No.

"All the more reason to get it over with," Shevraeth said with a grimace—and knew it was the right decision. Not because of any high-mindedness. In such a ridiculous situation there was no high-mindedness. But if he shuffled the problem onto Marec, it just postponed what he'd really rather get past if he could.

Marec opened his hands, a Marloven gesture that could mean a number of things separately—or all at once. Marec said, "As for the colts' strengths and weaknesses, I don't really know any more than you, situated as we are in the Pit. I just know that class has always been hot at hand."

"Right." Shevraeth thought, then said, "How about I scout them while you scout the territory. You have to know more about that than I do."

"Let's talk about the basic plan, then I'll know what kind of ground to pick."

めℂℛℰℭ⋈

The next day, just after archery drill, Shevraeth waited until Stad was away from the others, and said, "Marec and I have been made enemy commanders on a mixed-class run."

Stad grinned. "I heard. And?"

"So I've never seen the colts in training or action. Scouting 'em out. You seen 'em?"

Stad turned his way, trying to descry the foreigner's motivation. As usual, his face was about as expressive as the stones shimmering in the heat waves on the great court.

Stad paused to wipe his sleeve over his stinging eyes. At least the masters had been human enough to shift the afternoon schedule to archery, knife drill, and riding rather than lances or contact fighting, which were now first thing in the morning—at least until the heat broke.

Never mind that. Another speculative glance. "You know your main problem is going to be Van Marlovair."

"Yes—"

"Who is my cousin."

"I didn't know that."

And it was clear that he hadn't—the lift to his chin, to his eyelids, was about all the expression change Shevraeth ever showed, but Stad had been around him enough to pick up these signals.

"I'm not asking for gossip. I know he hates my guts—apparently because I committed the crime of being born foreign—but he'll have to live with it. I want to know what I can expect from them before I make my plans. Everyone says you've been running a lot of the upper school games this season. You have to have seen them in action."

"Fair enough. Van's their leader, has been all along. Not necessarily the best, just, they follow him. Even though he came a year early, because of . . ." Stad hesitated, hating to think of those very bad years, before Senrid was finally able to get rid of the Regent. How much turmoil there had been in the main part of the family, reaching out to touch the side-families, such as his own. Van—named for Senrid's father Indevan, just as Stad himself was—had lived to see his family threatened by the

Regent, followed by the overthrow of the government, and hard on that Norsunder's invasion.

Either he explained it all, or nothing.

All would take too long, and he wasn't sure he should. "Well. Events, you might say, and leave it at that. They're riders first of all. A lot of old history behind that. Marlovair has one of the largest territories in the kingdom. Part of that is given over to one of the biggest horse studs, which is where my family comes in. So they're traditionally good enough with weapons and so forth, but if you make any plan that resembles a charge, you've got 'em."

"Thank you." Shevraeth turned down one of the side-routes to the Puppy Pit.

"At least, technically you got 'em," Stad muttered to Shevraeth's retreating back. "What you're probably going to get is trouble." Shaking his head, he trotted off to his next drill.

᳐⧼ᘓ⟋⟍ᘔ⧽᳑

From Shevraeth's father:

> . . . *and reveling in the freedom and silence of our home, I had a chance to reflect over what I had been reading. It is as well that Galdran despises old records, for if he knew the half of what lies in his archive, he would probably set fire to it the same way we've heard the crazy Count of Tlanth ridded himself of his own library after the Countess's mysterious murder.*
>
> *But it is quite enlightening to see what voices from the past have to say on the matter of kingship. I found two records, one Colendi and one Sartoran, that echoed each other most curiously, and I wonder if these writers knew of one another. When you are home, I will put them*

*into your hands, and we can discourse on the probabilities as we sift the texts for clues. I will not tell you, therefore, what conclusion your mother reached, which is different from my own.*

*Let me observe only that it is given to few to be able to transform human interests into matters of kingship with justice and with grace, especially the grace to deal well with those whose place in life requires daily attendance on the monarch. It is these long days in court that most tellingly show the human being beneath the shrouding of symbolism.*

*Too much humanity can mean too much familiarity, which is harmless enough. Yet such a ruler can become a nonentity—or a jest—if he cannot enforce his will. Either that, or he becomes a tyrant . . .*

From Russav Savona:

*. . . your father just told me he's going to claim hip problems require him to withdraw to rest at Renselaeus, and so I'm here to scrawl out whatever nonsense I can think of before he returns. I wonder if it's true? About his hip—you see I am writing fast. I realize now that, long as I've known your father, he's never actually told us outright how he got wounded—and why the healers cannot restore him completely. Do you know? Or should I not ask? I can wait until you get home—there is no burning desire to uncover the details of something that was apparently grim enough to inspire him, in later years, to send his only son to that haven of rest and relaxation, Marloven Hess. Or has your endless drill become a matter of mild effort and maximum tedium, as*

*have the card parties Galdran has come more and more to favor? You shall see, when you come home at last, how skillfully I lose. I try not to imagine a lifetime of this tedium wearing us away.*

*No. Scratch unpleasant matters. Move instead to more amiable topics. Such as the regatta last night. The Marquise of Merindar might be about as pleasant as ice down the back of the neck, but one has to admit that when she gives a party, she gives the best. Strange, how mage-fire displays and music work on people! Last night Tamara kissed me. Today she hates me. No jokes about mage-fire, Danric. Though I will admit one is nearly as much fun as the other, especially if she'll kiss me again when we make up the quarrel. What caused the quarrel? My observation—I thought safely neutral—that Renna will probably be the first of us to marry. Now, you ask, how could that spark Tamara's own style of lightning and thunder? I mean to find out, even if it brings on my sorry head more of Tamara's lightning and thunder . . .*

The Princess wrote lightly of similar subjects, describing the masquerade where Savona had only mentioned it. No subject to distress her son. But at the end:

*My reading has offered this insight: the greatest periods of theater in Sartor and Colend appear to have coincided with periods of greatest social reserve, when unguarded expression cost you status and even place. The free play of emotions upon the stage apparently was so beguiling that courtiers who were said to be so sophisticated and subtle and long-seeing followed players off the stage, expecting their stage characters to be the same as real life . . .*

# Twenty-eight

Not that Shevraeth quite understood what she meant. He would think about it, of course. His mother never talked nonsense, except in court. But his mind wanted to linger on kisses rather than court masks and stage emotions, as he and the other boys trudged through the hot morning to the wargame site. He'd always expected Savona to be the first one with any success at romance—not that he'd thought about kissing girls except as a vague and remote possibility, belonging to the hazy future.

But that caused him to think about kissing Senelac as he toiled through the shimmering heat beside Marec, the colts of both houses chattering ahead of them, shoving and head-cuffing and elbowing one another to the sounds of nasal, voice-cracking laughter. Their own class followed behind, their voices a degree lower, the rough-housing less emphatic. Why did younger boys notice the heat less? Or maybe it wasn't the heat so much as constant shorted sleep . . .

Shevraeth shut them all out and reviewed his plans once more. After they'd agreed on the basics, he and Marec had by mutual consent stopped talking about it, so they could face one another in the field with some measure of surprise.

Shevraeth's intention was to lay out the basic strategy in as few commands as possible. He'd noticed that too many orders left people confused if events didn't follow the plan, which happened more often than not. Instead, he'd keep it simple, see what happened, and then decide what to do next.

By the time camp was set up and the blinding-bright rays of sunlight were straight overhead, his mind was sharply focused on the here and now.

For the first time, he was in command. As he faced the rows of boys his own age and a little younger sitting in the sun-hardened dirt before their tents, it just seemed utterly amazing that he was standing here, trying to formulate words (though the past few nights he'd lain awake far too long doing just that) to convey his strategy.

He was, in short, commanding Marlovens. Boys, of course. In a game. But still. When he'd taken on his duties as Marquis, despite the high title and the fortune at his at least hypothetical command, even at age ten he'd known he was just overseeing the smooth flow of events that his father had ordained years ago. Any real problem would be negotiated between adults before a decision by his father. Always carefully explained, of course. But the power of decision had never been his.

Now he was in charge.

His gaze rested last on Marlovair's resentful eyes, his sneer-twisted mouth.

*Keep it short.*

"They are defending," he said. "We are attacking."

The boys stirred.

"In this game, we're not just capturing their command, we have to occupy their position. They're uphill, we're down, they can see, we can't, so though we can take prisoners I don't want us to have to weaken our forces with all the guards it would take to keep 'em. Therefore you go for the kill."

Another stir. That meant chalking their wooden weapons, so the chalk marks showed on their clothes. It also promised the prospect of lots of duels.

"We'll have most of you strung out to charge, with a second line behind. Make as much noise as possible. Spread out.

Because to either side we'll have two covert teams, one just three, and one big one. The small one is a decoy if our main charge is in trouble. The small team makes a lot of noise so they'll think you're all we have. We split their forces then, using our bigger covert team as flying wedge. You run for the clearing atop the hill, which is where they've marked their outer wall. You go for the kill, capture the commander, and squat."

Shevraeth saw the smiles—except in Marlovair's face—and issued his third order, which was his big mistake: "I'll lead from the back, where I can see. But if you riding captains see the initiative, you take it."

It was permissible. It even made sense. From the rear he could see his forces deploy up the hill, and he could signal the decoy, or shift the chargers, or go up the side and reinforce the big covert team if needed. Leading from the front was great on a plain, if your men needed to see the leader at the charge.

What Shevraeth had assumed was that if he led—that is, if he was in sight, the implication being the others followed him—Marlovair might not be able to resist trying to lose, to make him look bad. Shevraeth had seen similar games on a social level, at home.

But here he utterly misjudged Marlovair, who would never throw a game, for any reason. He did not think that far ahead—and wouldn't for a few years—he only wanted to be winning, and to be seen winning by the second year colts.

And so what Indevan Marlovair heard was that the outlander in permitting the riding captains initiative, and in leading from the rear, was afraid to lead. In someone he respected, he might find the sense in it, but in this outlander who swaggered like a rad but scorned the rads' prerogatives, well, in other words, the outlander was a coward.

The trouble did not manifest immediately.

Marlovair was desperate to win, so the game got off to a fast start. Shevraeth experienced a rushing of exhilaration through blood and nerve at the sight of his army launching forward at his command, carrying out his will. They yelled and shouted wildly, and the two covert teams were gratifyingly invisible.

But the plan began to falter when Marec launched a wedge straight down the middle to break the charge. The outer wings of the charge swept out to flank them, but the defenders matched pace. Everyone spread out, the bushes thrashing wildly, as both sides tried to outflank the others.

Shevraeth faltered when dust puffs and shivering shrubs spread outward beyond what he'd assumed would be the boundaries—and sure enough, desperate toots on the enemy horn, followed by Stad's voice, meant the enemy had stumbled on Shevraeth's big decoy team.

Shevraeth launched himself up the hill at his fastest, with the idea of reforming them and running an oblique charge. He'd use his flushed decoys—anything to keep attention away from his small group of coverts, now his only fallback force. But Marec had already twigged to the idea, and sent searchers. By the time Shevraeth—out of breath, his eyes half-blinded with stinging sweat—reached the thrashing shrubs where the defenders were trying to take everyone prisoner, and the attackers to get kill points, another wild and triumphant toot sounded from the other side of the hill, closely followed by a cacophony of shouts and yells.

He turned to motion for a horn, realized the boy with the horn had joined the second wave of chargers. No horn—no one could see him—how could he signal?

Shevraeth plunged into the middle of the wild scramble, yelling hoarsely with the idea of drawing his army to himself, and away from the coverts. All he succeeded at was drawing the enemy, who saw the rumpled sash he wore as commander and wanted the credit of taking him down. All dove at him, many colliding and falling into the scratchy shrubs as they howled, kicked, and grappled. Shevraeth warded them off, leaped over struggling figures, a surge of anger giving him a brief renewal of strength. Stupid—stupid—didn't bring a riding as guards, the plan fell apart and he'd forgotten that they couldn't see him—

The sickening sensation of impending loss wrenched him when the bushes to his left hissed and thrashed, and three of Marec's defenders emerged, these ones moving with wary control.

Three of his own boys appeared from just above them, led by Evrec, and with wild yells launched into them.

At least none of them were Marlovair—Shevraeth thought as Evrec motioned violently for him to run. If he were captured, there went the game, and so ridiculously early the entire school would be laughing.

Dizzy with thirst, and fury at himself, he backed up and thrust himself into a thick bush, which scratched his face and neck mercilessly, but it slowed the chasers.

He forced himself through, ducked down, and ran parallel to the battle, seeking . . . he didn't even know what he was seeking.

Yes. The coverts. See if any of them were left, reinforce them.

Oh, but wait, he couldn't be just a single person, he had to collect an honor guard. He looked around in despair, rubbing his eyes—*why can't I see*—

The racing trumpet chords of a retreat sounded from below, quickly caught up by all the trumpeters. Shevraeth threw back his head, and saw that not only had the sun vanished behind the hill, but a layer of cloud had obscured the light. It felt as if the game had been mere moments, but it had gone on all afternoon.

Cries of disappointment and protest rose from all over the hill, followed by the noise of nearly seventy-five boys stampeding down to camp. Shevraeth's head now pounded rhythmically but he forced himself to listen to the chatter, in case there was some scrap he could use in reforming his plans for the morrow. He didn't have to see Pereth, the senior boy in charge of the exercise, to know he'd lost points so far.

The chatter was the usual, with an odd undercurrent that he finally recognized, the buzzing sound the smaller boys made that was supposed to emulate the sound of a rabbit shivering in fear. A coward.

He flung back his head, sweeping his gaze around, and there was Marlovair—and was that the rabbit face? They did that by lifting their upper lip so their two front teeth were bared, a stupid sort of face, but one absolutely guaranteed to start a scrap in the lower school, and even among some of the older boys.

Was Marlovair's lip lifted? The light was fading fast, the boys turning into silhouettes in various shades of gray as color leached into shadow.

Shevraeth suspected that yes, it had been.

He was right.

The trouble developed rapidly. The boys went about evening chores, the commanders now back to being rads, overseeing dinner. Shevraeth kept hearing quick buzzes just behind him, or just out of sight around the side of a tent, followed by snickers that gradually became louder and more daring.

It was his turn to oversee supper cleanup. He was resolutely impartial in dividing up the chores. Marlovair and his cronies did not react overtly, they just dragged their heels, asked for orders to be repeated, and as darkness closed in, their resistance became more obvious. They were watched avidly by the others of their group, who were more than ready for some fine entertainment, and resentfully by the other colt House, who counted up every evidence of Marlovair's and his friends' arrogance and swank. Why was the foreigner letting them get away with that rabbit buzz? Could the foreigner really be a coward?

Shevraeth's headache had worsened to a skull-hammering intensity. He longed to lie down and shut his eyes, though the scratches on his face and neck were by now hot stings that he knew would torment him all night long. Anything, though, *anything*, for a semblance of peace.

It was just then that Marlovair became aware of the other colts' mounting resentment and he chose to switch from covert to overt. When Shevraeth gave the order to clear the last of the dishes, he lagged with deliberate slowness. As if wading through a river.

Shevraeth shut his eyes. "Put. The. Cook pots. Away. Now."

Marlovair whirled around. They stood in the big cook tent, four of them, and him. The light a single lantern, its flickering flame like needles in Shevraeth's eyes.

"Or what?" Marlovair said. "Will I be cleaning shoes?"

And his friends snickered.

Shevraeth felt the words shape—he was just about to send all four to gather everyone's shoes and go to the stream to scrub them, except it was senseless, it was far too much and so he'd look stupid, he'd lose authority by overusing it. So what should he do?

*Anything* he did would be wrong. He should have waited them out . . . should have . . .

But there was no more *should have*. There were just these four younger boys, grinning avidly, and at the mouth of the tent—because tents don't block sound—more boys, some angry, some curious, all ready to be entertained. The rules kept them silent, but in the air was expectancy, because Marlovair had answered back to an order. You didn't do that.

You didn't do that unless you wanted a breeze.

So *that* was behind the scorn, the insubordination.

Shevraeth opened his eyes.

His heartbeats stitched the silence into a long seam as all around boys crowded, and Shevraeth remembered, for the first time in weeks, the stupid stick stuck through his sash.

He almost laughed, though that would have hurt his head too much. He said, "Permit me to comprehend. You want me to hit you?"

Marlovair stood silently, a sneer on his freckled face. Of course he wouldn't answer that, and if Shevraeth demanded an answer, he would lose yet more of his diminishing authority, not at the sand trickle by which he was losing now, but in great heaping handfuls.

Rage surged through him, first hot and then cold, so cold. He drawled, "I am amazed. You, presumably a thinking being, are actually endeavoring to provoke me to *hit you with a stick*."

Marlovair, not quite fourteen, gave the only possible answer for the thirteen year old whose sense of right and order has been rattled about fairly severely over the past few years: "*You* wouldn't dare." Then he added with deliberate contempt, "Shevraeth Radlav."

Shevraeth's hand moved before he even thought. The wand snapped free of his sash, and all those months of training drove his arm up and around so that the wood whistled a curious moaning note. He took a step toward Marlovair and struck the wand straight across the boy's bony shoulder-blades with so loud a crack everyone in sight jumped. The impact reverberated up Shevraeth's hand, followed by the urge to fling the stick—rub his hand as if to rid it of the horror of the contact with Marlovair's scrawny body beneath the wood.

Marlovair's eyes widened in shock and his skin blanched to the color of paper. He took an inadvertent step forward, then his face flooded with color, and his lips compressed, his eyes gleamed with pain-tears but he glared, hard, and Shevraeth knew if he apologized, the boy won this impossible contest. Even though he'd already won in Shevraeth's inner conflict, but if Shevraeth backed down now, he'd lose the last vestige of authority, and so he forced himself to put the hated stick back in his sash, and forced himself to say—though his throat was so dry his voice husked—"Of course I dare."

Then he pointed to the pots, put his hands behind his back, and he gripped them together to hide the shaking.

And the sound of another wand whistling nearly caused him to whirl; there was another crack—a wand hitting the tent—followed by Pereth saying, "So no one has any chores? I can fix that." And he issued a steady stream of orders, loading the audience with most of the rest of the evening's work.

The sound of scampering feet, rustling clothing, whispers, soon diminished, and from just behind Shevraeth came the senior's calm voice, "Are those pots stashed yet?"

Marlovair moved with slow, painstaking care; one of his friends wordlessly took the pot from his hands and put it away, as the other two hastily finished stacking the pots for morning. Then, two sidling looks Shevraeth's way, two looking downward, they filed out, and vanished.

Shevraeth forced himself to face the senior radlav.

Pereth said mildly, "We usually practice on our own hand, or leg, to get just a sting." He smacked his wand against his hand, then thrust it through his sash. "I'll take over here. You go plan tomorrow's campaign."

Shevraeth made it to his tent before his guts began to heave, but at least there was the mercy of the Waste Spell, and so he did not puke all over himself. He just sat on his bedroll, shivering, retching and whispering the spell, until at last he collapsed, bathed in cold sweat, his head a fireball of pain, but through it all came the inane taunt of moral defeat, of personal weakness: *I hit him. I hit him. I hit him.*

# Twenty-nine

Shevraeth was aware of Marec entering their tent only when something warm bumped his hand, and Marec murmured in a low, cheery voice, "Looks to me like a prime headache on you. Of course you forgot the first rule of summer games—"

And Shevraeth realized that yes, he had. He'd come straight off the game into his supervising duties, without stopping at the stream for a drink. Even though he'd had a desperate thirst, and a vile-tasting mouth, ever since . . . whenever it was.

He forced himself to sit up, despite the heave of his stomach and the renewed hammer in his head. First sips then gulps of hot, bitter willow-steep burned his mouth without really satisfying the thirst, but he drank it all anyway, then, gasping for breath, lay back down.

He was not aware of Marec vanishing and reappearing until the cup, cold and wet this time, nudged his fingers. It was full of water, fresh from the stream. Another effort, though this time slightly easier as he sat up and drank. As he lay back down his overheated body burst out in sweat at last, leaving him shivering for a short time, but that, too, diminished, and gradually the pain lessened to a mere candle compared to its previous sun.

When Marec returned for the third time, he heard the muted crunch of heels on dirt, the sough of the tent-flap lifting, and the rustle of Marec's clothes as he sat on his bedroll. "Here's a bread-and-cheese," he said.

Shevraeth eased himself up—and realized he was going to live after all.

Too bad.

"Thanks." He took the sandwich and braced for questions.

Marec yawned. "Pereth gave you advance to the point where our second defense broke your regroup. Said to tell you to get shut-eye now, because he's going to plant the flags the moment he's got some sun, so we can get at it early, maybe finish by noon, before the heat gets too bad."

"Right," Shevraeth said around his sandwich. And because he was not a coward, "Marec, I hit that boy as hard as I could."

"Yep. You did."

"Should I report myself to Keriam? I don't want to leave that to Pereth."

"Pereth has to anyway. My advice is, let it be."

"But I hit him with all my strength. That's not right."

"No. But you only did it once, and every single person here knows why. I think most were hoping you'd go berserk and lambaste him. Everyone except Pereth—only because he'd have to stop it—and Van's particular friends. This is nothing new, and there are enough witnesses to the cause. You may's well just let it be. Concentrate on how you're going to fight me tomorrow, or we're going to grind you into the dust. I still have Stad, and we wounded Evrec."

Marec grinned and got up to leave.

Shevraeth said, "Is there a night watch?"

"Not for you. Pereth had specific orders for you to rack out, since you probably made the night easier for us. It being a star night."

Star night—oh, yes. Shevraeth's overnights so far had mostly been cloudy or rainy nights, except for a couple his first year. Like everything else licit or illicit, there were unspoken but definite rules for tent raids. Dark nights were considered only a challenge for small boys as they were too easy, and you couldn't see the apparently side-splitting effect of a collapsed tent thrashing about as its occupants tried to fight their way out. Rainy nights had been deemed over the years to lie outside the rules (unless a definite declaration of war), but starry nights gave the sneak a challenge, and the results the fine visual edge.

Shevraeth lay back down gratefully, and did not stir when Pereth and Marec decided just before midnight that the colts had probably decided against these night festivities. The anti-Marlovair faction were too subdued. As for Marlovair, he'd declared (when he could trust himself to speak) that if That Rabbit Shevraeth could deal out welters for nothing, who knew what might happen if they were caught doing something?

ઠ૦૯૨૪૦૦૯૪

When dawn blued the air outside the tent, Marec and Shevraeth worked together to pack up their stuff so they wouldn't have to in the heat of day. They walked together to the cook tent, where a few early boys had gathered, most but not all on various morning duties.

The boys saw the two army commanders together, and conversation ended abruptly. Shevraeth knew what they were talking about. He had already withdrawn behind the court mask, though he felt his ears redden, but his hair had gotten so shaggy he hoped no one noticed.

In silence one of the boys on duty passed mugs of coffee, then Pereth came striding round one of the tents. "Just got the markers set up. Shevraeth, you're ahead on advance points, Marec, you evened up with the breaking of the second assault, so the first move goes to you. Marec, you've got four dead, Shevraeth, you seven. All the wounded have arm and leg bands."

Both signified assent with lifted hands, food was passed out, and Shevraeth forced himself to focus on the shambles of his plans. The points on advance were unexpected—so he hadn't been quite as bad as he'd thought. That meant they'd be closer to the summit. So what could he do with his remaining forces?

As soon as breakfast was done—and it was a hasty meal—the eleven 'dead' dismally faced the task of collecting the camp's neatly-rolled tents, bedrolls and gear and stowing them for ease of pack-up when the horses were brought to pick them up and take them back to the academy. The sun had reached the top of the hill by then, the edges of shiny leaves already glittering with the promise of glare and heat.

Pereth called the combatants together. "I'll call a halt at noon," he warned. "If there hasn't been a win, we'll count points then. But mid-morning there will be a truce, and everyone is to get back down to the stream to water up. Then return to your places, so mark them, mind, soon's you hear the signal." He waved at the boy with the trumpet.

At the peal Marec's crowd gave a shout and began racing up the hill to the summit, where they'd hold their war conference.

Shevraeth's army followed more quietly to the base of the hill, where there was a grassy sward. He stopped and faced them. They all stopped, most sitting on the grass, all attention on him. He rejected the impulse to talk over their heads to the hazy fields beyond, and forced himself to scan them. Sullenness was what he expected to see in Marlovair, and did. Marlovair's two particular friends were equally hostile. He'd braced himself to see it also in the rest, but their attitude was more subdued, some wary, others uneasy. And some were grinning, still inwardly cherishing the memory of Mouth Marlovair getting what he deserved.

"From what I can see," Shevraeth began, "our markers are fairly close to the boundaries of their castle. So I think the best thing to do is try a single charge. Everybody, because they'll probably be expecting a sneak-attack on the flank. We won't get away with that again. However, what we can try is a row behind the front chargers, running obliquely—light cav after heavy—who will concentrate on their left flank . . ."

ఌఞ౫ఠౚ

"... which is usually the weakest part of any line," Shevraeth finished the next day in command class. "All the written records in the library mention that everyone's instinct is to fight to the right. Unless you're facing an outer wing made entirely up of left-handers. Which has happened."

Keriam signified assent.

"But Marec was prepared for an oblique attack, and had his own second wing waiting for something of the sort. The result was a melee fairly fast. We did get a few of our best over the line, but most of ours were taken prisoner by Marec's ridings all working as tight units. We pushed, they pushed, we did gain ground where the landslide made defense tougher, but we lost on points."

Keriam lifted a hand in agreement with his assessment, then glanced Marec's way. Marec had already given his view of the battle. "Anything to add?"

"No, that's an accurate summation."

"All right." Keriam flicked a look toward the back of the room, where—they all knew, though everyone studiously avoided turning to stare—Senrid sat on the last bench, a slate on his lap. But it was just for support, as he was writing with pen and ink. They could hear the rapid scratches of his pen. "What do you each perceive as your weak points?"

Marec said, "Terrain first, for me. I really thought they could see more than they did. If I hadn't been on my rock, I couldn't have seen everything and commanded. And of course if we'd had the jelly-bag arrows on this game, I'd have been turfed first thing. In short, I won mostly because I could see better than anyone, and could toot my signals to my ridings."

Keriam smiled briefly. The only reason they hadn't been permitted the jelly-bags was that the practice helms and quilting the boys had to wear under their tunics would have slain most of them in the fierce heat; even tipped with the little papers full of jelly, the arrows could hurt when they struck.

"Shevraeth?"

"Two major mistakes." He frowned, picking his words. "First, I didn't have good backup plans. But even if I had, I forgot about communications."

Keriam snapped his fingers, his way of indicating approval. "Comms, and scouts," he said.

Shevraeth did not feel the least gratified. He was utterly disgusted with himself for his loss of control. He had expected, and felt he had earned, a dressing down in front of all the others. That had not happened.

Then, even if there had been no Marlovair, there was no excuse for forgetting a concept he'd learned from his father before he'd even come here. *Maintain the inside line of communication.* He'd always thought of it in political terms, further, his command the day before had been conceived in isolation—he didn't know his army, and hadn't even considered amending that fault, like Marec had, by setting up specific lines of communication.

"What is the very first lesson I taught you?" Keriam asked. "You can probably recite the sound of it, because I know you were paying attention, but perhaps now you've experienced the sense."

Shevraeth said, "Command is control of comms."

"What does that mean, now that you've had your first experience?"

Shevraeth did not speak immediately as his mind sifted through all the talk of the past few months—the necessity of line-of-sight, the need to reduce the proliferation of reports which in turn proliferated decisions to be made, which in turn forced the commander to lag behind events.

The others waited, still and polite because of the king sitting back there, until Shevraeth was ready to speak. The only sounds were the creak of a bench, the scrape of a heel, hastily stilled, as someone shifted. He said, slowly, "Command has to be exercised continuously, so one not only needs a good comms setup, but a way to protect it despite the change of events?"

"Good, good," Keriam began, but then the slate hit the bench from the back, and he abandoned whatever it was he'd planned to say as Senrid came forward, looking young, thin, and nervy.

*Now for the dressing down,* Shevraeth thought, and braced himself. It was no more than he deserved for his loss of control.

But Senrid did not even look at him. Everyone in the room could feel his tension as he began to pace back and forth, a quick step.

He said, "Keriam's also told you over and over the purpose of this place." A wide-arm gesture over the entire academy, then his gaze took in the entire class. "Right? What is it?"

A silence—shifty looks—rubbed hands down trouser legs—bit lips—then Stad said, "Training and drill are the only weapons we have against the chaos of battle."

Senrid whirled, paced restlessly back. "You know that. I know that. We grow up hearing it. We read it in old records. But like Keriam said to Shevraeth just now, what does it mean?" And when no one volunteered, he said, "You've got to see it. Perhaps if you turn it around. You are told that training and drill lead eventually to command, but the way you need to see it, I am becoming convinced, is that the success of command, given all other aspects being equal, is, oh, how shall I put it—measured exactly by the *lessening* of the information needed for performance at any level."

Senrid turned to Keriam. "Am I right? Do I make sense? I've been reading and reading on this subject. The more we drill for all eventualities, and that includes comm systems for every possible ground, the more likely it is we can move fast. Can anyone translate that back, what I mean is—" He gestured again, a fast, tense jab with spread fingers. "—how are you hearing that?"

They could all feel how important the question was to him, and every single one of them wondered what problem lay behind it.

Stad looked right and left, then muttered, "Forthan told me last year that command works best not when one man is brilliant, but when it's spread all the way down the line."

"Yes," Senrid exclaimed, bouncing lightly on his toes. "Yes! The more everyone knows not necessarily what to do—that's the commander's job—but how to do it, the fewer orders needed. *Think.* If someone has never, say, folded his shirt before, you have to tell him to shake it out, how to find the seam and fold along it, what to do with the sleeves. But if he knows how to fold, and you see something wrong with what he's doing. You don't have to tell him everything. All you have to say is *flatten the cuffs together* and he knows just what to do. See?" His chin lifted and his eyes narrowed with a distant focus. He seemed about to say something, but then, just as abruptly as he'd gotten up, he returned to his seat.

Keriam stepped forward again and said easily, "We're going to step up the games as soon as the weather breaks."

## ๛ CRROCR

"So what happened?" Senelac asked as they slid onto opposite chairs at a tiny table.

At Senelac's insistence they met at different eateries just about every time. Though they were permitted to socialize outside the academy—and Shevraeth had seen a few couples here and there during his rec periods—Senelac made it plain she did not want to be gossiped about.

The innkeeper of this new place, an older woman, gave them both incurious looks, her gaze flicking from their faces to their uniforms, and then dismissing them from her interest.

He was glad he'd gotten a haircut the day before, if for no reason better than the fact he knew he was almost indistinguishable from most of the other academy boys, and if he kept his words short, he could even pass for a time, at least, as a Marloven. It was always his accent that betrayed him, if he had to speak more than a few words.

The innkeeper took their order, then left.

Shevraeth said, "What didn't we cover in the—"

She waved a hand impatiently. "Not the war game. I was listening to the report. I want to know what happened with Brat Marlovair."

Shevraeth grimaced slightly. "I hit him. What more is there to say?"

"A lot. Word is, you gave him a welter."

He shook his head. "What do you want to hear, how much I hate transgressing my own moral code?"

She leaned on her elbows, her dark eyes flicking back and forth between his own. The shadows at the sides of her mouth—and, he realized, it was such an entrancing mouth, not too wide, not too narrow, the corners shadowed with just a hint of sardonic amusement—deepened to an ironic quirk. Then she said, "You really do think we're barbarians, don't you?"

The effect was like a bucket of ice-water somewhere in the region of his chest.

"No," he managed, and his faced burned. "No," he said again, and at her narrowed-eyed head-toss of disbelief he protested, "My standard for barbarity is pretty . . . royal these days, exampled in our own king."

That in turn surprised her, and all the scorn left her face. "Ah." She was about to ask more, then squashed down that impulse with a quick shake of her head, followed by, "So it's your personal moral code that's so superior to ours."

The faint lift to his brows, the widening of his gray eyes, signalled a hit. She felt a stab of remorse as he said soberly, "You did ask. Permit me to express myself a little differently. I lost control of my temper, and struck someone smaller than me who had no weapon in his hands."

She felt another retort forming, and let out her breath slowly instead. It was not his fault that she found herself thinking about him far too often. It was not his fault she couldn't stop studying the exact shade of his eyes—was it really gray, or just a pale, pale blue, and why did they seem to change color ever so subtly? Was his hair as soft as it looked?

The woman returned with their plates then. Because of the hot weather, both had chosen newly-baked bread stuffed with greens, a fresh-picked tomato, and sharp cheese. To wash it down there was a delicious punch made up of the juice of cranberries and lemon, mixed with just enough fermented ginger to give it all a pleasant bubbly zing. The inn's barrels, or whatever they made it in, had to be chilled by magic; the entire place, she saw, was drinking that punch almost exclusively, and she made a note to return here with the girls. Not him, not him.

They both turned to the food, each busy with their own thoughts. The snap of anger, of the possibility of quarrel, had subsided with her long breath, leaving him wondering what in his manner had angered her, and her with the intention to be fair. Or she'd lose his friendship through her own fault.

After a few bites, and a couple of sips of the cold drink that went so deliciously down, she said, "Some of the older women swear the weather will break by the time of your big game."

"I hope so," he said, relieved at her pleasant tone. "Or a week out in this sun will bake us into human semblances of this." He flicked the crispy end of his bread.

She uttered a make-peace laugh at the mild joke, then said, careful not to sound confrontational, "How about your telling me how it's losing control when you gave a whack—even a welter—to a brat who outraged the rules like he did?"

Shevraeth said, "What were you told about that incident?"

"A couple of versions. The most reliable, usually, is from Mad's cousin in the other colt House. He doesn't like Van, thinks he and his gang are way too full of rank-swank. They order the others around as if they were rads. Mad's cousin said Van and them were rabbiting you, but you ignored it, quite rightly. Then Van back-chatted an order. Absolutely dead-center-target against the rules, and you gave him a welter for it."

"I lost my temper and hit him as hard as I could."

She sat back, her sandwich forgotten in her hand. His tone was impossible to parse but his downward look, the slight length to his upper lip, made it fairly clear how angry he was with himself.

She said, "You hit him once. You were within the rules. He'd broken two of them, flouting an order and answering back. If Keriam thought you were going to make a habit of losing your temper, things might be different. As it is . . . well, you might not like 'em, but we do have rules. And none of the rules say anything about how hard you can hit."

Shevraeth's head dropped. She did not know whether he was hiding remorse or disgust. She sensed both. "I could tell you some grim stories about some of the Regent's pet bullies in the bad old days, and what they got away with. You can probably imagine. The rules now are strict enough, only three hits. The rads deal out what are called stingers, or a breeze in boy-slang. If you give out welters, then they're going to want to know why."

He opened his mouth, shut it, shook his head.

"Go on," she said.

"No, it might seem as if I judge when I just mean to question."

"I'll take whatever you say as meant."

"All right. So these rules regulate violence against one another, but isn't that another way to validate it?"

She pressed her lips together. Retorts were too easy, and she'd promised. So she thought through her response, then said, "The oldsters would all answer with the usual jaw. You know, 'War is a violent business.' But the king doesn't want war, he wants defense. So let me answer you with a question."

His expression was now wary. He would never suspend a sandwich in the air—his manners were too fine for that—but he had dropped his hands to the table, loose, a graceful curve of fingers that she had to force herself to look away from.

She said, "Does it hurt less when you use sarcasm as a weapon instead of a wand?"

His lips parted. He was about to say that he never used sarcasm as a weapon, but he knew he did. He always had when young, because he was so frequently the smallest, the weakest, he'd in fact prided himself on using wit as a weapon, darting his words with precision and skill, because his physical strength was so spindly.

And as for the incident with Marlovair, he remembered quite distinctly his corrosive tone, meant to be corrosive, when he said, *You, presumably a thinking being...*

"No, I don't suppose it does."

She changed the subject to their next command problem, and it wasn't until he was walking back alone in the simmering, moist heat held down by the lid of tiny cotton-puff clouds obscuring the sky, that he wondered why he couldn't tell her what he really thought. And though he contemplated this question all the way back to the Puppy Pit—passing by the colt territory, their voices carrying on the night air, their braying laughs sounding so . . . so *young*—he could not find any satisfactory answer.

What he did know was this. Though his striking that obnoxious boy had been deemed justifiable by the Marlovens, he could not permit time and distance to justify his own reaction. And time would, he knew enough about human nature by now. And distance. So what might happen in the future, if his father somehow put him in charge of, say, the Renselaeus Riders? He wouldn't ever experience any such punishment at home. Nor would it happen here—he was too careful, and supposing he did go mad and break the most fundamental rules, he suspected Senrid would get rid of him before putting him against a post like he'd done to his favorite Forthan. And in a way, it would make sense. Forthan's sufferings had been felt by almost every boy and girl witnessing. They were unlikely to empathize with a foreigner in the same situation.

And so, though he had no inclinations whatsoever toward self-destruction, he waited until the scrubs were finally asleep, and Marec and Lennac out for their free time, then he walked out just beyond the courtyard where sound would be muffled, the hated stick in hand. *Mother*, he thought, *I betrayed my own honor in forgetting my vow to you.* Then, drawing a deep breath, he used all the force of his arm to whack the wand down across the inside of his other arm.

The resulting pain made his knees buckle, a lung-seizing bolt of agony through every nerve. His heart labored until he managed, with effort, to draw in a shuddering breath. Just like Marlovair. It took all his remaining strength to walk back to the barracks, but walk he did. He used his outgrown cambric shirt from the bottom of his trunk to staunch the beading blood until it stopped. And though Marlovair had no doubt drunk a healing mug of listerblossom that night, dispensed from the first aid the senior rad always brought, Shevraeth, did not grant himself the same respite.

At dawn he rose after a long, ceaselessly pain-throbbing night, and oversaw inspection, and then walked the boys to breakfast, and then he went to his day's work, making the same effort that he'd seen in the Marlovair boy that second day of the game, only now he knew in every bone and muscle what it felt like. And as the pain gradually began to fade away each day, he knew he would always remember.

He had no idea that the very slight favoring of his hurt arm, the tension in his riding, the marginal falling off in his speed at drill, was witnessed by those who watched the boys and girls for unspoken troubles, and it did not take long to figure the probable cause. But because he said nothing, nothing was said to him.

# Thirty

"Well," Mondar said, gently fingering his puffy lip. "It's like this, see—"

"They started it first," Tevac cut in, using his most earnest, pitiful-victim voice. His gaze flickered from one to the others of the three rads, who stared at him in disbelief. "They did, they did! And we were just upholding the House honor, y'see, after their sneak-attack on our boots—"

"Those rotten eggs," Mondar put in, scuffing his heels on the courtyard flagstones. He added helpfully, "You were on the colt run, so Stad was our commander—"

Tevac elbowed him hard, his face held stiffly straight forward, as if that would hide the movement. "Stad wouldn't let us use the stream to clean 'em out," Tevac said in an injured tone. "I can't believe any animals were anywhere near, drinking out of it."

Mondar continued, "Really rotten. Stenched us right out of our tents!"

"Worse than horse farts—"

"Worse than dog runs!"

"You can skip past the comparisons," Lennac ordered.

Tevac gave up trying to jolly the rads, who were totally incapable of understanding what was funny. "They knew no one has a cleaning frame on a run, so they *laughed* when we had to wad 'em out with grass! And we had to wear 'em anyway, and they stank worse'n—well, they stank!"

"And they were still laughing when we got back—and they got everyone laughing at us! On the parade ground!"

"Not a single sound, but real obvious—"

"—so's everyone else was laughing, too!"

Tevac watched closely. Shevraeth and Marec had been back from the colt run by then, and from their expressions they remembered the smirking looks, the muffled snickers, nothing outside the rules, but still very, very evident. What he didn't know was if Stad had told them the reason. In his experience the rads all blabbed among themselves, but didn't tell you what they knew unless they were about to drop on you.

"But we couldn't do anything on the parade ground," Mondar said, testing the terrain. "So there we were—"

"—everyone laughing—"

"—we had to defend ourselves—"

The earnest voices rose, loud and shrill. Silhouettes bobbed in the darkening barracks windows on the other side of the courtyard (obviously trying to hear the defense) then, on a surreptitious gesture from Tevac, abruptly ducked down again.

The rads took no notice.

"So." Mondar was just winding up to a martyred finish. "I felt we just had to defend our honor—"

Lennac snapped his fingers.

Mondar and Tevac clapped their mouths shut.

"Let's sum it up. This feud with Scout-hound House began with the eggs, you say?"

Mondar and Tevac nodded vigorously, eyes round. Innocence unjustly accused, absolutely, totally, completely. Then Tevac said tentatively, "Maybe with the oatmeal."

"I remember the peppered oatmeal. Unprovoked, you say?"

Two less certain nods. Tevac's eyes shifted as he considered possible holes in his defense.

Shevraeth murmured, "Permit me to jog your memories. Was there not something about the baths, the day Marec and I were with our House against the seniors?"

Mondar grinned—until Tevac elbowed him even more forcefully in the side. Mondar woofed softly, and his eyes watered as he hastily assumed a solemn expression.

"As in taking their togs away? And throwing them in the stable-yard midden pile waiting for the wand?" Marec reminded them. "You have to realize, even if we didn't see it—" He closed his mouth lest the laugh escape.

"We did hear about it," Shevraeth said gently, his court mask at its blandest.

Mondar snickered uneasily.

"It does seem interesting that these disasters all appear to happen when Marec and Shevraeth are away with their House," Lennac observed. "And I am out in the fields with the seniors."

"In-teresting," Marec repeated. His tone was not promising.

Tevac checked the rads' faces, saw equal degrees of flat disbelief, and scrambled to rescue the situation. "Well, the clothes just needed to be wanded. They were perfectly all right. Unlike our stomachs, after they peppered our oatmeal. *That* was before the egg attack, you'll remember."

"You know for certain they did it?" Lennac asked.

Tevac snorted in scorn. "How could we not, the way Nath was crowing at archery practice. So of course we had to do *something*. You know, on account of honor."

Marec turned away. Lennac said with a blank face, "And you will instruct me in just how your honor was upheld at the, ah—"

"Spectacle?" Shevraeth murmured, gaze lifted to the sentry wall, the ever-ready guards pacing against the emerging stars.

"Yes, thank you, the *spectacle* of an entire class of boys, wearing only towels, hotfooting it from the baths to their barracks? Also, maybe more important, was this foray before or after the eggs-in-boots reprisal? You seem to be wavering a little on your report of the sequence of events."

Tevac's gaze had gone diffuse, as if the sadness he contemplated lay beyond the rim of the world. "We got our honor back in how loud everybody laughed, especially when Dorthad dropped his towel."

"You know what they're calling him now?" Mondar snickered again. "Moonrise Dorth—" He caught another elbow prod straight in the solar plexus that knocked his breath out.

Tevac said pleadingly, "*You* were there! You saw how the *entire mess hall* laughed when we ate that oatmeal—"

Lennac tapped his wand on his palm.

The scrubs shut up.

"If I let you gas on we will be here another month. Here's what it comes to. Stings turn into raids, which turn into skirmishes, such as that scragging outside the stables after mess this morning." Lennac indicated Mondar's split lip and Tevac's rapidly darkening eye. "This year is not going to end with all the scrubs going home with black eyes and broken limbs, do you hear me? So your new orders are the same ones Scout-hound House are hearing right now. You will leave them alone on the academy run. You will leave their clothing untouched. And the food. Nothing will happen to their tents. Or their wooden weapons, so the snap-vine oil I saw under Kandac's cold weather uniform during inspection, for example, will not be greasing anything but your own gear. Mess hall. Any problems, *any*, and you go back to mess-gag for the remainder of the year. Am I understood?"

Two palms thumped skinny chests.

"Dismissed."

In relief the two raced back inside to report their version of the rads' reactions to the other boys all crouched beneath the windows, doing their best to hear.

Lennac glanced up at the torches, just lit, as the castle bell tolled sunset, echoed within moments by the city bell tower. "That should settle them down," he said to Marec, then turned his thumb toward his chest and then at Shevraeth. "Shevraeth and I have orders to report castle-side."

Marec raised his brows, but said nothing as he returned inside to a relatively quiet, meditative barracks.

Shevraeth and Lennac left, walking swiftly through the leaves skittering over the stones, chased by a cold wind that promised rain soon, coming out of the north.

"You know what this summons is about?" Shevraeth asked, hopping over a startled cat that scrambled across their path.

"No," Lennac admitted, turning one palm upward. "But I know who. It's not Keriam, but the king."

"Ah." Shevraeth was now intensely curious.

They saluted the sentries on the wall above, then dashed into the mossy old archway leading from the academy to the castle, their boots ringing on the stones.

Lennac took the lead. They did not go inside the Residence, as Shevraeth had gone before when he was interviewed by Senrid. They made their way to Keriam's tower, the wind strengthening as thin gray clouds streamed overhead.

Full dark had fallen when they reached the door and saluted the guards. Lennac dashed up the circular stairs as one long familiar with the place, but Shevraeth followed more slowly. He'd been climbing these stairs to attend command class each week, but it still felt strange in some way he couldn't define to be here. The strange feeling was heightened as the torches, tattered by the fitful wind, cast shifting light over the ancient stones.

Keriam's office was closed. There was another room one landing higher. This one had windows open on all sides, looking back over the castle, the academy, the western side of the city where the communal truck gardens abutted the grazing grounds, and northward over the enormous stable yard belonging to the Guard.

Shevraeth stepped into a plainly furnished chamber. Senrid sat backward in a chair, his chin resting on his forearms.

On a plain plank table Sartora—Liere—perched, her scrawny arms locked round her knees, her bare toes curved over the edge of the table.

She shook with silent laughter as Lennac said, ". . . and then they carried the war to the enemy, making a commando raid on the bath house. The House had to run back to barracks wearing only towels. While everyone was returning for midday mess, which was of course why they'd gone to the baths. The stones hot, y'see, and apparently Tand Dorthad was so busy hopping and trying to spot one of our boys for later scragging that he tripped and dropped his towel."

Liere smacked her hand over her face. Her shoulders shook.

"Their rads had to go wand the clothes and haul them back. You can imagine how pleased they were at this. We squared it with Handauc—our next run with the pups, we will take their night watches."

Senrid grinned, lifted a hand.

Lennac glanced Liere's way, then lowered his voice slightly. "For the rest of the week everyone kept asking the Scout-hound barracks scrubs if they were on their butt-watch or their stink-watch."

Liere squeaked faintly, sounding like a one-day old kitten.

Lennac, familiar with her, said, "Go ahead and laugh, Sartora. You can be sure both boys' and girls' sides were howling about it—we could scarcely keep order that night."

"That *is* her big laugh, Lennac," Senrid said. "Her mighty mind powers, as our mutual friend C.J. says, do not extend to villainous guffaws. Carry on. Was the oatmeal a real thing, or did they make that up?"

"Oh, no. The Scout-hounds got into the mess hall right before we did. Which often happens—or did—their being just a few steps closer. Near as we can figure, as the last boy passed down the row he must have dropped a fist of hot-pepper into the oatmeal then gave it a stir because we all got a stomach-roaring load."

"Euw." Liere shook with laughter again.

"Right. We all got it," Lennac said grimly, and Shevraeth's mouth puckered in memory. "So that's when I got together with Handauc, while both houses were busy at ride-and-shoot, and we tried to lay down some rules, but the boys in both houses keep getting around them."

"Summation?" Senrid asked.

"Han says he's sure Branid Jath is getting his ideas from his brother over on Guard-side—I remember he was always working up stings, when I was in the Puppy Pit—but in our House, it's Tevac on his own inventing the ideas, and Mondar is always willing to scout for him or act as his shield arm."

"Ah," Senrid said, rising to his feet. "Skip up to today." He had begun pacing, quick steps, back and forth from window to door. "Not what happened—Keriam sent me Handauc's report just before he left. What you told them. Try to be exact."

Lennac frowned with effort, and repeated his orders slowly, then turned Shevraeth's way. "Is that right?"

Shevraeth had been listening carefully. His father might not have put him in the way of this level of military training, but he had been exacting when he required one to listen and then repeat what one heard. "Yes."

Senrid flicked his fingers open. "Then let me tell you this. If they break orders, you do what you like with them. But don't you see, Lennac, what you left out?"

"Huh?" Lennac's honest face was puzzled. He rubbed his knuckles against his jaw.

"Think." Senrid jerked a thumb toward the window, and the roofs of the academy beyond. "You were just a first-year scrub when Ndarga ran the barracks raid on Regent's House?"

Lennac winced. No one liked remembering what the Regent had done to Ndarga after that daring raid on his favored seniors, hand-picked to be in the best barracks, the one to which he gave his name. But then his expression lightened—he shifted from memory to idea. "You think Tevac will think of it?"

"I'm almost sure. If he does, send him to me. I'll give him a suitable punishment in the eyes of the others, for the rules must be kept, but it will be training." And he made a quick sketch in the air, what looked like three lines, with his finger wiggling briefly at the end of two of the lines.

Lennac pursed his lips in a silent whistle. "Oh, yes." And he saluted, the smack of his hand against his tunic underscoring his conviction.

Senrid stopped behind his chair, thumping his fist lightly on the chair back. "Go ahead and take your liberty-watch, Lennac. I'm going to keep Shevraeth here for a bit, since he's the only ready-to-hand foreigner we've got."

Lennac saluted and vanished through the open door. His footsteps rapidly diminished, then Liere dropped her legs down and hopped from the table. "Fenis is back," she said, cocking her head.

"Gonna get a riding lesson?" Senrid asked.

"At night," Liere answered. "I want to learn how to ride at—" Her brow wrinkled and her eyes blanked.

Shevraeth realized she was listening on some plane unavailable to him—and Senrid, also with that blank look, was answering.

The moment lasted only a heartbeat or two, then Liere gave Shevraeth a shy smile and flitted through the door, her bare feet soundless on the steps.

Senrid said, "I didn't lie to Lennac, though I misled him. He probably thinks we're talking languages and so forth. He can't know—none of them can know—but I want you to lead an attack on the city."

Shevraeth repeated, "Attack?" Then realized of course, he meant a war game of some sort.

"Covert attack. Yes. I need to plan the defense of the city, though if Norsunder gets this far, we're probably lost. I don't know. But I have to try, don't you see? But I can't find any records for the situation we're in now." He was pacing again, quick steps, a fist thumping table, chair, window sill, then back again, as he passed. "You because no one will expect you, and because you don't really know the city yet, am I right?"

Shevraeth hesitated. He'd been to a number of eateries and inns, of course, but Senelac had always had the lead, and his attention had been on her, not on their route. He'd only noticed somewhat vaguely that they seldom went the same way any second time. "That's right," he said finally.

"Excellent. First game, see, the commander doesn't know the city. Keriam is in the process of finding you some attackers—never mind what we're looking for. They will only be told their commander is at the academy, and nothing else. They'll accept you as their commander because they will have Keriam's word that it's by my order. One thing you can attest to in our favor is that if Marlovens are given a clear chain of command they generally fall right in. So you are going to take down the city however you can."

"But—what about the city people?"

"Oh, they'll go right along. Most of 'em with enthusiasm. Before my uncle, apparently all-city drills were more or less a regular occurrence, going way back. If we shut down business the crown pays for food and drink, makes it a special occasion. The city folk used to love getting involved, and I don't think it'll be any different now. I'll give you the list of symbols—they'll all know them, too. Like, your people will have strips of red cloth if you discover you have to set fire to a room or a house. Citizens have to stop and count to a certain number for fighting a wood-structure fire, and a different number, lower, for stone. Everyone uses wood weapons, well chalked. You take an arm or leg hit, you can move, but not use the limb. Hits in kill parts, you're supposed to fall in place and wait until the bells for the end, because they have to practice getting around bodies. Though older people don't have to lie on stones. They can tie their kill cloth around a footstool or chair and put it out in their place."

Shevraeth winced. Then, trying to hide his reaction, he said, "But is it really covert if they know the attack is coming—if they are watching for it?"

"No and yes. Yes, because I want them in the habit of watching. Norsundrians will not dress like us, they almost never use disguise. There's too much, oh, historical terror attached to the sight of those gray uniforms. I will give the city a real surprise attack, but after we have a few of these planned-for ones. Right now, I want it as real as we can get it, short of hurting anyone."

"Understood."

"But you have to think like a Norsundrian. You don't care about life, you have a goal: to do whatever it takes to capture this city with a small force. This first game, you'll be limited—it's to be a covert attack. Supposing they sent their warriors over the border one at a time—assuming they break my wards and . . . well, never mind the magic end. But they don't want to raise an alarm. Depending on how this one goes, next we'll do a full-on war attack, the entire academy against the city, and in that one we'll assume they'll have made maps, so the boys knowing the city will be appropriate. D'ya see?"

Shevraeth whooshed out his breath. "A Norsundrian, am I?"

Senrid did not smile. "Good practice for you. If—when—they come, your own kingdom will not be exempt."

"Right." Shevraeth said, trying out the idea, "If I think like an attacker, then I can . . . plan for defense at home." *And Galdran will have me assassinated, if I am too competent?*

*Later. Later.*

"That's the idea." Senrid dropped into his chair, but his hands were still restless. "Soon as Keriam sends me the signal that he has his people, I'll set a day. The first one, no one in the city can move until someone comes with the word, or they see the enemy. We'll provide you with some kind of outfit to mark you and your command as the enemy, leave that to me. Your job is to plan what a Norsundrian would do, and how to do it, without actually seeing the city—my ancestors have always been untrusting, and never permitted city maps to be made. You notice there are few street signs. In the past, when the bells rang for attack, there was always someone whose job it was to remove the ones near them. Not that the castle can be hidden, but anything that slows an enemy down is a good defensive tactic."

Shevraeth thought, *The first goal of a Norsundrian would be to kill you—unless they want you to be twisted to their service. I don't know which one is worse.* He said, "Are you playing, too?"

"Absolutely. I expect you to come after me. If you do win, at least I get a chance to learn something, and not in a Norsundrian dungeon." His tight-cornered grin flashed, and Shevraeth realized the whispers about Senrid were indeed true. He had indeed been in a Norsundrian dungeon. And had somehow gotten out alive.

Senrid went on, "Guard captains as well—if you can find 'em. If it's going to work, the game has to be bigger than the all-academy game out on the fields." His voice lowered, husky with strain. "I've got to learn how to defend this city. If I can." He looked away, then up. "When Siamis came, they used a combination of magic and then warriors. I think I have the magic end worked out—my friend Hibern and some others have been playing around with wards and so forth—but we need plans for the fighting part."

Shevraeth hesitated.

"Speak," Senrid said impatiently.

"Well, I do not wish to seem to impugn your thinking, but don't you have an experienced commander who could give you plans based on experience?"

Now Senrid was drumming with his knuckles on the table. "In a word, no. Keriam is all I have left of the competent army leaders. Though I've got good captains, all of them are on duty at the borders. Forthan would be running it, but he's not back yet from where I sent him, and he's the best of the young ones. You have to realize that the army at command level is mostly young. My uncle saw to it that all the good ones either suffered heroic accidents in the field, or else were quietly assassinated, leaving mostly old men who could keep their heads down and endure. And then there were the stinkers who supported him. Gone, now. This, too, is a Marloven tradition, though you won't see it lauded in the records. Kill off the good commanders who don't back you soon's you get power."

The Regent sounded like Galdran. *We are not so very different after all, Remalna and Marloven Hess.* And again Shevraeth appreciated the reach of his father's vision.

"I know I have smart boys in the academy with more experience at command than you, but I really think you are smart enough to put your mind to this matter—and you are not familiar with the city as they all are. Right now that's what I want. A Norsundrian won't know the city, so I want to hear about trying to sneak through it from your point-of-view. Might help us plan a better defense. So will you do it?"

The situation, the new possibilities in the real world, Senrid's tension, all compounded Shevraeth's own unease. "Right. All right. Have you any records on battles specifically with Norsunder?"

"Not much. You'd think we had, wouldn't you? Maybe my uncle destroyed them. Anyway, Hibern, the friend I mentioned before. She's off studying magic, said she'd search the archives in Sartor. She has talked with Queen Yustnesveas of Sartor, who is a scholar and mage more than she is a queen. Yet. Anyway, Hibern believes she'll let her loose in their archives, no problem."

Shevraeth tried to hide his amazement at Senrid's world-wide reach. He didn't brag, these famous names and places were just part of his life.

So was the threat.

"You'll keep this one unspoken, right?"

Shevraeth lifted his hands, gesturing from old habit in truth mode. "Of course. So if the academy gets a defensive assignment, I go along with it?"

"Absolutely. Keriam will see to it your assignment will be something that makes it possible to sneak away without letting down your riding. So. If Hibern gets back before we pick a date, I'll let you know what she finds. Any last questions?"

"No."

Senrid slapped the table with a flat hand, and then got to his feet. His restlessness made Shevraeth restless. He gripped his hands tightly behind his back.

Senrid said, "Ask me anything. Lennac and Marec will probably ask about your interview. You have to have an answer for their questions or they will suspect something."

"Very we—ah, what was this?" Shevraeth made the three lines in the air. "Tevac being in my charge."

"Ah." Senrid grabbed up a pen lying at the other end of the table, dipped it in the inkwell, scratched on a piece of paper that had cryptic numbers and signs on it in the same neat hand Shevraeth had seen on the map so long ago.

Senrid drew a line with a slight curving hook at one end, then just under it a parallel line with an almond-shape at the end under the first line's hook. Then below that, the third line, ending in an odd bracketing version of one of the Marloven letters. It was a highly stylized shape of a speeding raptor, beak open—that was the bracket—an inimical eye above. Yet if you turned it sideways, there were three letters of the Marloven alphabet, stylized, but recognizable, with long tails.

"Symbol for those we call the king's scouts," Senrid said. "More like a secret arm. Short chain of command—their orders come directly from me. Parallel to the military, so I can put them above or below any rank, for temporary orders, at need. But they usually act alone, or at most in twos or threes."

"You mean spies?" Shevraeth asked, but before his natural distaste could show in his face, once again his father's words whispered in his mind, from long ago: *May as well call these trusted servants of mine couriers, though they are really spies. They don't trouble anyone unless attacked, but they gather information and bring it to me.*

Images of quiet, bearded Leffain flickered through his mind, quick as fireflies in the wind. How he knew Marloven. How he talked to every single person on the ship on their journey west on the Sartoran Sea. How he chatted at every inn they stopped at, and once or twice had vanished, leaving Shevraeth to study or sleep or just roam about sight-seeing, and he'd never explained where he was.

Senrid was watching him closely. "They were spies and assassins in the past, and their history has varied according to the kings who used them. My uncles' scouts all vanished the week before I took the throne."

"Vanished?"

"Killed. But not on my order—I hadn't known what to do about them—they were hand-chosen by Uncle Tdanerend, you see, and trained to think themselves above any moral constraint, their only limit the Regent's will. Very secret. Keriam didn't even know them all. But someone not only knew them all, had them taken out in a single week. And I don't know by whose command any more than I know who did the deed."

Silence. A night bird cried in the distance, its low sound faint through the open window. Shevraeth's hands had gone cold; this was probably the most frightening thing he had learned in two years of grim lessons.

His throat was dry. "So you don't know if was an ally or an enemy with his own plans."

"Right. But failing more information, I've been building my own scout arm. People quick to think, to look outside the rules, while still maintaining honor. Good at action. I don't want assassins, I want people who not only get news, but can figure out a way to solve a problem with whatever is at hand."

"People? Or men."

"People." Senrid's quick smile this time was bland.

By now Shevraeth's mind was on the verge of dizziness, though not quite that—it was the effect of too many new ideas, chased by a rapid series of reactions. He'd not gotten used to it by now, but he recognized it.

Senrid, still short, younger than Shevraeth, looked like a boy in everything but his eyes. "So if Tevac does what I think he's going to, it proves he knows how to think around the rules. I'll see that he gets the training he needs. Got enough?"

"History," Shevraeth said. "And the meaning of words."

Senrid flicked up his hand in salute.

Shevraeth bumped his fist against his heart, the salute instinctive now, and left.

He stopped just inside the academy walls, picked a fence out of the line of sight of the academy barracks, and sat down to think it all through as the wind steadily turned more moist, and clouds piled overhead.

When the first spatters of rain began, he ran the last few steps to the Puppy Pit.

Which was quiet except for the slow breathing of small boys in sleep.

Lennac and Marec were lying in wait in Marec's room, a single candle burning on Marec's tiny camp table as they played a game of cards'n'shards.

"What was all that about?" Marec asked, throwing the hand-painted cards on the table. "He kept you a long time."

"Oh, we didn't talk much. I took a walk, then sat. It's perfect weather out there. Was, until the rain began." By now it was a steady tippety-tap against the windows.

Marec said, testing, "Word is, the king's been out of the kingdom a lot. Did he go to yours?"

"Not that he said. We talked some history. And also about the meaning of words."

Marec rolled his eyes. "Better you than me."

Lennac lifted his brows, but didn't say anything.

∞(R?E)∞

*Father: my next assignment is as a Norsundrian commander. I am to attack Choreid Dhelerei, perhaps the most guarded city in the world, outside of Narad in Chwahirsland and perhaps one or two others in the northern half of the world. Yes, you did read those words. After I recovered from the shock, my reaction was twofold: fear that I will not be adequate to the task, and determination that I will use for Remalna whatever I end up learning. Senrid said Remalna will not be exempt from any attack, if Norsunder does come. No, he said when. Anyway I cannot ask anyone here for advice, as my being commander is secret. So if you have any thoughts to share, here is the brief outline of what I will be doing . . .*

*. . . and so, my son, I will study the family papers for descriptions of Norsunder's taking of Sartor a century ago. I have not reread them—it was heart-breaking—but I will begin studying them tonight with your assignment in mind.*
*Russav and your mother send their greetings; Galdran has been keeping everyone close at hand. Perhaps related to that—he does not want anyone on the roads seeing it, that much is clear—I have another report to make. This is another of those situations in which one truly hates to be proved right. But word has reached me—and I waited only until I could send a courier to testify to its truth or falsity—that Galdran has ordered the renovation of Chovilun Fortress, so long left in disuse as it is not a home,*

*or even a center for overseeing a county or duchy. It has historically had one function: to house warriors. No, two functions: that extensive dungeon under ground, from which, as you will remember from your lessons, great numbers of prisoners never again emerged.*

# Thirty-one

"In history class they were talking about the Vasande Leror conflict. But no one gave any details," Shevraeth said to Senelac. "I checked the map, saw that it's a tiny country—it's half the size of mine, and I thought we were small—to the east of us here. But anyway, apparently the former Regent sent people to take it, or take the royal city, or what exactly happened? The master didn't say, and I was afraid to ask lest they don't go into details before the foreigner."

"No, it's more that everyone knows them, and many of us have relatives involved. My big brother was there. And, well, most everyone is pretty ashamed of it, in short."

Stad grimaced. "Though the truth is, the Regent gave shameful orders. The light cavalry tried to postpone their carrying out by a lot of unnecessary riding around in the depth of winter. The king was missing at the time, you see, and the Regent had assumed the crown at last." He opened a hand toward Senelac. "But—well, wasn't your oldest brother part of the riding who found the king?"

Senelac jerked her chin up. She wasn't sure how she felt being caught talking to the foreigner like this. Though there was nothing wrong: they were outside the academy, they both had before them slates full of the cryptic markings that anyone (such as Stad and Marec, for instance, who had stumbled on them while in search of pastry on their own free watch) would immediately recognize were part of the command class problem, which was to figure out a way to attack the city, and then how to defend against their own attack. So if there was nothing wrong, she had to identify why she was so annoyed.

Stad went on, "Only a half-dozen Lerorans were killed, in spite of the Regent's orders for a blood bath, but the truth is, anyone who has to obey shameful orders later feels shame when the necessity to obey is gone."

"There were plenty," Marec said, unwontedly sober, "who supported the Regent. Though they hated him as much as anyone did. But their own actions might make them accountable if he were replaced."

The three Marlovans watched the foreigner for signs because the truth was, they'd inherited a bit of their families' shame for the regency years. But though Shevraeth did not evidence any contempt, or disgust, or even a sense of judgment, he was sickened. His court mask thus protected them all; meanwhile, his foremost emotion was a kind of horror as he envisioned the disaster Senrid had faced once his uncle was gone.

Temporarily gone. He'd been sent back by Norsunder at the beginning of the Siamis year, that he knew from Forthan—though by then the Regent's will had been suborned, and he was more or less a puppet. And that was another appalling thing to contemplate.

Senelac said briskly, "Anyway, it fell out well enough, considering. For our king and the Leroran king are friends, so there won't be any more of that."

Marec grinned. "Though how they can call so small a piece of land a kingdom is beyond me. It's smaller than most jarlates."

Senelac returned his grin. "My brother said their royal castle is smaller than the academy stable—and about as comfortable."

"Speaking of defense." Stad tapped their slates. "We were just in search of pastry in order to fortify us against the sorry fact that we're grassed at this particular problem."

Shevraeth usually did not take the initiative, but he knew that this problem was set to help him. He meant to use the opportunity.

So he set aside the dirty dishes and pulled his slate forward. "We've been coming to a similar conclusion. You can hold a walled city against a siege if there isn't a powerful Norsundrian mage along to breach the walls, but covert infiltration seems to be a bigger threat than an enormous army."

Senelac's annoyance had vanished. Marec and Stad seemed to be utterly unaware of any reason for her to be sitting with Shevraeth beyond class preparation. Boys, she knew, were not subtle. If they thought there was any spark between Shevraeth and herself, they would have been smirking, nudging the foreigner, making what they fondly assumed were funny cracks. Nothing whatsoever. Phew.

But she'd never come back to this bakery with Shevraeth, that was for certain.

Stad hunched forward, drawing the others unconsciously inward. The sounds of others chatting, the clink of spoons against ceramic dishes, the clunk of mugs on wooden tables, all faded into the background as four smart minds tried to find ways to defend a city against evil infiltrators.

⋙ ❦ ⋘

*. . . but I never expected it to be fun. I'm sure my father will agree that invasion defense games might become a necessity in Renselaeus if Galdran's acquisitiveness worsens. You must be there—I think you'll have as much fun as I did.*

*No—I can hear you saying "But I haven't your training." Do you think that availed me anything my first, second, or third try? Yes, there have been several. Why I haven't had the time to write. Despite the flat-out failure of my first attempt (we were caught almost before we got in the gates) Senrid wanted me to keep at it, after he'd redesigned the rules. So we tried with the city knowing—they sat on their rooftops watching us—then with the city not knowing. That time we made it much farther in. Both times we were all dressed in black, including masks, so of course I had us going in at night. But the city is lit by glow-torches and globes all over, so there really are few dark corners. One thing Senrid is testing is whether the lights favor the inhabitants or invaders. Already there are no street signs at all. The Wand Guild has been hired to direct lost traders. The judgment is still not in on the matter of lighting, though he seems to be favoring a lit city unless there is danger, and then dark all over, except where the danger is reported, which, you might imagine, calls for a complicated warning system . . .*

The fourth attempt, Senrid did not want the city forewarned. This time he let the invaders, who now knew one another after having worked together over several weeks, dress civilian. The idea now was that Norsunder's mysterious leaders might try a covert snatch or assassination.

Shevraeth had gotten used to his job as Evil Invader, and so his plan was a lot more bold than any of his previous attempts.

He ordered most of his team to set fires at crucial junctures all over the city just after the midnight bells, and while the city was busy dealing with the threat of fire (he could hear people impatiently shouting out numbers in cadence as they went through the motions of fire drill—wood fires 500 counts, small fires in stone places 200 counts—as he slipped along fences and rooftops) Shevraeth led his chosen pair of Norsundrian assassins toward the castle.

And so while Senrid's doubled castle guard watched the city Shevraeth and his two assassins drifted in through the ancient archway—the old stone smelling of moss in the cold air—that connected the castle to the academy. They came out not far from the massive buildings that made up the throne room and the great hall, joined by an archway big enough to permit full ridings in days of yore.

They avoided the throne room, choosing the hall—to find that the doors had been bolted. Shevraeth flicked up two fingers, barely visible in the ruddy flicker of mage-torches. The three were dressed in black, though if they got inside, their first job was to find servant clothing.

Two fingers: Plan Two. Kitchens.

None of them knew the exact layout of the castle. Surely Norsunder didn't have a plan of the castle either. So how would Norsundrians find the kitchens? Like anyone else, using a combination of sense and their noses. The kitchens had to be somewhere midway between the great hall, which is where the jarls were served meals each New Year's Convocation, and the Residence.

They encountered more small courtyards than they would have believed possible. The castle was much larger than it seemed even looming above the north end of the academy, but the nose part of their plan did not betray them. The toughest challenge was staying out of sight of the sentries. They had to slink along the walls from shadow to shadow, freezing in place as sentries patrolled the endless walks overhead. The sentries were alert, and regular, and so the invaders' progress was a grindingly frustrating series of fits and starts.

But make it they did. Somewhere someone was slow-cooking herb-braised chicken, and the savory scent drew them as unerringly as footsteps painted on the flagstones.

They reached the bakehouse, and one of the doors was even unlocked. There was a torch high on an adjacent wall. No sentry immediately in view. One by one they slipped in.

Empty. The Fire Sticks had been diminished to mere licks of flame, the food to braise through the night and morning. Another look of triumph between Shevraeth and his assassins, who were young men having left the academy within the past five years. Despite the problems besetting the academy under the Regent, Senrid seemed to feel that these two had gained superlative skills. Shevraeth knew them only as Jarend and Keth.

He made a gesture down his length, they signified assent with two fingers upraised, and on tiptoe they each picked one of the three doors and eased it open.

One was to a pantry where, from the smell, herbs were stored; that door was shut. The second was to another storage area with sacks and bags and barrels of foodstuffs.

The third was to a hallway, lit by a glowglobe—but Shevraeth, who had picked that door, heard the whisper of footsteps and eased it closed again. What now?

Jarend raised a hand in question toward the second door. Yes, that one ought to have more doors, if it was filled with flour and rice and vegetables. The bake house and the bread room would both need access.

Keth kept the bake house door open as Shevraeth ventured inside. Almost immediately he stepped out of the slant of light and knocked into something, but caught it: glass jar, filled with something that rattled. Set it gently onto the floor. Moving more slowly, his fingers extended, toes working along the cold, dry stone of the floor, he shuffled his way around the perimeter of the room, easing past the maze of narrow aisles made up of tall stacks of stored goods. What seemed an entire watch later his fingers bumped into a wall, and then he felt his way along until he reached a door frame, and at last, a latch.

He motioned the others inside. The two joined Shevraeth, and they tried the next door. Just a finger's breadth first, listening. Nothing.

Wider. A kitchen—dark. Smelled like cinnamon. They slipped inside, saw pans of bread dough rising under cloths; Shevraeth checked one. Thin twists of dough. So no one was expected back for a while—these had probably just been set out. Jarend and Keth looked around. No aprons or clothes.

But there had to be a preparation room, Shevraeth thought, looking around. Here were tins and trays readied for the morning baking, with the first bread of the day rising. So . . . yes, that room over there should be the prep room, because it, too, had a door that would open into the other end of the storage room.

He pointed, Keth and Jarend moved to other doors to guard. Shevraeth eased into an enormous prep room. On either side of him, shelves of linens. Within ten heartbeats, the three had pulled off their black tunics and masks, and wore aprons hastily tied over their rumpled plain shirts.

They dashed across the room, which was dimly lit by torchlight through high windows, to another door—a hall. Empty. They'd just all slipped out when they heard footsteps. Back inside the bread room.

On the next foray they made it to a stair before they heard footsteps—retreat—footsteps from below. Shevraeth pointed, one up, one down, orders he didn't need to make as Jarend was already running soundlessly upstairs to pause against the hidden crook of the landing, and Keth vanished outside the door below.

"Oh, burn and blast," came a muffled voice from below.

Above, Jarend whipped his wooden knife lightly across the neck of a hefty woman who backed up a step in surprise, nearly stumbled, and then glared at Jarend as she sat down on the step.

The three ran up past her as she crossed her arms across an impressive bosom and sent an unequivocal look of disgust after them—she had to stay silent and dead, when it was clear she would have loved to have discovered them and made a blow for the Forces of Good.

Down a narrow hallway, and they encountered two or three other servants, all of them tired, on their way to retire for the night. They 'killed' them all—but of course the recumbent bodies were soon discovered, and the alarm went up as the 'dead' servants returned to work.

After that the search was on, and they just reached the stairway to the Residence before the Guard sandwiched them.

Senrid was grimly pleased by how far they'd gotten, and promptly reordered his whole castle's patrol system.

Shevraeth's next invasion was short-lived. This time they attacked the far gate, but everyone was on the watch for a ruse, and the alarm bells rang as soon as they reached the very first castle courtyard, where they discovered new lights burning. Guards pounced as they vaulted down from the wall. Everyone was relieved. The weather was a thin, chilly sleet, which leached all possible fun from the exercise.

The next attack was led by Forthan, who had returned from wherever he had been sent.

With Forthan, the objective shifted. Now Norsunder was expected to know the city, and to have a leader well-versed in military actions both overt and covert. Shevraeth was no longer in charge, but he was tapped to serve on the attack squad.

Shevraeth discovered he was both relieved and a little disappointed.

The disappointment vanished when, at their first meeting, Forthan said, "Unlike Norsundrians, let me make it clear, any good ideas, you bark 'em out. We have to give the guard and the city a hard run, or we're not doing our job. Now, what have you observed so far?"

Shevraeth, Keth, Jarend, and some of the others all spoke in turn, Forthan listening solemnly, head bent, his strong, rough-palmed hands dangling loose between his knees. They were camped on the grounds just outside the academy, where the little boys usually had their afternoon games. No one could see or hear them. By now, of course, the other seniors knew that Shevraeth had been made part of the attack team, which had surprised some, disgusted others, and gratified his friends. It also increased their expectancy—Shevraeth realized that they all wanted to be called upon to attack their royal city. They considered it a great honor—and a fun prospect.

"Here's our plan," Forthan said, when everyone had spoken. "We're going to infiltrate just before dawn. Come in with the market people. Then most will attack the castle in force. I want three of you to sweep behind and take the king from the other end, as covertly as you can. Shevraeth, Jarend, Keth, you three have been running together, so take this first one, will you? I'm going to command the diversion." He grinned. "We're gonna make this one hard, loud, and nasty. I want bodies piled—just the way Norsunder will come against us."

The men smacked hands against chests, echoed a moment later by Shevraeth, who didn't think, just acted.

This time they made it all the way.

Bells had been ringing, guards summoned to their stations. The bell-signal was the one for a major attack. Clearly the assumption was that the attackers were throwing everything behind their assault on the gates.

So the king worked on in his office as the King's Guard converged on the city gates, where a mass melee was taking place, the 'dead' having to pay for treats for the 'defenders' later on.

The castle was quiet—until the three kicked the door open and charged.

Shevraeth hesitated a heartbeat, not knowing if he ought to tackle the king of the Marlovens—what the repercussions might be. But the other two had no such hesitation, and Shevraeth realized when he saw the two spread to trap Senrid between them that they were deadly serious.

Keth feinted, Senrid vaulted over his desk, sending his own papers up in snow flurries. Jarend launched over a chair and tackled him with a sickening thud. They hit the ground with twin "Woof!"s.

Then Senrid turned into a squirming, kicking, punching bundle of fury that the larger Jarend struggled to contain. They were both crimson-faced with effort, and Jarend's nose was bleeding by the time he got Senrid pinned down, his face mashed into his rug, as the last of the papers swayed gently down to rest on his recumbent form.

"Okay," he said into the carpet. "Uh, that means let me up."

Jarend let go at once and extended a hand, which Senrid took. Restored to his feet, he revealed that he, too, had a bloody nose.

His door banged open a moment later, and Liere ran in. "Caught," she exclaimed. "I told you, I told you!" She pointed a finger, her voice as shrill as any ten year old girl. "I told you!"

Senrid responded with a breathtakingly vile curse, to which Liere paid no heed. "Told you, told you," she said, over and over.

"Good job, you three," Senrid said in a muffled voice, hand to nose, then he followed Liere out, and the three Norsundrians listened to their two kid voices diminishing.

Jarend said, "I hope that shows him."

Shevraeth switched his gaze to Keth, who flicked his hand open. Shevraeth was about to ask what he was missing, but the Marlovens' expressions smoothed to identical blankness.

"Let's go report," Jarend said. "Before Forthan kills off half the city."

He and Keth righted a chair that had been knocked over, but they left the papers where they were. No one wanted to be nosing through kingly business.

⊱❦⊰

"You did it," Senelac said, the moment she saw him.

It was two days later. They met under a tree across from a saddle-maker's. Her suggested meeting places had gotten harder to find, but on the other hand he knew the city a great deal better, and he rather liked the challenge of finding his way to them.

Not that that mattered. What did was how the chilly wind that smelled of oncoming rain brought out the glow in her face. The way the wind tousled her hair and pressed her tunic close, outlining her shape, made him go hot and cold inside.

"Don't talk yet." She raised a hand. "Let's get to the place." She set out at her usual fast stride, without looking back.

"There it is," she said abruptly, and soon they were sitting in a tiny eatery with low ceilings and little alcoves. It looked very old, but it was warm, and the food, though plain, was plentiful.

As soon as they were done eating she leaned forward and grinned at him. And said again, "You did it."

"You mean, captured the king? It was actually Forthan's plan, and Jarend made the capture."

She waggled her hand then lifted it—a gesture he knew by now was dismissal of extraneous details. "You attackers did it. You proved to him he can be taken. Oh," she said quickly, forestalling an imagined comment that he was not about to make, "he'll keep testing. Trying. This winter, those who stay over will be running city attacks, you can wager anything. But like Liere said, he knows he can be taken."

He sat back. "Bringing me to my own questions."

The innkeeper removed their dishes, and she put her elbows on the table, hands together into a fist, and rested her chin on them. "Questions?"

"Lots of them." And a pause.

"Go on," she invited.

"First, why is it so important that he learn he can be taken? I mean, isn't it obvious?"

Not obvious, from the way she shifted her gaze to the fire and frowned. Then she looked up. "There are two problems here, can you see? If Norsunder sends an army against us, that means they want this land, and we fight to the last man or woman to keep them from taking it. But if they send in covert teams, they want *him*. To twist to their purposes and use as a weapon, maybe with us behind him. They learned during the Siamis time that though we could be forced to take Tdanerend's orders again, at the risk of innocents being killed, nobody could make us fight well. It was a long, slow, silent war of attrition, is how my brother put it. Badly saddled horses, bad patrols that saw nothing, slow moving, everything utterly incompetent. They were too stretched to deal with us because the mages kept closing Norsunder's rifts, which meant they didn't have the forces they thought they'd have. Anyway, Senrid commanding us, now that's different. And they have to know it by now. So if they subvert him . . ."

"I see. He'd make a terrible weapon, marching against your neighbors at the head of this vast army."

"Exactly."

Shevraeth shook his head. "Then why did he stop growing? Smart as he is, and I've never met anyone smarter, if he's got all these problems, how can staying a boy possibly accomplish anything? I'd think he'd regret there isn't some way to grow faster."

"And then have to deal with being even more of a target? As well as, oh, personal reasons I don't quite understand and don't ask about. Not my business. But I do understand one thing. When he was a prisoner before, Detlev—he's even shadier than Siamis—said to him, 'You're not worth my time,' or something to that effect. Well, that was before Senrid helped Liere go up against Siamis. He doesn't want to be worth Detlev's time, and so he stopped growing as a way of hiding in plain sight—to seem not worth time, though of course he spends days and nights learning as fast as he can. But he wants them to think he's just a boy, they should wait, and if they do get him, well, about his only defense is to be a stupid, tiresome boy, until he can get away. But we don't want it to get that far. If they send coverts, we want him to run. He thinks running is cowardly. We think it's smart. If he's gone, we can play dead again."

"It's an insane burden," Shevraeth said.

"Yes, but it's one everyone is facing. Just, many don't see it. Can't, or won't," she answered soberly. "We Marlovens just stick out a little farther. But the danger is shared by all. Even the courtiers in Colend. And the Delfin Islanders there in the middle of the ocean." She jerked her thumb westward.

Shevraeth grimaced. The chill of the outside air seemed to have fingered its way in, breathing ice down the back of his neck. "Well, all the more reason to get busy on our last assignment," he said, pulling his slate in front of him.

The last command class would be held just after the academy games, which would also be discussed. It was the end of another year, one that had seemed both endless and swift.

&CR&ƆCR

There were two notable events that occurred after the last game, on which he was a riding leader for the losing army.

They marched back, having sustained two thunderstorms on the way. Shevraeth was then swept off to command class, so he was not on duty when, *some*how, Tevac and Mondar got half the scrubs organized and while everyone was either at the baths or in the city on liberty, they shifted all the furnishings of Scout-hound House out into their court, arranged just as they had been inside, the trunks all in the right place but open—just before a thunderstorm.

A score—but completely within the rules that Lennac had set.

The scrubs thus lost any chance of an end year scarfle, but they felt the triumph of that massive score against Scout-hound House would be sung about through history, so it was a fair trade.

The second thing occurred on Shevraeth's and Senelac's last meeting in the city. The weather was cold, rainy, but he was there anyway, and so was she. They talked over the game, laughed over the triumph over Scout-hound House. Tevac and Mondar had been ordered to shift it all back by themselves, and put each piece of sodden bedding and clothing through the cleaning frame—but the work was considered a banner of triumph. They talked about winter plans, she with her horses at home, he with the studies he planned to make here, and then they began their walk back.

And then Shevraeth said, awkwardly, flushing because he knew he sounded awkward, "I—I wanted to thank you for this year." Silence. "For sharing your ideas." Silence. "I've enjoyed these meetings. Here in the city. So much. Talking to you." Silence. He was too distracted to notice that she'd abruptly turned, leading the way down a narrow alley at a brisk pace. Despite the cold, dreary mizzle, his ears burned, his collar had suddenly become too tight. Feeling abysmally stupid, wishing he'd kept his mouth shut, he finished on a mumble, "And, well, just thanks."

They'd reached a little park. Most of the trees had already shed their leaves, though the perimeter was surrounded by thick shrubs. It was a secluded little spot in the midst of the city.

"The girls come here when they're twoing," she said briskly, and before he could react, she grabbed his head, pulled it down—their noses bumped, her fingers were cold—but he forgot that, forgot everything, when her soft lips met his in a long, warm, exhilarating kiss.

# Thirty-two

S he was gone the next day.

He was left to watch the packing, departure, and gradual emptying of the academy, until there were just a few of them left in the cold stone city under washing rain.

The command was handed down to shift their things to the senior barracks—where next year he'd be living. Strange, that idea.

Also strange was the order to report for new clothing. His wrists stuck out of his shirt cuffs, and the knees of his trousers had crept upward. So had everyone else's, so no one noticed.

When he went back to pick up his new clothes, he saw something added, something long and black. In wonder he picked up the long, very fine-woven woolen cloak characteristic of the seniors and the Guard. The wool, which naturally resisted wet, was reinforced by magic, which made the cloaks highly prized.

He looked up. The young Guard acting as quartermaster shrugged. "You'll be a senior come spring, might as well have it now. Next year you'll be doing night rides on the perimeter at games."

"Right," Shevraeth said, walking back to the senior barracks with the fine black wool carried in his arms. Despite the cold, he would not dare wear it, even though maybe five people might see him at most. He already knew how fast gossip spread.

There was no possibility he'd wear any of the senior gear until the orders came to move into the first year senior barracks. He was so used to how things worked by now he scarcely ever thought about invisible rules. Because by now, most of them had become visible.

&#8270;&#8270;&#8270;

One moment Russav Savona was savoring the delight of a fragrant girl in his arms—their lips met—a heartbeat after that pain flared across his vision, a bolt of lightning. Not from the kiss. He sprawled on the ground blinking up at a face crimson with rage.

"Anderic," Savona said, trying to regain his wits.

Renna had nearly fallen off the bench when Anderic shoved Savona. She jumped up. "You idiot!"

Anderic Gharivar snapped back, "You're only kissing him to make me jealous. Just like he's kissing you to make Tamara jealous. That's disgusting."

"To you," Renna retorted, her thin cheeks flashing red patches along the bones. She crossed her arms. "I assure you, it wasn't disgusting to me."

Savona got to his feet, dusting off his tunic. "Not to me either." He felt uncomfortable. In the year since Anderic had followed the new Baron Debegri to court, Savona had come to thoroughly dislike him. The fact that he was right only annoyed Savona more. "Take yourself off, Anderic. No one invited you to interfere."

Anderic flicked a sneer his way, then deliberately spat.

Renna whirled around. "How loathsome! Don't ever speak to me ag—"

Anderic caught her arm. She instantly began tugging to free herself.

"You—I won't—" he began, but was drowned out by her repeated "Let me go!"s.

Savona brought his fist down hard onto Anderic's arm. The other boy's hand spasmed, and Renna jerked her arm loose from his grip.

Anderic flung himself onto Savona, kicking, punching, howling curses. Savona got in as many punches as he took—but Anderic only got angrier. He strove to get his fingers round Savona's neck, shouting, "I'll kill you! I'll kill you!"

It's difficult to say how that fight would have resolved. Savona had not been all that angry when he began, because he knew he'd had mixed motives for a charming bit of dalliance that wasn't the least serious for either of them, but a fist in his eye and strong fingers clawing for his neck changed that.

Renna whirled around, reached down behind the bench, dipped her beautiful hat into the icy water, and flung the contents on them, splattering both boys equally.

The water had no effect.

What did was the voice of the king.

"What's all this?"

The boys dropped one another with more haste than grace—though those watching knew better than to laugh. The two bowed, water dripping off their noses (mixed with blood in Savona's case), and Renna curtseyed, her bared hair riffling in the wind, the ruined hat clutched tightly in her hand.

"Nothing, sire," she said, when she realized neither of the boys would speak first. "Just a disagreement."

"Over?" Galdran prompted, his eyes narrowing as he glanced at Renna's head. He did not like anyone bare-headed except at his invitation. How could they have missed him? He loomed there so huge and solid, his long red hair below the golden coronet lifting in the cold wind. He fingered his mustache, waiting for Renna to hat herself—and to answer.

She gritted her teeth and crammed the hat on her head. Water dripped into her eyes and off her nose. The brim drooped soggily down, blocking half her vision.

She heard a strangled "Whuff" behind her—someone trying valiantly not to snicker.

Savona said, "A disagreement about a kiss."

Anderic sent him a poisonous look, adding in a surly tone, "A person has a right to resent it when *he* kisses everyone in sight."

"So Savona lacks discrimination?" Galdran asked, laughing. *Har har*, a heavy sound—less humor than mockery. But it served as a reminder, and behind the three came the obedient, if forced, laughs.

"He can pester anyone else with his attentions. Not Renna. She and I have an understanding. She's just kissing him to rile me."

Renna flushed, her jaw locked against retorting.

"Well, Savona?" Galdran prompted.

Savona said, "No one was pestering anyone. Until he came along."

He immediately regretted it. He couldn't tell what Galdran wanted, but at the sudden smile on the king's face, the widening of his pale blue eyes, he knew that he'd fumbled into saying what the king had wanted to hear.

And sure enough. "So? Is that so? And no challenge? Have I a court full of cowards?"

Anderic sent a sullen look Savona's way, rubbing a stray lock of brown hair off his brow. "I'd like it fine to let a little of that hot blood."

"You already have." Savona rolled his eyes toward the sky as he mopped his nose with his besorcelled handkerchief.

Several muffled titters escaped from courtiers gathered behind. Savona rather thought one of those was Tamara's.

"Well, Savona?" came the hated voice. "Afraid to take up the challenge?"

What was there to say? "No." And, in a weak attempt to get them all away, so maybe the subject would be forgotten— "Here, I'm freezing. Why don't we change?"

"With such hot blood?" the king retorted. "Here's a challenge. Pay attention, *your grace*."

Savona said somewhat desperately, "We have to arrange seconds, weapons. Ground. And my eye—"

"Not," Galdran Merindar said, "with me here to assure fairness. You may send for weapons. This ground will do." He glanced up at the low white sky.

They all noticed the tiny white flakes beginning to drift down.

"No. Inside," the king declared. "As for that eye," he added with his usual cruel humor, "Would you stop defending me against invaders if someone from Denlieff hit you in the eye? I assure you, *he* wouldn't stop to wait for it to heal. My fencing hall. Now."

He used the verb forms of *must-be*; it was a royal order.

Everyone bowed. Galdran smiled, snapped his fingers, and one of the lackeys always at his heels sprang forward. "Matched swords," Galdran said without even looking around. "Meet us in the hall."

The servant, Savona's own age, sent him a frightened look, then ran off.

Savona sighed. He and Renna had chosen the bench beside the stream, a pretty corner of the garden only partially concealed—they'd wanted to be witnessed. The idea had been a bit of cuddle, a few kisses, and gossip flying out to where it would do the most good. Like to a certain blue-eyed, curly-haired girl who seemed to think everyone existed to wait upon her whim. Especially everyone male.

Savona glanced out of the corner of his good eye. Yes, there was Tamara, pale and furious as she glared at Renna.

Renna herself looked furious, as much as one could see of her beyond the drooping brim of her sodden hat. She glared at Anderic, who refused to look her way—all his fury was reserved for Savona.

Renna sighed, her insides cramping as they all followed the king inside. No one spoke, not with the king continually glancing back to see who was coming and who might try to peel off. Where had he come from, anyway? He was supposed to be in with the ambassadors.

They'd reached the king's rooms, which included the entire ground floor of the Residence as well as the series of beautifully decorated private rooms upstairs. The only rooms he never used were the library and archive.

They filed silently into the big fencing salle, a room with windows all down one side, a polished wooden floor. The room was bare except for a sitting platform down one side, with plain military-style cushions. All except for the grand one against the inner wall, from which the king could watch easily. It was next to the fireplace, which was bare. No Fire Stick wasted here, as Galdran was seldom in this room unless he commanded a practice for his own amusement.

The sound of feet pounding in the servants' hall just outside preceded two servants, their breath clouding as they ran to the king. One carried swords, the other was the original messenger, back for duty.

The king gestured flat-handed toward the two, who each took a sword in hand. Savona gave a thought of regret for the straw-colored raw-silk tunic, already blood-splashed from his nose. If he took it off to fight in shirt sleeves, he'd be even colder. Not good.

Anderic pawed uncertainly at his own tunic, which was made of royal blue silk. By the way he rubbed the thin fabric between his fingers, Savona suspected Anderic regretted the lack of padding. Savona wondered how much training he'd had—or not had. Anderic was a cousin to the Count of Mnend, ambitious, and had made it clear he was determined to marry well. "And he seems to think he's picked me, and I'm supposed to be grateful because I'm plain," Renna had said bitterly.

Savona had said with a laugh, "We'll fix that."

Well, they had. And now he faced Anderic as they measured their swords. The metal clanged and scraped, a sharp sound in the frosty air. No one spoke, there was no noise but the hiss and scrape of their feet on the floor.

The king said. "I do not wish to lose my court. First blood will suffice."

That ought to have been the choice of the challenged—though which of them that might be, neither knew. Anderic's brow quirked slightly as he glanced toward the king, then drew down as he settled into a fighting stance. At least some training, then.

Savona gripped the sword, surprised to find his hand sweaty despite the cold. He feinted, waited, and sure enough Anderic stamped in, swinging the sword in a wild attack. Savona blocked, stepped back, blocked. He hadn't had any serious practice for at least a year, maybe more. His arm muscles protested. But Anderic didn't seem to be any better. Savona grimaced, trying to see through his rapidly swelling eye as Anderic swung again. At least he was slow. He blocked again. Anderic came on a little faster. He was Savona's height and build, obviously strong. With a flush of annoyance he attacked again. Savona blocked, glancing past the blades at the king. Galdran observed with a narrow-eyed assessment that was far more dangerous than his horrible semblance of humor.

Savona made a couple of wild swings, the last one whistling a hand's-breadth over Anderic's head.

Galdran laughed, slapping his thigh.

Anderic swung, a fast, wild, deadly arc that would have half-decapitated Savona if he hadn't deflected it. As it was, the hit was so strong—so much stronger than practice hits—that he stumbled back, whereupon Anderic flashed the blade down and jabbed toward his belly.

Savona blocked it badly, but just in time. He leaned up and hissed, "Clown, idiot!" in Anderic's face.

Anderic lifted his upper lip, showing his teeth in a sneer. He mouthed the word "Coward!" and swung again.

So Savona settled grimly to the task of blocking the attack without making any kind of response. Galdran watched every move, his heavy face gradually tightening into the familiar lines of anger. Could Anderic not see it? Or did he think he was exempt? *Why do you think Debegri has his favor?* Savona thought, whirling around and then stumbling under another swing. *Because of his prowess?*

But then anyone who could be Debegri's friend—

Snap! The blade flashed at the very edge of Savona's vision, coming at his bad eye far too close—he got his blade up, which slipped in his hand. Again he just managed to block a bad hit, but he lost grip on his blade, which flew out of his hand. He felt the air of a cut just over his head as he stooped to pick it up.

The king said, "Here! We'll observe the rules, Gharivar!"

Anderic stamped in frustration, then flashed the sword point to the ground and stood at a semblance of military attention, breathing heavily.

Savona felt sick. Could the fellow not see the danger?

Obviously not. Time to end the farce.

To protect Anderic as well as to assuage his own feelings, he was going to win, but it couldn't be a clever win, it had to be by accident. Anderic was slower now. He was just as out of shape as Savona, but it was too late: the king was now leaning forward, watching every move.

Savona found his moment, stumbled, dropped his point after a feint and plowed it up Anderic's arm. He then dropped the blade, and stood there staring, trusting the king to halt the fool if he tried a lunge.

But Anderic was too surprised by the scrape. He flung up his sword, gasping for breath, and stared aghast at his arm.

The king said, "Hold! First blood to Savona."

"No!" Anderic cried. "It was an accident—no count!"

"I call it first blood," Galdran said.

"But your majesty, that's no win! The fellow can't even fight," Anderic retorted. "I swore to let some of his hot blood, and that's all I'll—"

"I declare the honor of the court satisfied," Galdran stated.

"Anderic," Debegri said from the doorway. "The king called a win."

Anderic swayed, blinking rapidly against the sweat in his eyes, then once again flashed down his point.

The king stood up. "My lords, are you satisfied as well?"

Savona bowed, not trusting his voice; Anderic said woodenly, "By your command, your majesty."

The king said, "You are all dismissed to make ready for supper, which I will host. Afterward we will game, and everyone, I trust, will be in charity."

This time everyone in the room bowed.

As they started out, the king said, "My lord Gharivar. You will wait. Is your wound deep?"

Savona forced himself to keep moving. Renna drifted up next to him. As soon as they were outside the salon, he whispered, "What did it look like?"

"Like he's an expert. He made it look like he was chasing you, toying with you."

Savona cursed under his breath.

Renna said, "Do you think—? No. He's a friend of his cousin . . ." A puzzled, anxious look followed. She couldn't believe anything bad would really happen. Not really, despite all the whispers and gossip. People just liked to gossip, put the worst face on stories, didn't they? Reasonable people didn't do wicked things, and she'd always refused to listen to such stories. Stop it by stopping your ears, that was the civilized way to handle nasty gossip.

By evening, though, they all knew that Anderic Gharivar had been sent home to recover from his wound.

Two days later Baron Debegri was seen storming out of the palace to the stable, his servants racing behind. In his wake the word spread: Anderic Gharivar had suffered a riding accident on a tricky hill, fell, and broke his neck.

Renna found Russav Savona out in the farthest part of the garden, just sitting, his hands between his knees, staring down at the half-frozen stream, his breath a steady puff.

He looked up sharply. His stricken face caused her tight control to break.

He held out his arms. This time there was no thought of passion, or pleasure, just the warmth of human comfort.

"My fault, my fault," she cried into his shoulder.

"Mine," he said, his voice husky. "I should have just let him knock me down."

"He was stupid," Renna cried fiercely. "He was arrogant and *stupid*. He wouldn't *listen*. He argued with the king in front of *everybody*. He—he—I danced with him because he was the baron's friend. I let him kiss me just once, because he made me laugh. He—he liked horses, he said, and—"

"Renna, it's not your fault."

"I shouldn't have flirted with him. He took it seriously."

"He wanted to. He was ambitious. He wanted to marry your family, not you. You told me so yourself."

She drew in a shaky breath. "I just can't believe—"

"Believe it. But believe all of it. It's the king, not you, who caused that. And it wasn't your flirting, or mine. It was because Anderic lost his temper, he looked too good fighting in Galdran's eyes, but above all he dared to argue."

Renna sobbed, sniffed juicily, then said, "I didn't believe those stories. I thought it was all talk, you know, by those who don't like the king. But he's the king! His brother Prince Canardan used to play in the castle garden with—with my father—"

"And Prince Canardan was exiled."

The new voice, cold, caused them to spring apart. There stood Tamara, her deep blue eyes wide, her diamond-decorated hair disheveled. She'd been running; the quick rise and fall of her bosom gave her away.

Savona kept his arms around Renna, who did not seem to be aware of his grip; over her head Savona's cold dark gaze met Tamara's wide blue eyes in challenge.

Renna was crying again. "Tamara, I didn't m-mean it to h-happen—"

Tamara had been about to unlimber a truly corrosive insult about flirts—she'd been thinking it up as she searched the garden. She'd seen Savona leave earlier, and Renna run after. But the looks on the two faces before her were not even remotely lover-like.

So she said, "I know. We're all at fault, a little. But Anderic was, too."

"I will never flirt again," Renna said, and Savona withdrew his arms; she didn't even notice. "Ever."

Tamara sat down on her other side. "It could just as easily have been the king ordering you to marry him. If Anderic had been quicker to obey, my aunt said, he could have moved in and taken your family's land within five years. And if you'd refused the king's wishes, it would have been you who'd have the riding accident on your way home. Even," Tamara said in a husky, low voice, "if you were not on a horse."

Renna covered her face with her mittened hands and cried harder.

Savona stood up. He lifted a hand, miming the fan pose for Two is Comfort. Tamara she gave him a curt little nod, and he passed quietly along the garden path.

# Thirty-three

*. . . and so I still feel sick about the whole affair. Maybe Anderic would have gotten himself killed some other way. Your mother says he was like Debegri—big, strong, fearless in the games, with a bad temper. But Debegri's instinct is to fawn and flatter, and Anderic was too honest for that. It's sickening. Court is full of music, good food, fine art, and rot in the hearts and minds of those in power. Your mother says that our job is to outlive the king so that we will be able to put the kingdom back together. I tell you, Danric, it is that, and only that, which keeps me from throwing myself into the river. I never want to see clown players again, not after having to live like one.*

Shevraeth pitched Savona's letter into the fire, wheeled to glare out the senior rec room window at the academy roofs painted in a hundred shades of white and gray and blue shadow. He wanted to be home with Savona—he didn't want to be home.

He struggled against the futility of anger. The courtyard was covered in a soft white snow blanket that obscured the stones where countless Marloven seniors had gathered for generations. One of his own forefathers had been out there, centuries ago—he found that difficult to imagine. But it was true.

The stone walls were ledged with smooth puffy white, and the huge tree that blocked the western sun in the summers, making rec time so pleasant out here, etched its barren branches against the sky, each outlined with glittering pale blue. The rooftops wore their snowy mantle—the world here was quiet, untouched by the destructive hand of man.

Except, of course, the intent of their training was destruction.

But for some reason it seemed, well, *cleaner* than Galdran's version.

He turned away. He missed Renselaeus—more each winter—but he did not miss court. And from the sound of it, court was where he would be forced to live. How would his father resolve these things? For of course he had a plan—though he didn't always share those plans until he deemed the time to be right.

*Come to the defense of the kingdom* . . . What exactly did that mean? Maybe it was time to ask in a letter. Though if he did, his father might tell him one reason, but not all his reasons—until he thought his son ready to hear them.

The mess bell rang, the echo softened by the heavy snowfall. What would court dinners be like? Sitting on cushions again, smelling the complicated sauces mixed with the fragrances men and women gave off from their clothing stored in herbs or dried flowers. Music playing. Stained glass. Oh, but there would be King Galdran, who, it seemed, would never get married and busy himself with a queen and eventually a family. Not if he couldn't find the perfect princess—one to bring wealth and prestige but no mind or will to stand against him.

When Shevraeth had left for Marloven Hess, he'd had no interest in such things, but now he understood his parents' oblique references to how the king would play families off against one another by seeming to court their daughters, while he still sent ambassadors out of the country in search of the right match.

But that was not nearly as odd as the idea of little Renna kissing someone. Renna! When he'd left she'd been exactly the same size and shape as he—a stick—and all she'd ever talked about was horses! When had she begun to notice boys?

He paced the short distance to the mess hall while thinking about the girls at court. He tried to imagine them not as brats more or less his size and shape, running about or riding in races but flirting. Kissing. Like Senelac—

Oh, *no one* was like Fenis Senelac—

He was halfway down the food line when footsteps broke his reverie. Shevraeth was surprised to discover Forthan's sober face.

Forthan piled three or four fresh rye-buns onto his tray, got an extra helping of cabbage-and-rice rolls, a brimming mug of turkey-barley soup, and followed Shevraeth to one of the tables. "I still think the food's better over here," he said as they set the trays down. "Though that's got to be in my head. Since I know two of the cooks, and they rotate between the Guard mess and the academy."

"Might be better if they're cooking for fewer," Shevraeth offered. He was about to add that his mother had talked about that once—ordering great dinners, and how careful one had to be because cooking for vast numbers could diminish the quality of the food as the number went up—but he bit the words back. He knew Forthan was not interested in the exigencies of ordering food for court parties.

"Shevraeth, we're going to be doing lance practice for the New Year's Convocation exhibition. You saw it last year, right?" On Shevraeth's nod, Forthan continued, "Why don't you come over Guard-side and practice with us?"

Lance drill. Ugh. Nobody had liked it last year—but then they had been doing them on the ground, then on the stationary saddles built along a low wall. First year seniors began doing them on horseback—and everybody had heard how spectacularly bad most seniors were. Which was why nobody saw them their first few months.

Forthan flashed his brief grin. "Yes, those with brothers or cousins will be training all winter at home. You get the advantage of learning it right the first time."

Shevraeth remembered, with gratitude, the sword-fighting lessons from horseback of the winter previous. "Thanks." Then, with dismay, "I won't have to exhibit, will I?"

Forthan chuckled. "Not likely. We have to look good. Beginners would be bound and gagged before anyone would let them out in front of the Jarls."

Shevraeth sighed with relief. "Thanks," he said again, and meant it.

Forthan ducked his head, then shifted the subject. "We're going to be attacking the city every other game this coming year," he said. "One out, one in. You'll be assigned at least one command."

Shevraeth ate without being aware of it, his mind running fast. "Whole academy?"

"Now and then. Sometimes seniors. Some covert, some overt. All surprises, from now on."

They embarked on various scenarios, the discussion much like command class; by the end of the meal, when Forthan left as quietly as he'd arrived, Shevraeth's mind was busy on plans.

<br>

ᔔᓄ**ᕀᔕᕀᔕ**ᓄᔕ

<br>

W inter passed swiftly. He practiced with the younger guards at lance drill, not just before New Year's, but also afterward. At first it seemed impossible he'd be able to maneuver the metal-reinforced lance, which was roughly twice the height of a man, while his horse moved under him. Every try left him wringing with sweat despite the bitter air, his stomach muscles aching, his legs and arms feeling like string. If he hadn't been given a solid fourteen-year-old war horse who was not quite ready to be retired to the horse stud and clover, but who was no longer used for the harder runs, he probably would have fallen out of the saddle more than he did.

He loathed lance practice—he knew he would never charge into battle with a lance. And even if, by some mad chance, he did, he'd never describe the cursed thing in a perfect circle, or do the up-and-overs and salutes. He knew that only the heavy cav used lances, or dragoons—rarely light cavalry, though that could vary—and that in a charge, after which they'd drop the lances and fight with conventional weapons.

But by the time the snows turned into sleet, then cold rain, and green shoots were seen on the muddy ground and fuzzing the trees, he realized the true purpose of those evolutions: strength. He had gotten used to jamming his feet heel-down in the saddle, his body a slant back to support the angle of the lance—and the corresponding strengthening of his body required that he get new clothes, though he'd only had these since late autumn. But it was time now for the white, cotton-linen shirts, and the fitted tunic of the senior.

The day before he got his new clothes—for there was the dress tunic as well as one for heavy work and one for summer heat—Keriam summoned him.

It was only when he made his way over to the castle that he realized he had not seen or heard of King Senrid all winter long. He'd glimpsed him once at the New Year's Exhibition, a tall, dark-haired girl beside him who everyone said was the mage Hibern. Liere hadn't been there, and Shevraeth hadn't gotten close enough for speaking.

Now he stepped into the Commander's office, and saw with a shock that Keriam's curling hair was much grayer. But the Commander's gaze was as keen as ever as the Commander said, "You have a couple of choices before you. First, would you like to be an aran radlav down in the Puppy Pit?"

"No." Shevraeth was afraid he sounded churlish. "That is, it was a valuable experience. Glad I did it. But I think I need the practice being with a House affords."

Keriam gave his short nod, one hand open. He accepted these words as reasonable.

"I should bring back that wand—"

"Not so fast," Keriam said with his rare, somewhat sardonic grin. "You'll still be commanding exercises. Also, for that matter, the king wants you in the senior command class. You and Stad will both be in it, and you'll be in his House, so make certain the two of you match watches so you can get away. We'll speak to Khaniver, who will be Thanar Valdlav this year."

Shevraeth's eyes narrowed, wondering if that meant the House rad was going to be someone who didn't like foreigners.

And Keriam said neutrally, "Gannan will be aran radlav for your House. He will be seconded by Stad, who will command the academy next year."

Gannan—who was not in command class at all. Shevraeth said nothing. At least he was sharing quarters with Stad again. "Marec?" he asked tentatively, not sure if asking about someone else was permitted.

"Aran radlav in colts," Keriam said, which was surprising. And, "He will make a superlative master here one day, if events do not force him into the field."

Shevraeth realized that yes, indeed, Marec would be a wonderful academy master. He was patient, even-tempered, never minded explaining things. Would even find several ways to express an idea until the small boys would get it. Marec had never talked much about the future—just assumed he would be a captain somewhere. Shevraeth wondered if Marec had ever considered being a master.

Shevraeth thought these matters over as he walked back to the academy. He was surprised that Keriam would come right out and tell him that Stad would be next year's Danas Valdlav, boy cavalry commander and leader of the school. Though Shevraeth thoroughly agreed. But wasn't that usually kept secret until right before the spring?

And who were they readying for Thanar Valdlav, the foot leader?

# Thirty-four

Though Shevraeth was secretly on the watch, he was still taken by surprise when the girls came back.

One day the mess was half-filled with arriving boys; the next when he entered the air smelled different, though he couldn't quite say how, until he heard the light voices of girls blending the unprepossessing bat-squeaks of scrubs and the nasal rumble and braying laughter of older boys.

He couldn't prevent just one look: ah, there she was.

Heat burned through his veins. He turned his back, lest everyone somehow see into his brain. Foremost in mind was the rules about girls. But right behind that was the never-stale memory of the sweetness of their parting kiss last autumn.

For a couple of days the girls were busy bringing the horses over from winter quarters, and tending to them. Meanwhile, the Houses were sorted out. Shevraeth was glad to see about half of his old bunkmates from his first year. They'd all reached the age where three years could make spectacular changes in growth and appearance. Vandaus was still pale-haired and short. He arrived with a box of books, allowed now that he was a first-year senior. Faldred arrived with an even bigger box.

Baudan had grown into a tall, husky boy with ears that stuck out, his voice shifting from a growl to a sudden squeak that made everyone laugh, especially him. Gannan was huge, splendid in build, strong as a tree, and, at least at first, wary and careful now that he was a rad. It did not take long to guess that now that he was an authority, he would not be looking for ways to get around the rules. He'd be a tiresome stickler in the exasperating manner typical of former slackers and cheats when they were co-opted into authority.

Nermand was middling in height, stocky, with a scowling demeanor. Sometime over the past year he'd fallen out with his old followers, and now was riding mate with Andaun. And Holdan had long since stopped being Gannan's follower. He had become one of the best riders of their year.

There was a lot of teasing when they saw one another in their new, fitted tunics, and the weapons belts instead of the old frayed cotton sashes. Most of them wore wands now, because part of being a senior was either training or rad duty.

It felt *strange* to be seniors.

The year officially started two days later. Their first morning, after the new Valdlavs held their first parade inspection, they had to report to the far field for lance training on horseback. The second year seniors sent them off with jeers, whistles, and hoots.

The practice was exactly as bad as the more experienced seniors gleefully predicted. Those who, like Shevraeth, had had lessons, were mostly knocked askew by the ones who hadn't. The chaos caused everyone to drop lances, or worse, whap them into boys or horses, sending all into a milling, shouting, exasperating confusion.

A very long watch later, they were all more or less in form on the first and simplest of the exercises. Those who'd slacked off all winter were crimson-faced with effort, and Shevraeth sympathized with how very, very sore they would be the next day.

He scarcely had time to rejoice inwardly that he would not be one of their number when Stad eased up next to him and murmured, "After dinner, Keriam's office."

Command class—already?

Suppertime arrived with impossible speed, though once the frenetic pace abated, he discovered that he was tired. Stad appeared next to him on the way to the mess hall. Shevraeth gave a furtive scan. Senelac was ahead of him in line, just getting her hot rolls. He dropped back a little on the pretence of brushing hay off his sleeve, so that he stood just outside of Stad's range of vision as she walked past—without a glance.

Not a word, not a single glance.

His insides flashed to snow cold and then to numb. He picked up his tray and followed Stad down the line, getting food at random. What had he done? He knew he hadn't said anything—

" . . . Shevraeth?"

Stad had asked him something. Not just asked, but repeated his question. "Pardon." He grimaced. "Lance practice," he said, picking a disaster at random.

Stad pursed his lips in a soundless whistle. "Get whacked in the head? I saw Hauth get thumped, and Andaun, of course." It was Andaun who had been knocked right out of the saddle.

Shevraeth hated being thought as clumsy as those others, but it was better than the truth. So he just bumped his forehead with his palm, which could have meant anything. He followed Stad past the silent lower school—oh, yes, first week mess-gag—then was distracted by a far too regular tinkle-clink, the tapping of a spoon against a drinking mug.

Shevraeth flicked a glance down the second years' table where he'd sat the year before. Marlovair and a couple of his friends beat codes on their dishes, their snickering only half muffled. When Marlovair twitched as though he felt he was being watched, Shevraeth shifted his glance away.

Stad sidestepped, gripped his tray in one hand, then swatted the back of his cousin's head as he passed. Marlovair opened his mouth, then shut it, rubbing the back of his head and scowling after Stad, who did not look back.

The second year colts began to eat with a sedulous air.

Stad led the way to the senior tables.

Shevraeth chose a spot with his back to the rest of the room, so he would not be able to see the girls.

As soon as they'd eaten they ran through the dusky twilight to Keriam's tower, where the windows were already glowing squares of light.

Keriam sat at his desk writing steadily until they were all gathered. Shevraeth and Stad sat all the way forward. As the others arrived Shevraeth listened to ring of heels on the stone floor, the rustle of cloth, the creak of the wooden benches as they sat. Even with the windows open Shevraeth could smell the new cloth of their tunics, the polish on their new, fine blackweave riding boots.

Other than a couple of furtive whispers once or twice, no one spoke. Shevraeth got the sense that the room was full—the sound of a room full of people, even when motionless, has a different quality than an empty room.

At some point he knew Senelac was in the room. His shoulder blades itched. But he did not turn around.

Senelac, who had chosen to sit at the very back, struggled not to peer between all those broad gray-covered shoulders to single out his. Finally she gave up. He was definitely taller, now. In fact, he was as tall as Forthan. The fitted uniform along the line of his shoulders—

*Arrrrrgh.*

She closed her eyes.

Presently Keriam glanced up. "The first year command class is going to continue the city attack drills. We might yet learn something, and it keeps morale up. People like to be doing, and like to see us doing. But half of you will have as your first assignment to set up a covert communication system—and the other half will try to break it."

He paused to let them consider it.

Shevraeth's first reaction was to ask why—it seemed too frivolous. Didn't they already have all kinds of communication systems?

Oh, but what if—

No, they weren't planning for *what if*.

They were planning for *when*.

As in, when Norsunder took the city.

A cold, sick feeling settled in his guts as Keriam went on to outline the instructions, and then he finished: "We will continue with field problems and solutions when the first games begin. But for now this is your assignment, so I've seen to it that you all are assigned a perimeter patrol watch per week. You're to see that those are minimally covered, and that your faces are seen at least once around the academy before you commence your exercise." Pause. "Questions?"

Nobody had any yet.

"Stad, remain behind. Since you'll be in charge of the first mission, you'll need a few words of instruction."

They filed out, except for Stad.

Shevraeth was full of questions, but none of them were the type of thing he could ask Keriam, at least not in front of the other seniors.

Because he'd been the first in, he was the last out except for Stad, already deep in conversation with Commander Keriam. He started slowly down the steps, aware now of the medallion swinging inside his shirt that he'd been living with for two years.

So he was startled when a hand gripped his arm, tugging him away from the turn through the archway that would lead back in the direction of the academy. He shifted, chopped down—and stopped his hand when it just touched Senelac's forearm. He stared down into her face, wits blown, replaced by a rush of warmth that melted away that earlier snow.

And she watched his expression go from blank to intent to the most wonderful surprise and happiness. It melted her, too.

She gritted her teeth against words, and tugged his arm again. His arm, which felt like shaped oak. He was, it seemed, even stronger than last summer; he must have spent the entire winter drilling. Though he still looked just tall and thin. No. She did a covert scan as they passed under the glowglobe outside of a boot-maker's shuttered shop. He wasn't thin, he was lean. She

thought hazily, he would never look like Gannan, all parade-
ground muscle. He was like the king, if the king ever grew up.
They were muscled like mountain cats.

He walked obediently enough beside her, and as soon as
they rounded a corner she stopped in an empty intersection
between the winter hay storage barns and the gear repair area,
and gave in to the temptation she had wrestled with all winter,
and kissed him again. And he kissed her right back, just as
fiercely.

It was just as fiery as the first time, and even sweeter.

She broke it off, her senses swimming, and groaned. "All
winter,'" she muttered, "I thought about you. But . . ." She cast a
short, sharp sigh. "And here we are again. All right. Let's see
how we do, then." She scowled. "But. If you ever go looking all
round for me again on academy-side, I will never speak to you
again. Ever. I will. Not. Risk my life's work for a few kisses."

It seemed natural to him that she'd take charge of
whatever relationship they had. He had no experience, she was
older, and seemed to know what she was doing—but he could
not hide his surprise. "Why would anyone care? No one will
ever see us doing anything wrong in the academy."

"You idiot," she said fiercely, jerked away, and stalked at
a headlong pace. He had to lengthen his stride to keep up. "You
keep forgetting you are the foreigner. Most are used to you being
here. I can see you are as well. But with all the troubles—Fath is
back for one purpose only, and that's to catch Forthan. If she
can, and—" She sighed again. "It's just that everyone is
watching everyone. And tempers are short because of the
threat."

He sensed she was hedging, that she protested all that
because there was a reason underneath all the talk. But whatever
it was, she obviously wasn't ready to tell him yet.

"I'll know all your schedules by tomorrow," she said,
after they'd walked a ways down an alley behind the big houses
on the main street. "I make the schedules for us this year. We
can meet in the city. Take a walk to the park." She grinned.

Last summer Shevraeth had learned that that innocuous phrase, overheard once or twice his first year and last year, meant people were twoing.

He was going to answer, but a dog barked at them. Through an open window upstairs came the rhythmic clatter of a loom. The sounds, innocuous as they were, broke the imagined perimeter of privacy and tightened Senelac up again.

She turned abruptly away before they reached the main street, so he walked alone down through the old, mossy-smelling, low tunnel to the academy.

# Thirty-five

"Shut up, shut up!" Gannan yelled, and when no one paid any heed, Stad stepped up to Gannan's shoulder and said in a normal voice, "Fine. Go ahead and burn the schedule, Gannan. They don't care."

"Why didn't you say we had the schedule already, Gannan?" Ventdor protested.

"Already? I thought it would be after inspection—" Hauth proclaimed to the rest of the room, not that anyone listened to him.

"We have to do some of that inspecting, remember, rock head?" Baudan retorted. "Or are you volunteering to do it all?"

"Shut up, road apples," Nermand began.

Gannan flicked a look at Stad, got a tiny nod, and held up the paper between forefingers and thumbs as if to begin ripping.

Instant silence.

Gannan flushed, wishing he could promise them a big scarfle if they'd just shut up about it, and do what they were told. Like he'd done last year, when he'd had to be a substitute rad. But it only worked on little boys. Now that they were all seniors and had liberty, and could bring food back to the rec room, who cared? How unfair was that, and how did the other senior rads manage?

He struggled with the impulse to issue threats—but he remembered quite well how he'd responded to rad threats, and he knew, and he knew the others knew, that he would never deal out breezes to fellow seniors, though he was legally allowed. Not that they'd do anything inside the barracks. They'd put up with it in here. But there'd be retribution out behind, with boy guards posted, and while Gannan was pretty sure he'd win against most, they'd all give him a hot time first. He did not want to risk running around with a black eye and getting laughed at. Because whether he won the fights or not, everyone would know it meant he couldn't control his own House.

He glared at them, realized they'd been waiting in silence, so he whooshed out the worst of his anger, then said, "Here's the schedule. Some of you will be rads on classes, which means you go there as soon as morning inspection is over."

Looks back and forth, a few comments began but when Stad, standing just behind Gannan, raised a hand, they stopped.

Gannan cleared his throat and began reading out the schedule. Shevraeth, who was glad that he'd have a couple of classes with Marec and Stad, expected to be in the senior classes in everything. What he did not expect was that he would be teaching the scrubs knife throwing. He'd known in a passive way that there wasn't anything more to be taught him in that. It was now a mere matter of practice, and he did it when he wanted to think, as all the moves had become pure habit. He always hit the target now, it had ceased to be a matter of moment last year. But he hadn't expected anyone to, well, notice. Which of course was absurd.

When Gannan finished they all clattered in their new, stiff boots off to breakfast. Shevraeth's mind promptly presented him with a vivid memory of last night's walk in the park.

And her threat beforehand. So he avoided any glances whatever at the girls' side, though at least during the first part of breakfast, he couldn't think of anything else. On his way out of the mess hall Shevraeth glimpsed Marec with the new colts, who were being kept still and silent at their table until the seniors left, the way he had his colt year. Marec gave him a brief grin, which Shevraeth returned, and then he was outside.

As they walked to the parade ground for inspection, they talked back and forth about schedules, including the fact that now, as seniors, they were expected to be doing those perimeter guard patrols during the first night watch. Only on games would they do the toughest watch, from midnight to first bell, as practice; the masters or last-year seniors would still handle those in the academy. Except, of course, if they got a gating like Sindan Hotears had earned for his House their first year as colts. Baudan wondered aloud—with grim pleasure—just how horrible that month had been to endure, and he wondered how creative the other seniors had gotten with expressing their displeasure with him.

Gannan wondered to himself just how humiliated their House rad had felt at not being able to control *anything*. He'd always wanted a wand—he'd so often dreamed all the details of beating a loudmouth into tears and terror—but he knew it would only work with the little boys. And then Keriam would drop on him. Not like the old days, his dad kept saying, and Gannan sighed.

&#8190;&#8466;&#8466;&#8190;

Shevraeth's first day as a teaching rad was easy enough. The master in charge took the first class, of course, showing the little boys how to grip the knife properly, and set them to the practice grip and swing. Shevraeth and a senior from the other house, with whom he'd be swapping off this duty, observed and at the master's request Shevraeth demonstrated by throwing a series of knives into a narrow post set up for the purpose, each landing in a precise row a hand's width apart. Right hand then left. These things had become so habitual he was more amused by the boys' wide-eyed awe than he was impressed by his own expertise.

They'd be expected to run the classes the way the master did. The boys were worried about defaulters but the rads worried about the boys making them look bad if they learned sloppily or the class got out of control.

And so the day sped by.

And then another.

And another . . .

Firstday evening the next week, the command class met again to hold their first exercise. Shevraeth was in the half chosen to play Norsundrians. The problem was to design a communications system, the setup was to get a message from the castle out to the guardhouses around the city.

Stad's idea was to send three messages. His team had debated hotly on whether there should be two blanks and one real one, or two false and a real, everyone saying that if the enemy finds one then everyone is put at risk. Two fake ones would lower the risk. Except, Stad pointed out, there was risk in *everything*. Meanwhile three, carried covertly, would get the message out faster.

So three were sent—and three were captured, one as soon as he left the palace, one along the road, and Shevraeth's group, watching over the farthest guardhouse from the surrounding rooftops, spotted the messenger, swung down with well-trained rapidity, surrounded their quarry and landed on him hard.

"Hey!" he yelped, his voice muffled by a layer of two muscular bodies.

"Get him up," the second year senior in command of their riding said briskly. "And we'll get his message out of him."

"We can't raise a ruckus here on the street," the other senior said—with difficulty, as he was on top of the writhing pile.

Shevraeth glanced around at the empty street; light glowed in an upstairs window over the big ironmongery on the nearer corner.

He didn't need to speak. All of them had the same thought at once: not wanting to explain their noise to a huge ironmonger. If he was really fond of his sleep he might not let them get to the part about king's business.

So the two seniors gagged their prisoner and all helped bear him off, still kicking and writhing mightily, to the side of one of the city's two rivers, which had a long swathe of green between the water and the nearest buildings. There they thumped their prisoner onto the grass.

"Give it up or we'll get it out of you," the riding captain said, ripping free the gag.

"Pooh! Pah!" The prisoner spat. "What was that? It was full of fuzz!"

"My sash from last year. Tucked it in my pocket just in case. Bit linty. Sorry."

"Norsundrians won't apologize for lint, fat wit," the other second year senior exclaimed in disgust. "They'll get right to the tortures."

"Tortures? Hey! Nobody said anything about—"

"We're Norsundrians, dolt! Of course there'll be tortures!"

The prisoner scowled, then yanked from inside his tunic a folded paper. "Let's just say you did 'em, then. I dunno if I'd ever hold out for torture. I guess it depends on how angry I'd be. Or how important it is, but one thing for sure." He turned the scowl upward. "I am not going to sit here and let you give me skull raps and rug burns and all the rest until I rat."

The seniors hesitated, and Shevraeth ventured a comment, "Wouldn't they search him first anyway?"

"True," the riding captain commented. "But the torture idea sounded like more fun."

The prisoner muttered a couple of choice epithets.

"So what is it, anyway," the second senior asked, squinting at the letter in the faint light of a corner glowglobe.

They all got up, including the prisoner, and moved to the light. The message was written in an alphabet none of them recognized.

"Code," the prisoner said in gloomy satisfaction. "And no, they didn't tell me what it said, only whom to take it to."

"So that's what we'd torture you to get, then," the captain said. "Then dump your body." He looked up. "Everyone agreed?"

They all nodded, and returned at a loping run to Keriam's tower, where they found the others already gathered, everyone talking at once.

Senrid was there, perched on the edge of Keriam's desk, a foot swinging as his head made minute jerks back and forth, his eyes narrowed and intent as he tracked at least three conversations.

Keriam loomed out of the crowd. "Ah. Here's our last group. Report?"

The senior said, "We stationed ourselves around the southmost guardhouse, where we'd been assigned to watch, and as soon as we saw our man here in uniform skulking along the road we dropped on him. Got this." He held up the message. "We would have tortured him to find out who was to receive it. He didn't know what the message contained."

Again everyone started talking at once, but this time Senrid flipped up his hand, and they all shut up abruptly.

"No written codes," Senrid said, holding up a finger. Then another. "If someone can read it, they can be tortured for it. And what if the senders don't find out, then the code becomes a tool for the enemy, not for us. No uniforms, dead of night will be bad unless our people can stay unseen. No fellows who look like obvious couriers. Good enough for the first mission—we've found out a whole lot about what won't work, even if we still don't know what will."

"More safeguards—"

"Couriers who know each other—"

"Light of day?"

"Disguises—"

"Those assigned to patrol go be seen, then get some sleep. All of you," Keriam ordered.

They trooped out, still talking, though in low voices.

The first year seniors formed around Stad, Senelac just behind them.

Stad said, "Torture is going to be the threat no matter what. I'll wager anything they try magic next. We won't be involved in that."

"Unless it's magic and us, combined," someone said. And added with grim humor, "So the mages sit tight and we still get the torture threat. Because you know it will be us, and not them, doing runner duty."

Some of them separated off. Senelac waited until she and Shevraeth were alone. "He's almost right," she said. "But what do you want to wager it's us, and not you, who'll be running messages?"

Shevraeth looked over. "You girls?"

She smiled. "Yes. And we'll be better at it."

He did not ask how she felt about torture. Her chin was up, her dark eyes wide and her smile the tight-cornered grin she got when she was thinking headlong. He already knew the answer: whatever fears she had wouldn't be shared, and she'd go right like that, wide-eyed, smiling, into danger, because that's what Marlovens did. That's what Senelacs did.

# Thirty-six

*Russav: I cannot believe how many days have slipped past. This spring has been so busy I fall into bed asleep before I hit the pillow, and it seems I draw a single breath before the morning bells have us up at dawn. Just last night Vandaus, who's about the most even-tempered fellow I've ever known, was grousing that there's no use in having a senior rec room when we never even get to step in it—except to sweep before inspection.*

*Things in no particular order. Teaching small boys to throw knives is nothing I ever thought I'd be doing. But it's fun. Except when I'm trying not to laugh.*

*Lance practice on war horses is another laugh. When it's not painful.*

*We did another comm run. Now they've got all these safeguards built in. It's an elaborate system. It broke down, in fact, because not everyone remembered all the rules. So we're going to have to drill before the runs, and they're adding more rules.*

*My first overnight as a rad is day after tomorrow. So I get tomorrow night off . . .*

Shevraeth stopped, pen hovering above the page—a slow drip of ink formed, and he hastily dropped the pen into the well.

No, he just couldn't write about Senelac and 'taking a walk in the park.' That part of their twoing was wonderful—but the rest . . .

He frowned. Savona did write about his struggles with Tamara.

He'd been destroying the letters, so it was not likely there'd be gossip.

> *The Marloven girl I've mentioned before. She reminds me of Tamara. Not just dark curly hair, though Senelac's is as short as ours. The resemblance is more in that sense of your being on a runaway horse, when you told me about Tamara's temper. It's not temper in Senelac, at least not the way I think of temper. Cursing, fists, throwing things. But I don't know what to liken it to. We'll be talking easy as a canter on an open road about command class, and battles, and family histories, but if I stray into Colendi history—any kind of parallels—she just shuts up. Not just that, she gets impatient. What seems so interesting to me is obviously boring. How can that be when we share so many other interests? But it's true.*
>
> *And if we see one another at the academy— and it happens—she walks by without a word or a look, as if I'm not there. I know why, and the reasons are good. Well, I don't know about the word 'good' in reference to war, and how females fit into it, and all that. Say, her reasons make sense. Yet, I still am bothered because there are others twoing, and they sometimes smile across a room. Nothing more. No one really notices, unless you're already thinking about these things. And a smile doesn't break any rule—*

Tang tang! Tang tang!

Shevraeth sighed, twisted the letter into a corkscrew—despite the last words still being wet—shoved it into the box, and sent it. It was either that or destroy it. He never left letters lying in his box unfinished if they mentioned his private life. It might be two weeks before he had a chance to write again. And two more weeks, if not longer, before Savona could answer, because he knew the existence of the golden box at the other end still had to be hidden from the king.

He threw the box into his storage chest and ran out, straightening his tunic and shoving the stupid brass-topped wand into his belt as he ran.

At least he did not have lance practice today; but the rest of the day was full enough. He ran down to the Puppy Pit, aware of the sun on the back of his neck. After the cold of winter, the sun had gained strength again. He supervised knife throwing, then ran back for his staff and sword practice, then archery, and the midday meal, after which he discovered the day had grown so warm he was sweaty, so he crossed the short distance to the senior barracks, delighting in its proximity. He dashed through the cleaning frame, felt the morning's grit vanish, and changed to his lighter summer tunic. Then paused, just looking around. The bright slants of light through the windows, making dots of fire of the lazy dust motes drifting in the air; the beds, alternating between sunlit and shadow, were all empty.

So he checked his gold box, not really expecting a message, of course, now that court was again required to convene at Athanarel Palace. In spring and summer he could go weeks and even a month without one. But to his surprise, there was already one from Savona.

*Danric: Tamara and the runaway horse was a better metaphor than I had first imagined. No, I will not bore on about my business until I at least acknowledge what you wrote me about.*

*I know only what little you've told me about this girl of yours, so you have only yourself to blame if I'm misjudging the situation. But it sounds from here like you don't share similar interests so much as you share some of hers, and she likes that, but she doesn't share any of yours.*

*Or maybe my view's fractured from the latest way Tamara's taken a hammer to it. Though she's been blabbing all over court that I am too selfish to live. You be the judge. We're getting along fine, more than fine out in the orchard, fragrant air, soft grass. Lemon-curd and kisses, that sums up Tamara in a good mood. And the mood stays good as long as we talk about court, and what she thinks of this boy, or that girl, or that couple. What clever thing she said at the ball. At the regatta. At the point-to-point. At the card party. Her new clothes, her hair (she got the hairdresser to do some spell and changed it from black to gold), what jewels go best in gold hair, who copies her styles and what she thinks of that . . .*

*I said, I like to touch your hair. I like the way it smells. But do we have to talk about it? Mistake! She says I only want kisses, I don't want to know what she thinks. Vastly unfair since she's been talking for two bells. I say yes I do and she says who had the best hair-dress last night and I know the right answer to that one! I say you, and she says oh yes then describe it. And when I say that I can't describe anyone's hair, I don't even remember what my own looked like, she says that's proof "you boys" only want one thing and dusts off, leaving me thinking, two bells worth of talk for about two kisses.*

*Tell me your girl isn't just the same.*

Shevraeth tried to imagine Senelac gossiping about girls' head-dresses, and laughed aloud at the unlikely picture. He turned the letter over and scrawled hastily, *If Senelac ever talks about any royal court—or her hair—then I'll eat horse feed for a month. Tamara as I remember her and Senelac have fewer interests in common than either of us could possibly be accused of having with either of them. Does that make sense? I don't have time to stop and parse.*

Twist, send.

Then he was off again to afternoon classes.

The next evening was his night off. He paid more attention to the set of his tunic and to brushing his hair than he ever did during the day, and then he was off through the tunnel to the eatery Senelac had chosen for their meeting place.

With a mood of pleasant expectation he made his way southward down the main street, then paused in surprise when he heard "Shevraeth!"—not a female voice, but male.

He looked round. "Marec!"

Both of them reacted in surprise—Marec to see Shevraeth crossing the street toward an eatery with such a happy smile of anticipation, and Shevraeth to see his old friend tired and tense.

"Going into Lancer's?" Marec said, indicating the eatery, from which promising smells of braised chicken emanated.

Shevraeth found lying unpleasant at any time, but when he saw the hopeful expression puckering Marec's tense forehead, he flicked out his hand in assent. Why not add Marec to the party? This was perfectly legitimate—broke no rules. He was on liberty, and girls and boys could meet anywhere outside of the academy. In fact, last year, hadn't the three of them sat together over command class problems? Of course, command class had been the night before, and Marec and Senelac were actually on the opposing team for the next communication run, but they could talk generally, couldn't they? And then he could walk out with Senelac after?

At any rate, he would not stiff-arm a friend who clearly wanted company.

"Come on in," he said. And with a smile, "Tomorrow it's camp grub, so tonight it's real food."

Marec gave a tight half-smile, and they made their way in. The place had become popular ever since the introduction of a new pastry that Shevraeth could have identified for the locals as a famed Colendi layered cake—a simplified version. But to the Marlovens it was a new, exotic treat, the flavoring of crushed almond-paste, the light whipped custard made with distilled vanilla bean and a touch of ground cinnamon, all in between layers of cake, something that hadn't crossed the border in centuries. Every time the Marlovens went to war against their neighbors, the restricted trade treaties after they were beaten back had choked off import of fine things like vanilla, and the next few generations were back to honey-tarts and berry-bread.

Not that you could smell the dessert. The delicious aromas were of hot olive oil used to crisp potato-and-onion slices, as well as the chicken braised in beer, and the fish poached in white wine and herbs.

The owners had responded to their new popularity by squeezing in more tables, and hiring some locals to make music. The sound of a young girl singing ancient ballads to the accompaniment of a drum and flute caused many of the younger journeymen and women to pull up chairs and join in, some with hand drums brought for the purpose. They took up most of the far wall. By unspoken but mutual consent Shevraeth and Marec chose a table close to the door. The constant comings and goings were somewhat distracting but at least they could hear one another.

Also, Shevraeth could keep an eye on the door.

A woman in an apron shouldered through the crowd. "Fish or chicken?"

"Chicken for me," Shevraeth said, and when Marec just waved a hand, he added, "Two. We'll have ale with it, and the pastry at the end."

Marec hunched over, fingers tapping restlessly in time to the drum beat on the far side of the room.

"It's not going well with the new colts?" Shevraeth asked.

Marec looked pained. "Are you blind?" He groped with a hand, then shook his head. "No. Sorry. I forget. I know how much you House seniors are working, and tomorrow you'll get an all-night patrol. But you really don't know what's going on?"

Shevraeth opened his hand. "I don't. Should I? In truth, I thought this year so far was shaping up to be as easy a year as last."

"For you seniors it is. Though it won't be when the rot spreads." Marec sighed. "It's the second year colts." A quick look. "No, it's Marlovair. He and his soul-rotted horse apple followers. I think they want to ruin everything and everyone. Drawing not just all the their year—both Houses—into their fights, but now they're trying to strong-arm the first year colts in—"

Shevraeth grimaced. "I had no idea. My regular rad duties are with the scrubs."

Marec said in a low, bleak voice, "I don't think I can hold them from following. And I'm not alone. But it's far, far worse for Evrec."

Who was the aran radlav for the second year colts, Shevraeth remembered. Evrec, Stad's best friend, and the toughest of their entire class—except for Stad. The two had had a friendly rivalry going since they were scrubs, meant to shape them into the best. And they were the best. So . . . what had happened?

"That's a tough group, but I thought Evrec was tough. Everyone says he and Stad are tougher than the seniors the year ahead of us."

"They are." Marec bent forward. "But. The other colt rads think Command will put Stad in with the second years, and take Evrec out. Evrec!"

"Why?" Shevraeth whistled soundlessly. Of course. "Evrec isn't from a high ranking family, I gather?"

"Saddle-makers." Marec made a fist, thumping it lightly on the table as he muttered, "Every night ends with the breezes blowing, but those boys just get worse. Never anything that would get them sent up to the tower."

"So it's a deliberate campaign?"

"Oh, yes. Must have plotted it all winter long. They're determined to ruin Evrec. I don't think they'd even respect Forthan. After all, he committed the cowardly crime of being born to farm people."

A flicker of movement, and Shevraeth looked up. Senelac paused in the doorway. He smiled, about to welcome her, when she shook her head, backed away, and was gone a moment later.

Marec's gaze was on the rough grain of the old table, and he did not notice.

Shevraeth's good mood evaporated. "What does Keriam say?"

"No one has ratted to Command, of course. Or to Stad. We're supposed to be able to solve academy problems ourselves. When Command steps in, it means we've lost control. Remember how savage Zheirban was, the year Forthan got caned? Well, I didn't realize it at the time. But I know what he felt like, we all do. If we can't hold 'em, how do we hold a rough patrol in war time? Evrec is sick about it. We all are. We meet every night, with Evrec and without. He's been asking our help, he doesn't swank about saying he'll go it alone like some idiot in a hero ballad, and so we try different things—"

The food clattered down in front of them, swiftly followed by the *tunk* of beer mugs, and Marec sighed. "Oh, never mind. It's not like you can do anything. Just, you be on the watch tomorrow. And it's a two-nighter! Or maybe they won't be so full of swank, being with Stad in command of the exercise. Still. There's talk of going back to the old way—two masters as well as two seniors on each game."

Two years ago Shevraeth would have shrugged. Now he understood the disgrace everyone would feel that they could not continue with last year's single master overseeing two senior rads on two-class overnights. Two masters would put everyone back to the rules of Shevraeth's first colt year.

"Those boys were in the Puppy Pit the year Sindan forced Forthan into that cursed brushfire," Shevraeth said. "You'd think they'd remember what happened as the result of getting the entire academy involved in their quarrel."

Marec sighed so hard he blew a potato crisp off his plate. He plucked it up then waved it in the air as he said, "Oh, but this is *different*." And popped it in his mouth.

Shevraeth laid his spoon neatly on his plate, wondering when he'd eat with a fork again, then leaned back. "How could they possibly justify that? Trouble is trouble. And wasn't the Sindan problem something or other to do with rank?"

"In a way." Marec wrinkled his nose. "That time, it was more like rank wafting you past the standards. It was the way things were done under the Regent, d'you see? If a family of rank supported the Regent, their sons would get command even if they slacked off through their years here. Forthan moving up through the ranks shocked them. But last year, they accepted it—their fathers have now seen Forthan in action at the Convocation games, and in various field exercises over the kingdom, with the Guard. Forthan's rep overcame his background."

Shevraeth knew that last year, Forthan had been gone a lot—which of course was one of the reasons he'd gotten to command the covert attacks on the city.

"But, see, this year Stad is the assistant rad in our own House—and everyone knows that when you're a rad in the first-year seniors, who aren't supposed to need a rad, that's as high as you'll ever go. Though there isn't any rule, it's just a tradition, that if you aren't going to be a Valdlav, you finish as a senior rad so you get some credit. He should have been over the second years or even the first, like me. Everyone knows I'll never be a Valdlav, but I don't care, I don't want to command an army. The Valdlavs are just about guaranteed higher command, if they haven't an inherited rank waiting. Like Zheirban." He made a rueful shrug.

Shevraeth's lips parted. His tongue had begun to shape the words—*But Stad will be Danas Valdlav next year*—then he remembered where he'd heard that. From Keriam, in his office. With no witnesses.

Shevraeth had assumed it was so obvious a choice that it had become general knowledge. But if Marec didn't know it, then . . .

Another test?

Keriam had not said, "You are not to tell anyone."

Shevraeth did not hear Marec, who was muttering curses about the obnoxious second year colts who thought they could run the academy. Shevraeth was stunned to realize that he did indeed have the inside line of communication, at least in one sense.

The spoken rules were: next year's appointments were made on First Day. Unspoken rules were obviously quite different—that some knew Command's thinking far ahead of time.

So . . . what to do? If he told Marec and swore him to secrecy, then he put Marec in a terrible position.

He said, carefully, "So that means, if Stad is put over the colts, it's not really because he handles them any better than you do, it is because of his family being related to an ancient one. And that means, if the commanders do decide to put him in as Valdlav next year, these boys will think it was their pressure that accomplished it, am I right? Because they forced the change into the traditional pattern?"

Marec made the arrow-to-the-mark gesture.

"But—" *But Keriam has to know what's really causing the problems. He and the king*, Shevraeth thought. He gulped ale so he wouldn't say the words crowding from brain to lips, and drank too big a swallow. His nose and eyes stung. He wiped his eyes with his sleeve, then discovered Marec eyeing him narrowly.

"Do you know something?"

"Only that I do not, ever, want to be a rad over those second year loudmouths," Shevraeth retorted. "The idea puts me off food, and we haven't even had the pastry. Ah, here it comes."

Marec glared at his pastry. "Here's my thinking. Well, my mother helped me to it. When I got home that year."

Shevraeth knew immediately what year he meant.

Marec turned the plate round and round with his strong fingers as he muttered to the pastry, "M'dad wouldn't talk to me about it. Forthan. What happened. I thought he was ashamed of *me*. My mother told me that everyone our age and older wears Forthan's scars on our spirits, including my dad. Forthan was the only one to walk away free of that, though nobody would have traded places with him for a heartbeat. But he paid the price of someone else's wrong, and he knew it. Oh, he let his temper get the best of him, so he wasn't entirely free, but the cause had been just. And all knew it. Even Sindan admitted it, when the other seniors sent him to Norsunder for the rest of the year. I think some still won't talk to him, is what I hear."

Shevraeth leaned forward, hearing the rapid rush of whispered words with some difficulty, as the drum beats and chorus rose and fell in the background, a minor key plainchant that was both compelling and sinister.

"My mother said the little boys don't know empathy, except for their close friends. Or family." The word *empathy* was taken almost wholesale from Sartoran—but it had a Marloven pronunciation.

So the Marlovens knew the term, and the emotion, they just didn't talk about it, Shevraeth thought. So different from the Colendi, and as Marec morosely bit into his pastry at last, Shevraeth remembered his father saying a long time ago, *The Colendi have at least twenty terms for variations on empathy. But many of those are not actually empathetic, and perhaps only a Colendi can fully understand them: "empathy-false, empathy-in superiority, empathy inferiority, empathy in condescension, empathy in shared guilt," are just a few of the distinctions. What it means is, they make war with words and the feelings that words evoke. Never forget that if events to transpire to send you to Alsais.*

Shevraeth said easily, "If your colts ever do straighten up, this cake here would probably go down in history as the prime scarfle."

Marec's brows went up. "It would, wouldn't it?" He frowned. "They're gonna earn it first."

ನಂ(ಐ೪೦)ಛ

Shevraeth was still wondering why Senelac had vanished the night before, as he rode slowly behind the marching boys the next day. This was his first game as a senior rad, riding a horse and wearing the black woolen cloak whose water resistant qualities were enhanced by magic against the threatening rain.

Stad was the commander on this two-night game. The perfect behavior of Marlovair's House would have astonished Shevraeth before his talk with Marec. He rode at the back, accompanying the supply wagon, and watched the second year colts marching in perfect order. Usually the column was staggered—still in pairs, but friends clumped closer together, others lagging father behind so they could chat and not be overheard. The dust kicked up by shuffling feet hanging in the air, rising higher when the goal neared and they picked up their pace.

Shevraeth gazed up the straight column, everyone in Jump House—Marlovair's House name this year, he had no idea what had brought that about—marching in step, each squared spear-length behind the boy in front. The other House, not to be outdone, were almost as parade-ground perfect.

Shevraeth shook his head. Meant nothing good. He peered through the golden dust to where Stad rode at the front next to Master Askan, who was right now the only master with them. They'd been told at the breakfast briefing that if needed, another would be along after the day's lessons were finished. There weren't any free masters as there usually were. One had been sent on an unidentified errand by Commander Keriam, and another had been given leave to go home to attend his wife's childbirth.

Keriam had said, "I will ride out myself if we cannot free up a master, and you feel there is need."

He had not said that in front of the boys, only to Master Askan and the senior radlavs. Shevraeth had thought he might have spoken in front of the boys as an oblique threat, but he realized now that to the colts it would not have been oblique at all. It would mean that the commander himself felt the need to stir on their behalf—and they'd take that as triumph, as a proof of the success of their campaign. Just as the older boys serving as rads would take it as a reprimand—that they might not have control over their charges.

Shevraeth shaded his eyes, trying to pick out Marlovair's skinny form. There he was, marching along—setting the step, in fact—face straight forward. Other than his obvious pleasure in stamping along, expressed in the rigidity of his arms and the emphatic thump of his feet, there was nothing to be read there. Not that he could comprehend a boy who would court a public caning and think himself a hero. Shevraeth sighed, and felt his mare shift her weight. She bobbed her head, ears flicking back, as Shevraeth thought ironically that last night he'd been so certain he'd at last mastered understanding of these people, but today he felt just as alienated as his first year.

So what was Stad thinking?

Stad, at the front, was furious.

He had not spoken a word to Master Askan the entire ride. But as they neared the turn-off to the field they'd selected as their game site, he said, "Permission to alter the plans?"

Master Askan cast a glance his way, saw the locked jaw and white, compressed lips of cold rage. "To?"

Stad turned a bleak face his way. "River."

Master Askan said mildly, "Warm as it is here, you know the water's still mostly snow melt."

Stad's lips curled. "Yes."

Master Askan was silent for a long moment, then said, "Van, you know I can't let you dunk those hot heads in snowmelt, satisfying as it would be."

Stad muttered under his breath, very aware of the banner-bearers riding the regulation ten paces behind, "Look, Uncle Kett, Cousin Van's near to ruined me."

Master Askan was Stad's uncle by marriage, through sisters. It was common—inevitable, really—that boys and now girls coming through the academy were going to have relatives as masters, or, eventually, mistresses. Everyone knew it, everyone knew who was who, everyone acted as if they had never met outside the academy gates. The masters were addressed by their titles, the boys and girls by their family names, and that was that.

But these two were alone right now, facing a difficult problem. Master Askan would never have alluded to it, but Stad, by addressing him by the family title, made the conversation personal.

Master Askan said over his shoulder to the banner bearers, "Shift in plans." His hand flicked out, palm down, and they halted obediently, causing the long column to lurch to a standstill, everyone semaphoring "What?" and "I dunno!" with their eyes, as they were being too obedient for the usual covert whispers.

So it was not just Master Askan and Stad who rode ahead to confer, it was Kettrid Askan and his nephew Indevan Stad.

The boy who had been so silent faced his uncle in open misery, and a rushing tumble of words came out so fast it was difficult to make them out. "They've ruined me. If I get shifted to the lower Houses, they win, and I can't see any way around it, honor demands if I get—you know—next year, I'd have to refuse. And you know what happens if you refuse a command. Oh, not that the king would do anything to me for that. I know that. He has to know what's going on. But on the other hand, he couldn't put me anywhere of importance in the army, not with that gossip sticking to the bottoms of my shoes. I'd stink wherever I go in future. Oh, Uncle, I'm so angry I can't think, I just want to run those brats through the cold water until they drop, and then kick them into running more."

He flipped out a hand.

"Look at 'em! No elbow fights, no talking, none of the usual fooling about that we don't pay any attention to on long marches. Marching strictly reg—because they think they are going to win, because I'm in command today. Like they put me here, not like I earned it. I hate it, and I want to make them as miserable as—" He stopped abruptly, face turned away. By his own code, he'd strayed into whining.

Master Askan took his time surveying the line. The perfect double line, varying shades of blond heads gleaming in the hazy sunlight, the quiet breeze rustling the two banners. Not a peep. Indevan Marlovair at the front of his House, face rigidly forward. The haze, the glare, the slowly settling dust made it difficult to see his expression, but was that a smirk of triumph or just a squint against the westering sun?

He would not tell Van what Keriam had said about the matter—"This is actually the best kind of command problem, the one you didn't plan for"—or the king's response—"Let Van Stad solve it himself, if he can."

Master Askan made a business of rubbing his thinning hair back off his forehead. He did not want to give the final command here, so when his nephew frowned, staring through his horse's ears, his mouth half open, he sat back and waited.

And Van looked up, and smiled. "Right. You don't spend your men in a fit of temper. Thank you. I think I ought to have doused my own head. We may's well camp here. It'll do as well as our usual site. And I have a different plan."

"Do it," Master Askan said in his master's voice, so the private moment was over.

They rode back to the line. Stad raised his fist, circled it in the air, then pointed toward the riverside. There they would camp. Usually this area was used in late summer, for water training. What was going on?

As the line began to move forward, it was not so perfect as before because few could resist just a comment, just a question, just an expression, and multiplied by twos, the whispers rustled in a susurrus down the line, where Shevraeth rode, thinking, *There's going to be trouble.*

# Thirty-seven

Van Marlovair's mood swooped about like a hawk in the sky.

He woke on fire with anticipation at the prospect of the best overnight game *ever*. Anticipation, and triumph. He was proving that his father was right. That the Marlovairs were born to command! He—he alone—was getting the *entire academy* to change. Didn't that mean, in a sort of way, that he was really in command? Oh, just in a way, and he'd never say it, even to his best riding-mate, Keth Jastan. It would sound so full of swank if said out loud. But still, he was in command, and by getting everybody behind him, he was going to make them put people born to leadership back into leadership. And all by proving that leaders led!

It was as simple as that. His dad had even said—in a way—it was his *duty*. "The king is after all just a boy. Oh, he's smart, and moreover, he's got a temper. So you don't tell him what his duty is. You just get everyone who sees it behind you, and that will in turn influence him to attend to it."

That's what Dad had said last year, before Marlovair came to start his colt year in the upper academy.

And it was working!

It was working, but it sure was not easy. Marlovair had to bite his tongue so often, to ignore good opportunities for scraps and jests, and he had to honey-bun some real horse apples at rec time, and pretend he liked their company. Just because they happened to be born to important families.

His mood swung again, drifting downward on a cold draft as Landeth began making that irritating noise with his tongue on the roof of his mouth, the galloping sound. That hadn't been funny since they were all first-year scrubs, but he still did it all the time, and those fatwit followers of his, Olavir and Penderic, loved it when he did it after lights out. Even though it had been centuries since it fooled the rads into going round and round the tents to figure out who it was.

Still. Landeth and the two idiots had scarfled the very best tent site for him, right across from the cook tent so they'd always be first in line for grub, just as he'd commanded. So he'd have to pretend not to notice.

As he lined up with the rest of Jump House to wait for their assignments, he fought down the urge to pull Keth aside and put together a plan to scrag Landeth, Olavir, and Penderic accident-a-purpose during the night maneuvers, just because they were annoying. Since there couldn't be any tent or bed or gear scrags. On this game no scrags, no raids, no stings, everyone parade-ground perfect, under the command of a *real* leader, his own cousin, Van Stad. Best in the academy. That was The Plan.

Marlovair took his place at the front of the line, Keth beside him, and Snakeface and Toss—his honor guard, he liked to think of them—behind. He listened in satisfaction as the others lined up behind Toss and Snakeface, no talking, just the shuffle of feet on grass, and one muffled sneeze.

And there was Cousin Van, who looked just like a hero of the old ballads. Not a single glance toward Jump House, but of course he wouldn't do that, not in front of everyone. He was the tallest, and everyone knew he was the best rider in the entire academy, though some idiots talked about Holdan. That stupid foreigner at his right looked like a scrub next to Cousin Van. How Marlovair hated that foreigner. Every time he saw him, his shoulder-blades stung in memory. He sneered as much as he dared, hoping the foreigner would look his way.

"Tonight's assignments," Cousin Van said. "We'll start with boundary scouts and riding captains conferring—no, no," he said impatiently as several people started moving, Marlovair among them. "I am picking the riding captains. I don't care what you decided in your Houses. I'm the commander, after all, am I not?"

No one spoke. The only sound was a snort from a horse on the picket line adjacent the rushing river, and a bird whortling in the distant hedgerow.

Cousin Van gave them a grim smile. With an internal shrug, Marlovair went back to glaring at the foreigner. *Come on, come one, one look, just one. See what I think of you, you road apple—*

"Marlovair."

Van Marlovair jumped, his gaze snapping to his cousin, who said, "You may take that attitude to the cook tent, and work off your sulks with cooking rice balls. You'd best have all the washing done by midnight, because that will be your guard watch."

Marlovair gasped. A joke, surely?

A couple of ill-muffled snickers behind him made it very clear how many thought that the joke, if there was one, was on him.

Marlovair did not hear all the names of his riding, but from the soft sighs, the shifts from foot to foot around him, he knew that none of his own mates had been named for the fun chore of boundary scouting. The rest of the assignments went out for a night-time game of flag-prisoner. Not just the usual scouting drill, done a million times, only worthwhile if you could pull a scrag, but a real game. And here he was, stuck on cook drudge!

A *fun* game. But, Marlovair told himself as they were dismissed, it was kind of a babyish game. Taking prisoners—making raids and escape attempts—not a *real* war game. The *men* didn't play at prisoner-raids. So obviously Cousin Van was giving the lesser boys a scrub game, while the future leaders were getting their chores out of the way. Yes, that was it! Everyone had to do some chores, so they were getting theirs over now . . . only what was that about a midnight patrol? Oh, surely he meant wing captain or advance scout on a night raid!

Making rice balls was tedious but easy. You just had to get the fire going, the cauldron on the boil, and the rice put in to steam while they got the big iron pans ready with crushed olives heating up on them. Then you got the onion browning gently while you separated off the cabbage leaves and dunked them into the ensorcelled bucket, ready for the rice to be plopped in the middle of each cabbage leaf with its pile of browned onion, a hunk of cheese on that, and then the whole rolled in the cabbage and set to crisp up on the pans.

There was little talking among the cooks, who listened wistfully, longingly, or resentfully—depending upon their natures—to the laughter and yells of the flag-game as the shadows lengthened, melded, and then strengthened into the blue of nightfall.

At last, at last, they were done. And not too long before the watch change. The boys stampeded back, then they were too busy to think as everyone had to get their share, after which the cook dishes all had to be dunked and stacked for morning.

Marlovair and his cooks were just looking wearily around the neat cook tent when Stad appeared at the tent flap, the lantern light on his face from the side made his expression seem hard.

"Attention," he said, before anyone could speak.

Now they couldn't, unless asked a question.

"You're now on guard duty. You two under the wing captain on the search team, for we're running a rescue game tonight. You are all prison guards," he said, sweeping the rest of the cook riding with one hand—leaving only Marlovair.

Stad turned his way. "And you are stock-post on the picket."

Without waiting for a response, he whirled, batted aside the tent flap, and was gone.

Stock post on the picket. That meant just standing there all night! No one made night raids on horses except on the big games with the seniors.

Marlovair stared at the swinging tent flap, waiting for it to lift again, for Cousin Van to re-enter, smiling, and say, "Stung ya! You really believed it! Now go take command of the raid team."

But nothing happened until the other boys began to move. Marlovair felt their covert stares, but he ignored them. Shock, disgust, anger, and underneath it the sickness of betrayal were so strong he couldn't seem to think past it.

A shout from outside, "Get moving!" snapped him into motion.

His jaw tightened. A challenge, maybe? They had set out to be perfect, so even if he didn't get to be a roving guard on the game, or even a guard protecting whoever was the prisoner they were rescuing (which was fun if the search team came your way, because you got to scrap), he'd just be the best horse picket ever. And Cousin Van would feel really bad when he discovered who had gotten him his position of command, oh, yes he would.

Marlovair stood by the animals, watching in every direction. For a time he wondered if Cousin Van would send some sort of sneak attack that he alone could repel, and thus earn House points, but nothing ever happened.

The sky gradually clouded over. Occasionally the cold breeze brought distant shouts as the attack team breached the perimeter of the POW camp. Excited voices rose, the words smothered by distance, followed by hooting and cackling laughter. Then torchlight bobbed about wildly. Finally the lights moved toward camp. Centuries later a pair of boys from Squirrel House showed up for the second bell to dawn watch, which meant they wouldn't have to do morning chores.

"You're relieved," one said shortly.

"You have the post," Marlovair answered in a formal voice.

They didn't respond. He bit down on questions about the game and walked away. His shoulders twitched when he heard a whisper, then a snicker.

He made his way to his tent, where half the others were already asleep. Puzzled, angry, worried by turns, he dropped into sleep—and then jerked awake when a rough hand punched his shoulder. The bleak, blue light of a rainy dawn outlined Stad, who said, "Cook tent."

"What?" Marlovair squawked, sitting up in his bedroll.

Stad said softly, though by now everyone in the tent was awake, their open, staring eyes reflecting the blue-gray light, "Are you arguing with an order?"

"No."

It was within the rules—but barely.

Marlovair got up, dressed hastily in the cold air, neatened his bedroll, and stamped to the cook tent—to be told by those already up that he had water-carrying duty. And so he got stuck lugging pails and pails of water from the river to the cook tent.

So he had to slosh back to the river and get water in the magic pails, while everyone else was busy getting the day's orders.

When he was done, it was back to horse-picket duty as the real game was set up. By now he knew that the impossible had happened. Instead of making Marlovair into second in command in all but name, Cousin Van—Stad—had made him a butt. Why? *Why?*

Everyone was still on their best behavior, thus he was forced to follow his own campaign, which had become a disaster. He couldn't even make his feelings known by covert resistance, because he wasn't ever in speaking distance of Toss or Snakeface, who were apparently (as far as he could see from across the fields) opposing captains on the day game-raid. No one else spoke to him, so he couldn't talk, much less command.

And at dinner, again he was on water duty, and again all alone. Alone slogging back and forth to the freezing river water, bringing back water for all the tents. The rain had ended, leaving a clear, balmy night, but he was still wet, and still numb from all that water duty. No one *ever* had cook tent three times on one game, unless he, or they, had ten or more defaulters. But was Master Askan around to see or hear, and land on Stad for his total unfairness? He was not. His silhouette was way out there in the soft rain as he rode the perimeter, looking for non-existent danger.

After water duty, Marlovair was stuck right back on horse-picket, marching straight out in his still-wet clothes, his fingers like numb icicles by midnight.

This time, it was Stad himself who came to relieve him. "Go to sleep," he ordered, after the formal phrases of watch change.

Sick, betrayed, Marlovair burst out, "Why?"

Stad whirled around. For a long, sickening time, Marlovair gritted his teeth. By now the beautiful glass castle of his future expectations had been shattered, and he waited miserably for the breeze he'd just earned for backchat to an order.

But Stad snorted, then said, "Because, you little wolf turd, you've come within a heartbeat of destroying my life. And you're so full of swank you don't even see it."

Pain flashed through nerves and brain, leaving Marlovair sick and numb with shock.

Stad said in a low, soft voice, "I have worked hard all my life. I earned my position. I practiced all winter every year to keep up with the best. To be better than the best. And every spring when I came back I got up before dawn to get extra practice. Every day. Eight years. So I'd be the best. And all—all! For *nothing*. Because of *you*."

"But—"

"Shut up. I don't give a spit for what you think." Stad actually turned his head and spat into the grass, and the deliberate rudeness was more shocking than any epithet. "No one would tell me. It's tradition, we don't rat out friends, we don't rat against families. I thought you boys were just acting like the scrubs because you're stiff-rumps about rank and that idiocy."

"But rank means leadersh—"

Stad flicked up the back of his hand with deliberate, unsmiling violence. Marlovair's teeth clicked.

"Evrec—my riding mate for eight years—wasn't even talking to me any more. And all these looks from everyone down in lower Houses—but I've been so busy with—with *real* things. So I can't blame anyone I know, but here's the truth. I didn't find out what you've really been doing until just a few days ago. Evrec wouldn't rat. I couldn't even find Marec, he was so busy avoiding me. I almost had to use a knife to get Baudan to tell me."

Marlovair kicked at the turf. "But—*you* should be rad in our House. Or even Squirrel House. Which means next year you'll be Danas Valdlav—"

"Shut *up*. Do you think I'd take it if it came to me like *this*? Do you really think it would mean anything to me that I got what I worked for all my life just because of who my relatives were in the past? Or worse, because a pile of stinking horse apples like you and your House made life impossible for everyone else, so Keriam was forced to make a change just so everyone can get back to what we're *supposed* to be doing, which is learning to fight Norsunder?"

"But you're just a second-rad in the seniors! That always means—"

"I'm a rad in the seniors because that's where I'm needed. That's what command structure means. Not flags, not marching with you first in order because of your family name. It means putting the right man in the right place. They decided they needed me as second-rad in the seniors. So I serve." Stad's voice sharpened.

Marlovair trembled. He couldn't speak. He knew his voice would shake.

Stad smacked his fist into his palm as he struggled for the right words. "If the king sends me to defend the west. Say, in ten years. Not because he has faith in my command. But because there are too many fools like you in the army who will only rally under a Jarl or someone related to a Jarl. If he has to send someone like Ret Forthan to do the real work, while I parade around with the banners of our ancestors and spout old ballads. Do you think I want that? I want him to tell me to command in the west because I can. Because he knows I can, and so he can send Forthan to the east, and he'll know he can."

"But I just—Dad even said—the king—"

Stad turned away, his entire body stiff with fury. Then he rounded on Marlovair. "And you—*You!* Have been trying your hardest to take my earned command away from me. Because if they pull Evrec and put me in his place, I have to obey. But if I get Valdlav after that—because of that—I will turn it down. And I wanted you to feel, just for one day, what that will be—oh, I've said enough."

He turned his back, jerking his thumb toward the camp in dismissal.

Marlovair took a few loping steps toward the camp, but when the tightness in his throat and chest broke on a sob, he whirled about and raced parallel to the camp, just running, paying no attention to where he went, because his vision was blurred by tears.

When he found himself in the scratchy hedgerow beyond the camp boundary, he tried to force himself through with the intention of running himself to death. The stiff twigs and the sharp-edged leaves were too strong in their scratching resistance, so he just flung himself down and wept for the first time since he was small.

He cried until he felt empty inside, then rolled over, his head pounding in time with his heartbeat. When Cousin Van's words whispered over and over in his head, the tears welled again.

What now? Fall on his knife? Except you don't do that in the academy—that is, he could, but he knew no one would be impressed. Because he wasn't doing it *for* anything. There was no Norsundrian threatening *Talk! Or die.* He wasn't protecting anything except his own feelings. They'd call him a coward for that.

But how could he bear—

Footsteps. He sat up, struggling to contain his breathing.

Coming this way! The inner perimeter! The hedgerow had always been the camp perimeter when they came here. That meant he was out of bounds. By just a spear's length . . . which was the sort of back-of-the-hand rule-testing they'd been doing to Evrec for the past month. If he was caught here, Master Askan would think—

A silhouette emerged from the copse to the east, starlight clear on the features of the foreigner. Not Master Askan. It was none other than the stupid foreigner, the other rad on duty.

Oh, yes, there were far worse things to bear. And he'd just fallen into one of them.

He held his breath, but his chest hiccupped twice. The sound seemed louder than a thunderbolt. Yet the foreigner did not start, or speak, or even change his gait as he slowly approached, eyes sweeping northward and westward. He wasn't asleep on his feet, not with the starlight glowing as tiny pinpricks in his eyes. Maybe the idiot was squiffy with illegal drink, that would explain his blindness and deafness, except how could he walk so straight?

Step, step. The foreigner's feet rustled through the wet grass, passing not an arm's length from Marlovair, who lay absolutely still, his breath held almost to the fainting point—

Gulp!

Another hiccup!

But the step didn't falter, the pale blond head kept moving as he surveyed the darkness beyond the perimeter, everywhere except these bushes.

Marlovair lay until the footsteps had passed out of hearing, then sat up. The foreigner just kept marching slowly along the inner perimeter until he vanished into the darkness.

# Thirty-eight

If Marlovair went missing, Shevraeth knew he'd be in trouble for not reporting the breaking of bounds—after the lights out trumpet, yet—so he worried a little as he finished his round. His first instinct when he'd heard that wild weeping had been to make as much noise as he could as a warning to whoever it was to get back in bounds.

But Marlovair, as it turned out to be, didn't hear him until far too late. So Shevraeth had sustained a short, intense inward struggle between duty and what he knew his mother would expect.

A very short struggle. It only took two steps to realize that in a contest between rule-bound duty, where no life was in the balance, and mercy, he would always choose mercy. Even if it was for the most obnoxious brat he'd ever met. But the depth of that misery was not faked, not from a fourteen-year-old boy.

Shevraeth's anxiety only lasted until the end of the long, wearying patrol. On his soft-footed return through the camp just as dawn was lifting the eastern shadows, he peered through the open flap of the tent where he knew Marlovair was supposed to be, and though the inside was too dark to see any specific figures, it was easy to count the deep breathings he heard there. No one missing.

Later that morning, as the boys began breaking down the camp for the return to the academy Shevraeth sensed Marlovair studying him covertly, probably with anger, certainly with worry.

Marlovair would just have to figure out that no one would know, nothing would happen. It would no longer be an act of mercy if he said anything at all. It would be an intolerable gesture of moral ascendance—and after the way Stad had rough-ridden his own cousin all weekend, it didn't seem as if any more was needed on that score.

The boys finished loading the tents and cook gear onto the cart, and they started back. Many of the boys were still watching Marlovair for clues on behavior. He marched as silently, eyes front, as he had on the way to the camp, and so—gradually—everyone else fell in line as well. Stad rode alone at the front, and Shevraeth, not seeing any sign that he wanted company, dropped back to ride with Master Askan behind the tent cart.

⚜

Some days later, he and Senelac sat side by side on a rooftop.

It was the first warm evening of the season, the soft air drifting by with enticing smells from cookeries, underscored by the astringent freshness of the blooming plains. The entire city seemed to be outside, judging from the festival quality to the noise. Everyone welcomed the first hot days after a series of long rains.

"Our communications have gotten so complicated. I can see the reasoning. Should say, I remember the reasoning," Senelac corrected, bumping her shoulder against his.

They had been put on the same team for the latest comm run. Someone was entering the city, and had to make it to the king with a message. Senelac had abruptly told Shevraeth that she and he were teamed, and she'd picked the place for them to sit and watch over the stables—guarding against whoever the newest comm team had picked as courier.

He said, "First assumption. Norsunder can't torture a place."

"That's where everyone is agreed." She thumped against him again.

"After that is where we part," he responded, seeing at last where she was going.

She opened her palms in assent. It was strange, how she liked his proximity—and he definitely liked hers—but she kept her talk on business. How could Savona possibly have thought she was anything like Tamara, who seemed (from report) to have two subjects of conversation: herself, and court gossip?

Senelac breathed deeply. "Someone is making wine-sauce," she said on a sigh. "Now I'm hungry. Anyway, so we leave messages. We don't hand them off person to person. Less to see by chance, and one life at risk is preferable to two. But a place can't *do* anything. We know that's the weak part. Someone has to pick it up."

Shevraeth waggled a hand. "We do seem to keep circling that. I don't know if there's a way to get round it." He extended fingers as he counted conclusions after missions. "The easiest method, the golden cases, is apparently out because Norsunder seems to have ways of breaking the magic protections on them and waylaying messages. A code carried by hand on ordinary paper can be broken. A person who knows a code can be broken. So now we're doing this secondary code, with the pinholes, only known to those at the top—but what if a Norsundrian holds the paper up to a light? And it's going to happen, especially if they lurk about in the night as everyone seems to believe."

She shrugged, her shoulder thumping his arm again. She liked it when he thumped her back, something it was difficult to bring himself to do. Wrestling and playful punches and the like had been scolded out of him and his court friends by the time they were ten. You didn't bump princes, and princes ought not to let people thump them. You kept a personal distance—the higher your rank, the greater your distance.

*Probably self-preservation*, Shevraeth thought now, distracted. *Though it's come to be a marker of rank. Ordinary people can stand together, shoulder to shoulder, princes are solitary, surrounded by rings of servants guarding space. Kings with the most space of all.*

". . . and finally even a place is not risk-free. The enemy could be lying in wait."

Shevraeth had been over this ground so many times he was bored. He knew the subject of communication while under siege—or worse, occupation—was important, but it was also something he couldn't see using at home. Ever. So he said, "That's where we come back to every courier being known, rather than everyone unknown."

"The risk being exactly the same, just shifting from your friend being in danger to what if the unknown passing you the message is a fake?" And when he did not immediately answer, she chuckled. "You're sick of it."

"No I'm not."

'Yes you are. You get that flat tone when you're hiding your feelings, and why hide your feelings unless you're sick of the entire subject? Besides, most of us are too."

*Us.*

"Stad admitted it yesterday, when I saw him coming out of that conference with the seniors." She grinned. "And I asked him what he'd done on that last game of yours to get those Jump House brats in line, and he gated me so hard my nose and toes still hurt."

'Gated'—with a group, it meant shut in or shut out. With a person it meant what in court was called the cut, where you severed public notice of someone or someones, and not only did not speak, but walked right past as if they did not exist. The final cut was if you walked directly into the person's proximate space, knowing that they must drop back.

The Marlovens' metaphor was more literal, the closing of a gate or door on one. The 'cut'—meaning a sword—in court culture was centuries away from actual steel, but just as inimical in effect.

"You were there," she persisted. "You were the only other rad. You must have seen or heard something."

He wondered why instinct prompted him not to tell her. They had shared many academy confidences, and nothing untoward had happened. "I was almost always on the other side of the camp, or perimeter, or asleep when Stad and Master Askan were on guard," he said.

She sighed. "And you and Stad never, ever talk, though you live in the same House. All right, shut me out."

"Stad is not talking about that to anyone," Shevraeth said. "In fact, he's not talking at all. His liberty time comes, he just disappears."

Senelac's profile, torchlit, was sober against the stone of the tower next to the building they sat atop of. "You know something?" She clasped her hands around her knees. "In the olden days, this whole section all belonged to the women. It was they who guarded the city. Not the men. They were always riding around, guarding the country." She shook her head. "I don't know what it all means, except maybe we've gone backward."

He was silent.

She gazed at him, narrow-eyed, "And you're thinking . . . what, that war with anyone, men or women, is backward. Right?"

"Right," he admitted, his tone apologetic.

She pursed her lips, and then laughed softly. "I just wish you could convince Norsunder of that." The end-of-mission signal, a single trumpet-blare, echoed down the stone streets, and Senelac said in a different voice, "The runner was Lis Kasrec. She obviously got caught. Come on, the night is still young, let's go to the park." She gripped the front of his tunic and gave him a smacking kiss.

# Thirty-nine

. . . *Galdran watched us like a hawk watches a mouse while riding the air currents above. It was so obvious to us all that the princess did not like him. She even seemed a little afraid of him, and if so, who could blame her? There were no wagers on whether or not there would be royal wedding negotiations. Then the king glowered around, Deric's grandmother saying he was looking for someone to blame if the princess goes home without accepting his suit. Both Olervecs insist that old Countess of Orbanith muttered over iced fruit that even when the Merindars were teens, everyone preferred Canardan, who was only a second son, to Galdran, future crown or no. Tamara backed it up. She said half the table heard, but she seems too old, and too tough, to care.*

*But here's the worst thing, Danric. The Marquise is back from Sartor, and has been ever-present during this royal visit, arranging all Galdran's entertainments herself. All of them splendid, even spectacular. And she is so deft a host she earns your mother's respect. Galdran stamps and glowers. The Marquise drifts about and smiles on everyone. How can so large a woman move so quick, and more to the point, so silent? She scares me as much as the king does. I can't tell you why. But I'll show you. Just last night I slipped out for some water during a concert. It was far too hot in that hall. On my return, suddenly there's the Marquise, right there before the door. She takes my arm and invites me for a night walk in her garden, and while we're looking at her roses, which look like ghostly blobs in the moonlight—I'll never like roses again—she's going on about her dear daughter and how difficult it is to find young men whose tastes are as delicate and refined as hers, and I think I'm dancing around all those pitfalls without committing myself when she comes out with: "Have you had opportunity to correspond with your young friend, the Marquis of Shevraeth?"*

*I almost fell into the fishpond with surprise. I galloped mentally back, wondering what we've said, and she just waited, so I ventured what I thought was a safe comment, "I believe he occasionally writes to his father."*

*She just smiled. I will go before any court of inquiry and attest upon my honor she was calling me a liar in her head, and Danric, much as I embrace you as my brother and friend, your letters will now be burned as soon as I read them. Almost before! Almost before! Though the only ones I kept were the ones about your lady friend—and sparse enough have you been with detail—(unlike Your Obedient Servant to Command) she smirked like she knew everything. I did burn those letters before going to bed. And since then I cannot go into my rooms without that sense that her fingers have been everywhere. Like an army of invisible slugs have left their trail over every one of my things, discernible only in the realm of the mind.*

*Anyway, she was not done with me.*

*"I shall have to put my question to Prince Alaerec, then," she says to me. "Fialma has expressed a wish to correspond with the young Marquis—wherever he is. It might be quite illuminating to discover faraway places through his eyes, and they might practice their Court Sartoran with one another."*

*Warm as it was, I make my earnest vow I felt the chill of mid-winter!*

੨ᎣᏒᎦᎧᏣ

Ndand Maddar and Fenis Senelac watched from inside the barn as Fath led several of the younger girls across the stable's outer court toward the two pale blond heads just visible among all the horses left by the seniors.

"Fath is after Shevraeth?" Mad asked in disbelief. "Or is she on morning retrieval?"

Senelac crossed her arms, her profile scornful. "If she twiddles her hair, she's after him, not sweaty horses."

As the seniors dismounted subsequent to their dawn lance practice, the younger girls obediently led away their mounts by their halters. They left a clear field of view to where Shem leaned against the gate talking to Shevraeth, who, Mad was quite aware, had grown amazingly tall. His head bent courteously as he listened to Shem, but she couldn't tell if his smile was one of pleasure or politeness.

Then came Fath, running her fingers through her loose curls. They did not hear what she said, they only heard her fluting voice, but Mad saw the change in Shevraeth's expression, and thought, yes, he was talking to Shem in pleasure because this one is his polite touch-me-not face.

Senelac said, "I just hate it when he does that."

Mad jerked round, staring at her friend in mute amazement.

Senelac's cheeks reddened. "I mean when he turns that look on me. He's quite welcome to use it on Fath, and the more the better."

"He uses it on *you*?"

Senelac grimaced. "Oh, sometimes I ask for it, no mistake. I cut him off as rudely as I can if he talks about wherever-it-is. And I've got him fairly well trained by now. But if he slips up and I frost him, he's never impolite, never insists, never calls me on it. Just gives me that look." She jerked her thumb over her shoulder.

Mad glanced back. Shem had squared off with Fath, both of them trying to outtalk one another.

Mad chuckled. "Why is it that everyone wants his attention? He's not half so handsome as Van Stad. I mean, he's easy on the eyes, but so are most of the seniors. You think it's that he's a foreigner?" *Or is it that whatever you want, the other girls want?*

But Mad knew Fenis Senelac did not think that way. Fath might wish she was the leader of the girls, but Senelac just was. And whatever interested her became interesting to everyone else.

Senelac's shoulder jerked up. "He moves like a foreigner, still. Elegant, that's what Sartora called it. She said it's taught to nobles in foreign courts. Who needs 'elegant' in the field? Yet it does look good, especially when it's not done to swank, and he doesn't do it to swank. It's just *him*. And he still has that accent. It gets stronger when he's—" She tipped a hand. "Feelings get past that blank face of his."

"Yes. And every girl here considers it adorable. You did, too, as I recall. So why the sour face? Familiarity made him contemptible?"

Senelac flicked a look at Mad, and saw the mocking quirk to her mouth. That was why they were best friends. They had exactly the same sense of the absurd. Especially about themselves, Senelac thought.

"No." Then added as two more senior girls joined Fath and Shem, one flicking her hair absently, the other letting loose with a look-at-me trilling laugh that both Mad and Senelac considered loud and shrill. "He wears this medallion under his clothes. All the time."

"I know, you told me that last year. You said it was probably from some girl back in his old country, and so you weren't going to let yourself get close. But you wouldn't actually *ask* him the truth of that," Mad added, her sarcasm now trenchant.

Senelac watched Shevraeth lift his eyes, ever so briefly, and yes—they found her even though she stood in the shadows. She felt the impact of his gaze as she always did. And she saw his breath catch, and knew he felt it as well.

She turned her back on him, though it took all her strength. "I wasn't going to tell you. Wasn't going to tell anyone. I . . . mentioned it, never mind the rest of the conversation, when Sartora was here last. She might have the powerful mind of an Old Sartoran. If such really did exist the way the stories go. But she's just a little scrub in all the ways that count. She looked at me with the innocent surprise of a first-year in the Puppy Pit and said, *But Senrid gave him that to wear. It's a transfer token. To take him home if Norsunder invades.*"

Mad opened her hand. "All right. That makes sense. What doesn't make sense is why you're still sending him dirty looks."

Senelac gritted her teeth, then said with an exasperated sigh, "Oh, Mad, are you ten years old, too? Because one day he's going to use it. He's going to go home."

Mad whistled under her breath. "But I thought—"

"What, that he'd stay? Give up his life wherever?" Senelac asked derisively.

"So you're angry because you think he's trifling with you?" Mad asked in complete disbelief.

"No. I'm trifling with him. And he knows it. I told him so from the start."

The mess bell clanged then.

Senelac turned away. "Go get your breakfast," she muttered, and ran out to the corral where the experienced trainers were dealing with the I-dare-you antics of the seven month olds, whose lunges, bites, and kicks could kill you before they learned the boundaries of horse and human personal space.

Leaving Mad to walk soberly toward the mess hall alone. *You said it but you don't believe it. I don't think you ever did. You thought he'd stay.*

*No, you thought he'd stay for you.*

When Maddar reached the gate she stopped in front of Fath and said in a field command voice that cut effectively through the chatter, "Breakfast! Scat!"

Shevraeth, trained to be polite, turned away in relief. He could not quite bring himself to abruptly leave when people, especially girls, were talking to him.

They ran off, and his dilemma shifted. He did not want to call attention to himself by being late to mess. Why had all those girls come crowding up? He liked Shem. She gave him excellent advice on which of the seniors' mounts was best for which terrain and fighting style. But lately they all seemed to want to come up and just chat, always about horses or food or exercises, all academy things, all well within the rules. And he liked talking to girls, he liked looking at them, and no one ever said or did anything that would cause trouble . . . but they didn't crowd around the other fellows. Maybe some new unspoken rule was forming? And he broke it just by answering back?

He'd just looked for a single heartbeat toward Senelac— surely that was not a problem as these others were all blattering away—and she'd turned her back on him.

Grimacing, he cut across the parade ground, where he passed a forlorn figure busy with a broom. It was Tevac, his wrists protruding bonily from his shapeless tunic as he stolidly whisked the broom over the flagstones. Particularly aggravated rads were fond of the late summer winds and drifts of leaves, which combined to make this particular punishment for an abundance of personal defaulters a brisk and entertaining exercise. Entertaining for aggravated rads and gloating classmates, that is, as the winds scattered the leaves hither and yon.

"Bell rang," he said to Tevac. "Didn't you hear it?"

"Have to finish." Tevac sighed.

Shevraeth paused, taking in the size of the court. It seemed exponentially larger without the entire academy gathered in it.

He whistled. "Alone?"

Tevac thumped the broom on the stones, the other hand out wide.

"Must have been some sting!"

Tevac tried for carelessness as he said, "Pepper in Jump House's drawers."

Shevraeth let out a surprised laugh. "That was you? Of course that was you."

Tevac tried not to grin, then gave up. He knew Shevraeth wouldn't be impressed by his victim pose. Not after all those stings last year. "Think they are so hot—" He smacked his own behind.

Shevraeth did not ask for the reasoning behind this thinking. He wasn't certain he wanted to know the eleven-year-old logic behind pepper in underclothes. The second year colts had already had enough trouble, in Shevraeth's private opinion. Since the two-night campout he'd seen them mending horse gear, scrubbing, sweeping, and doing the most tedious drill when others had rec time. So he shook his head, took a step, paused, then turned back. "I have to ask. And I don't know why, as I am certain the answer will be a piece of knowledge I will never put to use. But. Does pepper in your drawers really make your parts hot?"

Tevac snickered. "Itches."

Shevraeth paused, contemplating the horror of itching while standing still on parade—trying to concentrate on wooden weapons whistling past your ears—riding practice. Especially riding practice.

"That," he said, "is lethal. Keriam is more merciful than I; you would have been sweeping the entire city if you'd tried that last year."

Tevac snickered, and Shevraeth ran on, thinking about just how unpopular Marlovair and his riding-mates had managed to make themselves from masters and rads to scrubs.

He was stopped again, this time by Gannan, who bustled round a corner, flung out a long arm, and when Shevraeth came to an abrupt halt, said, "Stad and Landeth Elder were looking for you. They need you to run as senior rad on a pup overnight. Andaun broke his arm on the way in from lance practice."

"Horse all right?"

"Not the least hurt. Andaun dropped his point, caught it in a vine he didn't see, and—" Gannan wrenched his arm up in dramatic demonstration. "Since it's the pups going, you wouldn't have afternoon knife classes, and Ventdor is going to cover the colt class."

Shevraeth brushed his hand over his tunic in salute and continued on. Now he'd have to eat fast.

He rode out not long after Landeth and the two Houses of pups had marched out, easily catching up. The fields used for the smallest boys were very close to the academy, which was why a master was seldom assigned to the overnights after the very first one or two. The neat lines of small boys had long since straggled into shoving, hopping, chattering clumps, their high voices and energy boundless despite the summery heat.

By now Shevraeth was long familiar with all the regular campsites. The lower academy seldom was taken anywhere new. That remained for the all-academy game at the end of the year.

"Where to?" he asked Landeth, who was a second year senior Shevraeth knew by sight. They'd never exchanged more than a few words, always on the practice field.

Who grimaced. "Dish Field."

Of course. That was probably why Landeth hadn't found any volunteers, and so the first available rad who knew scrubs had to be ordered out. This was the very first overnight practice field to which Shevraeth had been taken two years before. It was the field used most often for the lower Houses, and the games were pretty much always related to the latest drills. Not a problem for the boys—who would do fine—but who would also be saving up that boundless energy for sneak attacks on one another during what would surely be a star night, which meant night guard would be long and tedious.

They arrived shortly before sunset, and supervised the boys in setting up the tents. Shevraeth had forgotten how terrible the smallest boys were at that—even by their second year, they had improved considerably. The sun had finally sunk into the west, closing a simmering day, when at last the tents and bedrolls passed inspection, and it was time for cook duties. The rads had to closely supervise with boys this young, inexperienced, and prone at the slightest opportunity to turn chores into mayhem.

Always simple food for the smallest boys. This first night, just slices of travel bread and cheese, the bread heavily studded with currants to make it a little more savory. The boys tore into it with the uncomplicated hunger of the very young.

"Plan?" Shevraeth asked Landeth.

Landeth watched the boys chomping away with the steady scrutiny of experience as he talked. "Usual. Ridings, emphasis on scouting and flank guarding."

"Flag game for tomorrow," Shevraeth said, hand out in acknowledgement of the expected. "Why not a night game to wear 'em out tonight?"

Landeth tipped his head. "You haven't been with the first-year pups much, have you?"

"Marec and I were Pit rads last year. I know well that they are looking for any opportunity to sting us, one another, the tents, probably the grass and sky, if they can just get outside of the light. I came up with this idea too late in the year to use it—"

"Of course." Landeth flashed an ironic grin.

"—but why not use it now? The problem seems to be keeping them within the torch perimeter, but away from the campsite."

Landeth snorted. "If you can do that—well, let's hear it."

Shevraeth had played seek-the-treasure with the other court children when young, memories he'd dredged up while working on the command class communications problems. Though none of his solutions had helped with command class, he'd wondered if one of the oldest favorites might appeal to scrubs. "Suppose we make up messages. In code. And hide them. But only one is the real one—and they have to break the codes . . ."

Landeth's bushy red brows rose. "You don't mean the scout-and-track."

"Codes. I don't know why I didn't think of it before. They all love codes, if they think there's some secret or reward. But we lay them out like the clues for the tracking exercise. It's a kind of seek-and-find, not tracking people, but clues, they have to figure them out, then hunt for more clues."

"It's brilliant," Landeth said. "What about the code? We aren't prepared."

"I think I can put something together really fast," Shevraeth said, considering what had worked and what hadn't on the comm games.

Landeth snorted a laugh. "You've got until we're done with cook-wash and perimeter setup. How much of a perimeter do you need?"

They discussed the landmarks as the light began to fade, then Shevraeth withdrew into the rad tent to get his end done. It was full dark when he finished staking down the torches and hiding the last of the messages; he'd been careful to keep the tents between him and the boys, who were busy singing ballads and thumping hand drums, organized by Landeth.

When he returned, they ended the last song. Landeth divided them, Shevraeth explained the rules, and released them. They exploded out into the huge square marked off by ruddy torchlight, and soon their cries, laughter, and excited commands to one another, threats, and insults (to which no one listened) rose on the soft summer air.

The game lasted until far beyond the usual scrub night games. The boys kept at it until they heard the faint echo of the watch bells for midnight. Landeth called a halt. Despite the yells of disappointment, most of them were drooping. They'd managed to find most of the hidden pieces of paper, and had divided themselves into ridings—some to decode, others to raid the enemies' papers (preferably ones nearly decoded)—which meant that some of the papers traded back and forth without much headway made on the codes. This was the cause of the shrillest confrontations, for some were entirely subsumed by the challenge of the codes, others by the irresistible urge to scarfle someone else's work without having to do any decoding themselves. Thus no one won, but they had worked hard, and so were given House points, which pleased them all.

The House rads got them established in their tents, the rads on midnight outer perimeter patrol took off, and the rads with morning duty went to catch some rest.

Landeth and Shevraeth sat by the campfire and brewed up some coffee.

The usual snickers, insults, and attempts at contests lasted a very short time before the shrill cries of "Shut up! I want to sleep!" signalled an end to the long day.

Complete quiet descended with suspicious speed, but when Shevraeth and Landeth, both experienced in the unsubtle subterfuges of small boys, checked the tents, it was to find the deep, even breathing of exhausted slumber.

Back at the campfire, Landeth said, "That was inspired. For that, I'll take the inner perimeter dead watch. I got to sleep in anyway, and of course you didn't."

Shevraeth withdrew to the tent, leaving Landeth to a quiet night.

# Forty

Senelac grinned. "It was a great idea. Caris tells me her brother and Marec and the others down in the lower academy from pups to colts are busy putting together paper chases as if they've just been invented, and weren't popular when our grandparents were young." She eyed Shevraeth, who gave her that faint smile that meant he was sitting on some sort of story, probably about his young days.

The usual spurt of resentment burned through her, to be determinedly dismissed.

She looked up into his sun-browned face, his light gray eyes, the pale drift of fine, silky hair across his brow. Listened to the sound of his breathing as they walked aimlessly along the river's edge. He looked like a Marloven, he should *be* one. Oh, she knew how stupid it was to hope one day he'd decide to stay, that he would not go back to wherever-it-was with the bad king and the silly girls who didn't know the difference between a bow and an arrow.

Shevraeth had no idea what she was thinking. She never talked about her emotions, or shared anything beyond their life here at the academy. So he had no idea why she stiffened and turned cold this time. The last time she'd frosted him was after he'd accidentally encountered Marec, just before that whole Marlovair mess. Senelac afterward had said that if she wanted to get together with two people instead of one—and have Everyone

Talking About It—she would set it up beforehand. End of conversation, end of day.

Gate.

Shevraeth had been careful since. If he was meeting her, he treated his departure like a covert exercise, taking care to avoid anyone else he knew. Even though they were not breaking any rules. Spoken rules. Unspoken . . . well, he had a good sense of the academy ones, but he obviously had plenty to learn about the unspoken rules between girls and boys, because he still could not figure out where the problem was.

As they paced side by side in silence, but not the companionable silence when she thumped up against his arm, he worked mentally back through what he'd said and she'd said. Everything had been great all evening until she brought up the scrubs' treasure hunt. He hadn't made any comment at all about home, or any of the things she got prickly over. So . . . what happened?

He began to wonder if he was imagining things when they neared a curve of the river that lay adjacent to the alleyway they all called Academy Run. It was a short cut to the academy tunnel, and when the watch bells caught someone short at the end of their liberty watch, you'd often see seniors sprinting at top speed to get back in bounds before the bells' echo went silent.

Senelac gave him a brisk wave, meant to be casual but it was far too abrupt for that. She vanished into a crowd of prentices celebrating someone's promotion.

Walking along down the alley, Shevraeth felt his mood cool from anticipation to bitterness. How could he have done something when he'd done nothing?

"Shevraeth!"

He turned around, relieved to be interrupted. The left-hand boundary of Academy Run was the massive city wall. To the right streets angled off, shops below and living quarters above, most of the windows open to the balmy night air. People-shaped silhouettes moved about in the upper story of a flax-weaver's shop. Laughter floated out, and the chink of crockery, but the young men's voices he'd heard had not come from there.

Another laugh. He turned all the way around, to discover five or six fellows in guard uniforms coming up the alley, one talking, the rest laughing as they passed into the shafts of golden light slanting down from the flax-weaver's.

"Shevraeth!"

That was Lennac, who beckoned for him to join them. Forthan walked by Lennac's side.

Shevraeth waited until they caught up. Now he recognized them all from lance practice over winter. They were new to the King's Guard, academy seniors last year or the year before. Joking comments revealed they were just walking back after a day of liberty in the guards' favorite pleasure house, Lennac having won in a long gambling session.

"You're allowed to gamble for money in the Guard, I take it," Shevraeth asked.

"Of course," Lennac said with the pride of a new guard.

One of the others snorted. "They'd do it anyway."

In the academy, you could wager for chores, or for things, but actual money changing hands had a stiff punishment, one that was never waived. Gambling for money in the academy was not done, hadn't been even in the worst days of the Regent. That much Shevraeth had learned.

A shout from the flax-weavers above caused them all to look up.

"Must be some wedding," one fellow observed.

"Hackle-change," the fifth fellow said, as another shout burst from all the open windows, followed by the sound of a drum and then rhythmic stamping. Seeing various looks of question (but comprehension from Forthan and one other) he said, "You know they sun-bleach flax."

Grunts and murmurs of assent.

"Best flax is bleached for a year. Then, mid-summer, they change the old hackles for the new. Celebrate. Weavers take off the hackled flax, which is now soft and white as yeath hair. Ready to commence weaving. Big celebration first."

Nods and shrugs of polite acceptance underscored most of the fellows' indifference to how flax became linen.

Lennac said to Shevraeth, "Anyway, among us. Academy boys doing our two years of King's Guard before we're made patrol captains. If we gamble, the winner spends it on the others. Big dinner. Drink. Fun."

Forthan put in, "The lifers spit at this rule. Half the fun of gambling for them is fighting, sometimes dueling."

Lennac said, "But us. We've been playing with one another for years."

The fifth fellow hiccupped. "'less you hate someone," he slurred wisely. "Strip him o'his earnings. Spend liberty on his butt inna guard barracks. Hah!"

"I don't gamble with anyone I hate." One of the guards smacked a fist into the other palm. "If I want trouble with him, I can find another way."

Shevraeth said, "I never thought of that before. Gambling, I mean. Money. Why not money?"

Lennac explained, "Unpaid gambling debts in the very old days didn't just cause dueling between seniors. Enough causes for that. They sparked off family feuds when fathers came to collect their boys at the end of harvest season."

Clan wars, Shevraeth thought. Ah. That possibly explained some of the unexplained references in the histories he'd read.

Today's winnings had apparently been equal to Lennac's innate generosity. Shevraeth sensed that they were all agreeably tipsy. While Lennac was enlarging on the more spectacular family feuds of history the one who hadn't spoken began smacking his hands in a galloping rhythm against every wooden fence or window they passed, and when Lennac finished talking, the fellow started to sing.

At once the others joined. The fellow continued whacking everything they passed, keeping time, as they shouted out an old ballad.

*. . . they rode the four horses and galloped the river. . .*

Forthan stepped up next to Shevraeth, his manner that of someone desiring private speech. Shevraeth obligingly slowed his steps.

*. . . Sword and shield clashing, blue sparks a-rising. . .*

As the chorus soared in loud, enthusiastic but tuneless voices around them, Forthan murmured, "You'll be finding out tomorrow, but get your sleep tonight. Tomorrow night command meeting. We'll all be there."

Just like that, the tension of impending trouble was back.

"Might be a long meeting," Forthan observed.

Shevraeth flicked him a glance. So obvious a statement in so meditative a voice meant in anyone else that there was something quite unrelated on Forthan's mind.

Shevraeth did not really know Forthan, not even after spending a winter tutoring him. What little he did know was straightforward, without social artifice.

Yet that flick revealed a fellow who was so uncomfortable his entire demeanor seemed uncertain. What military threat or difficulty could possibly unsettle *him*? Shevraeth was just thinking he did not want to know when Forthan mumbled, " . . . girls."

*Hoofbeats athunder, arrows like lightning.*

Shevraeth said, "Girls?"

Forthan gave him a quick, doubtful look, almost a wince, and it was then that Shevraeth finally understood that there was no military crisis involving the girls, but this was a personal question.

He slowed his steps even more, Forthan matching his pace, and Forthan said, after a quick look at his friends, "They talk to you. How?"

The friends were shouting the song, sometimes joined by people in windows above, amid laughter, as the one fellow drummed tattoos on every window or fence he encountered, then hopped on to the next.

Shevraeth bit back a sarcastic retort, *They open their mouths and shape the words.* Not to Forthan, who was . . . serious about this question. "Do you mean, why am I popular, or what do I say to them when they come round? Because I don't actually do anything to make them come round. I think—I think I'm popular because . . . because one of their leaders seems to like me."

"Senelac." Forthan breathed the name, and Shevraeth's blood ran to ice.

*Flanking the enemy, swift as a hawk.*

Not just his blood. His mind numbed, as if he'd stepped into a rushing stream and slipped over a waterfall. He began to babble, not really considering what he said. "I was raised chattering with girls. And boys. Chatter being the mode, without much matter. With most of the girls here, just asking a historical question or something about the horses bridges an awkward moment. But it's true there aren't many of those, they mostly just . . . talk. And I listen, and answer, because they—most of them—like to talk, and like me to listen."

Forthan's unwavering attention made Shevraeth feel extraordinarily awkward. He sensed that Forthan was lending his stupid words far too much import, as if trying to descry more meaning than Shevraeth intended.

*Valor makes victory, the price is our blood.*

And so he considered what Forthan was really asking, which was not 'how to talk to girls.' Shevraeth would no more send Forthan to Senrid's library to memorize impressive historical facts as conversation openers than Forthan would obey.

Not that it took long to consider. Forthan's tightened mouth, his lowered eyes when Shevraeth mentioned Senelac and her knowledge of history made it fairly clear what was really being asked, but the truth . . . it did hurt.

An act of mercy every day. Not that he needed his mother's admonition. He owed Forthan and Senelac the honor of the truth.

And so, with a fair assumption of his customary casual voice, he added, "Senelac seems to be their Danas Valdlav without their having one, so of course whatever, or in my case, whomever she takes an interest might draw the others, but since we aren't twoing—" He shrugged.

*Since we aren't twoing.* And saw revealed by the light of the sentry torches above them the impact in Forthan's face.

Shevraeth kept on talking, just chatter, mainly, about the academy horses and what the girls had told him. Nothing enlightening. Nothing Forthan did not know already, but it served to smooth away the terrible awkward moment, as if it hadn't happened. Because he'd answered the real question, the true question, the one Forthan could not bear to ask.

The academy tunnel was around the next corner, which Shevraeth was glad of. He brought his chatter to a close and flipped up his hand in farewell. Then veered off, unnoticed by the singers, who were now on verse fourteen of that bloodthirsty ballad.

Forthan raised his hand in silent salute.

# Forty-one

"... and I can't find them," Evrec said grimly.

"I'm going to thump Van blind," Stad retorted, flushing with anger.

They were the first ones at Keriam's office, Shevraeth having walked over with Stad from the senior barracks. They were on liberty, which made it easy to leave—most of the others on liberty were in the rec room, as it was raining outside.

Evrec had come straight over from the barracks, by special arrangement with his fellow rads, in order to talk to Stad.

He'd hesitated when he saw Shevraeth, but Stad had said, "Hasn't changed."

All three knew it meant: hadn't changed from his tight-lipped first year.

Evrec opened a hand, and then poured out in a disjointed flurry of words that Van Marlovair and his gang in Jump House had begun going missing during the rec time they only recently had begun to earn back. It was, strictly speaking, rec time, and therefore their time to do whatever they wanted, but rads always knew where their charges were, at least they did if they ventured out in large groups. The entire House had vanished. Not just Van's gang. All of them.

Stad smacked his hand into his palm. "And they've been so quiet. So good. Now what? I tell you, when I find my cousin—"

A quick step at the doorway. They turned their heads—and Senrid dashed in, then slowed, scanning them. "What is it?"

Stad flushed again, turning away as if he'd done something wrong.

Evrec stood up straight as though on parade. "Whole House missing," he admitted miserably.

Senrid said, "They have liberty?"

Evrec opened his hand in assent. Stad's brow furrowed in perplexity.

Because Senrid grinned. "It's all right. I know where they are. Best if you pretend you don't know. Remember, they're on their honor."

"Yes, but I can't find them," Evrec said. "And this is only their second rec watch. I don't dare ask all the others if they've seen 'em, then word gets around I've lost 'em."

Senrid's grin hadn't abated. "Leave it. You'll see. As long as they stick to being missing when on liberty, let it rest."

The two rads tapped their fingers against their chests, signifying orders received, though the angry flush had not yet faded from Stad's cheekbones.

Senrid seemed about to say something else, but the sound footsteps on the stairs caused him to shrug, then jump up to sit on the edge of Keriam's desk, one foot twitching back and forth, reminding Shevraeth of a cat's tail. His back to the window, he faced the room as most of the command class entered, followed swiftly by twos and threes, most of them a little breathless from running.

The watch change bell rang, Senrid cast a swift glance around. "Okay. You're all here."

Of course that meant everyone looked around. Senrid waited for the instinctive scan. Shevraeth looked around with the rest, and saw the two new girls sitting with Senelac over near the wall in the second row.

Senrid jumped down from the table and began his customary pacing back and forth as he said, "We're going to stop the comm runs. They just don't work. There has to be a way, but I don't know what, and no one has any better ideas than I do without resorting to magic. Which would be fine if there wasn't the problem with wards."

Furtive exchanges of looks: *Wards?*

"Think of 'em as magical walls." Senrid gestured with his hands. "Anyway, the comms are going back to the scouts. Yes, I know Norsunder has to have been behind all their deaths before. All we can hope is that they don't know the new ones. A few of my picks might surprise them." That sudden, unpleasant toothy grin. "So anyway, there's nasty rumor in the east. A renegade Chwahir who actually knows how to command. All I can gather is that Norsunder doesn't trust him because he's hard to control. They like efficient obedience. This Kessler Sonscarna is efficient at dealing death, but he's not so quick with the obedience."

Senrid paused for the inevitable rustles and whispers. "Yes, he's related to the terrible old king of Chwahirsland, and no, I don't know if they will sic him on us. My guess is, they want to use us, not slaughter us. Based on that guess, well, I've promised Keriam and the other commanders that I will run if Norsunder crosses the border in force. I know the Norsundrians want me—Detlev told me so before he got me last time."

Now they were all silent.

"So they won't get me." Senrid gave that grin again, but his fingers drummed on every surface within reach as he walked back and forth across the front of the room. "Nor are they going to get you, I've decided. They'd love to have all the training you get. Just take away your brains, and they've got ready-made low ranking commanders to fight and die for Norsunder."

More whispers, which ended with a shush from the back.

"Here's the new orders. You won't speak 'em until—if— when—it happens. When I disappear, that's the signal for you to take the entire academy and vanish. We're going to practice that in new games until . . . well, we'll see. Anyway, you're going to call it a game, and we're going to make it fun at first."

Shevraeth grimaced. He could hear tension in everyone's breathing around him. A game that wasn't a game—life and death, though they were all game-playing age. They shouldn't have to—

*Nobody should have to.*

*Pay attention!*

". . . hiding places, but also the skills of vanishing into crowds. That's what I'm forcing the cavalry to do. They are going to vanish, for they too are practicing. It's going to be part of training everywhere. Cav will blend themselves into horse studs, stables, training centers, ironmongeries. Foot command into cities, into the mines. Norsunder should not be able to lay a hand on anyone with training that they could enchant and use against us, or against outsiders. That's it. Rules for the first games will come down soon. Remember: to the academy, it's all new games, because everyone is sick of Dish Field and Sweat Hill and our traditional campsites. Don't use the word 'traditional.' Use the words 'old' and 'boring.' I know some of the older Jarls will be getting up on their hind legs and barking at me about tradition at the games, so I want their little boys, and the girls, too, all talking about old and boring camps, and new and exciting games. Nothing about tradition." He snapped his fingers. "That's all."

They got up, now everyone talking at once as they filed out. Shevraeth caught Senrid's gaze, and was not surprised to see the flick of a hand meaning 'stay.'

So he sat back down, waiting for the inevitable questions by some that required Senrid to repeat everything he'd just said. Some people need that, Shevraeth thought: everything repeated just to them. It must be reassuring. Or maybe they don't get all the new ideas on the first round.

But at last they'd cleared out, leaving Shevraeth alone with Senrid, who still shed tension like water off a dog's back.

When Senrid saw Shevraeth tense up, he tried to control his own emotions. This foreigner, related to him so distantly, hadn't made his unity—what the Old Sartorans called dena

Yeresbeth—but his kids probably would, if he ever had any. Meantime, he picked up on people's moods without being aware that he was doing so. Senrid had to work for a moment to get his own mental shields up.

He said, "A quick question." (Knowing the answer, but he'd learned it relaxed people a little when you follow the forms, especially when everything else was changing rapidly, and not necessarily for the better.) "You want to be sent back now?"

Shevraeth, as expected, rejected the idea before he even spoke. It was the twitch of irritation between his brows, the slight withdrawal, that expressed his opinion more forthrightly than the polite "No thank you" that he spoke.

Senrid also knew why. Three years here had not changed Vidanric Renselaeus's Remalnan loyalties a whit—but he'd been away long enough for the question not to call up automatic notions of patriotic duty. In fact, from what Senrid had learned about Remalna during a couple of covert visits, it would be difficult for anyone to feel any sense of patriotic duty . . . that is, not in the immediate sense. The kingdom was under worse threat from a rotten king—a king fast becoming *evil*—than from Norsunder, so of course Shevraeth didn't worry about going home to help defend it. He wouldn't be allowed to, and the king might arrange one of his 'accidents' if Shevraeth tried.

Shevraeth saw it first as a question of cowardice, and that much was habit of three years here.

As for the long-term sense of patriotic duty, well, that was why they were here right now, alone, with no witnesses so that Senrid could ask the question he'd been evolving in his mind off and on for the past year or so—ever since he'd figured out why the Sartoran-trained Prince of Renselaeus had really sent his son here.

He had chosen this day to ask his question, and this moment, because he wanted to be looking full in Shevraeth's face when he asked it.

Not that it was going to take question form.

"You understand the why of the new plan?" he began, approaching the matter obliquely.

Shevraeth's brows lifted at the sudden shift in subject, but the momentary resentment was gone. Shevraeth was not a resentful person by nature. "I believe so," he said with his customary caution. "The idea is to preserve lives by having the academy hide either in some remote place, or else in plain sight in some city, doing tasks related to what we—they—we have learned?"

"Yup," Senrid said. "It was Keriam's idea. And it took me a couple of years to get used to it, so that means it'll probably take ten—twenty—maybe a generation for Marlovens to get used to it. But here's the real plan, the plan behind the plan, you could say. I want the people to learn something besides fighting. Because, as a friend of mine who also got stuck with a throne at way too young an age pointed out to me not too long ago, if you train an army in nothing but fighting, well, they're going to want to fight, right? Which is why her kingdom—which is roughly three times the size of yours—hasn't a single warrior. Not even one. Whereas here, everyone, including me, are raised up thinking of war as a way of life."

Shevraeth's brow furrowed as he considered the insight, and Senrid sprung his trap.

"Which is what you are going to need to consider when you become king of Remalna."

And watched Shevraeth's face drain of color, followed by a flush of angry red. Anger—a repudiation so violent it was almost nausea—made him flinch back.

And Senrid struggled to hide his relief. He *had* judged right. He had, he had!

But he wasn't going to show that either.

Shevraeth raised a hand, struggling to assemble words strong enough to deny the very idea. Senrid cut him off with all the scoff he could muster. "Oh, spare us both the humble disclaimers. You reached the age you are now knowing you'd one day be a prince, so what's so stunning about a single rank-step up? Or are you ready to fight me in order to preserve the very idea of Galdran's royal rights?"

Shevraeth's mouth had opened. He shut it, and swallowed painfully.

"Go on," Senrid said, as if he'd spoken. "Why did your father send you here, if you really were going to go back and spend the rest of your life hiding all the skills you learned?"

Shevraeth swallowed again, shocked, sickened. "I am. Not. Going to go back and lead a revolution. Get people killed."

But Senrid just sat on the edge of his commander's desk, swinging his leg and smiling with the twisted, knowing smile of . . .

Of someone who had already trod every step of that path, and at a far younger age.

Senrid, watching carefully, saw realization cool Shevraeth's thoughts like snow on fire. Numbing snow, that chills you right down to the bone.

"One day," Senrid said softly, "Galdran is going to go too far. By that I mean he'll be threatening and endangering more lives than any revolution would. It happened here, with my uncle, and I had to act, ill-prepared as I was. Young as I was, though I never got much of what anyone else would call a childhood, which is mostly just protection from adult responsibility, far as I can see."

Shevraeth opened his hands, his gray eyes steady. "Go on."

No more of that courtly 'your majesty.' Good. "It might be the week you return. It might be in twenty years. Or, you may never have to do anything—he might challenge Norsunder, or try to scrape together an army and seek to smother the wrongs he's committed by making war against one of your neighbors, and conveniently die in battle. More likely he'll linger at the back and send that bully of a cousin, I forget his name, the one he made a baron last year. If I were him I'd look to Mardgar first, as they have the best harbor at your end of the continent. Though they are fiercely good at defending themselves—and he'd have to get through Renselaeus first, wouldn't he? So . . . what can you do to prevent that?"

Shevraeth swallowed again. His skull seemed to be ringing like a struck bell. Someone else said with his voice, "I can go back and train Renselaeus's Riders. So that no one crosses our borders."

"Exactly. Test all your ideas there. Try what works for the people you live among before you have to use it. Not many rulers ever get that chance."

Shevraeth looked stricken, so Senrid said, "Best get back now. You seniors will be running the first hiding games with the little ones first. Scarfle 'em good if they get by without being seen. Make the first and second year colts long to be in on the fun. Stad will have the plans. But everything else as always."

Shevraeth nodded absently. Senrid watched him go, relieved beyond measure. He'd initially taken Shevraeth into the academy because he was a distant relation—because he was curious how a distant relation would handle himself—because he wanted to test the academy with a foreigner among them—for many immediate reasons. He hadn't thought ahead about the future effects. Now he was learning to.

Shevraeth obviously had thought a lot about kingship in the theoretical sense. He was probably getting plenty of grim news from home, which was partly why Senrid had given him the magic case, so he wouldn't be worrying for the six months in between courier trips.

Senrid had made a lot of mistakes ever since he'd fallen into kingship, but this was one of the few things he was going to count as a success. Because when he snapped his verbal trap, Shevraeth's first reaction had not been the glory and glitter of crowns. His thoughts had gone straight to their neck-bending, back-breaking weight.

# Forty-two

Shevraeth never remembered walking back to the barracks, where the seniors were singing old songs and drumming. He was too busy arguing with Senrid in his head.

By the next day, while his body went through the motions of lance drill, contact fighting with the rest of his House, archery practice, knife fighting with the small boys, sword drill on foot and mounted, then cavalry maneuvers mounted, he had shifted to arguing with himself.

Of course his father wasn't cold-bloodedly raising him to take over the throne.

Well, it was true that Galdran Merindar was a rotten king.

Of course there were plenty of heirs, even if the king did not produce or name one. Galdran hadn't married yet, and what was he, fifty? Near it, anyway. And he hated his sister. Though that would not stop her from ruling, if he died. Either her or her children.

Fialma would be even worse as queen, but the Marquise was trying to marry her off to foreign princes to gain power and more wealth. Flauvic?

Shevraeth was stick-fighting from horseback with the second year colts as he considered Flauvic and Fialma Merindar.

Fialma had always been loud, nearly unmanageable, and cruel. The very first time he saw her, he remembered her shrill, shrieky voice when the court children were all going in to be served iced fruit on a hot summer's day, and she'd pushed her way past everyone saying that she was to go first because her uncle was the king, and one day she'd be a queen. And when one of the girls (he couldn't remember which) laughed at her, saying she couldn't marry her uncle, she'd screamed that she would be queen of Colend and pushed the girl into the ornamental pond. Then there was a flurry of adults and Fialma was borne away by her smiling mother.

The next day she'd been sulky but quiet, her eyes red. That had happened frequently; the girls later reported that Fialma tried to catch small animals in order to 'punish' them, and she only smiled if she caught one. By the time Vidanric was fifteen, all the local animals hated her even more than he did.

Flauvic had never done anything like that. But still, Shevraeth had never liked Flauvic. It wasn't just because the adults cooed about his prettiness and perfection. They'd cooed over how handsome Savona was, and above all they'd cooed over Tamara's beauty. Shevraeth never cared about how much the adults liked Savona's looks. If anything, he felt brotherly pride. As for Tamara, pretty or not, he had learned to stay away from her when she was temperamental, but he'd always liked her when she laughed and did generous things. Flauvic had never laughed—now that Shevraeth thought about it, he wondered why he'd never noticed. Flauvic had *never* laughed, young as he was. Smiled, yes. It was his mother's smile, cool and knowing, and it never reached their watchful Merindar eyes.

"Shevraeth. You all right?"

Shevraeth looked up. "Mmmm?"

Marec opened his hand toward the horse under Shevraeth. The animal gazed over the fence after the others, who had been freed to run around the paddock. The mare's ears twitched. A first year girl waited by the halter.

Senelac and the older girls were nowhere in sight.

"Oh." Shevraeth's face heated up. "Ah."

"So I repeat. You all right?" Marec said over his shoulder as he walked away.

"Oh, fine. Sure." Shevraeth leaped down, handed the reins to the waiting girl, and ran to catch up with him. "Just day-dreaming about—"

Marec grinned. "Girls."

Shevraeth forced a grin back. "Right."

The mess bell rang, and they found themselves surrounded by the rush of hungry boys. At the senior table talk was fast, covering games, lessons, and duty.

After lunch, it was Shevraeth's turn for perimeter patrol. He set out on his long walk all round the academy, his mind slipping right back into memory. Flauvic—who never did anything wrong, but who used sarcasm, in his soft, precise voice, as a weapon. Not that he did it often. But—

"Got you!"

"No, you didn't—"

"I *saw* you!"

The small boys snickered, running toward the passage between the lower and upper schools.

"You're dead," Shevraeth called, realizing where he was and what had happened. "If he saw you, you're dead."

The boys stuttered to a stop, one with mouth open, the other hopping about, crowing, "Five points for us! Five points for us! Five points for us, ha-ha, Sniffer!"

Sniffer ignored the enemy, scowling at Shevraeth. "What's the use of a game where you don't take prisoners, and get to fight free?"

"A game in which you're dead if they find you," Shevraeth said.

Sniffer sighed, and his rival followed him back to the barracks, teasing all the way.

Shevraeth continued on to the lower school. His ears registered the sound of a small boy breathing just above his head. Bad idea, to hide along a fence top—but it was not his part

SHERWOOD SMITH

to search or to comment on hiding places, only to see that the rules were obeyed.

The voices of small boys ricocheted off stone in the distance. Play, no problem. So he did not break stride as his mind ricocheted back to golden-eyed, statue-perfect Flauvic Merindar. Shevraeth recalled the relief he'd felt on learning that Flauvic was being sent to a foreign court to be a page. That had happened not long before his father sent him here to Marloven Hess. Flauvic had mostly ignored him, concentrating his knife-sharp tongue on Savona, the obvious leader of the boys. Until the last couple of years Flauvic had always won verbal duels because Savona lost his temper so easily—even though Flauvic was so much younger. Savona had finally learned to control his temper and even to turn Flauvic's fleering jabs into jokes. Then Flauvic was gone.

Gone to a foreign court, no doubt studying kingship. The Marquise would see that her son be named heir if she could. He was smart, he was being trained, and he was a Merindar.

So that was that.

. . . for the rest of the day.

When Shevraeth lay down to sleep that night, his body tired as always, his mind flared right up like a banked fire with a new log, this time presenting him with all the adults he knew. Why not any of them? Why, for that matter, he thought later, as he turned over for the fourth time, not his father himself? He was only ten years or so older than Galdran.

The urge to slip into the rec room and write a letter was strong enough to cause him to sit up in bed, but then he lay back again. If he was certain his father had the letter case, he would. But for the first time, he didn't want Savona reading a letter first. He wasn't even sure he wanted his mother reading it. The subject not only seemed fraught with danger but it was, well, kind of embarrassing, if anyone misunderstood. They might think he had suddenly decided he was going to be a king, when it wasn't that way at all.

He scowled at the rafters dimly edged by moon-shadow. He didn't even like the royal city all that much, and he certainly didn't know everything that being king entailed.

Well, one could learn. In fact, people did learn. Like Senrid, at a young age, after being deliberately kept from that knowledge by his uncle. Of course he was already king in name . . . but the Merindar family wasn't considered royal by long tradition. If any family was, it was the Calahanras family. But their last member had deliberately renounced her name when she married, and she was now dead.

*Which is why I am here in the first place*, Shevraeth thought. *If Galdran was shaping an accident for me, is it possible others were thinking about me as a possible candidate for king without my even knowing?*

He was going to have to talk to his father. But it was going to have to wait until he was home again, and they were face to face. The question of kings lay far, far in a hazy future. What lay ahead, and far too soon, was the prospect of being tipped out of bed as a slacker before running out to drill before breakfast.

&og;☊&cg;

Over the next stretch of weeks the furious inner debate dwindled to short spurts of memory.

In the meantime, Shevraeth decided the only thing he could do was read up on kings and kingship. He started his library habit again—at first furtively, because he did not want Senrid catching him there. He couldn't even articulate why, but in any case, there was no need for worry because gossip from the girls, who continued to surround him whenever he came by the stable (except for Senelac), made it clear that Senrid had not been in the kingdom at all of late.

So he revisited all the memoirs from Marloven kings. Not because he wanted to take them as models, but because at some time they were young, they must have wrestled with the notion of kingship and what was expected. Once he was back in Remalna, he would commence reading there—if, that is, he could slip into the archive with a frivolous-sounding reason.

There was another reason to be reading.

Senelac had always taken the initiative in setting their walks in the park. That was fine with him. She was older, more experienced, knew the customs of the country.

But she hadn't asked him when his free time was for . . . what, three weeks?

He counted up as he trod back from the library late one evening. Three, maybe four weeks. Pretty much ever since Senrid had started the hide-and-find games. The girls had their own games. "We'll be doing a seek on the girls late in summer," Stad had told them all, grinning. "And won't we run a gloat if we win."

"Won't they run a gloat if we lose," Shevraeth had retorted, to general laughter.

Nobody had seen a sign of them. As for the rest of the academy, there were some vigorous (inevitable) disputes among the younger Houses about the rules of these games. No one liked the "Once found, you're dead" rule because part of the fun of games for ages and ages had been after you were taken prisoner—you led revolts, you ran rescues and raids and escapes, back and forth, back and forth.

But the disputes were nothing the rads weren't used to handling. Gradually the intent of the games was changing, and rads were now ordered to tag as 'dead' anyone they spotted in a hiding place. The Houses now had to hide for a watch, and other Houses as well as rads were dispatched on seek-and-finds. Hiding places picked to allow a counter-attack were no longer favored. The hiding places were getting better. It was odd, in fact, to walk round an apparently empty academy, in apparent silence, and know that one was being observed.

*I might be a Norsundrian. Senrid thinks it's going to happen.*

It took only three tags before the small boys learned that their breathing could be heard when they lay overhead on the walls.

The uncomfortable thought vanished as he rounded a stone corner and ducked through the moss-ceilinged tunnel. As always he cut across the main parade ground so that his route would take him just past the stable. This habit shifted his thoughts to Senelac. He'd walked this way for two years when returning from the castle, just so he could catch a glimpse of the stable on the opposite point of the intersection before the mess hall hid it from view.

Gathering darkness hid him, so he did not turn his steps away. From here it was the shortest route. He could always ignore the stable, right?

But he didn't. And so he saw the two at the stable gate, so intent they appeared to be oblivious to everything else.

Forthan sat astride one of the newer three year olds, a mare just passing from yard training to rider training. She tossed her head and sidled. Senelac stood against the gate, her arms crossed as she talked to Forthan.

Both of them were ordinarily extremely observant, but this time the world had narrowed to just one another.

Shevraeth slowed his steps. Forthan swung down, holding the reins, his attitude sober. Intense. Senelac was not her usual efficient or lounging self. Her arms were tight, her profile as sober as his as they exchanged just a few words, then he pointed to the mare.

Girls working in the background did not seem to notice the pair, obviously seeing nothing amiss. Two or three fellows on the road paid them no attention as they passed.

Forthan handed over the reins—hands tense. Her hands were stiff as they took the reins. Then he walked off in the direction of the parade ground, which would lead toward the King's Guard barracks, and Senelac started the mare toward the barn.

Their heads turned—unwilling yet compelled—a last backward glance.

They straightened round again. Neither was smiling, but Shevraeth saw again and again the intensity of that glance, the way neither had been able to control the irresistible impulse that he had fought so many times.

Forthan vanished up the road without having seen Shevraeth—who probably could have stood on his head without catching his eye—and the gate was closed to the stable, Senelac gone from view.

*She never looked back for me.*

## Forty-three

"It's our turn for the hide-and-find outside of the academy," Gannan said to the boys gathered in the House meeting. "We're going to double it soon as we hear the signal. I mean fast. We can't let the colts or the scrubs find us. It would be too prime a score-off."

Noises of agreement rose all around.

Shevraeth knew that Stad had made the actual plans—such as they were—but he and the one or two others aware of the truth listened to Gannan as if the game orders were new.

"We'll retreat in a straight line back of Sweat Hill, which is probably as far as we can get on foot before nightfall, because we cannot have lights, of course. Then we'll lie up except for two scouting ahead for the next run. If we make it that far," Gannan said. "You all have to find a place to lie up for the night, and get what rest you can."

"What about food?" Baudan asked.

Stad stayed silent. Shevraeth suspected either he had forgotten to tell Gannan, or Gannan had forgotten to ask.

Gannan flicked a revealing glance Stad's way, then toward the window. "We're working on that," he said at last, with no conviction whatever.

But it seemed to be good enough for now. Shevraeth thought, *As long as someone seems to know what to do, most will follow along if they don't see a solution.*

"All right. Back to your duties, but as soon as you hear the signal, drop everything and run."

The signal for the new, longer hide-and-find games was just a quick double ring on the bells, what used to be the summons for duty runners to the commander's office.

The rules were, seekers had to wait until the next watch bell to go seeking. That was to simulate the Norsundrians arriving in force, sweeping ahead expecting a defense, and then finding the academy empty. They'd then have to assemble and dispatch search teams, all of which might reasonably take a watch.

But the academy all thought it was to give the hiders a fair chance to hide before they went out searching, since they'd gradually begun realizing that this was not in any way a seek-and-chase sort of game, the way they'd played for ages, but a one chance game. Not as fun as taking prisoners, raiding, rescuing, and breaking out . . . but if you caught someone, you got a lot more points for your House. And not only were there prime scarfles for winners, Keriam had arranged the type of incentive that caused everyone from ten to eighteen to strive with every bit of energy and enthusiasm: the Houses with the most points at week's end were free of chores the whole next week, forcing the losing Houses in each age group to do double chores.

Pause to imagine the devoted, no, the measureless intensity of the ten-eleven-twelve year old whose greatest pleasure in life is seeing a boy in a rival House sweeping your floor, straightening your bunk, and neatening your trunk. All while you unload generous helpings of critical commentary and suggestions that you have been cherishing all the long week while you had to listen to same, in silence, from *them*.

Gannan dismissed the seniors, and they departed, all talking, thinking ahead, trying to plan what they'd do to be ready. Gradually they were reabsorbed into the usual daily round, until just before supper, *ting-ting!*

They downed tools, weapons, gear, and ran.

Just before supper! The last thing Shevraeth heard, as he dropped his wooden sword into the rack and dashed out of the courtyard, was the nasal whoop of a colt, and a triumphant, "Guess who'll be good and hungry by the all-in bell?"

"Wonder whose nose the seniors stung?" someone else asked, laughing.

Shevraeth was out the gate by then and did not hear the answer. He forgot the second year colts as he ran alongside a wall, doing his best to stay out of sight of the wall-sentries.

As he sped by the stable he spotted several of his House passing through at a run, having come over the fence from where they'd been exercising the two year olds. The girls utterly ignored the boys as if they didn't exist. The horses twitched ears and tails, some of them stirring restlessly, but the girls' firm hands and calm voices brought their attention back to duty.

Shevraeth permitted himself one sweep—he couldn't help himself—and felt the usual tangle of regret and relief that Senelac was not there.

Then he was over the back fence, and into the grassy field, well-trampled by human and hoof prints from a season of maneuvers. Those gradually gave way as he ran, trying to stay in cover, with occasional glances back. He knew that their retreat was being watched from the towers, and anyone in command class who could be tracked continually by field glass would get defaulters.

So he picked low ground, along stream beds. Streams wandered, but were not too bad for running. Plus he could pause for gulps of water.

When the land began to rise he chose clumps of brush and the occasional copse of trees. The shadows began to blend everything together, making it difficult to see roots, animal holes, rocks. One of the first things the academy taught was an easy, loping run that they could use for almost an entire watch. It was not as fast as an all-out run, but it didn't leave one breathless and exhausted.

Finally the sun vanished behind the distant rolling hills, and the shadows deepened into dark. The sounds of other boys' breathing, the salt-tang of sweat on the air and the intermittent sound of footfalls hissing through summer-dry grasses gradually joined him.

They passed Sweat Hill while it was still twilight. They topped it and ran on as the light faded. They began to slow, everyone seeking a place to lie up before full dark. Now that they were out here without their usual camp lanterns and torches, they all realized just how difficult it was to find a hiding place when you just plain cannot see.

Shevraeth had thought this out, so he kept his eyes high. He knew the territory enough to remember a sizable stretch of woods just ahead. Many were also targeting the forest, though no one spoke.

Since there was no fighting back, they all wanted a hiding place with at least one escape route. Most were therefore ignoring the trees. But Shevraeth had spent much of his childhood in Renselaeus, high on a wooded mountain, and he and Savona had made a game of seeing how far they could travel through trees without touching the ground. He'd gotten good at gauging interwoven tree branches for this kind of aerial pathway—and yes, here was just what he needed.

Dark was fully on them as he felt his way up into a broad, smooth-barked tree. All he had to do was find a crook broad enough for him to trust for sleep. It was not hard. He was not all that high up, but he counted on hearing a search before he could see it (and they could see him) which would give him time to get higher into the tree and move along the branches.

He wedged himself in, staring up through the leaves at the faint stars, and drifted into a kind of half-sleep that broke when he tried to move. He jerked awake with a jolt, his body remembering quite well where he had so dangerously parked it. But when a wind rose, the swaying sent him more deeply into slumber, and the last thought he had before the torchlight and shouts midway through the night was, *Now I know why the dawnsingers live in trees.*

Voices and bobbing torches, brought him awake with a snort. He realized that he'd been drooling as well as snoring. But the rustle of leaves all around him, the shouts being general and not specific, calmed him down again. At least no one had pegged him by the sounds of his snores.

The search passed by, one torch bobbing not thirty paces away, as the colts called insults back and forth, laughing, and then passed on.

Shevraeth resettled himself, sleeping until the weak blue light of dawn. Time to move on as far as he could, and once he had to climb down, look for water for his parched tongue.

That was his plan, but he only made it scrambling through maybe eight or nine trees before there was a shout, "I've found one! In the trees! In the trees!"

Running footsteps to the right—so Evrec had (wisely) stationed sentinels along the search route.

He tried to lie flat, but the searchers circled in, and as the bright rim of the sun strengthened, they soon spotted him, gloating loudly as he climbed down.

"And that's five to us!"

"No, six," came a distant yell amid pelting footsteps. "They just found Andaun under a mat of grass."

At least, Shevraeth thought as he dropped to the ground and someone handed him a flask of water and a chunk of bread, Marlovair wasn't among the grinning circle.

&#8359; C<sub></sub>&#8359;

"*Y*ou've been avoiding me."

Shevraeth stopped so fast he almost stumbled.

He'd been sitting in the first row in Keriam's office, so he was the last one out, his thoughts on his new tree plan.

Senelac tightened her fists, angry with herself. She hadn't meant to say it.

Shevraeth's head whipped round, his body tense and still. A flash of summer-heat desire flashed through her.

Then came the face she hated, the blank, smooth, polite *courtier*. A word she'd never used in her life before he came here.

And then the courtier words, "I beg your pardon if I—"

"Don't." She hated herself for interrupting, because he never reacted like a Marloven, he was just so polite. So smooth and cool. It was like trying to stab through sheeted steel, except she didn't want to stab—she really didn't.

Then the skin behind her shoulder-blades crawled and she knew, somehow, that Forthan had heard her address Shevraeth. Ice chased fire through her nerve endings as Forthan ran down the steps, leaving her alone with Shevraeth.

They were the last after command class wrap up, which was why she'd spoken. And of course wished immediately she hadn't. Yes, she wanted to talk to him again, she couldn't stand the way he'd been ignoring her. Oh, but wasn't that best? No, it was different when she chose to ignore him because she knew he wasn't serious about Marloven Hess, the academy—her. He was serious about frivolous girls who couldn't do anything but lift a spoon, about courtiers in ribbons and lace, and serious about a king who was apparently even worse than the Regent. So she ignored him.

That did not give him the right to ignore *her*.

Her heart hammered her ribs, her palms damped. He just stood there, looking at her, like—

She gave in to impulse once more, and reached toward his hand.

His reaction was fast—he pulled away—but their knuckles collided, and she felt it. So did he. She saw it in the way his head jerked up slightly, causing his hair to drift down into his eyes. Heard it in his breathing. How could the fire possibly be there still? How could it be there for *two* fellows?

"Come on," she snapped, but didn't mean to snap. "You owe me at least a moment of talk."

No, he didn't. And she knew he knew it.

But as always, he did not give her the lie, or even call her on acting like a rotten beast. That was not *polite*.

She stomped to the stairway and down, intensely aware of his step, just behind, matching hers down the stair.

And they emerged to find Forthan waiting, alone.

She felt the look that passed between the two, and a new fear flared inside her, and she stepped back so she could see them both, while her inside voice wailed, *Why is everything so messy when I was so careful?*

Forthan turned away, walking rapidly toward the Guard-side. She let out a shaky breath at the tight set of his shoulders. How could you tell anyone that somehow a boy she'd always known and admired was suddenly a man—and altogether different? When had that happened?

She just knew that it had, and the fact that Ret Forthan had waited for her so patiently, so quietly, all these years, set her on fire all over again.

But if she turned around and just touched Shevraeth—

"Come on," she said rudely, hoping—fearing—hoping he would turn on his heel and go.

But he fell in step beside her.

All she'd intended was to get as far away from Guard territory as she could, but as she wrestled with that inner voice, and Shevraeth paced in silence beside her, *breathing*, she realized where their footsteps were taking them, just as simply and unswervingly as they always had.

*The self always knows what it wants,* her mother had said. *If you're wise, you will listen. It's our minds that play tricks on us. But if you're like everyone else, when you're young you won't be wise, because you'll think you're smarter than everyone else, and so you're going to make all the same mistakes we've all made.*

*Not me,* she'd said. *Not me.*

Score to you, Mama.

Senelac saw the park ahead. He'd followed, and once again her mind jolted, and so she tried to jolt him.

"That was a stupid idea, going up into trees." She stopped, shocked at her own tone of voice.

He stopped as well, and gazed down into her torchlit face, her eyes so wide he could see twin torches in them from the corbel overhead.

He said, with care, "No, the trees were not stupid. But being overheard was." He did not say that he was gong to find a way to make the tree plan work, but he didn't quite know how yet. These were descendents of plains riders, and so even his friends had laughed about going up trees. He hadn't defended it, not without testing his idea.

But he wasn't going to explain that to her, though last year he might have.

She saw his expression alter from remote to something harder to parse—thoughtful, maybe, or somber. "All right. I didn't mean to say that, anyway. I don't even know why we're here. No, I know we're here because I insisted—" She stopped. "There isn't going to be trouble between you and Ret, is there?"

"No," he said, and then his eyes narrowed. "Were you expecting any?"

She flushed. "I don't want it. If that's what you're really asking." The conversation was steadily getting more nightmarish—she had crossed some kind of boundary that she had not known was previously there until she crossed it.

He tipped his head back, then said in a considering voice, "Forthan knows who instigated this encounter of ours."

She dug her fingernails into her palms. "So you're saying I hurt him on purpose?"

"I'm saying what I said," he retorted lightly enough. "What I am implying is that he is aware I did not seek you out." He hesitated.

She said, "Go on. Say what you're going to say."

His polite gaze was resting somewhere over her head. "I told him some time ago that you are I aren't twoing. What I didn't tell him—I only realized it recently. Today, in fact. The reason we weren't twoing is because you were ashamed of me."

"Ashamed—?"

"That's what it seems like to me."

Her entire body flamed. "Your experience being so great," she said, and hated herself again, but by now she was almost desperate to see him lose control of his emotions the way she had, because why else did she have to keep wiping her eyes?

But he did not look at her defiant scrubbings of her sleeve across her eyes, he studied the row of torches on the battlement behind her head as he said in a ruminative voice, "What experience I have with girls is what you gave me. And I guess I didn't see it because . . ." *Because Vidanric Renselaeus, Marquis of Shevraeth, descendant of three kings, was not a Marloven.* ". . . I didn't think I'd done anything to be ashamed of."

"You make me sound horrible," she said, though she knew what she really meant was, *I sound horrible when you tell the truth.* "I'm not going to be able to fix things, am I?" She glared up at him through burning eyes.

"Fix?"

She struck her fist against her thigh. "Make it so there is no attraction to you. Like a closed door. I don't want to be divided between two people, especially one who will go to that—to your faraway home. I didn't want to care about anything but kisses and a few laughs, but you kept making me care. Now suddenly there's someone I will probably want to marry, but I don't want any other pull on my . . . *damn* these tears," she whispered fiercely. "On. My. Heart."

"So to make your own life more convenient you want me to pick a fight and be the villain," he said—unbelieving—but she did not deny it, because she realized it was true—in a sense.

And he knew it was wrong—in a sense.

But she did not speak, she just sniffed, and gulped, and wiped her eyes again.

He wanted so badly to kiss those tears from her eyes, he wanted to hold her. Even though she was rejecting all that he was except for the most trivial of ephemera, his looks. And even knowing it, there was still this flame of attraction between them.

The depth of unfairness turned the flame into anger just long enough for him to say, "Consider it done."

And walk away.

And keep walking despite the desolate sob behind him.

She'd chosen the one who could comfort her, and he was a good fellow. Probably the best one in this entire cursed kingdom. So she could go find him now.

Shevraeth kept walking to the great parade ground, which was empty. He crossed it under the ceaselessly vigilant eyes of the sentries on the battlements as they paced the worn, ancient stones, looking out for the ancient enemy that they knew was going to come. He walked until he reached the senior barracks. He passed that, too, and did not stop until he reached the outside wall of their court, with nothing beyond it but the paddocks for horse training, and beyond those, the wind soughing through the grasses all the way to the sea.

He leaned his hot forehead against the cool stones of the wall, and wept.

# Forty-four

Shevraeth hated the Summer Games.

It wasn't the games themselves. He had come to enjoy the competitions and demonstrations. It was the time in between that made him feel isolated and out of sorts, especially this year.

Though by summer's end the sharp pain that had knifed him every time he passed the stables, much less heard Senelac's voice in the mess hall (and he could not stop himself from listening for her quiet voice, her soft laugh) had dulled to an occasional ache. They'd taken care to avoid one another. He hadn't seen her at all. When the senior boys finally did hold their search game with the girls, it was to complete defeat. They never found a sign of the girls. The seniors were loud in their disappointment. For one thing, they'd had a bet going with the girls that resulted in a week of stable cleaning duty. And though Shevraeth made noises of disappointment along with the others, he was quite relieved, even though he had to rise early every day to wand out what seemed like endless stalls.

Fewer parents showed up for the Summer Games than did for Winter Convocation, which required all the Jarls to come to renew their vows to the king. But those parents who did come to the Summer Games wanted to be shown over the academy, or walk over it again if they'd attended, and so the talking, laughing, reminiscing voices of fathers—sometimes grandmothers and grandfathers—echoed off the stone, mingling with the talking, laughing, bragging voices of boys.

Shevraeth loathed the endless watches between the competitions, when the barracks were mostly packed up and half-empty, none of his friends about because they all seemed to be with their families. It was true that Marec and Stad had both offered to include Shevraeth with their families, but it took little imagination to envision everyone's awkwardness, the trivial conversation forced on all by the presence of a stranger. Maybe even being regarded as a peculiarity by relatives. And in Stad's family there'd be the added prospect of tension from his cousin's family, who were the principal branch. No and no and no.

He thanked them both, said that it would be wonderful if they all happened to find themselves in the same place at the same time—and saw to it that he never encountered any of them. Instead, once the seniors' lance demonstration was over he hid out in the castle's Residence wing, where absolutely no one went without invitation. There, in Senrid's library, he continued his hunt for books by or about rulers.

It was there that Senrid found him the last day.

Shevraeth was immediately embarrassed. He felt false, even arrogant. As if that kingship speculation was made more real by his reading.

But the sense that he'd been caught vanished like smoke when Senrid glanced down with immediate recognition at the book he was just replacing on the shelves. "Ah." He grinned. "I hoped you'd find that one. But that's about the last of the useful ones here. My uncle got to most of the good ones before I turned seven. He didn't want me getting dangerous ideas, like the king having to obey the laws he makes and enforces. So I borrowed some from friends in case you want to read 'em. But I don't have 'em here. I'm keeping them upstairs. There's a room next to my study. I hope you'll read those over winter. You can copy them out if you like, there's paper and pens and ink there. You can do that while the others are doing map work."

"Map work?" Shevraeth repeated, bewildered by Senrid's rapidly changing subjects.

"Yes. I asked Stad, Evrec, and a couple of the others to stay over the winter. Along with some of the younger commanders. What they're going to be doing is memorizing the kingdom map, and then putting together what we've learned since spring, and planning retreats. Next spring the games will change to how fast we can get away and not be spotted." Senrid opened a hand. "Anyway, far as they are concerned, you'll be busy studying history."

Shevraeth was almost heady with relief. Senrid seemed to have assumed that of course he would study kingship. In Senrid's context, he wasn't being arrogant, he was being practical.

The bells rang, and Senrid jumped up. "Come on, you have to watch the second year colts' demo."

The *colts?* A demo?

Senrid led the way down one of the old servants' backstairs. They emerged at the very back of the stands. Senrid did not go below to the raised platform on which the kings had traditionally been seated. He wedged in among the people in the back row, high above the parade ground, Shevraeth following.

They were just in time to see Marlovair and his House ride out. Usually second year colts didn't ride—but obviously something had been agreed between them and Keriam. Shevraeth remembered that conversation with Evrec before one of the command meetings, in which Senrid had said he knew what they were doing. So Senrid had been in on it as well.

And now everyone discovered what they had been doing in secret. They demonstrated, with exhilarating skill, trick riding of a kind Shevraeth had not imagined could even be done.

An old man a couple rows down cackled, "Just like the old days, just like the old days!"—as around him the crowd cheered and whistled.

Below, the boys leaped from horse to horse as the animals—all steady goers, Shevraeth recognized—galloped in a circle. They tumbled, they jumped down and up onto the next horse, and Marlovair and another boy even did handstands on the broad hindquarters of cantering horses, they tossed spears back and forth, and then—to drumming on the benches and shouts counterpoint to the horses' hooves—swords from hand to hand. Risking life and limb, Shevraeth thought, and for what? You couldn't do any of that in a fight . . . but you could do it if you wanted to regain the respect of your peers. Or regain your own self-respect.

The insight was new, tentative. As the demonstration came to an end amid wild cheers, Senrid murmured, "What do you think?"

Shevraeth considered his words.

Senrid flicked him an impatient glance, then jumped to his feet. Everyone around them obligingly moved aside. There was no bowing, none of the protocol for kings that Shevraeth had grown up thinking was required, but somehow everyone knew Senrid was there, and deferred without noise or elaborate gesture.

Shevraeth followed him through that back entrance into the castle.

Senrid said, "Well?"

"It was splendid," Shevraeth replied.

"But? I hear 'but' in your voice."

"Well, two things. If you will accept these as observations and not as cavils."

Senrid repressed a sigh. Shevraeth might look and sound and move like a Marloven, but he was still a courtier. And one would be a fool to fault him for resorting to his early training when he must not only return to it, but resume it or be killed. "Go on," was all he said.

"The skills are great to watch. But of what use? Second observation, despite their being useless, I saw some of the first year colts in the stands watching so closely you just know they're going to be trying the same tricks next spring. They looked like they were divided fairly equally between awe and envy. Is this sort of demonstration going to become a new rule, and will it require new and more spectacular trickery?"

Senrid flashed his grin. "You are the *only* one who saw that. The only one! That's exactly why my father forbade those tricks when he first came to the throne. Exhibitions were to be useful skills only, except for the riding patterns that go back to our forefathers. And those can be dangerous enough—as you know from lance practice."

"Ah."

"I gave them permission for a one-time. Regain their honor. You know what everyone said about 'em after they tried to run Evrec out. *Everyone* gated 'em. You probably didn't see much of that, but all the lower academy did, and they caught fire from all the little boys. So I made them a deal. If they got into any more trouble, no demo. If they did what they were told the remainder of the year, they got a one-time chance. No one will be permitted next year." Senrid's face tightened. "If we get a next year."

There was no answer to be made to that.

### ❧☙

*Danric? We just had our first big cold storm, knocking the leaves off the trees. The rest have turned. That makes it an entire season without a letter from you—a record even for you. If you are dead, find a way to let me know. Or would you see this? A dilemma. Yours to solve. You'll note my generosity here in writing to a dead man. Never let it be said I forget my friends whatever their state, regardless (pause to tuck behind my ear a single white rose) of how said friends treat me. So. News. Your father went off to Sartor to protect our trade, with Galdran's good will, I am relieved to report. Apparently the Marquise made enemies there— actually, according to the gossip, it was Fialma.*

*That's the real reason why they're here again. The ambassador's niece's maid, whose sister worked in the Merindar relations' house (got all that?) in Sartor reported that said relations booted her out with a lot of excuses about a hastily-arranged long-planned trip to somewhere or other. More gossip if you respond. This note is a test to see if the magic is still on this thing, and a prod to get you to reach for your pen again if it is.*

*Sorry, Russav. Nothing to say, and we had extra chores sending us constantly out of the academy boundaries. Too long to explain now. Then there were the Games to prepare for and do, and now I'm busy recopying books, which is using all my time. I haven't heard from my parents, so I'm assuming that I'm to spend the winter again.*

ഔ**രൂഴ**ൽ

The window rattled.

Shevraeth paused, his pen midway between the ink and the paper. The light in the window had weakened to the faint bluish light of a huge snow storm. He grimaced. The walk back to the senior barracks would seem as long as a day march in that.

Now that his attention was broken, he sat back and sighed, flexing his hands. He was actually enjoying this particular record from, according to Senrid, yet another relation, Valdon na Shagal, who'd ruled some form or another of the kingdom that Flauvic was in now. The record seemed to have fallen out of fashion, or else this copy was just really old, translated into a very old-fashioned form of Court Sartoran. It had been difficult at first, but Shevraeth had enjoyed the long-ago Valdon's voice so much he persisted far longer than he would have for someone less entertaining.

He regarded the ancient book. *Take Heed, My Heirs*! If you considered all descendants, maybe he was one of those heirs. Valdon's wife had been a Dei, his aunt married to someone whose name sounded uncomfortably like Marlovair, but wasn't. It wasn't Montredaun-An, either. Only written once, the name had an ink blotch, and so he could only guess at it.

He leaned back in his chair, stretching as he regarded a folding screen painted with graceful reeds, butterflies dancing above. This screen was new since Shevraeth's last visit in the Residence. Senrid had been rediscovering pieces of artwork his mother had brought to the castle on her marriage. According to Stad, the Regent had decreed it all be burned as 'civilian decadence' but Keriam had told certain servants to hide as much as they could.

Keriam again. One thing Shevraeth had discovered was that Keriam had not just run the academy, but had in a sense acted as father to Senrid after King Indevan was knifed by his own brother. Now here was evidence that Keriam had preserved a lot of the Montredaun-An family art and even some of the records. You could call him a kingmaker, though he hadn't picked the king. Or had he? He'd also led a part of the army when the Marlovens had revolted against the Regent. So he'd been important. Would his name be remembered as long as Senrid's might be, assuming of course (Senrid would be the first to say so) he didn't end up dead, having had one of the shortest reigns ever?

*What will be my place in history?*

Sudden laughter gusted from the main room on the other side of the screen. On the nearest wall there was a new tapestry as well. A new old one, he thought, regarding the old-fashioned clothes, the stiff, upright posture of the two leaders of opposing armies in a scene that could not possibly have happened. For one thing, no horse would tolerate someone sitting like that, especially in full armor—even at a treaty gathering—

More laughter, led by Stad's distinctive voice. Next year they would be second year seniors, the top of the school, as there would be no third year seniors. What would happen after that? Shevraeth wondered if he'd ever see any of these fellows again, supposing his father did summon him home at last. Would they all promise to write, and then feel it an awkward obligation as time went by? What do you say when you part with people you've lived with for nearly four years, and you suspect you'll never see them again?

The door opened and Senrid dashed in. "Give me that medallion." He held out his hand.

Shevraeth fished it out of his shirt and pulled the still-warm chain over his head. He tossed it to Senrid, feeling odd without it on him.

The metal and chain rang faintly as it landed on Senrid's palm. He sat down in the other chair, unrolled a piece of paper he'd been carrying, and bent over the medallion. For a time he whispered softly.

Shevraeth realized he was seeing magic done. Not that there was much to see, except for Senrid bent over the glinting gold on his palm, his lips moving, his eyes intent and steady. Tiny beads of sweat formed along his hairline. He dropped the paper, made a complicated gesture with his fingers too quick to follow. A brief snap of a weird scintillation not quite light, more felt than seen, then Senrid sat back and drew a long breath. Shut his eyes, drew another, then opened them; whatever cost the magic had taken from him had passed. "Put it back on." He tossed the medallion to Shevraeth's desk. As Shevraeth hung the chain round his neck once more, Senrid said, "I was in Sartor. Yustnesveas is sending people home."

*Yustnesveas.* The queen of Sartor, mentioned so casually by name, as if a casual friend.

"I discovered your father was there, and offered to transfer him to save him that long journey, or a smacking fee for magic transfer, and of course he agreed. And so I discovered, only because I don't trust any transfer Destination I don't know, that your ancient one in Renselaeus has a very new, and very lethal, ward on it."

Shevraeth stared, not knowing even how to frame a question, this 'ward' business was so far out of his experience.

Senrid gestured impatiently. "Never mind what it means. Except that you cannot use it until someone can remove that ward. So your medallion will transfer you to the next Destination I know of, which is at the port in Mardgar. I don't have time to find another closer."

Shevraeth shook his head. "If I can't get myself home from a few days' ride, then I'm hopeless."

Senrid grinned. "That's what I thought you'd say. Your father asked about you, of course. Said he left the letter case behind for your mother to use. I told him you were a total disgrace, you'd become fat as an alderman in charge of the guild dinners, and you were afraid of horses. He seemed satisfied."

Shevraeth snorted a laugh.

"I've got to get back to it. Two people are waiting for me somewhere else, but I wanted to get that done. No use wasting all that training, just to have you transferred from home to some dungeon somewhere, or even killed. But who in your Remalna would have access to that much magic?"

It was a rhetorical question, of course. Shevraeth hadn't been home since the spring of '39, and New Year's Week was almost on them, bringing them to 4742.

Senrid dashed out, leaving Shevraeth to tap his pen and frown at the record written by the long-ago king Valdon. It was a rhetorical question that was going to have to be answered. Some day. Along with so many other questions.

∞CR∞∞

   . . . *your father is now home from Sartor, darling boy, as perhaps you are aware. Sartor has a hundred years of interrupted trade to recover from, and there are rumors of more trouble with Norsunder that I fervently trust is just the usual "they say" without base. Your father reports that the*

*young queen is desperately trying to continue her
education in governing while events develop rapidly.
He also said that the arts are beginning to thrive
again, at least. Despite events, and the slowness of
arranging anything even as relatively simple as new
trade deals, he enjoyed himself in a way that has
become almost impossible at home, alas.*

*I miss you more than you can know, but I do
not want you feeling my motherly emotions as a
burden. So I talk out my motherly fuss at that
painting of you here in my room over the fireplace,
and wonder how you have changed, and look
forward to having a new one painted. Your father
said that you are to learn something about the
weaving of yeath fur cloaks, as you are (according
to the rumor we carefully let circle around court) off
on a mountaintop researching the clipping of yeath
fur as we are considering raising yeath on our
mountains here in Renselaeus . . .*

&#8286;CB&#8287;&#8258;

"That's an impressive stack of books." Stad smiled down at
Shevraeth's trunk. "I didn't know anyone could write that
fast."

"I didn't either," Shevraeth returned, running his hands
over the dozen books he'd spent the winter copying out.
Including the entertaining but sensible *Take Heed, my Heirs!*
"What's the word?"

"We stay here, of course. More to the point, we only
rearrange bunks if we want to, so you needn't pack and drag
unless you've got a hankering for a noisy corner."

Shevraeth kicked his trunk lid shut and waved at the two
windows between which his bunk was positioned. Plenty of air
when the weather was fine, but when it was cold, he wasn't right
under the draft that forced some of the boys, during cold snaps,

to sleep with their heads at the foot and their feet at the headboard. "One good thing about these winter-overs is we always get the best racks."

Stad grinned. Then jerked his thumb castleward. "Keriam will have us over tonight to set out radlav duties."

Shevraeth studied that smile, which was broad, almost a laugh. Stad's eyes crinkled, and—

Oh. "And so you're what, demoted to stable chores, right?"

Stad laughed, because now he could announce what before would have been swank: "No, but my first command will be to assign you there for a month."

Shevraeth laughed with Stad, reflecting that he found the joke itself less funny than the *idea* of the joke. Odd, the unsubtle cracks that Marlovens thought were the height of humor.

Stad added, "Evrec and I just got back. I really thought I was ruined last year. Dared not speak up." He cast a quick glance over his shoulder, but they were alone at this end of the barracks. "King made a deal with Van and the brats last spring, which kept them riding in line. He let 'em practice up that stunt riding display."

Shevraeth did not say that Senrid had explained that last summer. He just nodded, made appreciative noises, and listened as they walked to the mess hall, while Stad aired the ideas he'd been thinking about all winter, but had kept to himself until his appointment was official. As soon as the first parade and transfer of command was over, he and Evrec, who was Thanar Valdlav, had an enormous amount of extra work waiting for them—which they were itching to get at.

What amazed Shevraeth was how happy Stad was to be taking on this hideous number of extra chores. The rank could be best translated as More Hard Work Than Anyone Else.

But so would kingship, he was beginning to realize. More work, and the stakes were far higher if you erred.

# Forty-five

As promised, Keriam summoned the entire second year senior class to his office. The radlav assignments were distributed, few of them causing any surprise. Shevraeth found himself in charge of the knife throwing for the upper school. A first year senior would replace him in the lower school. Then Keriam reaffirmed the orders about the new games, which were to follow the pattern set up by the king last summer. The strategy was retreat. Fast, and unseen. There would be watchers posted on the walls and towers, and anyone spotted earned defaulters, from the lowest pups to the second year seniors.

"So it's more than a game, then?" Gannan asked, after exchanging uneasy glances with a couple of the seniors who were not in the command class.

Everyone else sat there looking attentive.

Keriam said, "It's serious enough that the time has come for the last part of the game strategy, which is the news—and you are not to speak of it outside this room—that this is not, in fact, a game at all."

The silence was so intense that the distant sound of little boys shrieking as they chased one another on one of the fields drifted in the open window.

"Norsunder is on the move. If the game bell rings an unscheduled game, you will know that it is the real threat. You will then drop everything. You will tell whoever you are supervising—you can see we cannot plan farther—what is happening, but you will reassure them that they all know exactly what to do. And you will lead the retreat to your cover. Right then, no stops in the barracks, nothing."

Silence, except for a few shifting uneasily.

"You senior rads are all going to pick a retreat route as well as whatever cover you favored last summer. You will stock your cover with a cache of supplies. The king will establish a communications link with you himself. Dismissed."

Somber-faced, eager to talk away from the listening ears of command, they thundered out, some of them moving stiffly in the year's new boots.

Keriam waved at Shevraeth to stay behind.

"I want you to know that, had events been otherwise, you would have given Evrec a close run for Thanar Valdlav. This means you would have had your pick of aran radlav positions in any of the Houses. But the King says you have to remain on detached in case we are forced on the academy retreat."

Detached, nickname for the support rad at any given drill, House, or overnight. Whoever the lead rad was, then, would have to command. Shevraeth was only lead on one: knife throwing.

"So if the retreat is sounded, my group goes with the master in charge, or if it's a class with no master, the primary rad?"

"Yes."

Shevraeth said everything that was proper, then left, feeling complimented, but mostly relieved. He did not want to be in command if the real retreat did happen.

And so, once the first day's inspection was over (Stad looking unwontedly serious as he made his way round the Houses) Shevraeth took up his new position in the knife court, facing a wary-eyed line of new seniors in their fitted tunics and belts, all of whom obviously thought they were quite adept at knife throwing. He wondered if it was just the presence of the presiding master that kept them in a quiet line, at least pretending to watch as he stepped to the mark to demonstrate.

He underestimated the effect of his skill. Shevraeth's years of throwing while his mind cut free and considered other things enabled him to nip up a knife from the rack and fling it with a casual crack of his wrist to thud squarely in the center of the target.

None of them could do that. They were quite determined as they demonstrated two throws apiece, one each hand. None of them could throw without taking that extra heartbeat to line up eye and hand. Shevraeth assigned them practice with handle throwing (taken from their belts) and blade throwing. By the end of the session their squint-eyed focus had dissolved into laughter and jibes when some of them threw wild, or worse, sent the knife knocking sideways into the target, to clatter ignominiously to the ground.

Not laughter and cracks *including* Shevraeth. Of course. It was more around him. But all in all, he thought as he walked them over to saber practice, it had gone better than he'd expected. Now to see if they took it out on him while he had to serve as post-target, as Gannan took command of the class.

Gannan put them through warm-ups, then paired them up for some fast drills. Shevraeth pulled on the padding required of all the post-targets. He took up a stance behind the hacked, splintery wood of the man-sized post stuck in the ground, two pieces to either side to represent arms.

Acting as post-target was not easy, despite the protection of the wood—because the entire purpose was to attack that wood. Shevraeth pulled on his gauntlets and picked up the heavy steel saber that the boys would attack.

One by one the boys came at him, long steel in hand for the first time, instead of the willow swords they'd been using for the previous years. Shevraeth extended the sword round the post, and initiated a bout. The post was not for refining technique, it was practice for the brutal part of sword work: block, extend, block, and he jerked his blade up as though in defeat, and the boy brought the sword down at the post with all his strength. He had to be fast and precise to simulate, as much as possible, real battle. In other words, killing the enemy.

Most of the boys' first blows just glanced off the wood, just as his own had last year. A lifetime of learning to pull one's blows made a real strike difficult, especially when one hadn't time to think about it.

By the end of a long session a few of them got the steel to sink far enough into the wood to raise a thin, acrid thread of smoke. The others sent up cheers.

The first one to achieve a hot hit was Marlovair.

Shevraeth was awash in sweat. He didn't know if Marlovair's strength, focus, and determination was a result of the new atmosphere of seriousness that had settled over the academy, or because Marlovair was, at one remove, striking at the foreigner. Oh, well, he suspected he *did* know the answer to that.

ఌ**ℭ₰ℰᏯ**ఌ

*I apologize for the long silence, my son. We had one of the king's spies with us as escort, and so none of us dared put pen to paper or reveal this gold case in any way. Here is the gist of it: rumors from refugees out of Sartor say that Siamis and even the evil Detlev have been seen in both Sartor and Sarendan. It makes sense that, if they strike, it will be at the heart of the world. We already know that Detlev is terribly adept at using our own symbols against us, and Siamis twists these same symbols, as well as people, to his own ends.*

*At any rate, the king was frightened enough. More to the point, the people have been clamoring in greater numbers so that even he cannot silence them, and he has sent all his forces to protect the borders. That means, of course, he is left unguarded (against us!) in Athanarel, which means he has sent us home, after a stirring speech about our duty to protect our own lands as he protects the borders. That suits us all. As if released from prison we have all ridden for our homes. But he sent 'escorts' with the chief of us, presumably to see us there, and our spies have just departed.*

*So we are home, for the duration, in Renselaeus. Russav will cross Shevraeth to spend time with us when he wishes. For now, at least, it seems the border between Savona and Shevraeth will not be watched.*

*Now to you. You are old enough, we feel, to make your own decision. If you can do good in the place that has given you its training these past years, stay. If it comes to defending our home, I can command. Were you here, it would take time to establish you in the place I have held so long, and that is not the ideal in a time of trouble. People trust what they know. Eventually you will indeed take my place—I trust at a more sedate pace. But if you desire to come home, you will, I assure you, be welcome, and you will take your place at my side. Choose the duty you can most effectively execute: that is, finally, all we can do in life.*

*Last, know waking and sleeping that I love you, as does your mother, and Russav sends his affection and wishes for your welfare.*

&#8286;C୪ℰ୦ଔ

Though there was now little chance Shevraeth would be leading a retreat, he still obeyed the orders, thinking that his trees (though rejected by absolutely everyone) could well provide a fallback, simply because they were so rejected. Surely the Norsundrians would expect Marlovens to take to the hills, or fields, or even caves if they made it all the way to the east, but never to trees.

When presented to Stad in this way, Stad agreed. In fact, he was so impressed with this thinking that he accompanied Shevraeth on a trial run, just the two of them. Shevraeth had begun to doubt his own wisdom late in the autumn as he experimented with moving swiftly and silently above ground. He'd forgotten about foliage, so busy he'd been, but the first leaves of spring renewed the overhead canopy so that the upper boughs were utterly hidden from sight.

Stad stood below a great oak, peering up the tree Shevraeth had just climbed. "Where are you?" he called finally.

And a voice echoed from not nearby, but downhill a considerable ways: "Here."

Stad whirled, gazing about. "Where?"

A sudden hissing thrash, and Shevraeth dropped onto the new grass at the bottom of the gentle rise. Stad ran to catch him up. "I did not hear you do that. I listened—I was right there."

"I figured out how to move. You stay along the big, broad lower branches. Some of them you don't even have to crawl, you can run."

Stad grimaced. "Run? In a tree? Not I!"

"Those branches are amazingly broad. But you do have to take your boots off. Thread your sash through the knife loops in each boot, and you can wear 'em over your back and move as fast as you like."

Stad grunted in approval. "Unlikely as it is we'd use it— you're support in just about every class, are you not?"

"Except knife throwing."

"Then you'd just tag on with the next court over."

"Right."

"But I still like this as a fallback," Stad said, staring upward. "We just don't know what's going to happen. Go ahead and stash caches in these trees. I imagine one could live up here for months," he added in wonder.

"There are entire tree cities up north, we're told. And over on Toar."

Stad flicked his hands open in that quick gesture so characteristic of Marlovens. "The dawnsingers. Well, if they can live in trees, we can, too, if put to it."

"One thing we won't have to cache is horse fodder."

"Horses! Horses in trees!" Stad gave a crack of laughter that rang through the silent glade.

Shevraeth joined the other rads in stashing supplies in their retreats. Meanwhile everyone kept busy with regular work plus retreat practice two mornings and one night a week as the spring spun away, the days gradually warming toward the lazy heat of summer.

Not that any of them were lazy—the atmosphere was too tense for that. The seniors, knowing that a single word out of place could be overheard and spread as fast as sound, kept tight-lipped on why the games had gotten so strict, but their tension, their lack of humor when the younger boys, bored by now, slacked off, caused a lot of speculation.

The boys had finally decided that the king was inventing some kind of new war game; because it was the king's, they cooperated, though there were rumbles among the first and second year colts, who were still testing the limits that Jump House had flouted the previous spring. Some bragged in barracks of hiding out somewhere in the academy instead of running half the night or morning, just to run back again.

Stad told the seniors to pass the word down that anyone who wasn't counted at the far end of the run would net himself a public beating. This order, plus the sudden disappearance of all the girls and the academy horses, caused a ripple of dismay through the academy.

Something was wrong, they could all feel it, but the masters (there were only four left now, the others being sent on unexplained errands) and the seniors said nothing, so the younger boys reacted characteristically: some by acting out in crazy ways, as if to force normalcy onto everyone else, even if it meant defaulters and breezes, others becoming silent and watchful, and a few talking wildly.

One very hot morning, so hot that Shevraeth was going to skip breakfast, he met Baudan just after he ducked inside the door. On Baudan's tray there was only a hunk of bread and cheese, and a brimming mug of water.

"No oatmeal?" Shevraeth asked.

"They didn't event cook it. Everyone's to have bread-and-cheese."

"Better than hot food," Shevraeth said, and Baudan followed him as he got his food and water. "And better than that, we're not out with the lances today."

"I almost wish we were," Baudan grumbled. "When it's this hot they're wild at the archery targets. Especially now that Tevac has 'em all convinced that the king is going to war."

"What?" Shevraeth exclaimed.

Baudan snickered. "What they can't decide is, which kingdom. And why. But some of their reasoning is better than any joke."

They walked to the senior table. "Like?"

"We're going to war against the south because the king's mother came from there, and she left it to him."

"Oh, and they hadn't noticed until now?"

Baudan grinned. "Right. And she wasn't the heir anyway."

"So they really must be listening in those history lectures."

"Oh, they do listen—some. Believe me, they're less ignorant than our own class was when we were pups. Then there's the insult-caused wars. Let's see . . . the king declared war because some king or other said he's too short to get on a horse without a ladder."

"A perfectly valid reason to go to war. If you are ten years old."

Baudan wiped his arm over his forehead "Too hot to think of the rest, but Hem knows, he was there."

Gannan loomed over them. "Listen, it's too hot for padding this morning, so we're to take sword classes over to the barns. Nermand and Hauth are already there, moving out all the gear. While the girls are gone, we're apparently to begin rebuilding the loose boxes."

"But everything else as is?" Shevraeth asked, thinking of knife target practice in the simmering heat, the sunlight glancing off the steel in eye-piercing shards. The new seniors would be wicked.

"Everything else as is," Gannan snapped. He was irritated by the heat, by the tension, and most of all by being ordered to lower himself to carpentry work.

Baudan rolled his eyes, and it was Shevraeth's turn to laugh.

The watch-change bell rang then, indicating the end of breakfast. Shevraeth stuffed the last of his bread into his mouth and loped off toward the practice courts. It was strange to be able to write every day to his father now. It was good, for they'd been discussing everything Shevraeth had read. But it was strange to get a note that his father had just penned, mentioned a long, cold rain falling—and not a hundred heart-beats after, there's Shevraeth sweltering away, reading it. He ought to ask for his father to include some rain drops next time.

*Why* was he thinking about rain? He was already thirsty when he reached the knife practice court, just ahead of Marlovair's crowd of new seniors. From the sound of their voices, they were arguing. Tempers hotter than the air. What sort of lesson could he offer them, he wondered as they shuffled in, some of them shoving back and forth with quick, irritated jerks of arms and shoulders.

He raised a hand to summon their attention when the double-tang sounded.

The boys ignored it; they were used to the double-tang for messengers. Shevraeth almost ignored it, his mind running irritably on other things—

Tang-tang!

"They're here," he said, not even aware of speaking. His nerves tingled with cold, as if he'd fallen into snow.

Three or four of the boys fell silent, staring at Shevraeth's blanched face.

"They're here," he said, louder.

"Who's here?" Marlovair retorted—then stepped back warily, on the look-out for Gannan or one of the other seniors who was a thought too ready with the willow wand at what they considered backtalk.

But they were alone, because Gannan's sword class was on the other side of the academy, at the stables.

"Norsunder," Shevraeth said.

# Forty-six

*T*ang-tang.
Third ring.

"Norsunder?" someone repeated. "That's not funny."

"No." Shevraeth lowered his hand, which had still been half-raised. He flexed his fingers. *They're here*. "But it's true."

Impossible! Impossible! He could feel them thinking it. He was thinking it himself. And Gannan was at the stable. He was here alone with the most hot-tempered, hard-to-handle class in the academy.

Already things were jagging out of the prepared-for groove. "Grab the knives," he ordered, though they were supposed to take nothing. But then he wasn't supposed to be alone with a group, either.

He lunged at the rack, slapping a knife into each boot and one into his sash beside the worthless wand. Weapons clattered as the other boys, now furiously whispering ("He's gone mad!" "No, there's something with the bells. We all knew something was wrong." "Quiet!" "Who're we gonna fight?"), armed themselves.

"Run," Shevraeth said when the rack was empty.

He bolted out of the court.

They were too well-trained not to follow. But Marlovair thumped directly alongside him. "What about Norsunder? You can't just say 'Norsunder' and expect us to—"

"War," Shevraeth said, aware of the medallion clunking against his chest at every step. He could leave by magic—he might be expected to leave by magic—but not before he'd handed off these boys, who knew nothing of the plans. "That signal was for a Norsunder attack. They're here."

"Here?" someone else said, voice cracking.

The boys tried to look around as they ran, two nearly stumbling.

"Maybe. Maybe at the border. In the country," Shevraeth said, without breaking stride—or looking back.

The word Norsunder having—for now—quashed any notion of rebellion in the ranks, the seniors followed Shevraeth as he ran his chosen route along one of the inner walls. They dove through the arch down by the lower academy, and outward along the back wall. Shevraeth tried once to gauge the castle walls, but the sun was too bright. Norsunder! Where?

His job was to stay unseen.

And so he did not try again to look back, but stayed low, and the other boys stayed low, following him in a snake line through the last bit of the academy. Just once they heard rapid steps—small boys, from the swift sound—but not a voice, and the steps vanished. Someone else's route, going who-knows-where.

They reached the outer fence of the riding paddocks. Temptation seized Shevraeth, almost unbearable—not 500 paces away rose the senior barracks. His trunk. All the books he'd so laboriously copied out. His letter case!

But he could not stop, and so, bitterly regretting everything he left behind, he cut to the stream, still bent low, and ran, arms swinging. He and his line raced alongside the water, Shevraeth glancing back once in a while to check on the others running at a back-aching crouch right behind.

They reached Shevraeth's designated first pause as dust clouded up just ahead, on the other side of the bend. He flung down a hand to stop his charges, then pointed at the dust.

He pointed at the stream edge, then flattened his hand. Most of the boys dropped down willingly, half of them stretching out crimson faces to the water. Marlovair, his thin face stubborn, made as if to follow, but Shevraeth gave him such a terrible look of taut-faced intent he stopped right where he was.

Shevraeth tiptoed up the rocky incline and peered through the shrubbery. Gannan, a master, and another senior vanished through the shrubbery toward the north. Should he shout?

No, the orders had been to stay quiet—and also not to double up. But Gannan's bunch were already doubled, all the classes assigned to carpentry. Already things had changed in small ways. But even so, he still knew exactly what to do. *Is that the real secret of command, then? When the impossible happens, you know what to do?*

There was no command class to ask, he was alone. And in charge.

*So do it!*

He slid back down in a small tumble of rocks, and reached the waiting boys.

"Eleveners?" Marlovair mouthed the word.

"No, some of us." Shevraeth kept his voice low. "Everyone has different hideys, you know that from all the games."

Marlovair jerked his head once. Then frowned. "Where's yours?"

"You'll see. Get a drink, and we're off."

He knelt down, splashed water over his head, then drank as much as he could hold. When he lifted his dripping head, one of Marlovair's friends whispered, "So where did the girls go?"

Marlovair snorted scornfully. "If this isn't just another game, of course they'd hide the horses so Norsunder can't get at them. I wager they're scattered from Vasande Leror to Methden."

"Let's go," Shevraeth said.

They were off again.

Stop, run, check. Stop, run, check.

⁊ᴑ(ᴚℰᴐᴖ

What the boys and Shevraeth could not know was that Norsunder had not sent warriors—this time. They sent mages.

After months of consultation with older, far-seeing mages, and some of the few adults in authority whom he was coming to trust, Senrid had been convinced that the mages would be followed by warriors if his magical protections, labored over so desperately for five years, were brought down.

Senrid had become convinced that if Norsunder sent warriors over the border their orders would be to force the Marlovens to do their conquering for them. The Norsundrians were too fractured among themselves, for the long, extended, bitter struggle to establish possession of Marloven Hess. Norsunder had to know—his own ancestor, Ivandred the Blood-Handed was still there—that Marlovens would resist down to the last child unless the Norsundrian leader was extremely clever as well as merciless.

So all across the kingdom Senrid's army was vanishing into defensive hideys to await further orders, while the unseen, sinister mages (and it might be only one, the terrible Detlev) tested the wards that Senrid and his mage allies had been working on for two years.

⁊ᴑ(ᴚℰᴐᴖ

Shevraeth and his charges reached the forest in mid-afternoon.

At first they were relieved at the relative coolness. It felt good to be out of the sun. There was even the faintest stirring of a breeze coming up the river bend.

But when Shevraeth stopped and said, "Here we are," it was to a circle of astonished faces.

And he watched his command dissolve as they exchanged glances of disbelief, affront, and anger.

"We're not going in trees," someone exclaimed. "We may as well surrender now, before Norsunder laughs us right off the branches!"

Shevraeth could evoke Stad's name. But he knew if he did then he'd given up his own authority to hide behind the Danas Valdlav's rank. And he'd have to use Stad's name constantly to reinforce orders—until even the name didn't work, which it wouldn't if Stad himself didn't show up.

Shevraeth straightened up. Inside his damp shirt the medallion clunked against his ribs. He let out his breath slowly. He could just vanish. If these boys revolted against his authority, he might as well use the spell and go home, because it would mean that despite nearly four years of training he had failed what he was here to learn.

"Find me," he said, and sprang into the tree.

He ran along the branches in his boots, his heart thundering in his ears.

As soon as he was out of sight, the boys burst into arguments, exclamations, and insults, Marlovair shouting "Shut up! Shut up! Wait, shut *up*!"

Apparently he had lost authority among his fellows since last year. Except for his riding-mates the others did not listen to him either. The voices were followed by grunts and thuds—fist fights.

Shevraeth cupped his hand round his mouth, shouting northward, "Find me!" The echo ricocheted away.

"Why?" someone wailed. "What's going on?"

"He's hiding right up there. What's the point of that?"

"Shut up! Find him! He's the only one who knows what's happening!"

The thuds of running feet was joined by violent thrashing in a tree farther back up hill.

"Hey, he's not here!"

"Go up higher, horse apple."

"I *am* high!"

"Hey, he's not here either!"

"Shevraeth, where are you?"

"Here." He shouted from a tree two hundred paces from where they crowded around, staring upward in futility. They all whirled around, their shock almost comical.

Then they stampeded his way. He moved back along the branches, as the boys dashed below. Some looked up as they ran, but none of them long enough to spot him.

"Where are you?"

"Here." He dropped down from the first tree he'd climbed.

They all turned as one, and ran back.

They stopped in a semi-circle, all semblance or order gone. Marlovair stood in the front, arms crossed, face red.

Shevraeth said, "You have two choices. You go up with me into the trees, where I have stashes for half a day's travel to the south. We won't touch the ground for that half day, which means any Norsundrians trying to track us on the ground will run around in circles."

Now they were listening, though most were wary, doubtful.

"I'll show you how to make a path on the branches. Without making noise. Or you go right ahead and run off. I'm not going to stop you. Maybe Norsunder will find you—maybe Stad. Which one, do you think, will be happier to see you running wild?"

"Trees?" came an insolent voice from the back.

"Shut. Up. Just shut up, Eveneth," Marlovair snapped. "Not like you had any better ideas." One last, long, unreadable glance Shevraeth's way, then Marlovair reached for a branch and hauled himself up.

And just like that, command snapped its invisible reins back into place.

Shevraeth waited until they were all somewhere on the two main branches of the enormous oak he'd picked as his trail head. He sat down and pulled off his boots, then removed his belt.

There were some joking whispers about stench and old socks but everyone else did the same, threaded their belts in the knife loops, and then slung their boots over their backs.

"What about our boot knives?" Eveneth asked, not quite as insolently as earlier.

"This." Shevraeth had taken off his tunic and laid it aside. He unbuttoned his cuffs and rolled his shirt to his upper arms, where the fabric pulled tight. Then he slid a knife into each rolled cuff.

"Not ideal," he said, trying not to laugh as the younger boys stared. It did look piratical, knives in your sleeves like that. "But since we don't have arm or wrist sheaths."

He spoke into a rustle of boys busy rolling shirt sleeves, some of them snickering softly. Shevraeth tied his tunic around his waist by the sleeves, then stood. "Now follow me."

At first he deliberately moved too quickly. They stopped talking, some bent double. Moving in trees was not easy at all. Then he slowed, demonstrating silently where he placed his foot, how he used his hands for balance on upper branches, sometimes swinging to a new bough. He had become so adept that he ran back and forth with unconscious and effortless ease as he checked on them.

The sight of him sauntering along branches two storeys off the ground heartened most of them. Trees! Who would ever hide in trees? But even the least imaginative of them thought of Norsundrians assuming the same thing and passing right below as they busily searched the ground.

"We're going to move far enough away from where we left prints," he said. "Then I'm going to take a party of two back, and if it's safe, we're going to make a trail down to the river. Let any Norsundrian scouts assume that we took a raft downriver."

Marlovair brushed two fingers against his shirt in a kind of salute, copied a heartbeat later by most of the rest. He, too, had re-established his old authority. Shevraeth had missed the transition, but right now it didn't matter.

They moved along the trees, the boys gradually getting more used to it, though they were hardly quiet. But they did not hear the sounds of pursuit, so Shevraeth said nothing.

The gathering shadows were making it tough to see when he called a halt. They'd reached his first cache. He would have liked to grab that and proceed to his second cache, to gain distance, but decided not to push too hard. Instead, he asked for a volunteer to stay in charge while he led the decoy party back. He got a gratifying number of hands, picked one, and so it went.

It was full dark when he and his two (one of them Marlovair, who had not spoken a word) made it back to the rest of the boys.

Shevraeth said, "We can either sleep in the tree—I've done it, it works—or on the ground, with watches posted. Tight perimeter. Not enough of us to risk being out of sight of one another."

Marlovair said, "If you're offering a choice, I'm for ground."

"Ground, ground," came the murmurs.

Shevraeth lifted his head, listening to the forest sounds. No raucous risings of disturbed birds, no galloping of hooves, no howls or whinnies. He sensed that they were the only humans in the wood. "Since we haven't heard or seen any pursuit, we'll sleep on the ground. But no fire."

They climbed down, leaves and twigs rustling. Everyone put their boots back on and belted up their tunics. Knives went into the belts beside the wands that half of them carried, being now second-rads. Then they settled close beneath the spreading oak.

In a low voice, as night birds wheeled overhead, Shevraeth told them about the command class meeting, and everything they'd been doing for the past year. What the king had said and what Keriam had said and what Stad had said. Except for muffled noises of disgust at being left out, they were fairly quiet. Everyone was trying to comprehend the idea of Norsunder actually invading. They all had knives, but—despite some hot talk about what they'd do to the Norsundrians if they caught up—Shevraeth could feel how frightened the boys were. It was easy to imagine lurking evil in the inky shadows. Moonlight limned the trees, rendering them large and mysterious and not very comforting.

But exhaustion from a full day of being on the run, followed by a meal of the thick, slightly stale trail bread that Shevraeth had stashed a couple of weeks before—intending to change it out once a month—defeated uneasiness, and they fell asleep one by one, most lying close by one another for comfort.

Shevraeth and two volunteers paced a close perimeter on watch, all three staying in a circle where they could see one another. Just like on camp games.

*Drill, plans in place. Everyone knowing what to do*, Shevraeth thought. *It makes all the difference between panic and purpose.*

Marlovair had insisted that he be the second watch, and Shevraeth agreed. Marlovair might not be aware of it, but Shevraeth knew that some of his regained authority was the direct result of Marlovair choosing to obey. The concept of command was no more tangible than air, but just as vital. But it did not, as Valdon Shagal had said in *Take Heed my Heirs!*, originate in your own mind, no matter how much you think it your right to have it. It originates in the minds of others, when they choose to obey. And as soon as you forget that fact, you start becoming a tyrant as you try to force those minds to align with yours.

When the moon had moved roughly halfway on its arc, Shevraeth declared a watch change. He left it to Marlovair to divide his fellow guards and set his knives carefully on the grass, then lay down within reach of them.

Urgent whispers jolted into his dreams, followed by a hiss, "It's the king!"

Shevraeth lunged up, remembered his knives. He fumbled on the grass, still half-asleep, then straightened up. There was Senrid's boyish face in the weak blue light of dawn.

Senrid was grinning. "It worked, it worked! Everyone is out, everyone is safe."

Marlovair rubbed his eyes. "So Norsunder really invaded?"

Shevraeth made a wry face, suppressing the urge to say, *Do you actually think I made that up?*

Senrid flexed his hands. "Mages only. And I don't think I can hold the wards." He hissed out his breath. "Two years of work. Might not last a day. That's Detlev for you. Look, Shevraeth, you have to get out now. I'll send your things when I can. Well done," he added, flashing another grin. Then he waved his hands. "But I can't hold 'em out any more. Go." And then in the formal voice, so everyone understood what was happening, "You are relieved."

"You have the post," Shevraeth responded as bewildered boys flipped gazes back and forth between them. Before anyone could say anything Shevraeth reached into his shirt, gripped the medallion, said the words.

The last thing he saw before the world was wrenched away was Marlovair's astonished face.

# Forty-seven

Painfully life, light, and sound coalesced into sense again, leaving Shevraeth feeling as if he'd been dragged over rocks by a runaway horse. He staggered, a hand took his arm in a kind but firm grip and helped him a few paces to—

A chair. He dropped into it, breathing hard against the surges of nausea that slowly receded. Someone put a warm cup of something clean-smelling into his fingers; he drank, and the last of the magical residue swept away.

"You transferred a long distance," a young woman said. She was maybe his age, and wore a green robe.

She spoke in Sartoran, the Sartoran accent of the Remalna side of the continent.

"I'm home," Shevraeth whispered.

The young woman shrugged faintly, and he realized he'd spoken in Marloven.

In Remalnan: "I did come a long way."

It felt strange to speak his home tongue again. He'd been writing it in letters, but he had not shaped the spoken words for so long the muscles around the front of his mouth felt clumsy.

"You're Remalnan." The young woman's freckled brow cleared. "You'll find your money-changer at the end of the street. Guild-approved," she added, giving him a second, puzzled stare as he stood up.

He knew where he was now. This was a magic-transfer Destination, probably in the Guild Hall, which was where most were located, unless owned by someone.

The air over the tiled floor flickered as if a thousand moths passed briefly into a ray of light, then a man appeared, short, fat, merchant robes. Another young person in green moved to help him to a chair to recover, and to clear the tiles in case someone else came through. No two could occupy the same space—that danger had long since been protected against—but the newcomer would force the old out if someone lingered, knocking them quite far if it was a long enough transfer.

Shevraeth walked out into a noisy street that smelled strongly of brine. The light was filtered through breaking clouds. The air was cool, and underneath the tang of the sea familiar scents teased at Shevraeth's memory. The sun was overhead—midday. *I am in candle time again, not bell time.*

Candle time. The urge to do something—to scout, to retrieve supplies, to run for weapons—still gripped Shevraeth with immediacy, as his mind struggled to accept the fact that Senrid, Marlovair, the first year seniors, and Marloven Hess were now four months' sea journey away. Unless he bought a transfer token—with what?

*And what would I do, become another thing for Senrid to worry about?* Shevraeth stared at the busy street unseeing, as he counted up facts one by one. Beginning with the realization he did not know the next stage in Senrid's plans, because Senrid had never included him in them. The troubles in Marloven Hess were now Marloven troubles. Shevraeth was home, one less trouble for Senrid to worry about.

Shevraeth had to accept it, and get on with his life.

At home.

*Home.* Despite all the dire letters, happiness made him smile. He'd see his parents again. Savona. His old ponies, his room above the waterfall, the quiet forests of Renselaeus. He'd hear his own language again. Home.

He stepped off the Guild Hall porch into the street, which was clogged with wagon, cart, horse, and foot traffic, people wearing a wild variety of colors and styles of clothes. Had he arrived in the middle of a festival?

No, he realized as he began to walk slowly along; these were everyday clothes. He was so used to the ubiquitous gray of Marloven Hess's enormous armed force in the royal city—the plain clothes of the civs. Around him rose the chatter of at least four languages.

He blinked. He walked. He breathed. But still did not feel quite real.

*Oh, but I am so close to home.*

So . . . how to get there? He had nothing whatsoever in the way of money. All he had were his clothes, the practice knife in his belt and the two in his boots. Oh, and the medallion.

His fingers closed around it. The magic was now gone from it. Untrained as he was, he could still sense by the lack of tingle in the metal that the magical spells on the heavy gold had been spent. Leaving a medallion of solid gold.

Maybe Senrid expected it back. If so, the Renselaeus family could easily replace it. But right now, it was time to sell it. Shevraeth remembered what the transfer chamber worker had told him, and set out down the street, utterly unaware of how people took one look at him and stayed out of his way.

The money changer had strung little flags over the door, representing the currencies they handled. The Remalnan green and gold was among them. Soon he was at the counter, smelling familiar spices, and speaking the language of home. The medallion brought a goodly sum; the proprietor offered as a matter of course to transfer a message through the Scribe Guild. Shevraeth agreed and paid the fee without demur.

What to say—in case there were Galdran spies along the message route?

Reality was shifting by slow degree.

On the paper he wrote: *Father, I'm in the Port of Ela, will arrange for a horse and start for home tomorrow. Unless you have other orders.*

He had gotten out of the habit of signing the letters he'd sent through his golden box, since there were only three people who had access to the magic. This letter would come through the Scribe Guild, so he must sign it. His fingers were ready to write *Shevraeth.* He caught himself, and penned deliberately, *Vidanric Renselaeus.* But it felt like he was writing about someone else.

He sealed the letter with waiting sealing wax and handed it off to be sent to his father through the Scribe Guild representative in Renselaeus. Then he asked who had the best riding horses. The proprietor called for his daughter, who emerged from the back, a pen stuck behind her ear. She gave him directions. He thanked them and left, and used more of the money to get himself a room at an inn that overlooked the harbor. He sat on the tiny terrace outside the room as he ate the meal he'd ordered. His eyes watered from spices that had become unfamiliar. It all tasted so good—so like home!

He stared out to sea, where the westering light spangled on the water. A mass of ships rolled gently on the waves, yards crossed, as they waited for the tide to change. Shevraeth— Vidanric—tried to gather his wits together into one place and one time. He still felt divided between two selves. Shevraeth had become comfortable, full of purpose. He had left Vidanric behind when he was fifteen. Being Vidanric again felt like pulling on old clothes that he'd long grown out of. He wondered if the messages had arrived yet, and what everyone was saying.

Where was everyone? Had Senrid taken the first year seniors to Stad? Was Forthan riding the border, watching for Norsundrian invaders?

Where was Senelac?

He put down his fork (forks again!) and rubbed his eyes. One thing, distance made no difference whatsoever to that kind of hurt. Good riddance, he thought with a pang of anger, but he pressed the palms of his hands against his temples, consciously forcing away the anger. He would not let himself start thinking of Fenis Senelac as a villain. There were too many good memories, and as for the end—well, she'd been as unhappy as he was.

He finished the food and ventured out to find the horse auction. It was mid-afternoon now. He wandered along the streets, guided by landmarks, until at last he reached the bazaar. It was located halfway up a hill, large and clean and airy, the animals looking well-fed, their feet well-cared for if perhaps not to the exacting standards of the Marloven girls. He watched as buyers and sellers dickered, handling the animals, riding, checking them over. To his eye they were hard-mouthed, uncouth.

The owner, an older man, was impatient at the young warrior's questions at first. But the questions kept coming, more and more specific about history and training. The man gradually became more deferential. When at last he was shown a young two-year-old that had been labeled on the high-spirited side, the warrior asked for a ride.

The animal seemed puzzled, slow, even uncertain, tossing its head and sidling. Vidanric fought his impatience, reminding himself that he'd been riding Marloven style for over three years. He gently but firmly repeated a simple command— knee, spoken command, praise when the horse moved—and felt a beginning response to his touch. He gave the horse a couple rounds in the paddock, and when he finally dismounted, discovered several people watching, their expressions difficult to parse. Shrugging, he thoroughly checked the horse over, liking its long legs, its intelligent response. Its coloring was nothing extraordinary: it was a dark gray with dapples that indicated it would lighten in color. After three years of mostly dun and fawn-colored Nelkereth racers with their beautiful arched necks, small heads, and perfectly proportioned limbs, it did not seem a beauty. But he did not care for that.

He was going home.

"I'll take this one. We'll train on the road." A wave of sadness gripped him, and he knew it for a reminder of the Marloven girls.

He would train this horse, and if he heard Senelac's voice as he remembered the Marloven methods, well, he could live with that.

"Yes, sir." The seller bowed repeatedly. "Yes, sir."

"I'll be by tomorrow morning," Vidanric said. "I'll want a feed bag, and gear for a cross-country ride."

A deep bow. Whispers from some of the others watching.

Strange. Everyone seemed strange. Bowing seemed strange.

*I've forgotten all our customs. Or maybe I never noticed half of what was around me*, he thought, striding off with a martial swing that caused heads to turn in his wake, as a young woman said to her companion, "Where do you learn to ride like *that*?"

৵ওঙে

The only other purchase he made was a sword. He felt a little foolish buying one, especially at first when he couldn't seem to find a decent cavalry blade, much less anything in Marloven steel. The straight sword he'd been used to as a small boy seemed unbearably clumsy. He had always known he'd have to come home to it again, but he hesitated, about to walk out, when the armorer—anxious for a sale—said, "Are ye looking for one of those big swords from foreign parts?"

"A cavalry sword." Vidanric gestured, flicking his fingers slightly outward at the tip.

"Ah! I do have one. Old. No one has ever wanted it, so I've kept it in the back. Bide here." The man ran into the dark room beyond, from which came the unmusical clangs of steel and a few thumps, then he emerged victorious, brandishing a dulled blade with a worn wooden handle.

Vidanric took it, frowning as he hefted it, then—with a care to either side—gave it an experimental swing or two. Not bad, actually—not well-balanced as he was used to, but heavy enough. Solid tang, handle fitted by someone who knew their business.

"I'll not charge for a sharpening." The man was obviously glad to get rid of something he must have bought from a traveler off a ship ages ago.

"Then I'll take it," Vidanric said, though it and the horse had seriously diminished his stock of coins. But all he had ahead of him was a few days' easy ride along the coast of Gil al Mardgar and he'd reach Renselaeus, which lay between the harbor and Remalna. If need be he could sleep outside, the weather was warm.

The next morning he paid off his shot at the inn, and arranged the saddle pad to carry the horse feed as well as allow easy access to his sword. He stopped at the Remalnan travelers' exchange, and was sharply disappointed to discover that there was no message for him. Not surprising, he told himself. His father probably didn't trust this method of communication any more than he did. His parents knew he was coming, that was good enough.

Galdran and his spying and threats were becoming more real as Marloven Hess's concerns gradually faded from his immediate thoughts. He wished again that he'd been able to stop at least for his gold case. Strange, how you go your entire life being used to messages traveling no faster than a messenger can ride or sail, but as soon as you get a magical aid, you adapt at once, and become impatient at its absence, when life reverts to its regular course.

He mounted up, taking a little time to work with his young horse, who seemed receptive to his touch and his voice. They threaded through the early morning traffic, moving slowly enough that Vidanric was able to listen to some of the talk around him. Most was about immediate and personal concerns, but twice he heard the word 'refugees' and once "If Sartor falls again—" but the rest of that sentence was about trade laws and how they'd change.

The horse was promisingly well-behaved despite slow oxen-drawn wagons taking, as only the heavy can, the very middle of the road, the shrieking children darting in and out of the crowds, boisterous sailors, dashing carriage horses, ordinary riding hacks, and stolid mules drawing carts. Vidanric could hardly wait to get out on the open road.

# Forty-eight

The coastal road was well tended by Gil al Mardgar's Road Guild. There were road-houses every so often, some of them no more than roofs on poles to pull under when a heavy rainfall occurred. Traffic was steady enough that Vidanric was never alone at any of these, though he used them several times as bands of rain swept through.

He fell into conversation during each of these stops as he (missing his rainproof cloak) and other travelers watched rain wash down the sides of the road. Everyone he met asked if he was a warrior on liberty from somewhere. The first two or three times he said "I'm going home to Remalna." Every time he gave that answer the conversation dried up.

Wondering if the cause was he or Remalna, the fourth time it happened, with a fellow his own age who was carrying a wagonload of rugs, he answered instead, "I just finished training. I'm just riding around to see the sights."

And the fellow opened up, talking about trade, horses, travel, which inns were good and which bad, and sights along the coastal roads. "You won't want to risk inland." He waved his hand. "Hear tell of brigands and the like inland, especially close to the border. You won't want to go into Remalna if you don't have to—everyone says the brigandage is on order of their king. Some say, in fact, he's the leader of 'em."

"Really?" Vidanric asked. "What do the people of Remalna say about that?"

The young man sidled glances at Vidanric's weapons, and stepped closer to the doorway. He looked uncomfortable. "Dunno, except the owner insists we pay to put our goods on boats, though it adds to the cost, and stay at sea along Remalna's coast. Then land at Nal Hamath or Tussora and go up-river."

"So Remalna is a nation of brigands?"

The young man made a little business of peering out from under the roof toward the sky. "Rain's lifting. Best be on my way. Look, all I'm saying is, you better have not just business well-established if you go to Remalna, but papers saying so. I don't point a finger at anyone, not at all, but there's bad news coming out of there. That's all, so take heed or take ire as you will."

"Thanks for the warning." Vidanric wondered what he had done to make the fellow so uneasy.

The traveler was not the last person to warn Vidanric against continuing on that road. Despite the rumors naming Remalna a nest of brigands, Vidanric cut inland. The first cause was an inn that gouged most of the rest of his money from him. If the rest of the inns along the common road were that grasping, he may as well sleep outside. He could see the purple line of Renselaeus on the northwestern horizon, too hazy for him to gauge distance with any accuracy. But it was there. And not too soon. He was out of money, except for a scattering of coppers that would get him another meal or two.

The day he cut inland, he rode steadily through the morning until hunger forced him into making an afternoon stop. Enticing smells emanated from the small inn at a crossroads village. He left the horse to be cared for by a pair of stableboys and stepped under the low roof into a small common room, where the local accent was enough like Rensare to wash Vidanric in as intense a wave of homesickness as anything he felt on first arriving at Marloven Hess's academy so long ago.

From the little village the mountains appeared larger, a solid wall that would soon swallow the afternoon sun. Vidanric ordered bread and soup (the cheapest offering of the three choices) and listened wistfully to the innkeeping family chattering with a room full of locals, the size of the crowd proof that the local brewery was especially good. Since he was effectively invisible, Vidanric concentrated on trying to identify the local dialect. *It's really all Sartoran way, way down underneath*, he thought. But enough regional differences for his patriotic ancestors to claim a name for their own dialect, raising it thus to the distinction of Language.

When one eats alone, there's no reason to linger. He mounted up and rode on, pacing the horse a trifle faster than he had before.

So far on the inland road he'd met very few people, and all those had been locals, most driving carts and wagons, and once a dust-covered carriage. Its windows were firmly curtained, behind which emerged a brief drift of laughter.

The sun had dropped behind the mountains, plunging the land abruptly into shadow, when he spied another horseman on the road ahead.

The rider was Russav, Duke of Savona, who spotted Vidanric at roughly the same time. Neither of them saw anything more than the shadowy outline of a male form on horseback, which did not raise much interest.

Savona had raced for days from post to post over the mountains, and then—after agonizing briefly—decided to take a shortcut, though everyone warned him of brigands infesting the lonely inland road. So far, the only danger seemed to be that his backside would be permanently bruised. Savona had not ridden so hard since he was a small boy, and he couldn't remember the last time he'd travelled all alone, without a gaggle of servants and spies surrounding him.

The first dozen times he'd spotted a rider coming from the direction of the harbor he'd stood in the stirrups, peering down the road. But it was always just another local.

This time he scarcely gave the rider a second glance. It had to be another local, this one in some sort of uniform. Though he rode like a—

Savona jibed at the bridle, sending his tired post horse skittering closer. The fading light didn't give much more detail, but that face—

That familiar face—

*"Danric?"*

The dark gray horse laid its ears flat as its rider drew in a sharp breath, his complexion going pale and then flooding with color.

Vidanric stared as the tall, broad-shouldered fellow in rich clothing and long flowing dark hair under a dashing, low-brimmed hat resolved into—

"Russav!"

Laughing, exclaiming—neither hearing the other—they flung themselves off their mounts. Savona gripped Vidanric by the back of the neck with one hand and pounded him with the other, his laughter sounding like sharp barks of joy.

Vidanric fended him off with one hand and took hold of his wrist with the other. Then they hugged, one massive squeeze that made their joints crackle and pop, and sprang apart as they both began shooting questions at the other. Realized neither could hear, and stopped.

Savona kept hold of Danric's shoulders as he held him off, staring into his face. "Life! How you have changed, Danric."

Vidanric grimaced. "Hair grows out quick enough."

Not just that, Savona was thinking, but he just shook his head. "Look, night comes fast in the mountains—in case you've forgotten. There is nothing behind me for half a day's ride, unfortunately. I was just cursing myself for taking this road, where there aren't any decent post horses to be had."

"Speaking of which, you'd better claim yours before he vanishes over the hills."

Indeed the post horse was walking downhill toward a stream below a clump of maple, the reins dragging. Savona bolted after, calling and waving his arms. The animal flicked its ears and trotted away.

Vidanric whistled. His gray pranced up, head lifting. He vaulted into the saddle and trotted after the skittish post horse, as Savona watched in amazement. It wasn't just his seat, it was how he held his hands—like there was a single line from his elbows to the horse's mouth. And the way he'd mounted, with a quick step and a leap—

Vidanric brought the escapee back, handing down the reins. "There's a small inn a ways back, where I had a decent meal. But I've run out of money, so I was going to sleep outside," he admitted.

Savona laughed. "You should have heard the warnings your father dinned into my ears about staying off these roads after dark, once I made it clear I was not going to lurk about hiding in your fortress over the falls. But there hasn't been the slightest whiff of the smallest bandit." Then, thinking of his haste, the innkeepers he'd cursed along the way (and would soon be seeing again) he amended somewhat sheepishly, "Though if you want to return by the coast, that's all right by me."

"Why, when it's so far out of the way?" Vidanric jerked his thumb back the way he'd come. "We'll go back to the inn for the night. It's too hilly to ride blind. Not safe for the animals. Tomorrow we can retrace your steps if the inland route really is faster."

Savona gave up, mentally reassigning his cache of coins for heavy bribery to innkeepers he'd cursed and hurried. "Is yon inn a byre?" Savona asked. "Of course it's a byre. They don't seem to have heard of posting inns hereabouts, or normal human comfort."

When they arrived at the small inn, all the locals fell silent as Savona strode in, looking as out of place in those plain, rough-hewn surroundings as, well, a duke in a countryside inn. As everyone watched, mugs here and there suspended midway between lips and table, he cast his hat and gloves onto the broad window sill, glanced around with cheerful dismay, and began pleasantly handing out orders that sent the entire innkeeping family scurrying. Vidanric heard the youngest child run out into the poultry yard piping, "Papa! The warrior is back, and he's got a *lord* with him!"

The regulars picked up their mugs and filed into the kitchen, some casting back glances of disbelief.

Vidanric sat down at a newly abandoned table. "We needn't rouse the entire village."

Savona laughed. "Why not? I've got plenty of money. May's well be comfortable." He kicked a rough-hewn table out of the way and dragged a chair close to the fire someone had just built. "Chairs! I feel like a world traveler already."

And with a casual, even breezy assurance that sounded to Vidanric like arrogance after three and a half years of rigidly non-aristocratic life, Savona took over the inn, first re-arranging the small common room to his satisfaction and then issuing a stream of orders about the dinner and the beds.

Vidanric would have demurred, but Savona finished off his long list of commands by slapping down a handful of six-sided gold coins onto the inn-keeper's serving table, waving lazily when they attempted to enumerate their charges. "Keep it! Keep it! Just hop to it. We're both tired and hungry."

The easy largesse brought smiles to the innkeepers' faces.

"Now we shall be comfortable," Savona declared. "And undisturbed." The voices rose in the kitchen as the locals wondered aloud what could have brought a lord to the village; by the next day, Savona's prestige would have expanded to include a coach-and-six, two trumpeters, and a dozen outriders in livery, their hair tied back in big ribbons.

Savona leaned forward. "Last I heard from you, you were there, busy with lances and all the rest of it. Why are you here so suddenly? What happened?"

Vidanric launched into his story, stopping and back-tracking frequently. It felt so good to talk again! Savona listened with admirable patience to the disjointed account, even when

Vidanric interrupted himself with "No, wait, I have to tell you this first."

While the recitation was going on, they had time to assess the other by the glow of lamps. Savona was so astonished at his oldest friend's changes he had to begin with Vidanric's few familiar features: his gray eyes, his pale hair. But the familiar gray eyes had narrowed in a way utterly unfamiliar, and the hair was worn short in a military cut. More, Vidanric had grown from a spindly weed with graceful hands to a height eye to eye with Savona. He was as lean as a knife, his manner a kind of leashed tension that was totally unfamiliar. *How are we going to hide three years of this kind of life from Galdran?* he thought, when Vidanric paused to drink, muscles straining against his sleeves when he lifted his arm.

Vidanric's thoughts were far more tangled. Savona looked, well, not soft, exactly—there was no fat whatsoever to that flat stomach—but he looked, oh, call it untrained. He looked like a civ. Like a lord, in fact—taking precedence as his right. And nobody seemed to mind.

During a brief silence just after the food was brought (all cooked to Savona's exact specifications) Vidanric entertained himself with just what would happen at the academy if someone—not Savona, no, but some unnamed fellow with long black hair, wearing velvet and lace to ride in—strode into the academy handing out orders right and left. *You'd learn all the shades of meaning of scrag,* he admitted to himself. *No, that's unfair, too. What's more, this is the kind of life I'm supposed to be leading.*

"I'm going to need new clothes, I guess," he said.

Savona laughed. "So I would think! But I'll take those riding boots, if you don't want 'em."

"Those stay. Gotten used to 'em." Vidanric stretched out one leg, regarding the scuffed, worn toes of his boot. "But I'm going to have to find a cobbler who can make them."

"Order me a pair."

They talked a while longer—clothes, fashions, food—nothing about home. By mutual agreement that would wait until they were alone on the road.

The candles had guttered low and Vidanric had lost track of what he was saying when they decided to retire. Savona followed him upstairs thinking that a couple glasses of wine had done a lot to make Danric, well, more *human*.

He grumpily changed his mind the next morning when noise outside his open window caused him to roll out of bed, pull on his trousers, and look out. He discovered Danric down in the court, fully dressed, the horses ready. Danric was in the act of shoving that long, curve-tipped sword back into the saddle sheath after what apparently had been a long drill.

"What did you do, get up before dawn?" Russav asked crossly.

Danric looked up, and grinned. "Yes."

"What? Life! Danric, you have gotten into some very bad habits."

"Think of it this way. Sooner we depart, the sooner we get home."

"Very well, very well."

And so they were soon on the road, as low clouds drifted overhead. Savona began the talk, complaining with long pent-up freedom about the king and all the court. Vidanric listened while they rode gradually upward, the ground rising in tree and shrub-dotted folds. He commented less and less, his attention shifting outward as he continually looked around.

Savona's diatribe against Galdran and court began to abate. He shifted to anecdotes, trying to dredge up the funniest ones he could remember. If he'd become a bore, he wished Vidanric would have said so, but he could take a hint.

Vidanric was unaware that he'd stopped listening. Signs of humanity were fewer as they progressed up the narrowing road. This was prime territory for ambush.

In the middle of one of Savona's more inspired descriptions of one of Galdran's card parties, Vidanric checked his sword to make certain it was loose in its saddle-sling.

Savona forced a laugh. "Hoping to fend off boredom? If you've had your fill of my natter, just say the word."

"I don't like this country," Vidanric returned, unsmiling. "In fact—"

He let the pause stretch into silence. Savona, uneasy now, was going to crack a joke when Vidanric flicked up a hand in a short, commanding gesture. Savona found himself reining in, his exclamation bit back. His horse's ears were twitching back and forth.

The bushes on either side of the road rustled wildly, and three armed men rushed out from either side, weapons raised.

Savona shouted—the men shouted—Savona groped for his sword—where was it?

His horse circle-danced in rising panic as Savona kneed one of his saddle bags to get at his rapier, which had slid under the pack. Shouts, clopping hooves, a nasty thunking noise and the clash and whirr of steel made his heart thunder.

He finally got the rapier out by yanking with both hands. He slewed around. Vidanric's arm was a blur of circles that ended in two sickening, blood-spraying chops. He stabbed one man, blocked a swinging stroke from the other side, whirled his sword into the attacker's throat. Blood sprayed darkly and the man choked, groaned, and crashed to the ground.

Savona gaped in mind-flown shock at six men lying lifeless in the road.

Six. Two with knives in their chests, one with the knife in his throat, three of them sword-hacked. Danric mopped with a shaking hand at the sweat running into his eyes, then he flicked a glance at the blood-smeared sword gripped in his right hand. He slipped out of the saddle, his haggard face going distinctly green, and dropped down to the ground with his head between his knees.

Savona said in a voice that sounded like someone else's in his ringing ears, "They're *dead*. You *killed* them."

Vidanric looked up, his face exhausted, his eyes dark with misery. "Didn't you hear them?" he returned, his voice husky. "They had orders to kill us both."

# Forty-nine

"What?" Savona exclaimed.

"You didn't hear them? They were shouting." Vidanric's voice was flat, his body shivering.

"Heard voices. Not words. Too busy wrestling with this." Savona flashed up the point of his rapier. "How could you stab three at once?"

Vidanric mimed knife-throwing. Then surged to his feet and with a sudden, swift strike buried the sword almost to the hilt in the loose soil beside the road.

When he pulled it free again, it was clean, except for one red streak. He plunged the sword into the ground again and again until it came forth clean, then he leaned against his horse, eyes closed, face still wan. "That one there." He pointed with the sword. "Came out of the shrubs. Said *Yellow hair—that's our boy.* And that one over there said *I want the lordling! He's gonna*—And that one said, *Don't play! Orders are, fast and dead!*" He wiped his hair back off his brow with trembling fingers, then retrieved one of the knives; Savona looked away as Vidanric cleaned that by stabbing it into the dirt. "So I took him out first. In an ambush . . ."

There came the sounds of the other two knives being retrieved and cleaned. ". . . You take out the leader first. Oh, Russav, I really think I'm going to faint." He folded abruptly again, head down, his breathing ragged.

*He's killed six men*, Savona thought, dazed. *They were going to kill us first, but still. Six people who woke up alive today. Ate. Laughed.*

*Planned our deaths.*

"Orders. To kill us." Vidanric's voice was muffled. He raised his face, and Savona saw the tear streaks that Vidanric did not try to hide. "Not their idea, then. Think what that means. Someone saw that message I wrote. Reported it to someone else. You were followed until you reached me."

"But—" Savona tried to get his brain to work. His thoughts skittered like frightened mice.

He turned his back on the dead, who were after all no more threat, though their terrible, lifeless sprawl was silent reminder that someone, somewhere, *wanted him dead.* Then drew in a deep breath. Now he was nauseated, and the edges of his vision flickered. He drew another breath. "But how would they know what you looked like?"

"Yellow hair is what he said." Vidanric shoved two of the knives into his boot tops, then wiped the last one over and over on grass before he put it in his belt.

"That would be an easy guess. Who could it be but Galdran?"

"It would fit the pattern of all those 'accidents,' wouldn't it? The point is, someone clever enough to have a spy either at the Scribe Guild or in our house, or my father would never have let you come after me."

Savona thought back, appalled. "You're right. We should get back—hold. I hear someone coming! Oh, Norsunder take it, where is that horse?" He spun in a circle, and nearly tripped over the forgotten blade in his hand.

Vidanric stood in the center of the road, sword held across his body in half-guard, his face pale but determined.

*I do not know you*, Savona thought bleakly. *Do I want to?* No, no, that was disloyal—Danric had saved their lives! He'd done the right thing! But—

Clopping and jingling harnesses preceded what turned
out to be a cart piled with barrels, driven by two big, burly men.
They saw the lone figure in the road holding a sword and one
reined hard as the other groped behind the driving bench for a
quarterstaff.

"Wait—wait," Savona yelled, running forward and
waving his rapier. "We're not thieves—*we* were ambushed." He
pointed the rapier back at the dead highwaymen. "They attacked
us."

The men, brothers from the look, gazed in astonishment
from the blood-splashed assassins to the disheveled young lord
to the pale-haired young fellow with the military haircut who
stood so silently in the road, sword at guard. The driver said,
"You're the two spent the night in Skyanee last night? Skyanee
Inn?"

The carter with the quarterstaff said, "I saw your horse
galloping down the road back that way." He thumbed back over
his shoulder.

Savona sighed. "I'll have to go find it. But first. Are you
locals? Do you know what we're supposed to do about brigands
who won't be attacking anyone any more?"

"That's an affair for the Road Guild and the local
magistrate," the other brother said. "The nearest of either is half
a day's ride away."

The brother with the cudgel fingered his weapon. "Where
are the rest of you?"

"Just us." Savona suppressed a weird urge to laugh.

The other twiddled fingers toward the dead. "The two of
*you* did for all of 'em?"

Savona said, "No. He did. I just fumbled around trying to
get this from the sheath. After which I lost my horse." He
brandished his rapier, then looked at it. "I don't suppose those
fellows would have stuck with dueling rules." He tipped his
head, unable to resist even so lame a joke.

Two sober heads shook slowly.

Vidanric dropped his head back, staring upward at the sky, then he brought his chin down with a jerk of decision. When he spoke, his voice was steady again, though absent of any emotion whatsoever. "We will do whatever is necessary."

And so it happened.

As the two rode off to find Savona's horse they held a quick conversation, deciding to leave Galdran's name out of the business—and their own. Word would inevitably travel cross country. You didn't take out a band of brigands, whoever they were, without people talking.

And so they followed the carters to the local town, and before the magistrate (hastily summoned from his dinner) Savona claimed to be from Tussora, Vidanric from Sarendan, which was known at this end of the continent for its army training at Obrin. Many kingdoms sent young men there, since the academy at Khanerenth was reputed to have been closed due to that kingdom's troubles.

The brigands had carried nothing except a hefty sack of new-struck Remalnan gold coins. The sight of those coins effectively ended the questioning. Savona and Vidanric recognized from the magistrate's grim expression that Remalnan coins on brigands were not unknown.

The magistrate ruled that since no witnesses could testify, they had to rely on evidence. After hearing the carters describe what they'd seen, he judged the deaths to have been self-defense. He finished with legal words to the effect that the bodies would be Disappeared, and the descriptions and clothing of the deceased written in the record for any families who might come seeking word of them. Then the two young men were sent on their way with a haste that indicated the local authorities did not want them lingering.

Savona was aware of whispers following in their wake through the small town. People came out to stare at the young warrior who'd done for six outlaws all by himself. If Vidanric was aware, he gave no sign of it. Just responded as little as possible, in that even, remote voice that made Savona increasingly uneasy.

Savona arranged to leave the post horse at the inn, with directions to the owner, and he used some of his stash to buy another horse. They rode on as soon as they'd eaten, stopping only to buy supplies for the animals. Savona listened as Vidanric answered questions with lie after lie: they were from Sarendan, they were going east along the mountains into Ergoramar.

For the rest of the day, Vidanric did not speak, but either watched the surrounding countryside with that narrow gaze, or else frowned between his horse's ears. Savona kept his peace. In truth, he had no idea what to say.

Vidanric broke the silence just before dark. "Here's what I think we should do," he said. "Buy extra food at the next place we can, after which we ought to leave the road. And cross the border under cover."

"Lead on," Savona said.

ಌⒸℛℰↃ

Over the next two days, Savona got a learn-as-you-go lesson in covert movement. He also got lessons in the style of sword fighting that Vidanric had been taught. Not that they could drill effectively with a heavy-bladed cavalry sword and thin-bladed dueling rapier, but Savona learned enough to realize that pretty much everything he'd ever been taught was useless except for dueling by the rules.

The weather stayed comfortable the first day, but the second gained considerably in heat. Summer had arrived at last. Vidanric took off his tunic and traveled in shirt and trousers. Savona found revealing the careful way Vidanric folded the grubby tunic away into his otherwise flat saddle-pack.

For most of the first day, Vidanric didn't talk except to instruct.

The second day the snows melted somewhere inside him, and he did not stop talking. Savona heard about kingship, command, the obligations of duty, the pressure of deciding for all the lives entrusted to one, and at night, under the forgiving starlight, in a low, swift, sometimes uneven voice Danric wondered if any of the men he'd killed had liked starlight, had been evil, what had Galdran told them? Did someone love them, and would grieve to discover they were dead?

To which Savona replied, "They took orders to kill two fellows not even of age, Danric. Fellows they didn't even know. So they got killed instead. I'm not saying it is right. I don't know what's right any more. Not the way we've been living. But I am saying you didn't murder them."

"No." Vidanric's voice was almost too low to hear. "I killed them. I did what I was trained to do. What my father sent me to learn. But I am going to have to question every single act. Or I will turn into—" He shook his head, his profile somber as he gazed out over the peaceful valley.

Savona sat companionably with him, offering what comfort he could.

Presently they slept.

The third day he was more like the Danric that Savona had first met on the road, talking normally, laughing, even. A few days later they reached a height from which they caught their first glimpse of Renselaeus's ruling city before the great falls. Vidanric had remembered his map from childhood, for which Savona was grateful. He also absorbed the implied lesson about knowing one's map.

When they reached the road up to the city they had been two weeks threading along animal trails through the mountains. The food they'd bought had gone stale, but they rationed it again and again until it was gone, after which they filled their stomachs with cold, clear spring water, and lots of wild-growing berries. Though they used the springs to wash as best they could, their clothing was grimy, and Savona shared the clothes he'd chosen without much thought, stuffing the dirty ones back into the saddle bags with rude jokes and laughter. He was relieved when Danric laughed with him.

With the sharing of Savona's clothes came the sharing of minds, and then hearts. By the time they reached the last mountain they had recovered all their old understanding and then surpassed it, reaching a new, adult consciousness. There was nothing, from strength to weakness, that either sought to hide from the other. They were no longer unthinking boys. They talked about fears, about failures, about the little triumphs that one usually keeps inside. Savona heard the entire story of Vidanric's relationship with Fenis Senelac, and Danric every flash and rumble of Savona's stormy relationship with Tamara Chamadis. More entertaining—leading to speculation about girls and their motives and intentions—Savona extravagantly described all his flirtations during the times Tamara and he were enemies . . . which never lasted, though each time they parted they swore it Was For Ever, and Do Not Speak To Me Again.

When the beautiful mountaintop palace of the Renselaeuses became visible, Vidanric withdrew once again behind that new, remote countenance.

After a while, Savona prodded him for a reason.

Vidanric said, "I'm angry with our border riders. They're slack."

Savona protested, "Hey! The Blues might not be up to your Marloven standards, but I assure you they aren't lying around drunk in some tavern."

"They should have seen us by now," Vidanric retorted. "If we can sneak up on my father, so can anyone."

Savona had no answer to that.

കൊ෨ൟ౨ఴ

That same morning Prince Alaerec found his wife sitting alone in her private chamber overlooking the falls, her hands gripping her upper arms tightly as she rocked gently back and forth.

"I am sorry, my darling." His breathing caught as he eased himself painfully onto the window seat next to her. "Do you wish to hear what I discovered?"

She turned her head, her eyes bleak. "I do not wish, but I must. We will share it together."

He raised a hand. "Nothing about Savona. Or Vidanric. I know no more than you at this moment. But . . . I realize I ought to have investigated long ago. I do not know why I did not. I thought the Scribe Guild was somehow above politics. They do take oaths. Still. The woman in the supervisory position who has served us these past ten years so blamelessly has a sister in service to the Merindars. To be precise, a scribe under the marquise."

Princess Elestra stiffened as though she'd been struck.

"I am certain of two things. First, that the Merindars must have heard about Vidanric's letter sent from the harbor. Second, I believe that the answer I made was never actually sent. I had one of my independent traders check. I just now received his note."

Her eyes closed. "It's been too many days. For the boys."

"There might be any number of reasons why the journey has taken so long."

The prince folded his arms around his wife's trembling body. After a time she relaxed against him. Neither spoke as the waters thundered and thundered beyond them, not until there was a rustle from outside the room, and someone scratched outside the tapestry.

The princess said, "Enter."

A footman ran in. "Arrivals on the road, your highness."

The prince and princess rose, their fingers intertwining. Bad news or good, they would face it together.

Hand in hand they entered the reception room off the main court. There was a great stirring of Blue Riders in their sturdy blue tunics who poured in, their manner excited. In the center of their group walked two mud-spattered, exceedingly grubby young men.

One was Savona. The other—tall, slender, straight, with short pale hair—familiar gray eyes—

"Oh, my son!" the princess cried, and flung herself into Vidanric's arms, crying and laughing together.

The prince limped up behind her, tears in his eyes. Wordlessly Vidanric extended his hands and pulled his father's thin, frail body in, so that they sandwiched the princess between them.

For a time they stood thus, the three of them, arms tangled about one another, too overcome for words. At last the prince lifted his head and faced Savona. "Thank you."

"Do not thank me. It was Danric who saved our lives," Savona said.

At that the little group fell apart, the princess smiling and wiping her eyes on her dainty lace sleeves.

"Father, here's my suggestion. One question and answer will not do, so why don't we bathe and meet you wherever you wish. Only I hope it will include food. We're both starving, as we came cross country. But I itch as much as I stink, and I want to burn these clothes I've been wearing the past two days."

"Hey," Savona protested. "Those are mine! A cleaning frame will do."

On unsteady laughter they all parted, the princess speeding on the light steps of joy to see to an instant, and substantial meal, the prince to his private chamber to await them.

When Vidanric reappeared, he wore his uniform, which had been put through the cleaning frame. He and Savona had resorted to the great bath, soaking away their aches. They joined Vidanric's parents, their hair still damp, Savona in one of his elegant suits.

"Dear boy, will you give us your report?" the prince asked.

Vidanric began in Marloven, stuttering to a halt as he blushed crimson. While his parents and Russav Savona watched, he had to make the mental shift to report mode in his own language.

But he found it, and began with a swift statement of result, then briefly filled in the details of his journey from the harbor, meeting Savona, the brigands, what they did afterward.

The Prince heard him out, then said, "I recently discovered that the Guild Scribe chief is connected to the Marquise of Merindar. I never thought to inquire about any of my scribes, who have always been exemplary until now. But when you did not answer my response to your note sent from the harbor, and then days went by—" He shook his head. "As well that I used my old contacts for private messages, and the Scribes for general communications. I very much fear that much of Renselaeus business has passed through at least one pair of Merindar hands."

Vidanric tossed his hair back from his eyes. "Father, that brings me to what I would not say below in the court, but I should not have been able to come thus upon you without being seen."

The Prince nodded slowly. "You are going to take over training the Blues, but you will have to contrive it from a distance. I suggest you train your equerries while you are away, and send them back to me. I will see that they train the rest, once I have ascertained who is trustworthy and who a plant."

"You cannot send him away again," the Princess cried, turning on her husband. Then she frowned. "Of course. If we have spies in the Scribe guild, and possibly inside the principality . . ."

"The Scribes can't know I'm here," Vidanric said.

"We may rejoice that no one saw Vidanric until he arrived at the palace today," the prince said. "I will vouch for the loyalty of the palace Blues. Some of the others? There has been little consistency in their hiring and training. That will have to change. Right now, though, he has to leave, because the king will be finding some excuse to comb through our land if he thinks the boys escaped his brigands."

The princess sighed, her thin fingers pressed to her temples. Then she opened her eyes. "Danric, dear, if you are to train the men, I desire you to train my women as well. Rinda Nessaren, my chief equerry, says her daughter Yora cries herself to sleep at night, wanting to defend the kingdom."

The Prince gave a nod of agreement.

"Whoever wants to learn." Vidanric thought of Senelac's goals for the girls of Marloven Hess. "Girl or boy, I don't care."

"Excellent," the Prince said. "Russav, you will go home tomorrow. You will never speak of being here at all. To anyone. If you never refer to what happened, the king can't, because he would reveal that he knew about the brigands. Danric, tonight we will have to ourselves, but tomorrow you will taken an honor guard of our best Blues and get yourself out of the kingdom the same way you entered it."

Vidanric's heart seemed to squeeze painfully in his chest. "Where do I go, Father?"

"Colend."

"But Norsunder—"

"We cannot let the troubles with them interfere with our plans. If the world erupts into general war, then everything changes. But—so far—indications are that there is at least as much trouble between the Norsundrian commanders as they are making with us. So far it seems to be a war of mages. While that is the case, it is far less likely that they will attempt to take Colend."

Savona frowned. "Why is that?"

Vidanric said, "Ah."

The prince nodded to Vidanric. "Tell him, my son."

Vidanric turned to Russav. "Consider the map. Colend has no defendable borders. Colend might be easy to take—I don't know what the status of their defenses are—but would be difficult to hold unless Norsunder has enormous occupying forces, because then they have to defend those open borders."

"Correct." The prince was pleased. "Vidanric. You are to make your way as swiftly as possible to Colend. You will take the most expensive lodging you can. My friend the Sartoran ambassador will introduce you to court, perhaps even to the young king, though he's been kept sequestered while the Regency Council rules. You will talk everywhere of oddities you've seen traveling. Leffain has been across the continent, and even over to Toar, writing you a travel diary specifically for this purpose. You will send the latest fashions back to us, here, which will pass through the Scribe Guild's hands."

"So you will not get rid of the Merindar spy?" Vidanric asked.

"No." The prince's smile was sardonic. "I will cherish her, for nothing is more useful than a known spy. If I get rid of her, I will only get another foisted on me. Instead, she will share with the king what I want him to see."

Politics. It seemed . . . dishonorable, somehow, after the straightforward days in Marloven Hess. *Straightforward and brutal*, Vidanric thought, remembering Sindan Hotears, and the result of his trouble-making. Militarily minded machinations were just as bad as political scheming. Was there no civilized method?

"After I discover who the spies are among the Blues, I will send them as couriers to Colend. You will then write letters to Russav, challenging his status as Remalna's chief fop and flirt. Your life's goal is to gain a reputation as the Marquis of Shevraeth, Colend's most famous fashion fribble. Before you come home, your reputation will be even worse than Savona's. The Marquis of Shevraeth will have a new identity entirely."

"Hah!" Savona laughed, teeth flashing.

*And so the title takes yet a new meaning*, Vidanric thought. "In short, every single thing I've learned over the last few years will be wrong."

The prince smiled. "True. And so you will learn again, not just the manners and mores, but how a different people cooperates among themselves to make a successful government."

Everyone under the same law, that's what Senrid's father had wanted. Shevraeth shook his head. "I can't believe the king will ever want anything I've learned."

"No." The prince's expression sobered.

"But the people might." The princess touched his hand. "It's easy to complain about the king. It's far more difficult to get everyone to agree on what ought to be done."

"So you, my son, will go to Colend. When your hair is grown out—I should think two, at most three years will do it— you will proceed home with a huge train of baggage and expensive but frivolous presents, as an excuse to hire at least fifty extra guards, and you will of course have your trained servants. You'll send equerries ahead to turn out the most famous, expensive posting houses. Your return is going to be gossiped about in every kingdom, making it impossible for you to be quietly ambushed. People will line the roads just to look at you."

The princess laid her hand on the prince's. "The point is this, there must be as great a difference as possible between you and the short-haired young man in the military tunic who killed six assassins. Which, you can be sure, will soon be rumored at twelve or even twenty."

The prince smiled at his wife, then said to his son, "When you arrive, your mother and I will be publicly insulted that you went to court first to show off your new finery." The Prince turned to Savona. "And you will become Danric's rival."

"Can we fight a duel?" Savona asked. "Please, let me challenge him to a duel."

Vidanric bowed. "At your service." Then grimaced. "That feels strange, bowing. But I guess I should get used to strange things. Like feeling like a fraud, because I'm about to become one."

"I prefer," the Princess said, "to think of it as hiding in plain sight."

The Prince bowed, gesturing with his hands in deferment to superior rank. She laughed softly, no more than a breath, and tapped the top of his hand with her fan. Vidanric realized he did not know the significance of the gesture.

Once again, much to learn.

"And when we fight our duel," Savona said evilly, "you are going to drop your sword at least twice."

# Fifty

"Did you hear that Shevraeth is coming home at last?" Pretty Lady Arasa announced breathlessly. The ribbons on her hat bounced as she tripped lightly along the stone path and joined the other young aristocrats in the garden behind Athanarel Palace in Remalna-city.

It was spring again, bringing everyone back to court after two years of being sequestered on their estates, and not hearing any news except what could be gleaned from traders passing through. During the time of the Norsundrian troubles in other lands, Galdran's warriors had guarded the borders and criss-crossed the kingdom. Under orders, they had stopped and searched any equerries seen along the roads—in case they were Norsundrian spies. People at the southeastern end of the kingdom had wondered why there might be enough Norsundrian spies in Renselaeus to require whole marching battalions going to that principality to search, but of course no one dared ask. Letters had been so discreet they were uninformative.

Young Lord Deric turned wide black eyes toward Savona, expressing excitement and a little apprehension.

Savona knew Deric was worried about accidents on the road. These days, everyone worried about accidents on the road. They had all returned as summoned, bringing their entire households, everyone armed right down to the cooks and tailors. Ostensibly against marauding brigands that the increasing numbers of warriors in green were supposed to guard against, but actually against the vagaries of their king.

Savona sighed, as Olervec watched him narrowly. "I am aware that Shevraeth proposes to return to Remalna at last," Savona said, his heart beating rapidly. So it begins! "I received a missive full of nothing else, just after New Year's Week. At least, as I apprehend. I fell asleep halfway through my perusal and it, ah, dropped into the fire."

Lady Fialma Merindar tittered, slapping his wrist with her fan. "Naughty," she said coyly. "Naughty!"

Savona forced a smile, took the fan from her fingers and playfully fanned her with it. She bridled, sending a scornful look of triumph at Tamara, who inspected the lace at her wrists. Fialma had returned to court with golden hair. Tamara's was black again.

"Where is Shevraeth now?" Lord Alcanad asked.

"I wonder what he looks like." Lady Arasa plopped down next to two serious young ladies, Nee and Elenet. "He used to be so twiggish."

"Probably branchish now," Tamara murmured.

Most of the others laughed. Fialma curled her lip.

"I wonder if he'll recognize *us*." Lady Renna twirled her fan to include them all.

"He's sure to recognize your riding." Nee was as usual the peacemaker, and Renna smiled, her fan flicking in the mode of Harmonic Agreement.

Typically Tamara ignored Nee, Fialma looked scornful, and Elenet kept her eyes lowered. Most of the other rankers ignored her, taking their cue—as usual—from Tamara. Nee might be Tamara's cousin, but from a lesser branch of the family.

"Well, we'll find out soon." Arasa swept her fan out in the arc of Anticipation. Then she tapped the fan against her chin, her head tipped in the charming mode of Rue. "Unless, of course, Shevraeth just goes up into Renselaeus and doesn't come down."

"No, he's on his way here." Fialma yawned.

Everyone stared at the surprising news—which was, of course, her intention.

"Heard my mother and my uncle discussing it over breakfast," she went on, enjoying the reminder of her superior rank. What was the use of an uncle as king unless you could use it? "You know nothing stirs in the kingdom without Uncle Galdran hearing first."

"Well then, we'll have to put together a welcome party, shall we?" Lord Geral leaned against the marble bench behind Renna. "Savona, you used to be at one other's side when we were small. You should give him a party."

Savona lifted his shoulders in a languid shrug, peripherally aware of Fialma's unwinking stare. "What if he's grown tedious? I do not want to give countenance to a bore."

"Can anyone grow tedious at Colend's court?" Deric spread his fan at the angle of Civil Incredulity. "I thought the Colendi would exile you for the crime of insufficient wit."

"Declarations of war for errors in style." Renna snapped her fan.

Tamara ignored them all, her trenchant blue gaze on Savona. "What if," she said sweetly, "he won't give countenance to *you*?"

Fialma stretched out her hand for her fan. "*I* give you countenance," she drawled, and drew the fan along Savona's cheek before flipping it open. She continued idly flapping the fan and watching Savona over it, as Trishe and Geral began putting together ideas for a welcome party—something that would be suitable for someone who'd been living for who knows how long at the glittering and infamous court at Colend.

Just as they were settling the main ideas, Fialma said in a bored voice, "Oh, I forgot. My mother is doing something or other."

Lady Trishe betrayed an angry flush, quickly hiding it behind her fan as she bent to straighten a flounce. When she rose, her cheeks were glowing from her stoop. She said in a sprightly voice, "Oh, that's even better. No one gives lovelier parties than the Marquise."

Savona shrugged, satisfied that everyone had noted his lack of interest or involvement. "Sun's out." He waved vaguely toward the departing clouds. "Who's for a ride?"

Half of them joined him. Fialma whisked herself off to report the conversation to her mother, the Marquise of Merindar.

And so the Marquise arranged a lavish welcome for the Marquis of Shevraeth, heir to Renselaeus. The general air of curiosity had sharpened to expectation in all, or nearly all. Savona continued to look, and sound bored.

Tamara had gone silent on the subject, but Arasa spread the word that Tamara had ordered the most spectacular gown ever seen—having gotten, from someone, a hint of what the very latest Colendi fashion was.

Elenet was not seen. Savona overheard from the sunny, uncomplicated Nee that she was painting the most beautiful fan she had ever made.

❧☙

The news of his approach heralded Vidanric's arrival. First news, and then a horde of servants who arrived, took over the Renselaeus suite at Athanarel Palace under the eye of the king's personal steward, and to the amusement of many and the covert disgust of some, proceeded to get rid of all the fine furniture they had had in there for years.

Whispers first swept round the palace like a wildfire that Shevraeth had brought in wooden furniture by the wagon-loads—no, worse, he'd had woods cut—no, but he'd bought half of Alsais—

That much at least seemed to be true. Not just servants but courtiers who could find any excuse whatever to be at the Residence wing of the palace witnessed a long parade of exquisite new furnishings, including rugs of fabulous and delicate weave. No wood, though, it was noticed, and some were even disappointed.

When the suite had been almost entirely redecorated, trunks and trunks of clothing of every type were lugged in, not just filling the heir's dressing room, but spilling over (it was eagerly said) into his parents' rooms.

In the middle of these trunks was a very plain, battered one, full of old uniforms and hand-written books, all under a folded cloak of unrelieved black. Galdran's spies, patiently sifting carefully through all these belongings, gave the battered trunk the most cursory of searches, assuming it was a servant's or scribe's stuff accidentally gotten among Shevraeth's belongings. The books were scrawled in some foreign tongue— perfectly useless.

Finally, the Marquis of Shevraeth himself arrived, driving in an open carriage.

The king of course did not go out to meet him: kings only met kings. But the Marquise of Merindar was there on the terrace, smiling, beautifully gowned, with her daughter next to her dressed in brilliants from head to toe.

They were the first to see a tall, languid figure emerge from the carriage, shrug off a driving cloak (which was caught from behind before it could fall to the ground, not that the young Marquis of Shevraeth bothered turning) and saunter at a leisurely pace up the steps. He looked around with an air of mild interest. As his head turned, they saw a criminally expensive hundred-facet diamond drop winking with glorious light in one ear. He wore a hat richly laced, four plumes curling down over his back. He perceived the marquise, paused, took off the hat, and bowed profoundly, his loose hair swinging down over his shoulders.

He advanced the rest of the way, removing fine silk travel gloves and taking her offered hand. He bowed again to salute it. He wore a signet of cobalt blue on a forefinger, and another, even more enormous diamond on the other hand. Nothing, they saw, on the heart finger.

"Marquise," he said in a soft drawl. "It is soooo good to be home. But fatiguing! I had to stop twice. Rain, you know. You will laugh when I admit I *can*not ride in a coach. Not ten paces, without untoward effect. Ah! Fialma! My dear, that lace—straight from Bermund, I see. *Most* beautiful. But I have some that even supercedes—you'll have it as a gift—no, no, no protest—it's a pleasure to give it to someone with such exquisite taste, I'm certain you are one of the rare beings who truly *understand* lace—ah, who else is here?"

They all came forward then, and he greeted everyone by name as they stared at his travel coat of pure, heavy satin in deep sunset blue. Who would wear satin to travel in?

But the embroidered vest beneath was even finer, chased with stylized cranes in flight, tiny sapphires at their eyes, and diamonds glittering discreetly at their wingtips. He carried a fan of white lilies painted over cream-white, the edges just discernible to the careful eye. He employed it languidly, flicking it so swiftly between modes that few could guess at the meaning, though they all tried.

And so it went. The thin, studious boy Vidanric Renselaeus had gone away, apparently to study trade, courts, and fashions, because he returned with a fund of stories about every ruler on the eastern end of the continent, plus the very latest in music, poems, plays, and of course clothes.

He never, they were to discover as the day faded into night and he emerged in a spectacular outfit of midnight blue with crimson and gold embroidery (tied over with ribbons)—never ever stopped talking about clothes. Well, unless it was about horse races. Apparently he had spent a great deal of his time riding steeplechase and point-to-point and garland-hunting.

They discovered by the next day that he could indeed outride most of them—he was most dashing on horseback—but as soon as he dismounted, the very first utterance out of his mouth was about his clothes.

Fialma, spying on her mother and uncle after Shevraeth presented himself to the king at formal court later that day, heard her uncle say, "He's an idiot."

The Marquise looked fondly at her brother. "You would like him to be an idiot, Galdran. Shall we wait upon the arrival of the prince and princess? I confess I am withholding judgment until I see them all together."

Galdran snorted. "War—Norsunder—changes of government, and all he can talk about is who is flirting with whom. Worse, what they were *wearing* when they did it. Idiot!"

Fialma fumed. Being a princess would be so much better than a duchess. She hoped her mother wasn't going to take against Shevraeth, at least while she had a chance of marriage. Renselaeus! She'd have her very own principality, and not even her mother could interfere with her there—once she was safely wed, and got rid of the old people somehow. She preferred poison if she could get it, but that stupid old man could barely walk, all he'd need to do is fall down some stairs.

She tiptoed away, holding her skirts against rustling, and got dressed for the Orbanith reception. She made certain she had the best seat so she could see everything. When the prince and princess appeared together, they obviously noted their son, but they trod across the room to sit on the opposite platform. Fialma gloated. He clearly didn't care a jot for the two old bores. He might even help her get rid of them!

The Marquise, the king, and many others watched covertly as Shevraeth made his way languidly to his parents, then bowed over the princess's hand. "Dear Mother," he drawled. "I am transported to see you well."

"Would it sound ungrateful," the Prince murmured just loud enough for the avid ears on either side to hear, "if I point out that you could have seen her well the sooner had you come directly home?"

"Oh, Father, the fatigue of those mountain roads! I knew you would be here—and, well, here you are, are you not?"

"Yes, dear," the Princess said, fluttering her fan. "He is here, is he not? Oh, Shevraeth, that earring! Are the boys wearing them in Colend? I remember when I was young everyone wore them in both ears."

The prince gave his wife an exquisite bow, and his son one of a shade too shallow a degree. "Permit me to leave you two to canvas all the fashions at your leisure."

And he moved across to where the Denlieff ambassador, a visitor from Lamanca, and Grumareth were busy taking out their gambling tokens.

The Marquise, Fialma was glad to see, showed her relaxed smile. And so Fialma turned her attention to cutting out Tamara Chamadis, who had disgustingly showed up in a stunning gown made all of lace, with cloth-of-gold beneath it, the whole making a crown of her pearl-and-diamond braided hair.

❧ ❦ ☙

The four met in the garden the next day, arriving by different routes.

The prince touched Vidanric's hand. "Well done, my son."

The Princess kissed him. "You have a headache, dear boy. I can see it in your eyes."

Both the prince and Savona were surprised by this observation, a surprise that intensified when Shevraeth said, "Yes. I don't know what it was. I had fun, but there was a moment when it suddenly ceased to be entertaining. I thought of the days, possibly the years stretching ahead, all of us acting out this pretense, and I—well, I lost courage. Forgive me. I had a notion how bad it has been, but nothing came close to the reality." He rubbed his temples. "In truth, I did not sleep all night. I—the fear in my old friends' eyes. Fear, and the way they watch one another. People with their brains and skills shouldn't be sitting about watching one another to see who vanishes next."

The prince said, "Yes. But not everyone in the kingdom sees it, and some who see it shrug and accept Galdran's behavior as part of their ambition to get what they can. Nothing can happen until we have a kingdom united in the determination for change. Grumareth and his cronies are still the greater number, and they are perfectly satisfied with things as they are."

The princess said, "Many believe that the Marquise of Merindar is the voice of sanity in the kingdom, and look to her for guidance."

"She scares me." Vidanric winced. "And Fialma is more detestable than I remembered."

"Nevertheless, she is going to be your chief flirt for the foreseeable. She's had no success finding a royal prince to marry, and she will carry tales of you to the king."

Vidanric said tiredly, "I know. I know. Oh, it is good to see you again—and there is much I can tell you about the things I learned in Colend."

The prince said, "But it will have to wait. Speaking of which, we must not be seen all together like this." He took his wife's arm and they passed on, leaving the two boys behind.

"Let's ride," Vidanric suggested.

Savona joined him. Neither spoke until they were riding the forest beyond the garden's outer wall. Even then Vidanric's gaze never stopped scanning. Finally he said, "I can't tell you how much I admire you for keeping a sense of humor."

Savona snorted. "Tell me about Colend. And the court beauties. I hope you had plenty of flirts. Catch up with the expert." He flicked his chest.

Vidanric laughed silently. "Flirts aplenty. For a time I was the latest curiosity, with my short hair and my provincial accent." He slewed round to face Savona with sudden seriousness. "And so I saw how beauty can be used as a weapon. I read once that assassins used to take a little poison each day to become inured. So it is with beauty."

"Ah." Savona nodded, and drew in a slow breath. "Tamara and the gold gown. A weapon aimed straight at you."

Despite his attempt at a light tone, Vidanric's gaze stayed both steady and acute. "What about you and Tamara?"

"What about us? Surely you had enough of an answer last night. A lifetime of flirting might have become a dull habit, and she thinks of me—if she thinks at all—with a kind of cousinly fondness."

"Do you really believe that?"

Savona dropped the pretence of lightness. "I don't know what I believe. But she'd make a beautiful princess one day."

Vidanric raised a hand in oath-salute. "Brother. Hear me. I'll dally with her if she wants—I'll flirt with them all, but there's going to be no heart in it." He hesitated, his hand taking the reins. "Here's my own truth. I could see last night that my parents both favor Elenet. She's smart, she's dedicated, she's got a fabulous eye for style." He reached into his pocket and drew out a fan of deep, deep blue, painted over in silver stars in an exact replica of the summer sky: blue and silver, Renselaeus colors. It had arrived at his table that morning, with a beautifully written quote from a famous Sartoran play. Nothing presumptuous or out of place—unlike Fialma's possessive attitude—just words of welcome, but the whole imbued with meaning. No, with *intent*. "My parents said nothing, but I could see how they watched the two of us together."

"We have years and years before we have to think like that," Savona protested, unsettled.

Vidanric turned the fan over and over in his hand, thinking back to the evening. Elenet's kindness to everyone, the calm good sense of her remarks—and, just once, the calculating glance she shot across the room when Vidanric was turning on the dance floor with Tamara.

He decided not to say anything. Tamara in her low cut golden gown and Elenet with her quiet deliberation were using the weapons they were permitted. He shouldn't resent it, but he did: that beauty, and art, and poetic words, should all be used as weapons. What should grace life and render uncomplicated joy became edged like cut glass. Scruffy-haired Fenis Senelac in her rumpled horsey-scented tunic seemed farther away than ever. She had hurt him, but she'd hurt herself, too. Her intentions, her motivations, even her conflict had been honest.

"I'll say this once more, then never again." Vidanric touched his hand to his heart. "I will flirt with Tamara because it's fun, because she seems to want to. Same with all the others. But I will never marry Tamara. I promise."

Savona shook his head. "I don't know what to say. Except maybe this conversation ought to happen more rightly in five or ten years."

"I don't see myself changing," Vidanric said. "More to the point, I don't want there to be this weapon lying between you and me. Even if I find myself in love with her—unlikely—there is a world full of other women. I won't marry her. That's it."

"Unlikely?" Savona struggled for lightness again.

"No fault in her. Just because I don't see myself falling in love again. I don't want to. The kingdom is far too unsettled for me to lose my wits over a woman. Perhaps I will never marry."

Now Savona laughed, long and hearty. "I can see it now! Your Marlovens ruined you. Just wait. One day some enormous girl with military musculature will gallop into court, and start commanding us all in a field voice. She'll have a rep for slaying her enemies all on her own, barehanded, before breakfast. You'll fall helpless at her booted feet and we will not be able to pry you away."

Vidanric snorted, midway between irritation and laughter. "I endeavor to be serious and you will not take me seriously."

*Because we cannot know what will happen,* Savona thought. *But at least you are back.* "We're going to make a wager," he chortled. "And oh, is it going to cost you when I win."

To the disgust of Vidanric Renselaeus, Marquis of Shevraeth, Savona laughed all the way back home.

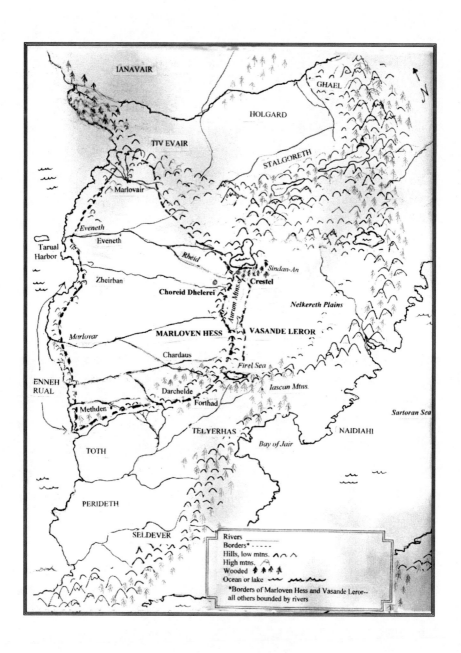